TRIALS OF TRIANGULUM

THE PRICE OF SURVIVAL

TRIALS OF TRIANGULUM

THE PRICE OF SURVIVAL

[signature: Jeremy D. Williams]

by Jeremy David Williams

This novel, my first, is dedicated to many people.

To those who held my hand every step of the way during publication, Dave, Patty, Sandy, Barry and Gaille.

To my parents, who, when I asked their advice concerning such a tremendous undertaking, said, "If you don't publish, you'll always regret it."

To Amy, for being a critical, helpful, and honest beta reader.

To Earl D. Spires Jr., for your work as a beta reader and a fellow novelist, always keeping me motivated.

And to Mrs. Fontaine, my high school English teacher. You inspired my writing more than you know. The rough draft of this novel was written during my senior year in high school. Thank you for not holding all of your students to the same standards, for we are not all alike.

And lastly, to all my readers. I don't yet know many of you, but you're about to learn a little about me. May your lives never be dull.

Qaz Assembly

Uns Solar System

Redron

Onuy Nebulae Cluster

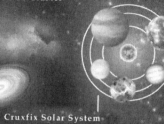

Cruxfix Solar System

Kriline Defense Barrier

Harza

Enarf

Braline Solar System

Nuin

Strunk Nebula

Sekurai Solar System

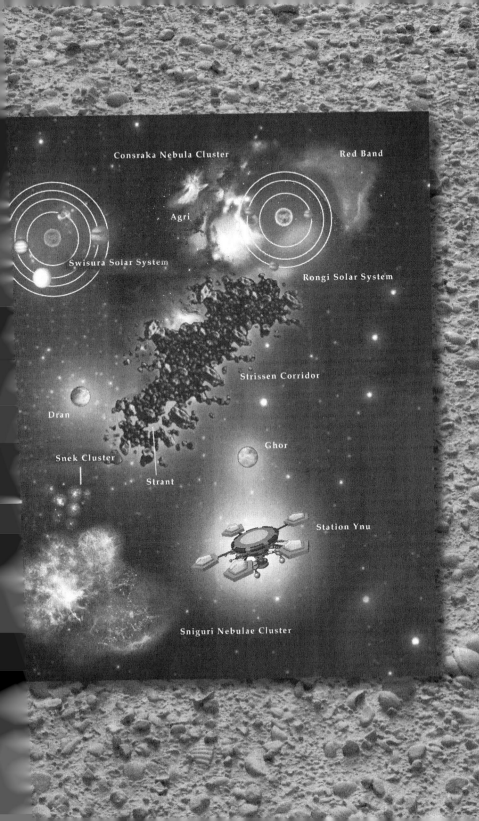

Contents

PRONUNCIATIONS OF TRIANGULUM NOUNS

The Orb Seekers

Karak Jewill	CARE-uk JEH-will
Field Marshal Notolla	NO-taw-la
The Low-High Hiram	HI-rum
Lithinia	le-THIN-ya
Surist	SURE-ist
The Duke of White	DOOK of WHYTE

Stone Globe

Levu Earsp	LEH-voo UHR-sp
General Regti	REGH-tee
Prak	PRACK
Nurisk	NUR-isk
Humwe	HUM-way
Kolij	kole-EEG

Other Characters

Praetor Jarob	JEHR-ub
Prelate Luric	LEUR-ick
Empress Mudin	MOOD-en
King Brale LXXII	BRAYL
Rorn	RORN
Narvok	NAR-vock
Scit	SKIT
Flahr Ky Gen	flar KYE gin
Tirsch	TURSH
Major Jehn	GIN
Captain Tegrun	TEE-grun
Commander Nal	NALL

Other Spatial Bodies & Phenomena

Qaz Assembly	KAZZ
Sniguri Nebula Cluster	snigg-YUR-ee
Harza	HAR-zuh
Redron	RED-run
Nuin	NEW-in
Strissen Corridor	STRIE-sin
Consraka Nebula Cluster	kun-SRAH-kuh
Snek Cluster	SNECK
Agri	AG-rih
Station Ynu	EE-neew
Onuy Nebulae	OWN-wee
Dran	DRANN
Ghor	GORR
Strant	STRANT
Red Band of Death	red band of death
Uns System	UHNS

Stars, Planets, Moons and Other Bodies & Phenomena of Solar Systems

Rongi System:	RON-jee
Tris	TRISS
Adcar	AD-kar
Zor	ZORR
Praw	PRAUGH
Baro	BAR-row
Brack	BRACK
Stren	STREHN
Vock I	VAHCK I
Vock II	VAHCK II

Spish	SPISH
Quati	KWA-tee
Fros	FROSS
Fergh	FURGG
Snog	SNOGG
Pern	PURN
ICE	Interplanetary Clear-Liquid Extraction

Braline System: BRAY-leen

Trak	TRACK
Vrondak	*VRON-dack*
Strana	*STRAH-na*
Verdin	*VUR-den*
Crasten	KRASS-tin
Prasten	PRASS-tin
Breduin	*BRED-oo-in*
Meri	*MEH-ree*
Meriet	MEH-ree-et
Strunk Nebula	STRUNCK
Kriline Defense Barrier	KRY-line
Enarf	EE-narph

Swisura System:

Jisk	JISK
Isk	ISK

Sekurai System:

Qu'uack	KOO-ahhck
Station Sek	*SECK*
Ei Cluster	*EE-aye*

Cruxfix System: CRUCKS-ficks

Crux I	CRUCKS I

Redron

Kriline Defense Barrier

Enarf

Braline Solar Sys

Nuin

Strunk Nebula

Chapter 1

MEETING OF THE BRALINE

The ancient Meeting Bell tolled—and it told. It tolled in its usual low, loud tone to announce an imminent gathering. The bell was only used in times of desperation and near hopelessness. It always announced the beginning of a meeting that could decide the future of the Braline people and their way of life. One way or another, the lives of everyone in their entire civilization were about to change. In this dark hour the bell's toll seemed a little lower and more ominous than usual, though it had been many years since it was rung at all. Also, it told. It told the people of more than an impending meeting, however. It chimed in the deepest recesses of their good natured and kindly hearts a bleak, black suspicion of something they feared more than their own individual deaths: an unknown future which included the possibility, and indeed the likelihood, of falling completely out of existence. The state of affairs was so severe that each planet had chosen to send one or two of their most trusted people to represent their planet's population at a special meeting called by King Brale LXXII.

"Welcome, Levu, my friend." The king moved more to the center of the room to greet Levu Earsp while his advisors continued to flit about on the other side of the room. "You're the first to arrive."

"I try not to be late," Levu said very sarcastically, but clinching his fist as he finished, "when our people's existence lies in scales of the justice of the universe." Levu leaned forward just a bit and dropped his packed bag to the floor with a groan showing that he was not quite as young as he once was.

"The scales are blind, you know?" the king asked as he raised an eyebrow. "They're impartial."

"I prefer my scales; somehow I always win." Levu straightened his wide brimmed hat. The king gave an approving smile and a chuckle. "How was your trip from the far side of the world, Levu?"

"Long. I was hoping my vacation would last more than a few hours."

"I am sorry, but things have changed. An unforeseeable occurrence has taken place, but more about that when the others arrive." The king put his arm around the shoulder of his most trusted friend.

One of the king's advisors called him aside. "Are you sure this is the man to lead a crew on such an important mission? He carries a gun." The advisor was sure to whisper as he pointed toward that apparently controversial item Levu carried on his belt.

"Levu executes his life with a finesse of thought and handles situations with great care," responded the king with an assuring furrow of his brow. "He is the best of us."

Levu, having overheard the question in the echoing hall, perched himself upon a chair with his legs crossed and laid out comfortably on the marble table. He became steely-eyed, and simply stated, "This laser is *made* a finesse weapon because I *never* miss. And this staff may be a walking stick, but it can also double as a weapon when necessary. In fact, I would rather use this because it can strike fear in the hearts of my enemies. Anyone can be scared of a man with a blaster, but, in an era of space travel and intergalactic war, it takes a special man to be able to frighten someone with a stick."

Others began to meander into the room all at once, already engrossed in their own conversations.

"Any luck with researches as to your past?" Humwe asked with genuine concern.

"I've had no success whatsoever." Nurisk took a somewhat defeated tone.

"Now that we are all gathered," King Brale moved toward the table, "we'll begin the meeting. First of all, I want to welcome you all to our system's planetary capital of Verdin. Levu Earsp, it is once again good to see you, my friend. Kolij, also from Verdin, I have heard much about your abilities from Levu. The two of you have served together several times in the past. It is a pleasure to have you here. Prak, from Strana, your reputation precedes you. Your works in the field of trade have helped to make your world and our system what they are today. We all sincerely appreciate your work to maintain the Kriline Defense Barrier, our solar system's best defense. Nurisk from Verdin, your traveling experience will be of great help in this meeting, and whatever is to come. General, you are here for obvious reasons. The assistance of your forces may be needed before this ordeal is over. And Humwe, it is good of you to come. I appreciate your being here. I only wish I could greet you all under less deadly circumstances."

The king paused a moment to look over at his three year old daughter playing with her doll. She couldn't know what was going on, but she'd detected her father's tension and wanted to stay with him. As he began to address the group it seemed as though the life was slipping right out of his eyes.

"We are faced with the greatest peril our people have seen since the last Sekurai War. Nuin, the colossal star that has maintained our solar system's gravitational equilibrium, has begun to destabilize. We have no idea how this happened; there were no foretelling signs. It could be part of yet another Sekurai plot to destroy us; we don't know. Due to the sizes and proximities of the two astronomical phenomena, Nuin, an enormous giant, has been the only thing offsetting the tremendous gravity of the black hole, Redron, since long before the Kriline Defense Barrier was put in place by our ancestors. Our entire solar system is being sucked into Redron, the largest black hole known to exist. We don't know exactly how much time we have until the gravity from the black hole becomes so great that our ships will not be able to escape it. We have some time, but not enough to evacuate our people. In fact, it's likely we could evacuate only the smallest fraction of one percent of our population if we started today and used every ship available. My advisors and I are unsure about what to do. One thing we do know is that we must act, but we must do so together, as one cohesive efficient unit. That is why you are all here. We need some sort of plan, or our civilization and culture will cease to exist."

There was a long silence while all were contemplating. Eventually General Regti spoke up. "Is there any way we could enhance our ship's engines so they wouldn't be so affected by the gravity well?"

"Kolij is the helmswoman here." Levu turned his unkempt beard toward his long-time friend. "She keeps up to date on propulsion theory."

"Any engine improvements that our scientists are working on are either in the preliminary stages and could not be ready for a few years, which is entirely too much time, or have been abandoned because they failed too many of their test runs." Kolij turned, deferring to the king. "Besides, that would only postpone the problem. Redron would suck us in eventually anyway."

"It might at least have bought us a little more time," Regti said.

"We have a large navy. Is there any way we could muster the firepower to destroy the black hole?" Prak asked.

"It's not possible to destroy a black hole. At least, not with any technology we have," Humwe said, with a bewildered look on his face. "I wouldn't even know where to begin."

"Why don't we just create a balancing solution?" Nurisk, the lone outsider in the group, asked innocently.

"What do you have in mind?" the king asked, excited for a suggestion.

"Nuin has been performing a service to us for a long time." Nurisk dropped a beefy arm onto the table. "We can try to replace it with another star." He raised his eyes to meet those of the others. "Or a black hole—anything that would perform the same function."

No one spoke.

After several moments, General Regti leaned toward the side of Nurisk's face, looked in his ear, and said, "I think the wheel stopped turning."

Nurisk rolled his eyes. "I'm serious," he said. "This system has been a LaGrange point between Redron and Nuin for longer than astronomic observances have been recorded. Our system sits much closer to Nuin than to Redron, but Redron's gravitational pull is greater. We've wound up in a precarious balance due to the settling nature of these gravitational forces." Nurisk wrinkled his forehead. "Why can't we do the same thing artificially?"

"Seldom is there a suitable artificial substitute or replacement for something of this nature," Kolij said as she shifted in her seat. "I think it would be a waste of what little time we have."

"How would we go about doing this anyway?" the king asked Nurisk.

"We'd need to draw in enough material that, when ignited, would create a new star," Nurisk's eyes met the king's. "This star would have its own gravity well. It could offset the pull of Redron."

"Could? What do you mean could?" Levu squinted.

"We would have to gather the right amount of material to create a star large enough, but not too large, to offset Redron." Nurisk spoke with his hands. "It would need to be of the same mass and density as Nuin. We would also have to draw the material to a specific point in space and ignite it there. If it were too close to Redron it would be sucked in along with us. If it were too far away, its gravitational pull would not be sufficient to keep us from being taken into the black hole."

"An artificial gravity device could be placed at the desired point in space to draw in as much material as possible," Levu suggested.

"It could then be ignited simply by firing a torpedo at the device," Regti said. "That part would be simple enough."

Kolij typed a few quick calculations on her computer pad. "I don't think we can even come close to having enough raw material to create a star." She shook her head.

"It might work, but the lack of material would be the greatest problem." Prak pushed up on his upper lip with the bottom one. "But I would offer a different solution."

"What would that be?" The king leaned in.

"What if we gathered some of the stray gases from around Nuin itself and ignited them after they'd been transferred back to the star?" Prak murmured as though thinking aloud. "This might reignite the star."

"That could work. We could collect the gases in cargo ships," Humwe said, "and then just send the ships into the core of Nuin. There's still enough heat in the star to destroy the ship."

"The engine core explosion would ignite the gases and very likely the rest of the star," Kolij said.

"There could be several problems with it, though." Levu pinched the excess skin around his neck. "We may not be able to gather enough of the gases to ignite the star. We also may run into the Sekurai while we're out there. Nuin is a little closer to their system, and we don't need to *add* to our problems."

"Nuin is also a few days away," the king said. "We would only have a few chances before it would either work or we would have to find a better use of what time we have. This second solution seems more plausible, but if it doesn't work we'll be out of time."

"I think we have to give these ideas a try," Levu said. "We don't seem to have many options."

After a moment of silence, the king said, "We have two options on the table. The first is to create a star large enough, but not too large, to offset Redron. The second is to ignite Nuin by bringing in gases from around the area in hopes of increasing her gravitational pull and bringing her back to life." He looked around the table at his advisors. No one spoke. "Since there appear to be no objections, I believe we should make an attempt to ignite Nuin. Keep your minds open to new possibilities, though, in case we're unsuccessful."

"I suggest we assemble a task force for this operation," Regti said with an authoritative tone as he pulled his shoulders back and nodded toward Levu. "This group can operate from a central command ship and coordinate the entire effort."

"How soon can we be ready?" Levu asked.

"I'll send ships to begin gathering material and have them bring it to the proper location at once," Regti said.

At this, the group rose and left the meeting room. General Regti would provide a cruiser. They would leave in that ship and head for Nuin with escorts and science vessels.

As Levu and his newly formed crew arrived on the scene at Nuin to take charge of the undertaking, they were met with a fleet of military ships that would provide defense during the operation. They didn't want to be caught off guard by any Sekurai patrols that might be in the area. The Sekurai were the worst enemy of the Braline, and of many people throughout the galaxy.

One by one, warships and cargo ships—those with the most powerful engines and most cargo space—made their way to Nuin, just outside the Braline System. They carried and towed via grapple cables asteroids, debris, and even old derelict ships to try to amass enough content to add to Nuin and reignite it. Artificial gravity modules were deployed and set into rotation within nebulae to gather the gases. This operation was far from simple, and even further from being a sure thing. The sight of the massive fleet was impressive with their home system in the background and the Strunk Nebula off to the side. The dying star, which was the lifeline of their entire existence, was off to the left, a pale version of its former glory.

Prak turned from his console to face Levu and report. "As we get better sensor readings from closer up, I'm reading the instability in Nuin. It's really odd."

"What do your sensors show?" Levu asked.

"Its mass is decreased by more than five percent. I can't offer an explanation as to how this happened," Prak continued, looking at the main view screen on the bridge, "but it appears the star has expelled a massive amount of material into space." Nuin, a red giant, had a large indentation on its lower half. Normally the star would have been spherical, but this empty spot left it with a blank area on one side.

"Where did it go?" Kolij asked.

"I can't say." Prak shrugged. "I've not seen anything like this before. It's too much material to have been burned off, so it must have gone somewhere, and I don't see how the star could have ejected that much material to begin with. The dislodged section, wherever it went, included part of the iron, cobalt, and manganese core."

"Levu," Nurisk said urgently, "I'm reading a few Sekurai scout ships just coming into range."

"Intercept them," Levu ordered, "and jam their transmissions."

"I'm already on it," Kolij replied as she engaged the ship's engines.

"Levu," General Regti said, "our place is here, supervising the operation of gathering material to reignite the star. We can't go chasing after a few Sekurai patrol ships. That's what our defense forces are for."

"Generally, I would agree," Levu said, "but if those ships detect us, which they probably already have, they'll try to get off a transmission to their superiors, and then they'll send more than we can deal with. The best way to ensure the success of this mission is to stop those ships. Order three wings of fighters to follow us after them."

"We're coming up on those enemy scouts," Kolij reported. "They don't seem at all interested in getting away from us."

"Surely, they're not that overconfident," Prak said. "We have the advantage here."

Everyone looked at Prak. The Sekurai were far ahead of the Braline in terms of technology, numbers, and training for warfare. War was the line of work of almost every Sekurai. Their entire civilization was driven by conquest. Prak knew this as well as any of them, but he suspected these scouts were merely a standard patrol that was far away from their home territory or any of their fleets.

"I'm detecting more Sekurai ships," Nurisk said. "They're meeting up with those scouts and heading this way."

"They have a few fighters, cruisers, and two escort ships," Kolij said.

"Escort ships mean a warship won't be far behind," Regti observed. "We're in over our heads."

"We have a mission to complete," Levu reminded his crew as he braced himself in his captain's chair. "We must protect the main effort. Attack those escort ships; use our maneuverability to our advantage."

"The fighters are targeting us; they're thinking the same thing we are," Kolij said.

"Then it'll be an old fashioned dog fight," Levu warned. "Have our fighters target theirs. Our escort ships will help us with—"

Two Sekurai cruisers attacked with heavy fire. Cruisers were a mid-range craft that packed more firepower than a fighter, but were faster and more maneuverable than an escort ship. The cruiser which carried Levu and his crew was under attack. They were hit from both sides and the ship shook violently. Sparks flew from wall-mounted consoles.

Levu and his crew found themselves under fire from two ships that were more maneuverable and out-gunned them in every way—as well as a whole wing of fighters that, while they were almost equal in terms of fighting force, were superior in speed and maneuverability.

"Our projected plasma defense shields are down to sixty-seven percent," Regti informed Levu.

"One thing at a time," Levu said calmly. "Kolij, match move for move with one of those Sekurai cruisers. Once we have the first one down, then move on to the second. Regti, as you get a shot, don't be shy about hammering them with everything you've got. Those escort ships will have to wait."

"Our fighters are being left alone for the most part," Prak observed.

"Have them target the enemy fighters," Levu said. "Maybe they can take some pressure off of us."

"Those escort ships are coming into range now," Nurisk said.

"Good." Levu smiled a cheeky grin.

"Good?" Regti said questioningly. "What's good about this?"

"Instruct our fighters to split up into two wings and send them in hot," Levu ordered. "Have them attack from equal but opposite sides of the escorts to try to push them closer together. Kolij, take us immediately between those escorts and slow up so as to allow the enemy fighters to almost overtake us. When I give the word, speed up and get us out of the line of fire. Nurisk, keep an eye on the power levels in those escorts. The timing here will be very important."

The ship rocked as cruisers closed in from behind and pelted the Braline cruiser. Levu was playing a dangerous game in trying to even the odds against his small force of inferior ships.

"I'm reading power buildups in the escort ships," Nurisk reported. "They're firing."

"Punch it!" Levu yelled.

Kolij literally pounded her fist on her console, and they sped up to get out of the line of fire. As the escorts fired with all weapons, their barrages nailed both of their own cruisers and they were completely obliterated. The resulting explosions of warheads, engine cores, and what oxygen was in those ships also ignited the plasma residue given off by the engines of the fighters that flanked the enemy cruisers. Not all of the escorts' fire was absorbed in this melee and conflagration though; some laser blasts and warheads hit the opposite escort. Now Levu and his defense wing could concentrate on the less maneuverable and damaged escorts to destroy them and then get back to the operation of reigniting Nuin. The process of outmaneuvering these ships was not a difficult one—until Kolij executed their attack runs and had to avoid oncoming fire while still keeping focused on hitting the enemy ships that were shooting at them.

"Levu," Prak said, "I'm picking up a Sekurai warship attacking the star-building effort."

"Get us back there! We'll have to let these escorts get away," Levu said with a loud growl. "Are they alone?"

"Yes, it's just the warship," Prak answered. "There are no other enemy ships. It must be the warship from the patrol group we just destroyed."

"Warships don't generally go out on patrol," General Regti observed.

"Then what do you suppose they were doing out here?" Levu asked.

"I don't know," Regti said with a concerned tone. "If they were expecting us, I think they would've been lying in the nebula waiting for us instead of just beyond sensor range. They also wouldn't have waited until the entire force connected with our operation was here; they would have just attacked each ship one by one as it came into the area. They certainly weren't acting normally either. Generally, warships and their escorts wouldn't have been out on standard patrol."

"The warship has inflicted massive damage on the cargo ships," Prak reported. "We have two warships currently in the area, but they're overwhelmed by the firepower of the Sekurai battle cruiser."

"Take us in, weapons hot," Levu said in a standard tone, not getting too fired up or lackadaisical. "Target their gun ports one by one."

The Braline cruiser went in, firing all weapons.

Kolij performed a conical corkscrew dive directed right at one of the many main guns on the dorsal side of the ship. On their way out of such a maneuver, she would repeat it while Regti targeted individual emplacements with the aft torpedoes. Kolij could avoid getting hit most of the time, but once in a while a proficient Sekurai gunner would connect with his battery.

They took one or two hits from the warship, and that's all it took to begin operating at decreased efficiency.

"Make one more run," Levu ordered. "Take out that last gun on this side."

"I don't think I can keep us from taking more hits," Kolij yelled over the warhead impacts and explosions going on all around them.

"Stay on it! Take it out! Focus on the goal!"

"Our weapons were disabled with that last hit," Regti reported as he tried in vain to operate his tactical console. "I have nothing left."

"Our engine capacity is also reduced," Kolij said with a defeated tone and then turned to Levu with desperately deferring eyes. "I don't think we're going to kill this monster."

"The fighter escorts could barely scratch the surface of the warship's shields and our two warships which came under attack first were knocked out of the fight, one of them destroyed, the other dead in space," Prak reported. Levu and his crew had to retreat out of weapons range. Fires began to break out due to overloaded systems and integral components having been hit in the fray.

"The last cargo ship trying to leave the area is under attack from the battle cruiser," Regti said as he waved smoke away from his face. "That ship has a crew of over two hundred men and women."

"Take us in," Levu said without hesitation as he walked over to Nurisk's console and began punching buttons. With his bridge going up in flames all around him, he stayed true to his task by inputting a program that would allow himself and his crew to escape while still protecting the last cargo ship. "Sit us directly in the line of fire between that warship and the cargo ship. Prepare all six escape pods."

"We're coming into their weapons range," Kolij said. "We might take a few more hits, but soon we won't be here to protect that cargo ship."

"Everyone to escape pod one now," Levu ordered.

"Everyone in the same one?" Regti asked with a perplexed look. "That's putting all our eggs in one basket, don't you think?"

"Yes," Levu answered Regti. "We're going to use the other five baskets as a shield while we get out of weapons range." Levu was the last to leave the bridge, as he should be, but he didn't stop and take one last look around his bridge or say anything sentimental. He just made his way to the first escape pod, got in, and jettisoned all pods into space. The escape pod that housed the crew took point, and the other five formed a wall between the first pod and the warship. As the other pods were blasted away, this bought them enough time to get out of weapons range of the warship. They had saved the last cargo ship and its crew, but the mission to reignite Nuin, which was highly unlikely to succeed even without Sekurai interference, had failed.

With his demonstration of inventing new tactics to try to win an uphill battle and also in risking his life, the lives of his crew, and allowing his ship to be destroyed to protect hundreds of others, Levu had demonstrated that he was willing to do whatever was necessary to serve his people. Levu looked back as the escape pod travelled out of range of the enemy warship. His mind was occupied by several thoughts. *I'm lucky to be alive. We are lucky to be alive. This didn't just happen by coincidence; there is more here than meets the eye; I must find out what. What will we do now? I must plan for the next stage of this process, but what will it be?* Levu held his clenched fist to his forehead. *I'm going home in utter defeat.*

Upon hearing of the failure of the mission, King Brale LXXII wondered if he might be the last of the Braline kings. He had reconvened the meeting with Levu and his crew to discuss other possibilities. The setting for the meeting was a table in the middle of the Royal Garden just outside the king's palace on Verdin, the political hub of the Braline System. This garden was adorned with the flora of as many of the regions of the various planets as the garden could contain and support. The table in the middle of the garden was a white, perfectly square granite structure with four legs, each having an intentionally aged look to them. These legs were, like the rest of the table, a regal sort of marbled white and very clean—until one looked at the graying mid-section of each of the legs. Upon still further examination, the portion of the legs nearest the floor was black and dirty.

"You did a hard thing, sacrificing your ship and putting yourself and your crew at risk in defenseless escape pods, but it was in the hope of saving hundreds of our people," the king said to Levu. "I only wish the mission had been a success."

"Do we have no good solutions?" Kolij asked. "We have not considered that we may need some help from others."

"We should try to do everything on our own that we can," Regti suggested with a prideful tone. "I prefer not to reveal our troubles to others. You never know who could be listening. We have already run into the Sekurai."

"We have tried our first plan," the king said. "Because it didn't work, I think we will seek help from more powerful and more knowledgeable people."

There was no longer time for reigniting Nuin and recreating the gravitational pull to offset Redron. After much consideration and debate, it was agreed by all that help was going to be necessary if they were to save their civilization. Some members of the group preferred to avoid this, but even they could not help but see the necessity. The conversation then turned into a discussion of whom to ask for advice or help.

"I think we should go to the Cruxfix System," Nurisk said. "They have massive libraries of information that may offer us some knowledge on how to deal with our current situation."

"Inster is no longer in charge there," Levu said, folding his hands on the table in front of himself. "Gronil, who was one of Inster's advisors, is now the leader there."

"Do you think they could help?" Prak asked.

"He is the best educated and wisest person I know, and their technology is ahead of ours. They may have options we don't. I can think of no one else who could help us." Nurisk leaned back in his seat. "It takes about a week to get there though."

"How much time are we predicting we have left?" Kolij asked as she looked to the king.

"We're thinking about a month, maybe a bit more," the king said. "We just can't be certain. There are too many variables. It depends on Nuin's rate of decay, and that can change daily."

"Should we all go to the Cruxfix System?" Levu asked as he looked around the table, meeting everyone's eyes. "Or do we leave part of our team here to investigate further options?"

"I would advise that whatever you do, you do it as a group," King Brale said. "You were sent or requested because you are the best. I will assist you in whatever ways I can, but there won't be many. I trust your judgment. The survival of our race is in your hands. Don't waste time and don't fail, or the consequences will be catastrophic."

"I will do everything I can to save my people. If it means going all over the galaxy trying to find a way, I'll do it. Nothing will stop me from fulfilling this oath," Levu pledged with certainty.

"I do this for posterity. Wherever you lead, I will follow—if it means saving our citizens," Humwe said. "Our people must go on," he finished with an intent whisper.

"It's not a question as to whether or not we should do this—it's an understood task," Nurisk added. "We must all do it."

General Regti rose from the table, standing tall. "My forces will begin evacuating as much of our populace as they can while we're away. I'm sure you'll need a tactical brain on this quest. I will go."

"We have been through difficult times together before. You know what you're doing, and you do it with a sound heart. I will follow you as well," Kolij stated as she looked at Levu.

"Well, that leaves me," Prak added, "and I'm in."

"It's good to hear that you're all doing what's best for your people. Our situation is bleak, but it just got a little brighter," King Brale said.

"I think we should leave as soon as possible," General Regti said.

"That is a good idea," Kolij added, "but 'as soon as possible' isn't going to be for a while because none of the Kriline Defense Barrier's openings are towards Gronil's Cruxfix System."

"Then the good and the bad are one," Levu said with a sigh. "We can't start at once, but we can say goodbye to our families and friends and let them know why we go, and that we may not return."

There was a long silence as everyone realized the gravity of their personal situations. They thought much about their families and the ones they would leave behind. If the mission was a failure, they might never see them again.

"This will also give us a chance to gather supplies for the journey. This trip may extend beyond the Cruxfix System," General Regti observed. "I have to pick out a ship for us that will make the journey."

"When will the next opening in the Barrier be towards the Cruxfix System?" Levu asked.

Kolij consulted her flight computer pad. "It will be a few days before we can leave."

"Then we'll all meet back here the day after tomorrow," Levu said. "I'll see you then. Come prepared for a long journey."

Everyone stood and made their way out of the garden. They had to prepare for the long road ahead.

Later that night, the king took some time to peruse some of the history of his line of kings. It was largely filled with positive accounts, as he hoped his reign would also be, but there were a few interesting notes, some of which struck a chord with him personally. He chronicled his thoughts and spoke as he wrote.

"The Braline are a civilization that has overcome many trials and torments in its long and peaceful history, and now we are on the brink of a slow and nearly certain destruction. We have one chance. We've never seen a more ominous set of circumstances than those which we now face in what will surely become our most desperate hour. All three inhabited planets in the system have been informed of the situation and told to pack—and pray. They were also told that only a fraction of a percent of our people would survive if evacuation of the solar system were decided to be the only option. In fact, if we have to evacuate, such a small number would survive that our culture would be practically destroyed. There would still be a sufficient number of us to successfully propagate our species, but our culture, art, architecture, literature, and all the things that make up the essence of our culture would be lost, right down to our very home. We are utterly unable to facilitate an evacuation of any greater proportion. Though we be a space-faring people, we are among the less powerful and less advanced solar systems in the known parts of the galaxy. I wonder what challenges await Levu and his brave crew." The king leaned back in his chair, staring and thinking.

Kolij and Levu had gone home to be with his family for a few days while they gathered supplies. He was in constant contact with General Regti about what class of ship they thought they should take. Kolij had no family to speak of and was glad to have been taken in. Her parents had been killed in the last Sekurai war. She and Levu had served together before on a few different occasions and knew each other quite well and had become close.

Levu was a disciplined, goal-oriented, principled man. A husband and father of three adult children, he'd developed a tremendous amount of patience over the years, though he still needed to retreat into solitude regularly.

Levu's wife was a loving, laughing sort of woman, just the kind Levu needed to return home to after a day of meetings or a long voyage. She was perfectly capable of running the business of family while he was away, but she was also ready for him to come home and take care of things too. Her food was a bit bland for Kolij's taste, but it was certainly passable.

"Where is your mission going to take you?" she asked of Levu as the two of them carried on a conversation around the supper table with their children and Kolij.

"The Cruxfix System," he replied.

"That's quite a trip!"

"Yeah. I hope it's a good one."

"I'd like to go to the Cruxfix System," the youngest, a boy of twenty-two, said.

"It's not exactly a joyride," Levu said curtly. "We have a mission to complete." After a brief pause, realizing he may have been a bit blunt, he calmed. "But I wish you could come along too."

"What ship are you taking?" Mrs. Earsp asked while keeping her eyes on her plate. This was a discussion that had been had many times between the two of them.

"Regti said he'd take care of it. He said he wanted to surprise everyone." Levu let out a long sigh and enviable eye roll. "I hate surprises."

Everyone chuckled a bit to lighten the tension, and also because it was amusing how much Levu hated surprises.

"How long will you be gone?"

"I have no idea," Levu said. "However long it takes. We may have to go further depending on what Gronil has to say." He swallowed his worry and looked at his wife.

"They could send someone else," she said.

"The king asked me to lead the mission. I don't want to sound like I'm bragging, but I'm the most logical choice." He looked at his loving wife. "You know that I love you more than life itself. All the things I've ever done have been for us. Not just for you and me, and not just for our family, but for my people. Our very existence hangs in the balance. This could wipe us out." Levu patted the head of the friendly family pet sitting by his side.

"If I were done at the Academy, perhaps I could go," the oldest son said.

"I'm sure you'll make a fine officer, as I once tried to be," Levu said, trying to be humble. "You can best serve your people by helping with the evacuation."

"*Our* people," the son corrected.

"No," Levu said. "They are *your* people. We must take personal ownership and responsibility for the things we do."

Their middle child, a daughter, feverishly took notes. She was an aspiring young author and hoped to chronicle all the current happenings for posterity, no matter how events played out. She made no comment, but rather just sat and listened and wrote down everything that was said.

"If it were just us here," Levu said looking around the table with the same young, shiny eyes that were so full of life when he married his beautiful bride, "then we'd load the next transport and leave, but there are bigger things than just us riding on this. I have to go."

Levu's wife looked back at him with a big smile that conveyed her intense pride.

Their children felt the same as their mother. They wished all was well and the dangerous mission wasn't necessary, but they understood the situation and knew he must do this. They all knew it had to be done. What they didn't know was what all would be involved, how far he and his crew would have to go, and the things they would do to complete their mission.

☓ ☓ ☓

Consraka Nebula Cluster

Red Band

Agri

Rongi Solar System

Chapter 2

RONGI COUNCIL

Praetor Jarob leaned on one of the pedestals upon which a flower vase sat and he looked around at nine leaders of the Rongi Solar System. Arranged in a semi-circle surrounding him, they were the brightest minds their people had to offer.

"This council is now raised to the level of organization." Praetor Jarob nodded toward each of the delegates. "I welcome you all here to this Council. The condition in which we find ourselves deserves no obfuscation or delay. Our solar system is in peril. We have been fortunate in that we've never had a long war or any terrible struggle outside our own solar system that has tested us. Many of those elsewhere in the galaxy would say this will be our weakness because we aren't used to fending for our lives, but fend we will."

"Fend?" Vladdy, the delegate from Vock II, murmured, stretching his V-shaped beard.

"I believe that our history of peace and good relationships with others shows that we make the best decisions and can overcome adverse situations." Jarob swept his long arms to include everyone in the group.

"Our scientists have informed me that a massive energy shockwave is on a direct course for Tris, our sun. This shockwave of stellar material seems to have been somehow captured by Tris's gravitational pull. It's something of a mystery to us as it's still a little way away, but one thing that is certain is that the sudden infusion of material into our star will have an unbalancing effect that will cascade through the star." Jarob leaned in closer to the group, his brown eyes large and round, and his voice soft. "This means that our sun will be destroyed."

Gasps and murmurs escaped from those gathered.

Jarob looked over at the wall upon which hung pictures of his predecessors as he waited for the group to quiet. "The Red Band, while not a terribly creative name, is what we have come to call this shockwave. We believe the Band's destructive force is due to large bursts of plasmatic energy, but we're not sure. We know troublingly little about it. Its fuel source and power levels are unknown. Its exact size and shape appear to vary somewhat as it wrangles through space, but what we do know is that it's going to collide with Tris, our sun, and alter the power and forces within the star. The entire star will become unstable and an instant supernova will be triggered."

"Obviously there is some hope or you would not have called us together," Karak Jewill broke in. "You would've just told us to pack our things and meet at a specified location." He tilted his head. "What do you have in mind?"

"Astute as usual, Karak," Jarob said. "We all may yet have to leave our homes. In fact, leaving is one of the two options I've discussed with my advisors. Unfortunately, the Band appeared on our long range sensors far too late and is moving at too great a speed to evacuate all our people. Nearly all of our population would still be in the system when the sun explodes. We estimate that only about 300,000 of thirty-six billion could be evacuated before the Band hits."

"Thus ends option one," Field Marshal Notolla said sarcastically. "Where would we go even if we could all get out?"

Praetor Jarob shrugged. "That's another issue. There's no place to run to even if we had the time," he said. "We've already weighed that option. And there is insufficient time to form relations with those in another system so that our people would be accepted. We rarely venture beyond our own star, so we don't even know of many other people—other than the Cruxfix, and only a select few of them."

"How much time do our astronomers suppose we might have until this Band hits Tris?" Karak asked.

"We figure about two lunar cycles, perhaps a little more, perhaps a little less," Jarob answered. "The Band's speed fluctuates slightly, as do its dimensions."

"You said there were two options," Hiram, an excellent helmsman from Pern, said. "I hope the next one is better."

"You're not going to like this one at all," the praetor warned. "As the duke will attest, there are many folktales on Vock I. In fact, there are more stories on this planet than on any other in our system. There is one that you all may or may not have heard. It's about the eight Orbs of Quality."

"Surely you're teasing," Smee Glars said. Smee was a grumpy man whose fuse was only slightly shorter than his stature. "I would laugh heartily if the situation weren't so bleak. It is, as you said, just a folktale. There's no scientific evidence those Orbs even exist." Smee scowled. "And if they do exist, where are they? Do they have the power described in mythology? If they do have that kind of power, is it enough to stop this Band?"

"There is often some truth to be found in the old stories," the duke of White interjected while raising his finger and adjusting himself in his seat, "and in times like these, we must cling to whatever hope we can find. As the curator of the Museum of Rongi History I can tell you my studies have shown that those people who clung to any hope they could find were the ones who most often prevailed."

"Yes, but even if the tale of the Orbs is based on fact, there are many questions to be asked. Do they still exist? If so, where? How can we find them? Are they just pretty rocks, or do they really have the powers the legends speak of?" Smee asked incredulously, shaking his head and turning up his ham-fisted hands with a shrug of his broad shoulders. "I'm very doubtful already."

"It appears some of us know more than others about these Orbs," Lithinia said. "I've never heard of them."

"You're right. Not everyone knows the tale," the praetor said. "We should all hear it. After all, it's the only option left to us. There's nothing we can do to stop the Band, and time is short." He nodded to the duke. "If you would, tell us the tale of the eight Orbs of Quality."

"Yes." Smee sneered. "Go ahead. Tell them the tall tale."

"I will." The duke leaned back in his chair. "The old stories say the eight Orbs of Quality are perfectly spherical rocks, each of them having a different color. Their colors are black, white, red, blue, yellow, green, orange, and purple, and these colors are of the deepest and purest hue imaginable; nothing compares. No one knows who or what created them, nor what they were used for. But, we do know the legends say they were created in the Cruxfix System many thousands of years ago.

"Their power was equivalent to their beauty. They each have a specific ability or power that enhances a certain quality of an Orb's possessor. These abilities are unknown today; that information has been lost and was not handed down through the years. We do know from the legends, if they are indeed true, that the Orbs merely enhanced abilities already present in the Orb owner. They did not give the possessor power or ability, but only offered clarity of thought where an aptitude was concerned."

Praetor Jarob looked around the room and saw the hold the story had on its listeners.

"The Orbs are very powerful, but not omnipotent. They are also not indestructible. They can be broken, but when any piece of a broken Orb comes in contact with another whole Orb, the broken Orb is forged again. But, the more Orbs that are broken, the more force is required to break another one. Thus, it would take a tremendous force to break the last one. If they're all broken, then they're lost forever, since there is no way to put them back together."

The duke looked around at his audience; all eyes urged him to continue. "The tale of the Orbs is not unique to our solar system, however. What few times we've ventured out of our own region of space, our explorers and other travelers have come back home with stories strikingly similar to this tale. Also, it's believed that the Orbs, some or all of them, have been at various locations throughout the galaxy. Little is known about the history of these Orbs other than tales, which are surely based on some fact due to their stories' similarities. This is all the information we have about the eight Orbs of Quality."

"And just how are we supposed to use these Orbs to stop this, this—Band of Death, or whatever it is?" Smee Glars waved an open hand up into the air. "How are they going to help anything?"

"I don't really know," the duke answered. "They are very powerful. I don't know how they'll help, but they're the only thing I can think of."

"If they're as powerful as you describe," Surist began, "then surely they have some sort of power source inside them. Perhaps when this power source is somehow unleashed on the Band, it will be neutralized."

"I'm hearing a lot of words like *if, perhaps,* and *somehow,*" Vladdy said. "*If* that's as close as we can come to a real solution, then *perhaps* we should come up with another way of stopping the Band—*somehow.*"

"You, the representatives of your planets, have heard our two options," Jarob said. "There are many stories about the Orbs, and judging from them, the Orbs might have the power to destroy the Band. We're all in this together. We must now decide whether to go on a journey to gather the Orbs or sacrifice many of our people in an evacuation attempt. I have already decided that Karak Jewill is the most qualified to lead an expedition, if that is what the Council decides. We will take some time away from the meeting now for you all to decide what you think is best for our people. We should all meet back here within the hour, for our decision must be quick, no matter what we decide."

Everyone but Karak, the duke, and Jarob left the room and went out into the adjoining hallway. The others split up. Some went for a walk, some went to their rooms, others just leaned up against the wall and pondered what they'd heard. Some of those who left the room did so shaking their heads, some in disbelief of the overall situation, some in defiance of the option presented. Others left the room already postulating what would be necessary to find the Orbs and bring them back. Where would they start? What if they ran into trouble? What if they got out into the depths of space and were attacked or their ship failed them?

At the end of the hour, all nine members of Rongi Council met back at the table in front of the praetor to state their decisions. Once they seated themselves, Jarob entered the area.

"What have you decided?" the praetor asked.

"I would encourage everyone to include themselves on the journey to save our people," Karak said. "Our civilization has never seen the level of destruction now staring at it. We must do everything in our power to continue our legacy for the future. We cannot simply sit and watch our society die."

"So many casualties among our people are unacceptable. I will join the group and give my services to Karak, a worthy leader," Lithinia said.

"I must admit that I have reservations about setting out on a journey with an uncertain end," Craden said. "We don't even know if these Orbs exist, let alone where they are or if they can help us. I have come to the decision that I will not risk wasting my time for such an endeavor. I will, however, offer my help in evacuating our system. I think that's the most practical thing we can do."

Field Marshal Notolla, seemingly irritated by what she'd just heard from Craden, stated, "My strategic abilities and tactical knowledge will be useful while looking for the Orbs, especially if we run into trouble. I will join your crew, Karak. My forces will also help with the evacuation and they will support us on the journey when we're near home."

"I have been in communication with my leaders and my constituents' other representatives as well," the duke of White said. "It is the decision of my superiors, and my own personal choice, that the seeking of these Orbs is our best chance. I, too, will join this team and pledge my allegiance to Karak."

"I'm afraid that I must agree with Craden," Vladdy said. "A long trek that may well be unsuccessful is not what we need right now. We must try to cut our losses. I will not join. But, I will assist with the evacuation of my world."

"What about the other inhabited planets in our system?" Jarob asked.

"Surely they can perform their own evacuation attempts," Vladdy answered.

Karak shifted violently in his seat. "I care greatly for all our people, despite their occasional opportunistically provincial outlook, an attitude I do not share." Though the Rongi had long ago developed a central government in their solar system, there were still many who tended toward blind small-mindedness. Helping someone outside your circle was a good thing, but to some it was entirely unnecessary and often viewed as a weakness or abandoning those to whom you were pledged and closest. Karak did not at all care for this approach to life. He preferred working with and moving as a team for the good of all concerned.

"I'm appalled that some of you are willing to settle for a miniscule percentage of our people surviving this impending calamity." Surist shook his head. "I am Surist, son of Hurid. My father, brother, and I would often leave Spish and go on long voyages like the one this may turn into. We would always do whatever we could to help our people. If they were here now, they would be as ashamed of you as I am! My father and brother died on the last trip we took, and I know they would want me to do this. I've traveled more and farther than any other Rongi. That's got to count for something. I will add myself to the crew of this voyage."

"You speak bold words, Surist," Smee said, "but I don't have many friends, save those whom I have the honor of working with on Interplanetary Clear-liquid Extraction. We melt ice and transport water throughout our solar system. We have our own ships for this, and we can evacuate ourselves; we have always taken care of ourselves. I hope you don't think me heartless, but I must tend to those who are closest to me first. I owe my loyalty to them, not to you."

"I am the Low-High Hiram, son of—my father," said Hiram as he leaned forward, mimicking Surist jokingly to lighten the tension. "No one can blame you for seeing to your closest people first. We must each make a choice, and this is yours. There is no right or wrong answer—at least not that I can see. I don't agree with your decision, but I understand it. I will join our group and will do whatever I can to help. I carry the title of the Low-High. This means that I am second in command on Pern. I answer only to our highest leader, the High-High. I am responsible for far more than just myself and my family and friends. I have an entire planet's population to think about, as we now have all Rongi people to consider."

"It looks like I have a six-man crew." Karak eyed Smee, obviously annoyed because some had chosen not to join the mission. "We have the best talent and a cause to galvanize us on this team. And, due to these things we shall be victorious. I think we should all inform our leaders and families of our situation."

"Agreed," Praetor Jarob said, "but it is late now. We should meet back here tomorrow to decide the finer things of this expedition. Sleep quickly, for we have come a long way, but we have not even begun to see how the odds are against us. Tomorrow you will decide how to proceed."

Everyone then filed out of the meeting room and went their separate ways to say their goodbyes, and to pack. Not one of the members knew what was in store for them and their quest, but they were going to try whatever it would take to succeed.

Karak, Jarob, and the duke met at the praetor's home for dinner that evening. Jarob's wife had prepared her stew, a hearty rib-sticking dish for which she'd won awards in the past and that was frequently requested when Jarob entertained either at home or the office.

"Delicious, as usual," Karak said as he pushed his third empty bowl away at the table. "Plenia, you never cease to amaze me."

"Indeed," the duke said as he used his tongue to dislodge one last piece of stew from between his teeth. "This is the first time I've had the honor of sampling your cooking." He turned to Jarob. "Do you hire her out?"

Jarob chuckled. "The short answer is—no. I've been asked that plenty of times. It was with that very line that I ingratiated myself to her mother years ago and I don't want to risk losing her due to her culinary skills." He then rose and pushed his chair in. "Let's move to the other room. It's more comfortable for an evening of heavy discussion."

Having poured themselves a drink and seated themselves in the comfy chairs of the next room in the house they began discussing their next moves.

"We leave tomorrow for the Cruxfix System," Karak said. "It's a long journey."

"I think you should stop at Pern for supplies on your way out of the system," Jarob suggested. "You can have a ship dock with you so you won't even have to land."

Karak nodded. "Duke," he said, "I will be relying on you for Orb information. It seems that they may be our best chance at stopping this Red Band."

"Unfortunately, I've already told you everything I know about the Orbs," the duke said. "I have nothing left to tell. It's essential that we make for the Cruxfix System to gather more information."

"Are we sure the Orbs were made there?" Jarob asked.

"That's what the legends tell us. Those legends are stories; they may not all be true. Though legends often have some basis in truth, they're often embellished or altered as they're told through the generations."

"I admit that I was somewhat annoyed that Craden, Smee, and Vladdy didn't want to join our quest," Karak said. "I hate the provincial nature of many of our people. I wanted to jump out of my chair and tell them how I really felt."

"You mean like you did with Smee the last time you and he were in a meeting together?" Jarob grinned.

"Yeah, something like that," Karak answered, annoyed that he had to admit that his anger was a larger component of his personality than it should sometimes be.

"What's this?" the duke asked, unaware of the previous encounter.

Karak and Jarob looked at each other with knowing smiles to see who would tell the story. Karak waved to Jarob and the praetor began. "During the dispute between Pern and the workers on ICE, Karak and Smee got into a heated debate. The shipping workers wanted increased compensation for having to travel all the way to Pern. It is farther away from ICE than any other planet in our system."

"They did have valid points," Karak conceded.

"Yes, the trip was longer. They were away from their families for a few extra days. Being cooped up in the tiny quarters, tiny bridge, tiny engine room, and even tinier corridors of those cargo ships is taxing, I know," Jarob agreed. "But, it's still a job that needs done."

"We tried to get them more time off to compensate," Karak said, "but ICE was then going to have to hire more people to cover the route. We tried to get them extended shore leave on Pern so they could have some time off the cargo ships in the middle of the voyage, but that was going to leave an empty cargo ship docked at Pern for a day or two instead of making another run. We tried to have a few more cargo ships built so the trips could be spread around to more crews, but that was going to take money, crew, resources, and more hectic maintenance schedules. Glars had an answer for everything. Everything we proposed wouldn't work for some reason or another. I got tired of excuses and that's when I lost my cool."

"So, he gets up," Jarob said with a laugh, "and he jumps on his chair and was about to start crawling on top of the table toward Smee." He could hardly contain his laughter. "He was yelling the entire time about how Smee was unwilling to compromise and was being unreasonable. When Smee saw how angry Karak was, I think he realized he'd made the wrong person mad, and he agreed to everything Karak suggested after all."

"Pretty soon every delivery crew from ICE wanted to make the Pern run instead of avoiding it." Karak laughed. "It went from the worst route to the best route because Smee got scared and agreed to everything I said."

For a moment they all shared a big laugh, but only until the weight of the current situation squared itself again on everyone's mind.

After a short pause, Karak continued. "I just didn't care for all the excuses. I was interested in getting the settlement worked out and moving on to the next goal. I can sit and talk and enjoy myself with the next man, but when there's work to do or a mission to accomplish, that has to be the goal. There's no time to waste. You just get down to business."

"They have to choose their own paths," Jarob said. "They have to walk it, so it is only right that they should choose it. I don't like their choices either, but they are what they are. They will help with evacuations, and that's good, but I agree they could do more."

"Is the evacuation already underway?" the duke asked as he turned toward Jarob.

"Yes, the initial stages have begun. We are in the difficult process of deciding who to evacuate. Evacuees will have to stay on their ships until we come up with a place to go."

"I hadn't even thought about that," the duke admitted. "How do you decide which three-hundred thousand people will be evacuated?"

"We're currently exploring several options. One of my advisors suggested that we draw lots. Another said we should load people of child-bearing ages who possess the greatest physical and mental assets our people have to offer. Yet another claimed we should evacuate those who are currently experts and the most seasoned in the fields that will serve us best as we try to rebuild our entire civilization. We haven't made a decision yet. Nothing is certain."

"One thing is certain," Karak said.

"What's that?" Jarob turned toward Karak.

"I need another drink."

Plenia, having heard this, came into the room and reached for Karak's glass.

"No," Karak said with a smile, "I really don't like to be served. Dinner was one thing, but I couldn't have cooked like that. I can get my own drink, however."

"What's certain for me is that my family just arrived from home," the duke said as he put his communicator back in his pocket after having looked at a message on it. "I'm having dessert with them. It may be the last time I get to see them for quite a while."

"Tell them 'hello' for us," Jarob said. Karak echoed the sentiment by raising newly refilled glass toward the duke with a smile.

After the duke had left, Jarob and Karak continued deep into the night with their discussions.

"It's not going to be like the last time I went through the Strissen Corridor, is it?" Karak asked, already knowing the answer.

"No, I fear not," Jarob answered, the weight of the situation finally hitting home with him. "That experience will merely have been a test run for a mission of this magnitude. Just in going to the Cruxfix System and back, you will have equaled the longest journey ever undertaken by one of our people."

"I almost didn't come back from that trip."

"I know. Your leadership paid off then, as much as your temper would with Smee later. I read your report, but I know some things don't make it into reports. What really happened out there?"

Karak just sat and stared blankly at nothing for a moment. Then he sat his glass down. "We were travelling through the Strissen Corridor, and a free-floating asteroid collided with us. Our helmsman wasn't paying attention, but honestly, it wasn't entirely his fault. He was performing a routine diagnostic, which is standard when you're cruising through an unknown region. That protocol is meant to ensure the ship is operating at peak efficiency while you're in strange space."

"Sure."

"Our starboard engine was destroyed, the shield generator system was fried, and power systems were overloaded all over the ship. Life support was barely functioning. We had more injured crew than healthy and I had to think fast. I took over the helm and turned us around slowly to head back home. I ordered that all non-essential areas be cordoned off and power to those decks cut completely."

"If it weren't for your quick thinking and leadership, you might not have made it home."

"I don't want to take any of the credit, let alone all of it. My crew, what was left of it, performed admirably. That's why I put them all in for commendations when we got back. I had to make an uplifting and positive speech right there on the bridge in the middle of the Strissen Corridor telling them we were going to make it home in one piece. I wasn't even sure it was true, but they had to believe it. As soon as we got out of the Corridor and within communications range, I sent a message for help. A warship met up with us two days later and took us into its bay. From there we began repairing the damage. You should have heard the yelling and language Field Marshal Notolla used when we finally got the ship back to the dock."

"You got your crew home."

"We didn't accomplish our mission to explore beyond the Corridor."

"No, but you weren't responsible for what happened either."

"Now I am going to be responsible for saving all our people."

"No pressure."

Karak smirked. "This is the biggest thing we've ever done," he said. "We're not ready."

"Get ready."

X X X

Chapter 3

TIME IS OF THE ESSENCE

The next day, the now cultivated group of the Rongi representatives gathered in the same place they had met before. The top order of business was to decide when they should leave on their quest, but first they would have to sort out a few other things.

Karak was clad in boots that had seen their share of the workload, pants that were charcoal in color whose cuffs were frayed and dirty and also somewhat worn at the knees. There were three things he hated: public appearances, public recognition, and being lied to. He hated when the attention was on him, good or bad. His goal in life was to do work; he had made no time for family. He simply wanted to accomplish the tasks that were set before him. He was first to speak.

"Now that we've decided that this endeavor is in the best interests of our people, we must discuss a few important things. First on the list is our destination. We don't know where the Orbs are, so we don't know where to begin our quest. I was hoping that the duke, our Orb expert, might have some input on this matter."

"Indeed, I do," the duke said as he straightened in his chair. "I believe we should make for the Cruxfix System. According to the stories, that's where they were created, and it's logical to assume they would know more about the Orbs than anyone else. They may know where the Orbs are, and they may be able to further educate us about them. It's also possible they can help us if our mission should become a longer and more serious commitment."

"We also know they are wise and helpful," Surist said, raising a stout hand. "They saved my life there so long ago. Inster was in charge when I was last there, but I believe he died a few years ago."

"Yes," Karak said, pointing to Surist in agreement. "I hear his chief advisor, Gronil, has succeeded him. I know little to nothing about him, but I can only assume he's a wise man and a good leader, if he's any representation of the Cruxfix people and their leaders as I have known them." He looked around at the group. "It's decided then; we will go to the Cruxfix System and plan the rest of our journey based on what we learn from them while we're there. The next order of business is to decide the time of our departure. We don't yet have all of our supplies, but time is of extreme importance. We must move with all expediency."

"The duke and I have conversed on this, and we have come to the conclusion that it would be best to take time and gather supplies," Hiram said quickly. "It would be counterproductive if we had to turn around and come back—or if we didn't have enough supplies to get to the Cruxfix System. I think once we've left we should not return until we have total success in this mission."

Notolla then squinted and furrowed her brow. "Surist and I thought it would be best if we got started as soon as possible. We're going to have to re-supply somewhere anyway. We have enough supplies to get to the Cruxfix System now. We can just go. Why take time to gather redundant supplies? We can't afford to waste any time."

"What if something happens and we don't have enough supplies?" Hiram asked. "It has already been mentioned that this mission may wind up taking much longer than we think. I don't want to run out of anything in the middle of something I don't understand in a place I don't know surrounded by people who may not like us. Space is full of perils; you should know this, Notolla."

"The praetor and I discussed this topic last night, and we agree with both sides of the issue," Karak said, pushing the air down with his hands in a calming way. "I've already sent orders to the planet Pern so we may pick up our remaining supplies on our way out of the system, but this still does not answer our question. When do we want to leave?"

"Since supplies are no longer an issue, I believe we should leave immediately," Lithinia added in a slightly higher octave. "We only have a couple of months, and we don't know if we can accomplish our mission even if the Orbs exist and can help us."

"Then upon this matter we are agreed also," Karak said. "I have been thinking about another point. We need a name for this group. This is not necessary for us, but it is for our people. They need something to call us. A name will provide a more mentally-tangible object, and that will provide them with a galvanizing hope. Does anyone have any suggestions?"

The duke shrugged. "It should be a name we can all relate to, and it should be of emotional value."

"How about the Weary Wanderers?" Lithinia asked with a smile. "That's likely to be our best description by the time we get back."

"We haven't even started yet," Karak said. "How can we be weary? If the people think we're already tired, they'll lose all faith before they ever have it."

Surist grinned. "I quite like the Galaxy Surfers."

"We will be swimming with sharks," Notolla said curtly, eyeing Surist as though she were a predator stalking her prey. "There are civilizations out there more advanced than ourselves. We may find enemies."

"I don't like the Galaxy Surfers," the duke said, not realizing that Surist was joking. "It sounds too much like Galactic Hippies, and besides, we're not on a pleasure cruise."

"Galactic Groupies!" Surist yelled. "That's it!"

"Can we vote him out of the group?" Notolla asked sarcastically.

"Heeeeeey," Surist complained mildly, feigning a whining offense. He was quiet for a while now, much to everyone's delight.

"What about just calling ourselves the Orb Seekers? That's what we are now," Hiram proposed.

After a moment of disbelief that someone had finally taken the question seriously, Karak said, "It sounds straightforward and simple, and these are qualities people will appreciate. Since there are no objections, we will henceforth be known as the Orb Seekers. Now, we need a mode of transportation."

A few members of the newly dubbed Orb Seekers looked in Surist's direction, almost hoping he would suggest something ridiculous like a caravan of camels.

Surist said nothing.

"I will take care of that. I already have a plan to see to our transportation needs," Notolla said with a sly smile. "I just have to inspect the ship and bring it here."

A few hours later, Lithinia and Surist were in the Memorial Scout, the local hotspot for information, an exciting story or two, although probably embellished, and good grub. They had discussed the group's plan and gone over potential flight plans, speculating about what obstacles they might run into. They had brought information on known cultures, rumors of cultures they hadn't met officially, all known information on the Orbs, astronomical charts, and previous mission reports. They'd discussed so many different options and possibilities, their attention was wavering and their eyes were beginning to glaze over. The enormity of this mission was only surpassed by the gravity of the situation.

The Memorial Scout was a large building which incorporated each level of architecture in the history of Vock I. Out front, the giant brass double doors spanned 36 feet tall and a dozen in width, but a more normal sized cut-out would open for regular foot traffic. Rarely did the doors become opened in their entirety. That was reserved for ceremonies celebrating the return of a crew after the completion of a difficult mission that advanced the cause of the Rongi exploration of space. On either side of the doors were eight giant columns that lead up to the eave overhanging the portico. These columns were just as tall and impressive as the doors. The establishment took up an entire block in the capital city on Vock I. The highly acclaimed facility was a usual meeting place for various things. It was one of the best known places in the Rongi System.

The Memorial Scout was built in dedication to the many explorers who had, for one reason or another, perished in the voyaging of the galaxy. Many of these explorers died in the early years of space exploration. They simply set a course away from their home and relayed information back home through a long web-like series of probes that had been deployed little by little with each mission of exploration. Many of those now seemingly ancient probes had long since ceased functioning, but a few still transmitted data.

Those explorers who did eventually return home had great and terrifying stories of the outer reaches of space. Some believed they had experienced something out there that messed with their minds and caused them to become unhinged. These former explorers would tell unbelievable stories and they were often passed off as crazy. Some of them did, of course, embellish their accounts, but one thing was sure, they were grateful for the dedication of the Memorial Scout and showed this gratitude with their frequent patronage. Surist was a regular and a staple customer, as well as well-known to everyone there. Some of the missions he and his brother and father had been on over the years were the stuff of legend.

"It might be a shorter journey if we were to pass through the Consraka Nebula Cluster," Lithinia suggested, unsure even of her own idea and knowing this would meet with instant and vehement disapproval.

"It would be death to do so," Surist interrupted with cold eyes. "There is a great and ancient beast there we don't want to disturb under normal circumstances, let alone the most dire."

"An ancient beast?" Lithinia questioned with a chuckle. "Are you just being silly again? I mean, yes, I've heard rumors, but nothing more, nothing conclusive."

"No," Surist said harshly and forebodingly issuing a blank look from his distant cold, brown eyes. "It's out there, I promise. You should ask Hiram. He's seen it on his quests."

"I see," Lithinia said lowly, conceding the idea. "I see that you're serious."

Surist's tone changed from grave to experienced. "No, I think we should start by going through the Strissen Corridor."

"Won't we be slowed by the gravity in the Corridor?"

"A lot will depend on the ship Notolla chooses for our journey."

"I hope we don't run into any of those more advanced civilizations she spoke of," Lithinia added, wringing her hands. "That could mean our expedition would be over almost before we even set out, let alone before we can finish it."

"Perhaps they'll be helpful and not enemies."

"I am a realist. They'll be a hindrance."

Surist sighed. "You're probably right."

They sipped their drinks for a while, thinking silently about what they might run across out in the depths of space with so much on the line. Surist had ventured a long way in his life, but the furthest he'd ever been was likely to be only the first leg of their journey, and Surist had travelled farther than any other Rongi who'd ever made it back home. They were scared, very scared. They were so scared, in fact, they would have admitted it.

At last Lithinia broke the silence. "Can I gather from your statements at the Council last night and today that you once lived in the Cruxfix System?" she asked, looking at Surist wide-eyed.

"Yes, I did for a very short time. They are an interesting people there—all highly educated and logical. In their history, they were explorers. But in modern times, they've rearranged their list of priorities. They now value the history of all people and the ability to learn from it. They believe that history holds the key to the future, and that to develop into our best futures, we must know ourselves now and in the past as best we can. Many people seek their counsel, as we are."

"Do you believe they will be able to guide us?" Lithinia asked.

"I do. All of the information we have suggests the Orbs were created there. If this is true, they may have some of the Orbs, or at least know their locations."

"How did you come to live with the people of the Cruxfix System?" Lithinia inquired, "What took you there?"

"Thirteen years ago, my father, brother, and I were on our way to the Cruxfix System. All we wanted to do was visit and learn a little more about their culture. On our previous journey, we had been in a scout ship when we discovered their system and opened communications with them. However, we were unable to land and make face-to-face contact, as we didn't have sufficient power to go there, visit, and still return home, so we could only talk for a short time. It was established early in our initial communications that our ships ran on indimite, a substance they no longer refined in the Cruxfix System, as their technology had developed beyond using it, so our ship couldn't be refueled for the return journey."

"You left home without the ability to refuel your ship." Lithinia's mouth hung open.

"Yes, our second trip was made with extra supplies so we could establish solid relations with them and also help them set up a system for refueling our ships. It was decided at a different council, similar to the one we've had here these last few days, that it would be a great thing to have a port of call, as it were, at which we could refuel and resupply and continue on a longer journey. On the second trip, we took an escort class vessel with a slower speed and a little less sensor range, but capable of carrying more supplies. Also, it was a little bit tougher ship.

"We were getting ready to land on this second journey when, for an unknown reason, our ship suffered a chain reaction of onboard systems failures," Surist continued, talking with his hands as he was prone to do. "We could do nothing to prevent the ship from crashing, so we tried to lessen the force of the impact as much as possible. Despite our efforts, our ship crashed violently, and it was later scrapped for spare parts—and only a few of those. Much of it was irreparably damaged. We crashed on the capital planet in the Cruxfix System. I was the only survivor. My father, brother, and our entire crew were killed. Luckily for me, I was not hurt so badly the doctors couldn't repair me. It took a long time to recover physically, but emotionally it took even longer. I've served as science officer on several missions of exploration outside the Rongi System. I have actually ventured farther out of Rongi space than anyone else ever has."

"How did you get back home?"

"While I was recuperating in their hospital, they went ahead and set up a specific landing pad to refuel and resupply any future ships of ours that might want or need to set down there. The people of the Cruxfix System were kinder than I could have imagined. They brought me home in one of their ships. They didn't have much of a navy, but they were willing to help."

Lithinia studied her drink, then spoke softly. "I'd only heard a few allusions to the event. I hadn't thought that it would have affected you in such a profound way. It must have taken a lot for you to return to the stars."

"I spent about a month in the hospital recovering. At first, after arriving back home, I refused to board a ship," Surist admitted with a bow of his head, "but later, I realized the ideals instilled in me by my father could not be denied and, in fact, must continue to be pursued. So I got back at the science officer's post on another ship and continued to explore. I suppose I'm stronger because of the experience."

"It takes great strength to recover from an ordeal such as the one you endured," Lithinia shook her head sadly. "I have no doubt your experience and good relations with the Cruxfix people will be of value on this mission."

The day after the group decided on a destination, their ship was ready to embark on its voyage. Field Marshal Notolla had procured and renamed a cruiser class vessel, the *Malus Tempus*, for their voyage. Rongi cruisers had a short but protruding nose flanked on either side by a wing containing two of the ship's six laser guns. In the nose were the bridge, main sensors, and several weapons, including the forward torpedo bay. In the aft of the vessel were the engines and the aft torpedo bay. On both sides of each wing were two more laser guns. The crew's quarters, medical facility, engineering section, and other non-command stations sat in the main body of the craft. The ship only required a crew of five to operate as it had advanced automation systems.

The entire ship could be controlled from the bridge. Cruisers were small but powerful for their size, and the *Malus Tempus* would be flown by the best crew in the fleet.

"I'm impressed with your choice, marshal," Karak said, nodding his head. "This ship will serve us well. She's perfect for our needs."

"She's ready to go on whatever voyage we want," Notolla said.

"Will it get us to the Cruxfix System?" Karak asked.

"It will get us farther than that," Notolla said loudly and with a smile nearly as big as the task before them. "You could fly this ship from here to the other side of known space if you wanted to. It will also defend us should we find ourselves in battle. I have personally seen to the outfitting of this craft with all its weapons. It will take us anywhere. The journey of a thousand miles may begin with a single step, but the journey across the galaxy begins by pushing the *start* button and setting a course."

"Well, there's no time like the present." Karak placed his dirty scuffed boot on the boarding ramp. "Shall we go?"

The Orb Seekers entered their new ship and headed for the bridge. Karak didn't want any kind of sendoff, just to be on his way and trying to accomplish his mission. A living area made up most of the crew quarters. These rooms included a few windows through which one could look out into space and some simple furniture, always dark blue. These fixtures consisted of a few chairs and what the duke termed a chesterfield. Lithinia insisted they were davenports. Hiram just called his a couch when they argued about it.

A small room was available for fixing personal meals and snacks, but all major dining was done in the larger kitchen, located just outside the infirmary. The proximity of these two areas was the central butt of many jokes.

Elsewhere on the *Malus Tempus* was the engineering section. This vital part of the ship was controlled directly from the bridge and only occasionally required a technician to perform repair and maintenance work, tasks any one of the crew could perform. Also located in the extreme rear of the ship was the shuttle bay where two small shuttles were kept. Shuttles were of a very similar shape and configuration as the *Malus Tempus* herself.

The bridge held a large window in the front and center just behind which sat the helm to the right and a science station to the left. In the middle was the captain's chair with control panels and display screens on both arms. Along the wall and to the left of the captain were the communications post and the second science officer's post. Behind the captain to the right was the tactical position where Notolla would be stationed.

Upon entering the command room, Hiram seated himself at the helm and, pointing to the large red button on the console, jokingly said, "And this, I presume, is the thruster control switch."

Notolla glared at him. "That's the activation switch for the self-destruct panel. I thought you knew how to pilot a ship. I thought you did this sort of thing for a living." Notolla's annoyance increased with each sentence.

"I was only joking," Hiram said as he effortlessly lifted the ship off the landing platform and piloted it into the atmosphere. "I assume we'll take the Strissen Corridor in order to avoid the Consraka Nebulae, Karak."

"Yes, that would be wise," Karak said definitively. "Irritating Agri is the last thing I want to do. You know, people, a cruiser has never been through the Strissen Corridor. We may find something new out here the scout ships haven't seen. Keep your eyes open to the sensor readings, science officers duke of White and Surist."

After they got the ship underway and picked up additional supplies at Pern by docking with a Rongi warship to save time by not having to land anywhere, they decided to take a look at their quarters. The identical rooms each had a chamber with a bed large enough for two people, though this wasn't exactly the kind of mission that called for bringing families along. Flanking the bed were small night tables holding artificial greenery. Empty shelves waited along the wall, which was in all other ways bare.

The *Malus Tempus* ventured on out of Rongi space and headed into the Strissen Corridor, an interesting phenomenon in its own right. They wouldn't have extra time to explore every little thing, but they would certainly be interested to see what the ship's advanced sensors were able to pick up. The sensors on scout and escort ships provided long range detection of incoming ships, but the sensors on a cruiser class vessel offered more range and greater depth of scanning ability. This was because the emitters in the sensor array were able to focus the sensor beam more narrowly, thus lessening the dissipation effect over longer distances. They were also able to scan on wavelengths other ships couldn't. The cruiser class of ships was still fairly new, and none had gone through the Strissen Corridor with its full sensor array scanning.

ꙕ ꙕ ꙕ

Chapter 4

THE HIGHS AND LOWS OF DUTY

At the same time the Orb Seekers began navigating the Strissen Corridor, the Braline were preparing to embark on their own journey. They had absolutely no idea what awaited them in the cold vastness of space. Though they had been as far as the Cruxfix System a time or two before, they hadn't dedicated as many resources to exploration as the Rongi—nor any other civilization in the known parts of the galaxy, for that matter. Their past had been consumed by defending their home from repeated brutal attacks by the Sekurai, their long-time and only rival in the galaxy.

Levu Earsp walked down a long hallway to a scheduled farewell dinner to send them off on their dangerous and uncertain mission. Humwe was going to the same place, and he met Levu on the way. The hallway was well adorned with large tapestries which, when seen and interpreted one by one, told stories of the old times. Some told of times before the Braline were a space-faring people and others were of more recent events. There were scenes in great detail about the wars the Braline had fought. Some of the most honored and revered people were pictured doing the great deeds that made them famous.

These tapestries were hung on long rods and featured elegantly braided tassels dangling from the bottom side. They were easily made out, but the dyes used to color the threads were such that they gave the appearance of slight fading. None of the tapestries were brightly colored; all were somewhat muted. This had the effect of inspiring one to stay and admire not only the craftsmanship, but also to take in the entire scene depicted on any one piece.

"Levu, I hear that General Regti has found a ship that will suit our needs," Humwe said excitedly, then lowered his voice. "I hope he's chosen well."

"It disturbs me that a tapestry such as these is being made for our journey." Levu nodded towards the nearest tapestry, ignoring Humwe. "After all, all of the people seen here are dead now. Some died of old age, yes, but most died in some kind of horrible or nasty way, either in battle or in some perilous accident." He paused and turned his attention to Humwe. "Yes, I've heard the same thing," Levu continued, finally acknowledging Humwe with a furrowed brow, "but he hasn't told anyone which ship it is, or even what its capabilities are."

"Perhaps he's planning to reveal it at the banquet tonight," Humwe suggested, opening his eyes just a bit wider than normal. "I hope he does. I would like to see it and get an idea of what we're getting ourselves into before we go star hopping."

"Whatever he's done, I hope it's ready to go. I want to leave as soon as the farewell party is over. He knows I don't like surprises," Levu said with a small eye roll.

Kolij joined them in the main corridor from a tributary hall. Her bright smile betrayed every emotion she was feeling at the moment. "Have you heard that Regti has a ship for us?"

"Humwe and I were just talking about it," Levu said. "You don't know anything about it, do you?"

"No," Kolij said. "I was hoping you would know something, since you'll be commanding it. He isn't allowing anyone near it."

"Where's everyone else?" Levu asked, looking around curiously with his hands turned up and arms partially outstretched. "Prak, Nurisk, and Regti should be here. We're supposed to make some kind of damned classy, overrated entrance to this banquet as a group." He scowled. "I hate fancy appearances," he growled as he tugged uncomfortably at his coat lapels, "almost as much as I hate surprises."

"General Regti reporting for damned classy, overrated entrance to farewell banquet," the general said sarcastically as he stepped out of a small room along the hallway.

"General, you know I hate surprises," Levu said with a sneer.

"Yes, but I couldn't resist. I'm told that Nurisk and Prak are already there waiting for us.

"Good," Levu said. "That means we don't have to be looked upon like gods when we walk through the door. Let's go."

"By the way, I am ready to die, like many of those in our tapestries, if it's necessary," Humwe said, finishing off the conversation he and Levu were having before Kolij joined them. "And I don't need any tapestry."

Levu just looked at Humwe and smiled. They both hoped it wouldn't come to their deaths, but they knew what was at stake might require drastic measures and could claim some lives in the attempt to save many, many more.

They entered the ballroom through a back door, which irritated King Brale to no end, and seated themselves in their designated spots next to their families. The frustration of the king was almost as much to Levu's liking as not having to take part in a fancy entrance.

The ballroom was a large circular room with a conical ceiling, the uppermost portion of which was made of multicolored stained glass arranged in a pattern that was a dazzling display of color and spatial orientation. The sizes and shapes of the glass pieces had been unplanned when the ceiling was built, which was widely considered to be the beauty of the structure. The room was centered by a circular table of the same shape and proportions as the room.

The meal was delicious and plentiful and included each person's requested foods, all Braline delicacies the group might not taste again for some time.

Everyone told stories of their accomplishments, battle scars, and just their lives in general. No doubt a seamstress had been among the invitees so notes could be taken on what should be added to the tapestry that was being made for this key event in Braline history. One of the most moving stories was of the building of the Kriline Defense Barrier. A large viewing screen was brought in to show the video accounts of the event. King Brale had the tapestry removed from its place of honor and brought in for all to see.

"The Kriline Defense Barrier," the king began, pointing to the tapestry, "is our primary defense. About a century and a half ago, a race previously unknown to us introduced themselves as the Sekurai and claimed to have come to offer peace. King Brale LXV was suspicious of these Sekurai. The Sekurai pushed hard for peace to be made and finalized. The king theorized that the Sekurai wanted to use the supplies of the Strunk Nebula, our chief source of indimite. Indimite, as you all know, is the main power source for many ships."

As the king continued, many of those assembled shifted in their seats because they'd heard this story many times before. "The king suspected ulterior motives on the part of the Sekurai. Ordinarily, my predecessor could have just refused peace—something we've never done—but in this case, the enemy was much more powerful and could force us to accept this "peace"—or they could simply go in and take the resources from the Strunk Nebula. There would have been little or nothing we could do to stop them.

"What was not agreed upon was how to solve the problem. Some thought open confrontation would do it, but the idea of open war was thrown out because our small, backward force would not stand a chance against the Sekurai fleet. Their ships were far more numerous and possessed greater firepower, had stronger defensive systems, and were led by more experienced officers. Their ships were more maneuverable and faster, as well. It was long considered that a large, three-dimensional minefield should be spread between the two systems. This would be effective for a time, but the minefield would eventually fall, and simply replacing the mines just prolonged the war. Also, the Sekurai could just go around the minefield and attack us anyway."

The king noticed he had Humwe's full attention; he hadn't heard the story before.

"One other idea was brought up, and it was the one, in conjunction with another, that was implemented. One of our representatives, Kriline, said asteroids should be brought from the solar system, and anywhere else they could be found, and placed just beyond the system in orbit in a spherical pattern around our small solar system. There would be small holes in a few places in this wall for outgoing ships and approved incoming ships. These holes would be mined and heavily guarded. A combination of tactics was applied. The minefield was set up to allow us to get the asteroids in place. We set all our ships to bringing the asteroids into orbit around the system and named the wall of asteroids after the man whose idea it was."

General Regti looked over at Kolij, alongside whom he'd fought the Sekurai in the last war. They knew all about the Kriline Defense Barrier.

"The Sekurai took this as an act of war and attacked the minefield. To go around the minefield would have left it in place, thus hampering future travel to and from our system, a region of space they wished to occupy. However, the mines did buy us time. The mines were all destroyed, but not without bringing heavy damage to the Sekurai fleet, for even though the Sekurai were far more powerful, our mines were so numerous they were able to lessen the Sekurai attack force and delay their strike for just long enough.

"The Sekurai then began attacking the Kriline Defense Barrier, which had been completed by the time the minefield was destroyed. Asteroids were hauled in from all over our space, made by blasting some of our uninhabited planets as well as those in other systems, and from everywhere else they could be found, including free-floating asteroids, but mostly from material being sucked in thus far short of the event horizon by the gravitational pull of Redron, the largest black hole known to exist. Redron was, and still is, viewed as a ravenous beast in the cold blackness of space because of all the material it consumes. To further make it difficult for potential invaders, the asteroids themselves were sent into a fast orbit, like a fan blade which, when still, covers only its area, but when in fast enough of a motion, affects a much greater area, thereby reducing the number of asteroids necessary to complete the structure while still causing massive navigational obstacles for anyone unwelcome wanting to enter through one of the apertures. It was an immense undertaking, but it was successful.

"Because the small holes in the structure were mined and supported by warships, they soon found that any ships that attacked it were utterly destroyed. The Kriline Defense Barrier saved the Braline people and it has been in place ever since."

Once the meal and presentation were complete, they all knew they had to get back to business. It was time to say goodbye to family and friends. Everyone looked around, not wanting to begin.

Eventually, General Regti stood. "I think we can postpone the inevitable for a few more minutes. Some of you have been rather skeptical of my suspicious activities recently," he said with a sly smile as he rubbed his palms together. "I've told some of you that I found a ship that should do better than any other. This is true, and I think it's now time to show it to you, and if you will follow me, I'll do just that."

They all ventured out of the ballroom and down the main hall, which opened directly onto a landing pad. When everyone saw the ship, they gasped. Its design was that of a side view of a pyramid. The ship, when looked at from above, was a right isosceles triangle and was colored blue and green. It was a giant wedge that would fly through space. In the nose, which is where the wings met at a ninety-degree angle, was the bridge, a missile launcher, the main sensor array, and two laser guns. At the aft of the ship spaced about one-third of the way in from the wing tips were the ship's two engines, boxes protruding downward from the body of the craft, which were subdivided into three smaller engine thrusters. The power channeled to each of these thrusters was variable and would allow for the ship to be turned. Also, at the rear of the ship were the aft missile launcher, aft guns, and a small shuttle bay which comprised much of the fairly small vessel.

"It's a new class of ship, a cross between an escort class and a cruiser," Regti said. "It's a smaller, more maneuverable vessel whose size and power output are between those of fighters and our current escorts. We've been working on a new ship for some time, and have performed many test runs. It has passed every test we could put it through. I can't tell you the ship's limits because we haven't found them yet. This ship is called the *Quia Vita* and it will bear us on our journey across the stars. It's equipped with two fore and two aft laser guns, as well as one on each side, dorsal and ventral. To compliment those, we have at our disposal fore and aft torpedo launchers.

"And the passengers that have been selected are the best minds in our culture," Regti continued. "The king, Levu, and I discussed the possibility of beginning evacuation efforts with our journey to the Cruxfix System. Our passengers are among our most precious cargo, along with the hopes and dreams of all our people. We will transport them to the Cruxfix System where they will take up residence and coordinate further evacuation efforts there as possibilities emerge in their study of the Cruxfix database."

"I am pleased with your choice," Levu said in a surprised tone. "It sounds like a good ship, but why haven't we heard of this new class of vessel?"

"We're trying to keep these things a secret," King Brale answered as he looked around, feigning slight paranoia. "There are still those in the universe who would take advantage of any knowledge they could obtain, and the Sekurai are sure to have spies everywhere. There will be time to ask questions of General Regti later. Now it's time for you to say your farewells and take off on your journey."

Everyone said their goodbyes; they shed some tears and coughed up a little laughter. None of them wanted to leave, but they knew they would die if they didn't, and perhaps even if they did.

As they turned to enter the ship, King Brale stopped them. "You have been chosen to represent our culture in the hour of our greatest need. Your journey will require the utmost levels of courage, patience, and preparation. You should go in hope and also in fear. Hope that you will succeed so you may never give in, and go in fear of what will happen should you fail. Let nothing deter you. Take any action necessary to achieve your goals. The price of survival is irrelevant so long as survival is the end. Remember what's at stake. Now is the time to hold nothing back. You are not only on a quest to preserve our very existence, but our culture, our legacy, and the posterity of our people for which you have all fought at various points throughout your lives."

After this short speech, the group bowed low to their king and turned to enter their ship, which would be their companion for however long it took to accomplish the task at hand. They knew they had to get to the Cruxfix System to get help in saving their people from the voracious appetite of Redron.

"Set course for the Cruxfix System," Levu said. "Hopefully, they can help us there."

The ship lifted off from the landing pad and ascended into space. "Setting course for the hole in the Cruxfix side of the Barrier," Kolij said.

"How long before we leave the system?" Levu asked.

"About two hours to clear the Barrier," Kolij responded. Knowing Levu as she did, she knew he would frequently ask "how long".

"This is the time I hate," Levu said. "Even if we were going to fail in our task, I would rather know now."

After the ship left the Kriline Defense Barrier, the crew went to investigate their quarters and the amenities of the ship. The quarters were quite plain, save a few things, but would serve their purposes well. Each crew member's residence consisted of a living area with a few end tables that flanked a few large cushiony chairs and a glass table with a wrought iron frame. Included, however, was a large fully stocked kitchen with everything one would need to prepare most of the more popular Braline culinary specialties.

The bedrooms were the plainest of all rooms. They were composed only of a bed and four walls. The room was only large enough for the bed to be shoved into a corner with a two foot walkway around the foot and one side. Throughout the quarters, though, smaller versions of the tapestries which lined the halls in the king's palace hung on the walls of the quarters.

The part of the ship that Levu was most pleased with was the hole in the floor just next to his captain's chair on the bridge. It was just the right size for his staff to fit in two feet deep. He never could get Regti to admit that he'd had the hole put there intentionally, but somehow he knew.

The bridge was very much to Levu's liking. The large view screen was directly in front of him with no officers' stations in front of the screen. Most ships in the Braline navy had stations between the captain and the screen. Levu didn't want any obstacles; he wanted to see everything all the time. The various positions and stations were scattered along the side walls and the rear wall of the bridge.

Late in day five of their journey, the *Quia Vita* was noticeably passing into the gravity well of Harza, a medium sized black hole. Harza was just a little more than halfway between the Braline System and the Cruxfix System.

"Levu," Humwe said, "we should adjust our course to go around the area of Harza that will affect us most."

"Won't going around it take extra time?" Levu raised a hand questioningly.

"No, we would be slowed down too much if we tried to go through. It would take longer to go through this part of Harza's gravitational field than to go around. I can plot a course that will take us on the most efficient route, keeping us from crossing the event horizon and being sucked in as well as not going too far out of our way and taking longer than necessary."

"Why is there always something in my way?" Levu whined as he grimaced. "Here we are on the cusp of the end of our civilization, the dawning of a new age, the changing of our universe, and we have to walk around a mud puddle. How much extra time will it take?"

"It will take about three or four hours more than we'd planned," Humwe said.

Kolij shifted uncomfortably in her seat at hearing this obstacle would claim several more hours of their time.

"Oh, very well, go around Harza," Levu acceded. "I just hope this little detour doesn't cause us to waste too much time. That would be very bad indeed."

As the *Quia Vita* executed a parabolic course around Harza instead of passing through a more significant portion of its gravitational pull, the crew were all highly anxious about their mission. This would not simply be a cruise across the galaxy.

ℵ ℵ ℵ

ra Solar System

Rongi Sol

Strissen Corridor

Dran

Ghor

k Cluster

Strant

Chapter 5

THE HALL OF ROCK

The Strissen Corridor is a long and deep tunnel surrounded on either side, above, and below by walls of asteroids that are so large and so compact that the spaces between them are not navigable. This entire phenomenon is encased in a fold in space. Once one enters this hall of rock, there are only two ways out of it: the way he came or the far end.

"Even at maximum speed, the *Malus Tempus* could not make the trip in less than a week," Hiram said while making constant adjustments to the ship's course, "and probably a little more, depending on how the currents and eddies knock us around along the way."

"An even stranger part of the Corridor—the walls of rock are held in place by a spatial tunnel," Karak added while stroking his chin and looking intently out of the bridge window. "I've been here before. This tunnel provides sufficient gravitational forces to hold the asteroids in place. The spatial tunnel is a corridor in itself. It's the fastest way out of Rongi space, and so makes the best route for us to take."

"So many asteroids have been taken into the spatial tunnel," the duke said, looking perplexedly at the readouts on his mapping computer, "but are kept on the perimeter of the tube by orbiting its center of gravity such that they've formed a hall of rock. However, there are asteroid collisions on the perimeter of the tube. Due to this, there will be free-floating asteroids in the middle of the tunnel, and navigation will be difficult and dangerous."

"This is another reason why our people haven't explored very much in this direction," Surist said. "There are so many hindrances to exploration around our system."

A quick maneuver jolted the crew. As soon as everyone was back in their seats, Hiram said, "The spatial currents which are funneled by the Corridor will actually move a ship more than its engines." He paused to concentrate as he looked upward out of the navigation window, checking to see if they were going to collide with a nearby asteroid. "That's the reason ships can't move as quickly outside the Corridor. The currents are not funneled outside the Corridor, and ships would take longer to pass through the region, even though the ride might be smoother."

"There is no good way through the Corridor, but going through is the best option," Karak added as he met Lithinia's wide eyes. "The journey through the Corridor will still take a little while, and it would be a bit rough, boring—if we can avoid a collision, and a lot like riding rapids," he continued as he sarcastically eyed the back of Hiram's head. "Either way, it'll be more of a navigational challenge than we need, especially considering the weight of our mission."

"I agree with Surist," Hiram said as he made more course adjustments. "The Strissen Corridor is one of several natural space formations that have led to our isolation."

"We have only found other civilizations on the other sides of such formations as the Strissen Corridor and the Consraka Nebula Cluster," Surist added, looking at the duke and Lithinia.

"I know this isolation has been, at various points throughout our history, the subject of much debate," the duke said. "Some of our people have wanted to expand our sphere of influence and knowledge and branch out into the vastness of space. And some are opposed this idea for some of the same reasons."

The *Malus Tempus* jolted again as Hiram made a last second course correction to avoid a collision.

"How far is it to the Cruxfix System?" Lithinia asked in a high-pitched voice.

"With the Cruxfix System days away but somewhere far off to our starboard side, Ghor, the second nearest star, is on the port side of the ship," Hiram said calmly and slowly. "Ghor and Dran, which is on the other side of the Corridor, are outside the Corridor and on opposite sides of it. Stray asteroids traveling through this region of space are caught up in the stars' pull and eventually also by the spatial tunnel and find themselves placed almost as if by hand into a position along the circular interior wall of the Corridor."

There was very little the group could do since they had no information. Sensors were harshly affected by the electromagnetic fields of the stars and the density of the asteroid walls. Constant adjustments had to be made to the ship's course due to the gravity of the stars and the shortened range of the sensors. The line of sight was very short and the crew dared not go any faster. Someone had to be at the helm the entire time; no course could be set and left on automatic. The ship was constantly being pulled off course because of the whipping of the currents inside the Corridor.

Their time was occupied by meditation, recreation, and making the *Malus Tempus* feel more like home. Some played games to pass the time, while others immersed themselves in the ship's records, trying to learn everything they could about the mission ahead. Each member of the Orb Seekers did, however, have a chance to get to know one another better. There were many hours spent in discussion as either the whole group on the bridge or just two or three members who had gathered to share stories. Each individual that had left someone behind back home told of their families and how much they would miss their loved ones.

"I'll miss my wife and kids," Hiram said as he stared blankly at his console. "They and piloting are everything to me."

Lithinia turned toward Surist. "What should we expect from the Cruxfix people?"

"They're highly intelligent and deliberate," Surist said. "We should expect them to come up with the answer to our troubles, but we will have to accomplish the task ourselves, whatever it may be. The Cruxfix people don't have much of a navy."

Just then Karak and Notolla came charging through the door. "You knew that card was there all the time!" Notolla shouted. She was still holding her losing hand.

"Of course I did," Karak said. "That's why I didn't take it, and that's why I won." Karak smiled and eyed Notolla from the side as he sat down in his captain's chair.

Field Marshal Notolla set aside her disdain for losing cards to Karak and struck up conversation with the rest of the crew. "The government has told the people that Brack is simply a wasteland and a barren world. This is true on the outside, but the largest part of the Rongi navy is housed beneath the surface, through the natural crevices of the planet. Spish is thought to house the entire military at docking stations and shipyards in orbit, but we would rather not have all of our forces in the same place at the same time. So we allow a small part of the fleet to be seen, while the larger portion is constantly being upgraded and augmented. There are hundreds of ships inside the planet. That's where the cruisers like the *Malus Tempus* were designed, built, tested, and commissioned for larger scale construction. This ship was one of the first of its class to come off the line.

"Brack is a desolate and inhospitable planet on the outside. Its atmosphere is so thin it's practically nonexistent, and we don't possess the technology to create an artificial atmosphere on that scale. However, we can create a containment field for a smaller atmosphere, and that's what we have done underneath Brack's surface."

When the duke questioned her about the need for such a large force, the marshal answered, "At present it's not necessary and it never has been, but we don't want to begin construction on a fleet when it's needed. By then it would be too late. Time may be of the essence, as it is in our current situation. We would rather have resources readily available should they be needed."

"So there is a navy that can help us if we should find ourselves in trouble?" the duke asked. "That should come in handy."

"Those ships are otherwise engaged," Karak responded quickly. "They're currently evacuating as many of our people as possible. They'll only be able to help us if we are close to home. If we run into anything this far out, we're on our own. There's no help at all for us until we reach the Cruxfix System."

"A few years ago," Lithinia said as her eyes met Notulla's, "our chief mining facility on Adcar was growing old and unsafe. We had to do something to build a new facility, but we knew it would be better if it were located nearer to the actual mining work. The most heavily mined area is mountainous, though, making the task nearly impossible. But, I came up with an idea that would allow the structure to be closer to the work, but safe at the same time."

"Lithinia is an expert on mining and construction," Karak said to no one in particular. "She comes from a long line of family members who've worked building and maintaining mining facilities.

Construction being her specialty, she's resourceful and can take various things to other dimensions of use by transcending their original purposes. That's why she's here."

The ship shifted harshly again as Hiram made yet another course change.

"Well," said Lithinia with a grin and a chuckle, "it's certainly not because I like traveling in a place where the ship could be torn apart by an oncoming asteroid or sucked into some uncharted gravity-well thing." She paused and looked around to make sure her humor was well-received. "It sounds like we may have done something similar to what was found under the surface of Brack. Instead of building a new installation, we carved one right out of a mountain. We chose the most stable mountain and left enough rock between corridors and rooms that it was almost as structurally sound as when we started. After I came up with this idea, I was transferred to the Creative Thinking Department on Adcar. We try to apply revolutionary techniques to achieve higher production and safer environments. I'm guessing many of the materials we mine on Adcar go to the augmentation, as you put it," Lithinia said as she nodded in the marshal's direction, "of our navy."

"They do," Notolla agreed.

"It puts everything into a different perspective," Karak said. "All of the sudden everyone realizes they're part of a machine that's bigger than any individual and his or her personal tasks. We're trying to prolong a civilization and all its greatness. The Rongi have more than just a physical existence in their people; we have the essence of life. We have quality, not just quantity. There is history, art, architecture, technology, and literature. We are doing what we have always done—trying to use the past to interpret the present and create the future.

"Every member of this group silently knows that the times of such unnecessary levels and quantities of self-interest, as are all too often present in our people, could be detrimental to our cause. They also know that those representatives at the council who chose not to join this mission made their decision based on exactly that kind of self-interest. It has always run in our people, this self-centeredness. We all have to come together for a common goal. If those who had chosen to stay behind had decided differently, they might now understand that much more can be accomplished when you allow yourself to become galvanized toward an end than will ever be possible when working alone." Everyone paused to consider Karak's words.

Surist broke the icy silence that had been created so quickly with a prefacing slap of his knee, "Hiram, tell us about yourself. I've heard many things about your skill at the helm. You're one of the few people to try to navigate the Consraka Nebulae, and even fewer to come back alive."

"Flying amongst the stars was always my greatest passion. I knew it was what I would do from a very early age." Hiram waved his hand dismissively. "My first job was loading cargo ships while I was enrolled in flight school. I was tired of just hearing about the adventures of the pilots; I wanted to experience those things too.

"Later, when I began to run longer and more complicated routes and pilot larger ships with crews, I decided to try to find a safe route through the Consraka Nebulae. I wanted to see if any of the cluster's sections of open space between the different nebulae went all the way through to the other side. For a long time now, our explorers have tried to find a way through without suffering the deleterious effects of some of the nebulae, and catching the attention of Agri."

Upon hearing that name, everyone sat up straighter, as though a sharp, cold object had just been stuck up inside the middle of every-one's back.

"If such a route could be found," Surist continued as he raised his nose in understanding, "our ships would not have to go around the cluster; they could go through it. We could open up trade with those on the other side of the cluster. It's interesting how we've only ever discovered civilizations in one direction from our own solar system."

"As Surist said," Hiram began again, "there've only been a hand-ful of people who have survived the journey through the Consraka Nebulae. Few have tried to get entirely through the cluster. Those who did were unsuccessful. In fact, no one has ever seen the other side of the cluster by passing through it. The only way we know its outer dimensions is through the information that Surist's father, Hurid, was able to provide when his team went around the nebulae.

"When I made the trip, I encountered Agri. Everyone always seems to find her, or rather she finds them. There has rarely been a trip into the cluster when Agri has not been encountered. She saw me and headed straight for me at about the same time I saw her." Hiram began motioning with his hands as he spoke. "I saw her large bird-like figure silhouetted against one of the blue nebulae. It was as though a large hawk was bearing down on me. I was only in a scout ship, but I think she would have bettered an explorer ship in size. I didn't stick around long enough to get a good look, though. We now know she won't pursue anyone out of the cluster. But," Hiram paused to take sip from his cup, "she'll kill you if you go inside."

"Didn't the military send anyone in with you?" Lithinia asked.

"No," Field Marshal Notolla said. "We didn't know how powerful she was."

"We had no idea whether or not our weapons would have any effect on her," Hiram continued. I immediately lit up my engines at maximum and she was still gaining on me. So, I redirected all of my ship's power to the engines. The only reason I got out was the heat my engines were emitting. She was faster, but she had to stay back from the heat. We learned two very important things that day. One is that she is susceptible to heat, and she either refuses to leave the cluster or is intelligent enough not to engage a small fleet of warships waiting just outside. This, and only this, allowed me to get to the fleet before she got to me. So, yes, I survived. More importantly, I brought back valuable information about Agri."

After what turned out to be a nine-day journey through the Strissen Corridor, the Orb Seekers' sensors came fully online and their engines were running at full thrust. "Karak, there's something on my sensors that our ships have never recorded in this sector of space," the duke reported. "It's on the edge of sensor range, and I can't quite make it out."

"We don't have time to investigate every little thing that comes into sensor range," Karak said. "Prepare to alter course once we're clear of the last of the corridor."

"I think we might want to take a look at it," the duke said. "The sensors are now identifying it as an abandoned station."

"We've never seen any station out here," Lithinia said. "Perhaps our sensor adjustments were just powerful enough to pick it up at long range. Either way, we don't have time to explore. We have a mission to get on with."

"Agreed," Karak responded. "Maintain our original flight plan and make for the Cruxfix System at maximum speed."

"Karak," Notolla broke in, "I think it might be in our best interests to investigate, at least on a small scale."

"Why?" Karak questioned, eyeing Notolla.

"I was just thinking this station is on the very edge of sensor range," Notolla responded. "Even if it is abandoned, information from their databanks could lead us to allies. If it's old, maybe their logs have information about the Orbs. The station could also become a port in a storm to run back to without going all the way back home if we get into trouble—a place to resupply later. It could also become a place to evacuate our people to if necessary. Right now, we are just loading people onto our ships, but they have nowhere to go."

Karak looked at the duke and Lithinia for the latest sensor report and for opinions.

"It makes sense," the duke said, "There could at least be information in their computers that could help us."

"We wouldn't have to take time for a full on exploration of the station and surrounding area," Lithinia added. "We could just go aboard and download their computers' information and try to make sense of it on our way to the Cruxfix System. We aren't even equipped for a full investigation anyway. That would usually involve several scout ships and even transports to carry officers to explore the station."

"How do we know it's abandoned?" Notolla questioned as a warning. "Appearing to be abandoned is the oldest trick in the book."

"That may be," the duke agreed, "but it may also possess some technology or information that could help us on our quest."

"What do your sensors read, Surist?" Karak asked.

"The station is completely inactive, but it is intact," Surist said, examining the readings at his console. "The hull is in good condition and has not been compromised. Its defenses seem to be offline."

"I'm not detecting any life signs," the duke said. "I'm not even detecting any energy signatures. There hasn't been any activity here for a very long time."

"That means this place must be very old," Notolla said as she looked up from her console in surprise. "Energy signatures from engines or weapons fire remain in an area for a long time."

"Exactly how long?" Karak asked.

"Well," Surist answered slowly, "there is nothing out here to expedite the dissipation or movement of such energy signatures. There are no solar winds; there aren't even any stars in the area. There's nothing out here. It's a very funny place for a space station."

"Yes," Karak said a little impatiently as he looked over at Surist, "I can see that. But, how long has the station been abandoned? I don't want to walk into a trap, and I don't want to waste time."

"There's only one way to answer these questions," Notolla said as she tilted her head toward Karak, "and you know what that is."

"Well," Karak started, "I can't say no to adventure. Let's see what's on that station, if anything. Plot an intercept course and take us in. Remember, anything we do on that station has to be proactive toward our mission—no wasting time. I'm allotting a few hours, not an entire day. We have urgent and pressing needs to tend to."

"Course laid in," Hiram said as he tapped the appropriate controls on his console. "We'll be there in less than an hour."

"Let me know if your sensors reveal any more information as we near the station," Karak said. "I don't want to walk into a surprise."

"Everything is likely to be a surprise on this mission," Surist said nonchalantly, "if my past explorations are any indication."

Karak glared at Surist.

⅄ ⅄ ⅄

Chapter 6

FINDERS KEEPERS

The abandoned space station was a large ovoid section laying almost horizontal relative to the *Malus Tempus*, but cocked just a little, with five irregular pentagonal platforms emanating from it at equal angles. It had a large number of defensive laser gun turrets as well as many warhead launchers, in addition to an intense, multilevel defense ring of gravity mines. Also around the station were several containers which were presumably for cargo, supplies, and, due to the seemingly military association of this heavily armed station, probably munitions, and a few small shipyards as well. The place seemed a veritable fortress beyond anything its Rongi investigators had ever seen.

"We're coming up on the station, Karak," Hiram reported.

"Duke, what are your sensors reading?" Karak asked, catching his science officer's eyes fixed on the window instead of his console.

"The place is abandoned. There's no activity whatsoever, and there are absolutely no signs that any activity has taken place anywhere near the station in a very long time," the duke said. "There are no power signatures, no movement, no communications, no life signs, nothing."

The closer the Orb Seekers got, the more answers they were able to gain. "Karak," Notolla said, "The station is inoperative and the minefield defense grid isn't working. Most of the containers outside the station are still intact, but nothing is known about their contents."

"Are the docking ports still operational?" Karak asked, swiveling around in his chair.

"Nothing appears to be mechanically wrong," Surist answered, "but they will require power. The station is entirely powerless now. An access code will be necessary to activate the mechanism, but we don't know what code to transmit. We can't even be sure their transceivers are working well enough to receive a message."

"If they have transceivers, they should be able to send messages as well as receive them," Lithinia said. "Perhaps we can initiate communications ourselves."

"The design of this station is completely unknown to me," Karak said. "I don't suppose that, from all your studies, you could give us any information, marshal."

"No, I've never seen anything like this," Notolla responded as she looked out the main window on the bridge. "I can tell you, though, that when the military wants to activate a ship or station that has no power, we initiate a power transfer beam and angle it into one of their receivers. Then we could try to send some messages and hope for an automated response that would indicate something about their language and perhaps the necessary code or signal to allow us to dock."

"After we've sent power to the station, if we were to transmit a distress signal and request to dock, it might allow it," Lithinia suggested.

"But there's no one on board," Hiram observed, raising an upturned and outstretched hand toward Lithinia. "Well, no one that we know of."

"It might work," Surist said. "Even our stations, which are less advanced than this one, have automated systems for things like communications."

"If that's the case," Notolla said, "once we've gained information, we may be able to convince the automated system to open up a docking port."

"Hiram, do you think you can pilot and dock the ship on manual?" Karak asked.

"Yes, but why?"

"If we can make the station think we actually do need help, our message will be more convincing. Its system may be programmed to scan for evidence of our alleged systems failures. Duke, take some systems offline," Karak ordered.

"I'm taking long range sensors and primary engines offline and setting life support to minimum," the duke said as he operated several controls on his console.

"I'm ready to send the power transfer beam, Karak," Surist said.

"Initiate the transfer," Karak ordered. "Notolla, keep an eye on the power levels of the station. We don't want to give it too much—just enough to respond to our message and open the docking port. If the station should have enough power to transfer to weapons, it might activate its defenses when the sensors reveal the presence of an unknown vessel. Lithinia, run any language, markings, panel readouts, or communications we find through a translation program in the computer. We'll need the computer to translate their language for us."

"I'll have the computer analyze it all," Lithinia said. "We have a little information from the Cruxfix people from the last time an explorer ship was sent there. Perhaps there's something there that can help."

"I hope so," Surist added, looking over at Lithinia, "but they didn't give us their entire database when they brought me home."

Notolla reported, "Another ten seconds should do, but I'm only guessing. We don't know much about these foreign systems. Ending power transfer—now."

"All right, Lithinia, start sending the following distress signal: 'This is the Rongi cruiser *Malus Tempus*. We are in need of assistance. We have just come through the asteroid corridor and several of our onboard systems have been damaged. We request permission to dock at your station for our repairs. Please acknowledge.'"

"I'm reading power transfers to the communications and docking systems," Surist reported, rubbing his hands together satisfactorily.

"Any power to weapons?" Karak asked somewhat urgently.

"None, just communications and the docks."

"We're receiving a message from the station, Karak," Lithinia said, "They're responding to us—in our own language."

"Put the message through on audio."

"Docking permitted," a gruff male voice said. "Proceed to the nearest docking port."

"Whoever once occupied this station was obviously quite like us," Notolla pointed out.

"It's the voice of an oxygen breathing being," Lithinia said, "and that would suggest that the atmosphere onboard will be suitable for us once power is restored."

"How do they know our language?" Karak asked. No one had an answer.

"I would recommend that we take some power coils with us in case we want to transfer some power to a system or two," Surist suggested. "We're going to have to bring up the station's displays."

"Agreed." Karak nodded at Lithinia. "Everyone should have one. See to it."

"The nearest dock is now open and the power from it has been transferred to life support on board the station," the duke said.

"Hiram, take us to the nearest docking port. Let's go see what's in there," Karak said. "Why was power transferred to life support automatically?"

"I suppose they know we're coming on board," the duke said.

"Yes," Karak responded, "but there's no one there to transfer the power to any other system—at least not that we know of." He turned back toward the main window on the bridge to look at the station suspiciously.

"Perhaps their computer has an artificial intelligence that can execute those kinds of decisions and commands," Lithinia suggested.

At this proposition, Karak furrowed his brow ominously, but proceeded anyway.

Upon entering the station, the crew found it more interesting than they had imagined. They also found the air to be quite stale. Fortunately, getting life support up and running was quick and easy since the station had already powered that system. To get the process started, they linked the ventilation ducts on the *Malus Tempus* to those onboard the station and began pumping fresh oxygen into the station. With a little work, the station was soon refreshing its own oxygen.

"We will split up into groups of two to gather information," Karak ordered. "Lithinia and I will go to the command center of the station to find as much information as possible about whom the station belonged to and why they abandoned it. Marshal Notolla and duke of White, you two go examine the weapons systems and determine the defensive capabilities of the station and whether or not they would be a threat to the *Malus Tempus*. Hiram and Surist, set out for the central power core section to see what it would take to get the station up and running."

Karak and Lithinia walked to the main command center only to find the door closed and locked. "These doors are several inches thick. It's too much to try to blast through. There is no other way to get inside that I can see," Karak said.

"I didn't bring my gun anyway," Lithinia said.

"How do you board a strange station without your blaster?" Karak asked curtly, his eyes narrow and piercing.

As he reached for his own gun, his hand was met only by his own empty holster. "We tell no one of this," he said with a serious smile.

"We'll have to hotwire the doors somehow. There's an access panel over here." Lithinia pointed to her right. "This is going to take some time."

Lithinia pulled the cover off the wall and revealed dozens of wires. Karak looked on with anticipation, waiting for Lithinia to get the doors open.

"I'm a communications officer, not an engineer," Lithinia said, trying to earn some patience.

Meanwhile, Notolla and the duke were able to ascertain the strengths and capabilities of the weapons. "Based on the number and power of these weapons, I would say this station was built for both launching assaults and defending itself against many enemies," Notolla said as she pored over the console they'd powered up. "It's like the stations we have planned to build in case we ever have to have an outpost near enemy territory—except this one is far more advanced than anything we've ever had."

"I have no problem with being prepared," the duke started, "but—"

"Good," Notolla interrupted then turned her glaring eyes at the duke. They gave a small sneer to each other.

"I know what you were going to say," Notolla said understandingly as she turned back to the computer console. "You don't like the idea of such a peaceful people as we having a large military, but I'm glad you don't mind being prepared for defense."

"Fair enough," the duke said. "A station close to the enemy would have to have good defenses," he said, "but would also have to be able to supply and house the ships necessary for a major offensive."

"Hence the shipyards outside," the marshal said. "I wonder if we can get the weapons online."

"I think we should wait to do that until we have control of the station," the duke advised. "You never know what the station might do with its weapons if it detects trespassers onboard. It probably has automatic internal defense systems too. We were allowed to dock here, but we weren't told we could go poking around all over the station like we are." The duke looked up and around as if the station were alive. "Let's not make it mad."

"Good thinking. We can access the weapons from command and control anyway. That is assuming that Karak and Lithinia can get the command area under control."

"What do the weapons systems look like over there?" the duke asked.

Notolla hooked her power coil up to what appeared to be the main console, which stood in front of a large display screen. "This screen is probably for monitoring the tactical status of the station," she said.

After a few minutes, the display began to light up and show the status of all the weapons on the station. "All of the weapons appear to be inactive because they have no power, but they are in good working order."

"Much like the docking system when we first arrived," the duke said with a puzzled look, "but if we've transferred power to the system to bring up the display, shouldn't the weapons also have power to them?"

"Yes, and we should find out why they don't before we leave here." Notolla sifted through the different displays. "Duke, look at this."

The duke walked over to the weapons console. "What have you found?"

"There is a different power system for the weapons themselves than there is for the weapon controls."

"Why would they have done that?" the duke asked.

"It's ingenious," Notolla said, raising her eyebrows. "One of the first systems targeted in battle is the weapons, but you don't try to knock out each individual gun port. If you did, you would destroy the station's weapons; the station would be defenseless once you took it over. Also, it would take a lot of time to destroy each individual turret. So you try to knock out the system, not the guns specifically."

"You would also want to avoid destroying the gun ports and mines if you were trying to take the station over and use it for yourself, so you want to knock out the control system," the duke added with an understanding nod. "Because they have a system for each, that problem could be avoided, but if one goes out doesn't the other go?"

"No," the marshal said, "that's the genius of it. You can knock out the weapons control system, but the guns themselves have an independent power source. They couldn't be trained on specific targets, but they would continue to pick out their own targets and fire. To take over this station, you would have to destroy each individual gun turret."

"We should report this," the duke said as he began to leave for the main command area. "We've done all we can here. Let's head for the command level."

"I believe I've found a way to get the station's power supplies recharging," Hiram said, "but it's going to take a while for the power level to get to where it must have been a long time ago. This station is very large and it was once very important to someone. These power stacks are enormous. This station was meant to take a beating and to survive a war of attrition in terms of power and supplies. All I really had to do was transfer some power from my coil to the control panel. The power ran out here a long time ago."

"They must have left something running when they evacuated," Surist said looking around at the central power core. "Do you get the feeling we're waking up a giant?"

"Why do you always do things like that?" Hiram turned and sneered at Surist.

"What?"

"Say those kinds of things to make the hair on the back of my neck stand up. You have a nasty habit of doing that. Can't anything ever be what it seems? We haven't found anything threatening here yet."

"Okay, I just like to be a realist," Surist said sarcastically and with a mischievous eye toward Hiram. "Perhaps this station won't swallow us up. Perhaps it will become your new best friend and tuck you into bed at night."

Hiram glared at Surist. "Are you done yet?"

"No, give me a minute and I'll think of something else to taunt you with," Surist laughed. "Oh, I've got it."

"Here we go," Hiram said, equally as sarcastic as Surist.

"Maybe this station will actually save us later on," Surist continued, unhindered by Hiram's annoyance. "Maybe it will actually be in the right place at the right time, which is interesting because it's in the middle of nowhere, and will deliver us from certain destruction."

"Sure," Hiram said, now completely dismissing Surist's silliness. "Okay."

"I imagine the marshal and duke have found a great deal of weapons technology and defensive abilities," Surist said, more serious now. "There would have to be a lot to account for the amounts of power that are produced and stored here."

"We can access this power from command," Hiram said. "I don't want to turn it on from here anyway, since we don't know if station control has been taken yet. It would be disastrous to start generating power and have no way of controlling it. Besides, we don't even know if Karak and Lithinia have been able to get into the command area yet."

"I would assume they have not," Surist said. "If they had, surely they would have told us. We'd better go report in. We'll do the rest of our job in the command center."

"Agreed."

"You know," Surist said, "you need to learn to have some fun."

Hiram sneered at Surist, but then realized he was right and shrugged.

Lithinia had been trying to hotwire the doors for about an hour when she finally crossed the correct wires and the doors opened. "There we go; we're in," she said with a sigh and leaned back against the wall. "It was a matter of finding the two wires that had power. The others wouldn't have power because there is no one in the command area to transfer power to them. The only reason these two had power is because when the previous inhabitants of the station left it, they had to seal the doors from the outside. All systems were shut down except those they couldn't access. The other systems were shut down from inside, but there was no one left inside to kill the power to these wires. When we transferred power from the *Malus Tempus,* that power would have been automatically directed to the last systems to be operational, you know, systems like docking ports and communications. The systems remaining operational would have used power until it was gone. It must have taken a while for a door switch to run the power down."

"I understand, Lithinia." Karak rolled his hand in the air impatiently. "Can we go in now?"

Karak and Lithinia entered the command level and transferred a little power to the main computer. Then they accessed the computer and its various files. They found information about places and things they didn't even know existed. By the time they had finished gathering the desired information, the rest of the crew had reported in and joined them.

"We have found some interesting information," Karak said to the rest of the crew. "This station has a name; that name is Ynu. It would appear this station once belonged to a race known as the Nilg. Based on the armaments on this station, we can deduce that they were a militaristic people, and the records confirm that. Do you know of these people, marshal?"

"Where's your gun, Karak?" the marshal asked.

"Have you ever heard of these people?" Karak asked again.

"How can you board a strange and possibly enemy space station unarmed?"

"Answer my question!"

"You forgot your gun." Notolla laughed.

"Yes," Karak admitted, annoyed he'd been caught unprepared. "I forgot my gun, but so did Lithinia," Karak said with a childish whine as he pointed to Lithinia's empty holster.

"You're in charge, though," Notolla said, laughing heartily. "You're not supposed to forget your gun, you of all people."

Karak just growled.

"I have never heard of them in all my studies," Notolla squeaked out, getting herself under control. "Their race is new to us."

"Exactly as Notolla and Surist reported," Karak continued, "this station was an outpost built for war. The Nilg were at war with the Sekurai, another race about whom we've heard nothing. And from what we can see from these files, we want to avoid these Sekurai at all costs.

"According to this database," Karak said as he viewed a screen at a console near him, "this outpost was the last known refuge of the Nilg. The rest of them were exterminated by the Sekurai. In fact, the Nilg were like us, peaceful, exploratory, but they were much more powerful—until they met the Sekurai. The Sekurai fought them wherever they could. It says here the Nilg were not only driven out of Sekurai space, they were hunted down in all corners of the known galaxy. The Sekurai are or were a warrior race; they live for war. They destroy everything they can. The Sekurai were faced with a real challenge in the Nilg."

"Are these Sekurai still out there?" Notolla asked.

"We don't know if the Sekurai were beaten after they destroyed all the Nilg people, if they simply died out, or if they're still in existence. However, we do know this station was on the very edge of Sekurai space. The Nilg used this base as an outpost to keep a close eye on the Sekurai navy, to be the first line of defense in case the enemy advanced on Nilg territory, and also to launch offensives into enemy space. According to station records, the Sekurai laid siege to this station many times and were not successful until it was the only thing in the galaxy that was still claimed by the Nilg."

"Do you mean the Nilg still fought here after their home world was taken over?" Notolla asked with a mildly surprised tone.

"No," Karak replied. "I mean the Nilg still fought here after their home world was destroyed. The entire planet was wiped out, reduced to rubble floating in space. As the report states, the planet was a 'lifeless rock less than half its original size' after the Sekurai laid siege to it. Evidently the Sekurai were not only powerful, but smart as well. They could not break this station's defenses, so they went far around it and attacked the Nilg home world head on. Then they doubled back and met another of their own fleets here to flank the station."

"But the station is intact and structurally sound," the duke said. "The Nilg must have left of their own free will."

"The attack was unsuccessful," Karak continued. "The Sekurai were inflicting almost no damage on the outpost, but they were sustaining heavy casualties. This was part of the Nilg civilization's downfall. They put everything into this station and had nothing left to guard anything else. They thought it would protect them forever, but they didn't think of the simple possibility of the Sekurai just going around the station. After a while, the Sekurai realized the small outpost could defend itself well, but it could not mount an offensive strong enough to threaten the Sekurai home, so they left it alone."

"I thought you said this station was partially for launching offensives," Notolla said.

"Apparently it could be a staging ground for such an attack, but the warships were not produced here, only fighters," Karak said as he continued reading the logs and database. "They could send sorties into Sekurai territory, but they could not mount a full scale assault without warships sent from elsewhere. Once those ships and shipyards in other areas of Nilg space were destroyed, they could no longer hope to defeat the Sekurai.

"The Nilg left the station because there was no need to stay. They'd lost everything except life, and that meant nothing to them at that point. So they just up and left in a ship, from which they later sent a message saying they had been found by the Sekurai. The transmission ends abruptly when the ship's shields failed and all systems were damaged. The station's long range sensors registered the destruction of the ship seconds later."

"Is there any indication as to how long ago these things happened?" Surist asked.

"Yes," Karak said, "according to these records, this station was evacuated approximately six hundred years ago. The lengths of their units of time are not exactly like ours, but they appear to be similar. That's why I can't be certain."

"We do know though," Lithinia said, "that the last of the Nilg had to have left at least five hundred of our years ago because the energy signatures that would have been left by a ship as powerful as those the Nilg had would have taken at least that long to dissipate."

"That's a very long time!" the duke exclaimed, his eyes growing wide.

"This station is in the middle of nowhere," Karak pointed out. "There's nothing here to expedite the dispersal of such energy signatures."

"Was there any other pertinent information in their database?" Hiram asked.

"There are a few things," Karak said as he picked up his pack of supplies, "but we can discuss them on the way to the Cruxfix System. I've had transferred to the *Malus Tempus* as much of the data as our computer will hold. The station's computer has been linked with our ship, and the displays and readouts are changed over to our standard layouts and our language."

"The *Malus Tempus's* computer doesn't have enough memory to store the entire database, but we can get a lot from here," Surist said.

"We're claiming Station Ynu for the Rongi System. It now belongs to us. I've already had Lithinia send a message to our government, and I expect they will send a crew and supplies to effectively run the station, though I have not yet received a reply stating this. The transceivers on this station can send and receive messages from here to home, a much longer range than the *Malus Tempus* has. I want the defense grid activated now that we have control of the station, but first I think we should recharge the power stacks. Once we have everything under control here, we will continue on our journey. When we leave, we will set the station on automatic and program it to accept our crews if and when they arrive."

A couple of hours later, the station and the defense grid were set on automatic. The *Malus Tempus* then set out for the Cruxfix System with the Orb Seekers on board. They'd learned a lot on this little stop, but it got them no closer to accomplishing their mission. It was viewed primarily as time wasted, except for the information they'd gained, which did little to further their mission. They would have to come back to Station Ynu to learn and do more later, once their mission was over and their people safe.

On the journey, Karak finished sharing the information he'd gathered from the station's database. "There were a few interesting things but nothing of real importance in the station's logs. First is the Onuy Nebulae, a small collection of three nebulae, the middle of which can hide a ship from another's sensors. The other two nebulae will tear down a ship's shields, overload systems, and cause structural damage until the ship is destroyed. The Onuy Nebulae are located on the other side of the Cruxfix System. Second, Harza, a black hole with normal black hole-like gravitational effects in sector F:5. Next, the Snek Cluster, a group of nine dwarf stars set closely together. These stars have an unknown affect but are almost entirely undetectable until one is already in the middle of them due to the strong gravitational pull from the cluster of stars. We should deduce from this that they have an undesired impact on sensors and engines due to gravity and radiation."

"I will add these features to our stellar map," Hiram said as he operated his console.

"Lastly, there is talk of another civilization. A people called the Braline are mentioned as living in a solar system not far from this Onuy Nebulae. They are said to be very primitive compared to the Nilg, but that was centuries ago. They were just achieving normal interplanetary communications at that time. That places their technological timeline close to our own. Nothing more is known about these people, but I would imagine we will find more information on them in the Cruxfix System."

As the *Malus Tempus* raced on toward the Cruxfix System, the Orb Seekers could only hope they hadn't wasted too much time. The Red Band was closing in on Tris and time was at a premium.

𝔁 𝔁 𝔁

Chapter 7

SURPRISES

The Orb Seekers blazed through three sectors of empty space over a period of about five days. Nothing unusual or unexpected had happened since they'd found the Nilg outpost Ynu and claimed it for the now expanding Rongi empire. An uneventful trip was best.

"Sensors show nothing out of the ordinary, Karak," Surist reported as he swiveled around in his station's chair. "We're passing through an area of space between the corner of the Strissen Corridor and the Sniguri Nebulae."

"What are the Sniguri Nebulae?" Lithinia asked, not looking up from her console.

"Sensors show the Sniguri Nebulae is a group of dangerous nebulae," Surist answered. "Any ship which stays inside the nebulae too long would have its shields ripped down by the destructive radiation, and its hull would then be broken down until the ship was destroyed." Surist looked up, then added dryly, "I suggest we avoid this phenomenon."

"It isn't common for all nebulae in a cluster to be dangerous," Marshal Notolla said. "Generally some are harmful, of course, but some nebulae are enhancing to a ship's systems and others are neutral. I've never heard of a cluster whose nebulae were all dangerous."

"I agree that it's unusual," Surist said. "Nevertheless, these are all nebulae to avoid. We would not be able to stay in there for very long."

"The nebulae are not in our path anyway," Hiram said with a slightly dismissive tone and wave of his long-fingered Rongi hand. "We don't have to worry about them now."

"True," Karak said. "We don't have time to investigate everything. Station Ynu has taken up enough time already. Take all the readings you can. We don't have time to explore it now, but maybe a science ship can come back and answer some of these questions later. What have sensors picked up beyond the nebulae?"

The duke responded, "Sensors are only able to provide us with the edge of the nebulae. They are unable to—"

"What is it?" Karak demanded.

"My sensor range is shortening rapidly," the duke answered.

"Mine too." Surist leaned forward to examine the system readouts more closely. "Range is at half a sector and dropping. Sensor range is down to one quarter of a sector—now only half that."

"We're flying blind now," the duke said as he held his hands out in front of him, palms facing forward.

"Why is this happening?" Karak asked. "Report!"

"We had three small dwarf stars in a triangle formation in our shortened sensor range just before it all went blank," Surist said as he checked the last sensor record. "They weren't registering on my sensors a few seconds ago. The effect started suddenly."

"Our engines are also down by about fifty percent," Hiram reported. "It started about the same time the sensors went down."

"Do you think we've found that Snek Cluster the Nilg records spoke of?" Lithinia asked.

"It's possible," Karak said. "The way we didn't see them until we were already encompassed by them supports that theory. How long until we're clear of these stars?"

"Unknown," Surist said. "We will be clear of these three in about three hours, but we don't know if the others, assuming this is the Snek Cluster, lay beyond. It could take much longer."

"If there are more dwarves out there, they will probably continue to wreak havoc with our systems as well," Hiram said. "There's no telling how long it could take to get through."

"We don't have time for this," Karak growled. "Put all available power to sensors and engines."

"Two more dwarves up ahead," the duke reported urgently, looking out of the main window on the bridge. "This will increase our passing time to about eight hours, twice the normal time."

"Hiram, keep a close watch out for all the small rocks orbiting those stars," Karak instructed. "With maneuvering ability down, we will have to adjust more quickly, and I don't want to hit any asteroids."

"I have them in sight," Hiram said nonchalantly. "I can avoid them."

"Is there any way we can get out of this predicament?" Karak asked.

"We can plot an arcing course towards the Cruxfix System and out of the cluster to get out more quickly. If we did, we wouldn't have to take the time to back out of it to gain full power."

"Very well," Karak said. "Do it."

Six hours later, two more dwarf stars were detected on the sensors, whose efficiency had increased slightly as they slowly began to clear the first dwarves. The engines also regained some of their efficiency as the *Malus Tempus* put greater distance between herself and the previous stars. The sensor range expanded slowly but steadily, and they could now navigate a little more freely. It was now clear they had gone through part of the Snek Cluster and around the rest of it, and its effects were as bad as the Orb Seekers had anticipated. They had now been set back several additional hours and had to take a less than direct route.

"Hopefully we will continue on towards our destination unhindered," Hiram said once the *Malus Tempus* had passed beyond the effects of the Snek Cluster.

"I'll second that motion," Karak mumbled dryly as he leaned back in his chair and stroked his chin.

"Systems have been gaining in efficiency and are nearly at full strength again. In two hours, we'll be clear of the cluster and our systems should all be at full power and on our way to the Cruxfix System," Surist said.

"Good," Karak said. "Get us there as quickly as possible."

A few days later, the *Malus Tempus* approached the border of the Cruxfix System. The crew were ready for a rest. They quite enjoyed their new and hopefully temporary home onboard the *Malus Tempus*, a fine ship indeed, but they didn't wish to be confined to it for the rest of their days. Setting their feet on the ground would be most welcome. A good meal and some pleasant hospitality would be appreciated as well.

"We're approaching the Cruxfix System," Surist reported. "We should be ready to land on Crux I in about 30 minutes."

"Karak, we're detecting several small scout class ships," the duke said. "They're on an intercept course!"

"Why?" Karak asked. "Have we done something wrong?"

"They're sending a message," Lithinia said, "and they don't sound nice."

"Put it through."

"This is a Cruxfix patrol group," the voice said over the communications system. "You have entered our space from an unauthorized direction. You are ordered to leave our space immediately. If you do not comply, we will use force."

"Karak," Surist said somewhat urgently, "they've launched fighters. There are four heading towards us. I think they might be serious."

"Open a channel to the lead scout ship," Karak said. "Send this message. 'This is the Rongi Cruiser *Malus Tempus*. We are on an urgent mission of mercy. We're here to talk to Gronil. We mean no offense—'"

The ship shook. An explosion sounded from outside.

"What was that?" Lithinia asked.

"They are serious," Notolla said. "They fired a warning shot. We sustained a glancing hit to our shields—no real damage. They really don't want us here. Should I return fire?"

"No!" Karak said with certainty. "We will not escalate this situation. Bring us to a full stop. Tell them we will answer any questions they may have and we will not advance until they're satisfied with our answers."

"This is the leader of the Cruxfix patrol group. What is this mercy mission of yours that's so important?"

"Our solar system is suffering a natural disaster of galactic proportions and we need to see Gronil for advice," Karak replied.

"Who are you, and why have you entered our space from an unauthorized direction?"

"I am Karak Jewill, ambassador from the planet Vock II to a special Rongi Council and leader of the Orb . . . . this group. I didn't know there was an authorized or unauthorized direction from which to enter your space. We took the shortest safe route from our system to this one. May we speak with Gronil now?"

"Absolutely not! You don't just enter our space unannounced and uninvited from an unauthorized direction and then talk to our prime leader."

"Perhaps I could try," Surist offered. "I have been here before. Surely someone remembers my name."

Karak gave a sarcastic motion of his mouth as he demonstratively waved his arm in an invitation for Surist to speak.

"I am Surist, son of Hurid, aboard the *Malus Tempus*. I have been to your system before. The ship which carried my father, brother, and myself, along with our crew, crashed here thirteen years ago. Someone will remember my name and the event I've described. We've come here needing advice and information."

"I'll have to check," the scout leader responded. "Wait a few moments."

"Thank you," Surist responded.

"Why didn't you want to tell him we're the Orb Seekers when you first introduced yourself?" the duke asked of Karak.

"He doesn't need to know how much we know," Karak said. "I don't expect problems here, but you never know. They did fire a warning shot at us, and that's not something I expected from these people."

"They may not want us searching for the Orbs." Surist looked across the bridge at the duke. "You did tell us they were said to be a source of great power and were dispersed lest they fall into the wrong hands."

A short time later the scout leader came back. "I have been able to confirm your name and story about the crash thirteen years ago. You may land on Crux I at the landing pad farthest from the capital. It's the one fitted to refuel your ship. Proceed directly there. I apologize for the harsh way in which you were greeted. Everything will be explained after you've landed."

After an hour of waiting for other traffic, the Orb Seekers were able to land on Crux I. Once disembarked, guards stopped them at the door.

"I told you, I don't know why you weren't told about our coming," Karak said. "We were shot at while trying to land and given the third, fourth, and fifth degrees. Isn't there any communication here? This is supposed to be an enlightened civilization."

"We can't just let someone in here," the guard said. "We don't have any information about your arrival, and until we do, you can't go in."

"We are on a mission of mercy," Karak said. "Why don't you go ask Gronil about this? It was he who granted us permission to land."

While the guard went to speak with Gronil, the Orb Seekers sat outside the building waiting for a response. They couldn't help but take notice of the city around them. It was absolutely and undisputedly beautiful. Nowhere was there any litter of any kind. The buildings were tall, but thin and majestic.

The duke wondered how such tall and narrow buildings could stand. "Their underground structural supports must go nearly as deep as the buildings are tall," he surmised. While the buildings of the cities within the Rongi System showed on the outside what kinds of materials had been used to construct them, these buildings were covered or plated in some obviously abundant material that shrouded their frames.

Even Lithinia, the foremost authority on matters of construction in the Rongi System, hadn't a clue what kind of material these buildings might be made of. "To be so tall and yet so thin, they'd have to be made of something stronger than anything we possess."

The buildings—or whatever coated them—were of as many different colors as could be imagined. The entire city was a veritable rainbow. These colors were all somewhat muted with a pastel-like quality.

"I know the Orbs are said to be a deep color," the duke said, "but could they possibly be any more impressive than this?"

They sat down to take it all in and talk for a bit.

"Hiram, have you seen to getting the ship ready and supplied for the next leg of our journey, whatever it may be?" Karak asked.

"Yes," he responded with an eye roll. "That's one thing that Gronil's people have been most efficient with so far. I spoke with an official at the landing pad. They're resupplying and refueling the ship as well as repairing any systems that may be in need of touching up after our passage through the Strissen Corridor and the Sniguri Cluster. I also asked them to take a look at the outer hull just in case that warning shot singed the paint."

A few minutes later, the guard returned and admitted the Orb Seekers to see Gronil. "It's about time," Karak said showing the first signs of losing his temper due to the tremendous weight of the situation.

"I'm sorry about the delay, sir," the guard said, "but you landed before the scouts were able to tell me that Gronil had agreed to meet with you. I have arranged for an escort to take you to Gronil's office."

The group was soon met by another guard who was clad differently than the others they'd seen. This one wore a uniform that seemed to represent a time many centuries in Crux's past. While the other guards wore the kind of suit you would expect to see an officer on a warship wearing, this guard wore a thicker, almost armored shirt that featured two wide silver bands, one coming from over each shoulder and crossing at the chest. These two bands were solid silver in color and showed no other decoration—not what the Orb Seekers expected from Gronil's innermost guards. The room they were escorted to was a large, square, ordinary room, also not what they envisioned to be at the heart of the largest and most reliable library system known to exist. A long rectangular table stood in the middle near a wall with various end tables along that wall. The end of the room to which they were ushered held a group of comfortable-looking chairs.

Gronil entered the room in a long white robe with purple trim. "I must apologize for the inconveniences you must have been put through in trying to land here. Our security is a bit tight on that edge of our space." He scratched the scalp beneath his dark brown hair with the top of his bright red walking stick. He made his way across the room and seated himself in his chair—the chair that was larger and more ornate than the rest—and greeted his guests. Each arm of the chair was carved in the shape of a lion's head with determined eyes and showing many teeth as though in mid-pounce upon its prey. Above Gronil's head, the back of the chair bulged out in a perfect half sphere. This chair was not entirely upholstered like the rest of the chairs. The seat and back were heavily cushioned, but the wooden legs as well as the outer frame of the back were exposed. These exposed wooden parts were decorative in design, showing masterful carving skills. Nothing in particular was carved, merely a series of shapes making concentric rings all over the back of what could only be best described as a throne. "How are you, Karak of the Rongi System?" he asked.

"We're not entirely well. Why is there an unauthorized direction from which to enter your system?" Karak squinted. "We were completely unaware and were actually shot at upon entering your space."

"I do apologize for any inconvenience. I will explain our security purposes later. I have, indeed, heard that you are not well. What exactly is the nature of the problem, and what can I do to help you and your group?"

"Our solar system is under a threat like no other. A great shockwave of deadly energy approaches our sun, Tris. This Band possesses immense power and will destroy Tris, which, of course, will have a devastating effect on our entire solar system. We have examined all options and have concluded the only place we can go for advice is here, to you."

"What options have you considered?" Gronil asked.

"We have very little time. Our navy is currently trying to evacuate as many of our people as possible," Karak said, "but the best predictions say we will only be able to save at most three hundred thousand of our total populace. Not only can we not get enough people out, but we have nowhere to go. There are almost thirty-two billion people in our system. We've heard the tales of the eight Orbs of Quality. They seem to be our only hope of saving our people. Do you think they can help us?"

"You came all this way for something you didn't even know existed? You came all this way for a next-to-nothing chance? The trip must have taken you a couple of weeks, at least. This shows great need on your part, but the eight Orbs of Quality are a very serious matter. Do you know what you've gotten yourselves into?"

"We know that we have only one chance, unless you have another idea, and even if they don't exist, we have to try to save our people," the duke said and then raised a hand to his chest. "I am the duke of White."

"The duke of White?" Gronil looked directly at him. "That's an interesting title. What does it mean and what do you do?"

"I am the head of the Trade and Finance department on Vock I, as well as the curator of the Museum of Rongi History. I have an office in each of those facilities. Those in my position have always been called the dukes of White, but no one knows why. It's an ancient title with implications that none remember, and its roots have thus far been untraceable. The duke of White is never called by his name."

"None of us even know his name," Karak said.

"My wife and I have three children, all girls. I spend a lot of time at the office—and the other office," the duke dryly added with a blank stare and a sigh. Everyone managed a short chuckle.

"This solar system is in no position to support another thirty-two billion people," Gronil said. "I wish it were. We could try to help those of your population who can escape, but that doesn't help the immediate issue of the billions who will die if we don't stop this spatial phenomenon."

"Since you say the Orbs are a serious matter, we must assume they do exist. Will you help us?" Lithinia asked.

"We don't make the knowledge of the Orbs public to just anyone." Gronil hesitated. "The Orbs do exist and their storied power is true. These things must be a relief to you."

"Indeed they are," Notolla said with a sigh.

Gronil looked at the desperate people before him, thinking what he should do. "You are honorable and peace-loving people. We will share the knowledge of the Orbs with you.

"There may be a few things you did not know, though. The Orbs were created here a thousand years ago in a time of horrible war." He closed his eyes and shook his head at the thought. "It was hoped their power might put an end to it and set us on a path of peace. It worked, but we soon realized they could be used for evil as well as good. Their secret was hidden and kept only within a certain order of our society. We dared not destroy them all for fear they may one day be needed again and they were scattered across the planet. When we achieved space travel, we scattered them in our own solar system, and then later, they were sent to the furthest corners of known space. It was on this journey to scatter the Orbs that we learned much of the information that we have amassed in the generations since. It was then, also, that we reprioritized our society and began to focus on learning and knowledge instead of expansion and the wielding of influence."

"We know there are eight Orbs," the duke of White said, "and we've heard they have powers of some kind."

"There are eight Orbs of Quality, and each bears the power to influence its possessor where a certain quality is concerned. Each of these Orbs is a certain color. The White Orb, when its power is accessed by its possessor, gives him a better sense of clarity when decisions of morality must be made. It helps to make one's thoughts clearer where right and wrong are concerned and less hindered by the minutia that seems to surround us in our lives. You see, these Orbs have never been used for ill purposes, but they could be used in such ways if they fell into the wrong hands. The Blue Orb exudes to its possessor intuition where matters of health are concerned. The Red Orb is militarily inclined. It will allow for greater clarity in battle and a heightened sense of the outcome of a battle and a clearer sense of strategy. Then there is the Black Orb, which will enhance leadership qualities to a point where a leader can lead or govern more effectively for good or ill. The Green Orb, when its power is exercised, will offer instincts concerning the growth of life—or its destruction. The Purple Orb allows one to better perceive a sense of foresight. It allows its possessor to make logical decisions based on the circumstances of the current situation. Next, the Orange Orb encourages insight to make decisions accurately and solve or create problems using a more pronounced inclination for creative thinking. Last, the Yellow Orb will present its intuition for the accomplishing of goals." Gronil looked at the group in front of him. "Those are the qualities of the Orbs," he said. "Have you heard that the Orbs can be broken and then forged again?"

"Yes, we have heard that," the duke answered.

"One thing I don't understand," Gronil questioned, "is how the Orbs can help you. How do you plan to use them to stop this Red Band?"

"We planned on gathering them together and releasing them into the Band," Lithinia answered. "Our hope is that the Band's power, when it encounters the powerful Orbs, will be offset and nullified, thus dissipating the wave."

"I have no idea if that will work," Gronil said blankly. "It could work, I suppose. The power matrices in each of the Orbs could generate sufficient offsetting energy to dissipate the wave. It may also destroy all of the Orbs and not work at all. It may dissipate the Band *and* destroy the Orbs. I've never even seen one of the Orbs, but I can't imagine their story ending."

"We know it's a possibility the Orbs could be destroyed," Karak admitted, "but we are out of options and out of time. We can't let anything stop us. We will go to any end to save our people."

"I fear you may be tested strongly. This is no small quest. You may have to decide how far you will go and what you will do. You come from peaceful people," Gronil said, "but you may have to do not so peaceful things in order to accomplish your goal."

"We must stop at nothing," Karak said determinedly.

"Seven of the Orbs are broken," Gronil continued after a pause while he considered Karak's situation and his resolve. "The only one still intact is the Green Orb. It's enshrined as a god on a planet in the Swisura System, which is on the other side of the Uns System. That will be where you'll have to start. But enough about the Orbs for now. You're tired from your long journey. You should rest."

"We would all approve of a rest," Karak said. "If we should run into problems along the way, will you help us militarily? Will you allow us to consider you a supply point for this expedition?"

"I knew you would ask this much of me and my people. I cannot help you militarily. We are only mildly powerful in such ways. You are likely to run into people we could not begin to combat. We are a people of information, not war. That brings me to one of your other questions. The reason that entry into our system is prohibited from the direction you came is because there is a severely militaristic race known as the Sekurai in that direction."

The members of the Orb Seekers looked at each other halfway knowingly.

"I see you have heard of these Sekurai," Gronil said, having observed their expressions. "I didn't know your people had ventured so far from your home."

"We haven't," Karak confessed, "but we ran across an old, abandoned space station on our way here. We found that it once belonged to a race known as the Nilg."

"I see," Gronil said. "That explains it. Those two peoples fought a war long ago. The Nilg were completely destroyed by that war."

"We know," the duke added. "We reactivated the station and downloaded as much of their memory core as our databanks could hold."

"Well," Gronil said with a sigh, "the Nilg may be gone, but the Sekurai are still alive and strong. We must guard against attack from them. They've never shown us aggression, but that's because we are of little threat to them. Still, we must try to defend ourselves should they attack. We have allied ourselves with the only power in the galaxy that is equal to them, the Swisura. Any attack on us by the Sekurai would be met with retaliation from them."

"That's the system you mentioned earlier concerning the location of the Orb that's still whole," Surist said, opening his hand towards Gronil.

"Yes," Gronil said, "and as to your other question, you may come here and supply yourselves as much as you like. Also, I will have the locations of the eight Orbs and other information sent to your ship's computer. You'll have to go find the Green Orb first, since it's the one that's still in one piece. When you find a piece of an Orb, touch it to any whole Orb, and the broken one will be reassembled. Even if the pieces of a broken Orb are spread across the galaxy, the pieces will be almost instantaneously relocated to the point of contact with the whole Orb and in their respective places within the Orb they're re-forging."

Gronil leaned back in his chair and folded his hands. "As I said, seven of the Orbs are broken. This is to further prevent their power from being misused. As any Orb is broken, the others become harder to break. This last one that's still intact will be nearly impossible to break, though it can be done. This is not to say they're fragile when all eight are whole. They are rock, after all."

"Thank you for your help. You don't know what this will mean to our people," Karak said.

"I sincerely hope you don't have to destroy the Orbs; I would like to see them remain in existence in case they should ever be needed again. Also, they are a singular point of archaeological history that I would like to lay my eyes upon, since I have never seen even one of them. But, if you have no choice other than to destroy them, at least it will have been done out of necessity and in the doing of good deeds. The people of your system must be saved from this impending calamity. You will want to leave as soon as possible." Gronil stood and tapped his staff on the stone floor. "We will send you off with a great banquet tomorrow."

The Orb Seekers stood. As they were leaving the room, Gronil stopped Karak. He motioned Karak to come to his side and spoke lowly to display the seriousness of what he was saying. "There's something else about the Orbs." Gronil put his hand on Karak's shoulder. "You may want to think twice before embarking on this quest. If even one of the Orbs, should fall into the wrong hands, more than just your own solar system will be destroyed. Some things that are lost need to be found, but some things that are lost are lost for a reason. Perhaps by being lost they are protected from people, or people from them. Something that has been lost for so long should not lightly be sought. The Orbs were lost for a reason."

"If you decide to continue, you must gather all eight Orbs. This task cannot be completed with any other number; seven will not do. The Orbs' power matrices generate a harmonious bond between them. This bond does not initiate until all are gathered in one place. An Orb's individually unique powers can still be accessed even if you have only that one Orb, but this monumental task of destroying the Band, if they can do it at all, will only be within the scope of the power of all the Orbs gathered at once. Keep this foremost in your minds as you consider your options."

The next day, the *Malus Tempus* was supplied and ready to leave. Each of the crew members was seated at the large table in the room they had met with Gronil the day before. They had all slept well, glad to be out of the *Malus Tempus* for a time. Their quarters had been large and roomy, quite the contrast from those on any ship. They feasted on all sorts of delectable food and drink, and sampled cuisine from several different cultures they'd never even heard of. They shared in great fellowship with each other and with some people they didn't even know. Moods and spirits were high. Everything was going as well as it could.

Gronil made a short speech to end the feast and send the group on its way. "You're about to experience a lifetime of events in a very short time. I hope you are prepared for what may lie ahead of you. Your trail will be perilous and there will be many hard times. I only hope you come through them alive and well. Take the utmost caution and remember my warning. You may have to push yourself well beyond what you would, under normal circumstances, consider appropriate. You may have to make decisions that will haunt you for the rest of your lives. Life is long; work is hard; consequences are severe and long-lasting. At some point in every civilization, the price of survival is high. You will have to decide how far you will go and how much you will compromise."

His words did not fall on deaf ears, but they were not understood, not even in the slightest.

✕ ✕ ✕

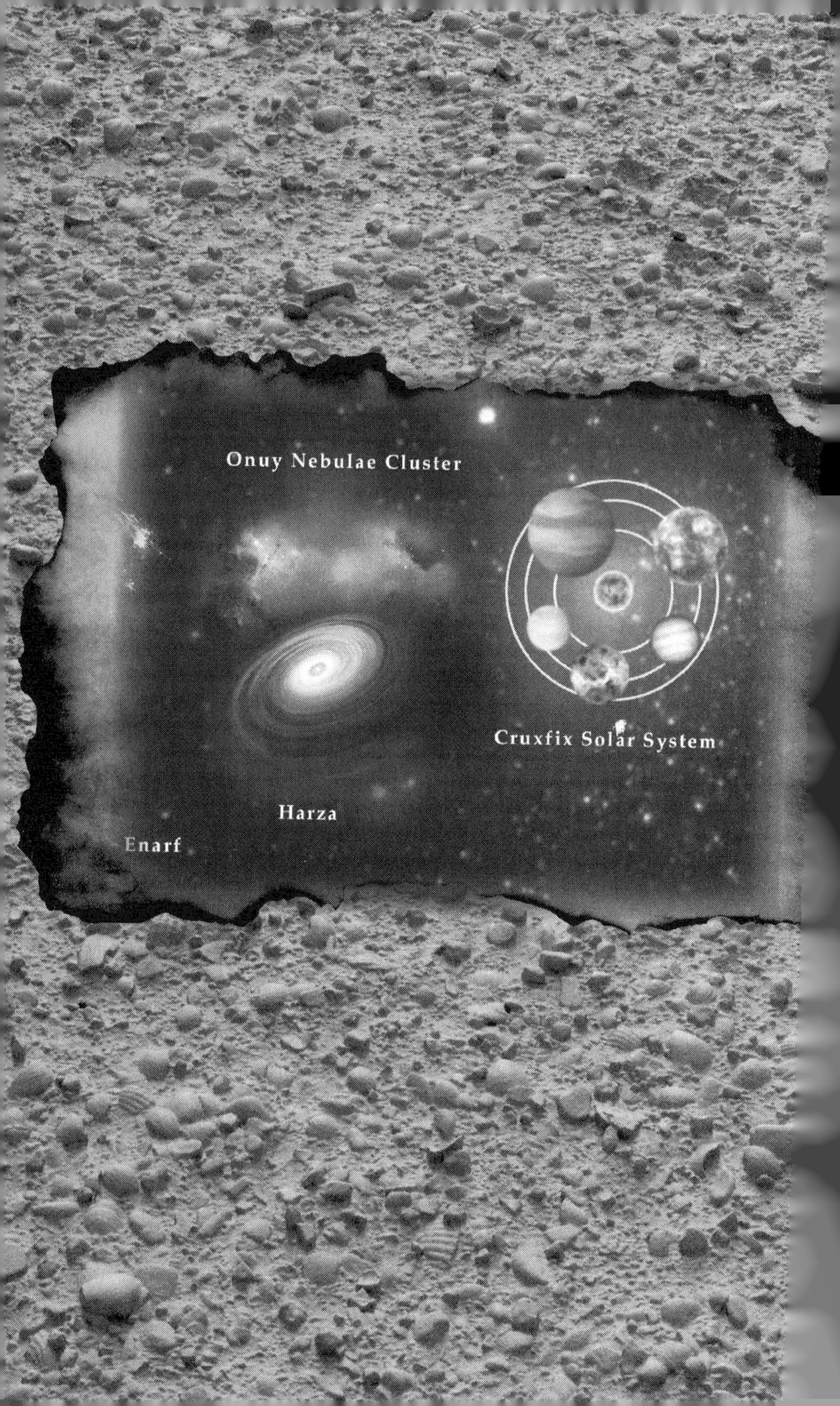
Onuy Nebulae Cluster
Cruxfix Solar System
Harza
Enarf

Chapter 8

A WARM WELCOME

Once the black hole, Harza, had been dealt with, the *Quia Vita* was able to continue to the Cruxfix System uninhibited. It would still be a couple of days until the ship would arrive at its destination. Levu had checked the ship quite thoroughly and found nothing to occupy his time nor his crew's. General Regti had done a very thorough job of seeing that everything was ready for the journey that lay ahead. The ship was well armed and well stocked.

"I hope we don't run into any Sekurai patrols," Nurisk said as he eyed Regti, the self-appointed tactical officer.

"That's unlikely for several reasons," Regti reassured the crew. "They're likely to be engaged elsewhere in their usual militaristic conquests, and the closer we get to the Cruxfix System, the less likely any Sekurai encounters will be. Although I'm sure the Sekurai hold great interest in the Cruxfix libraries and desire to possess them in order to find new peoples to conquer and new knowledge with which to do so, they know an attack on the Cruxfix System would result in an immediate and severe response from the Swisura, the Sekurai's greatest rival."

"Those two powers are head and shoulders above the rest of us in terms of power and defensive capability," Levu added. "The Sekurai could wind up losing men, ships, and territory if they tempted the Swisura into conflict."

"At least something holds them in check," Humwe said thankfully and with wide eyes.

"How long until we reach the Cruxfix System?" Levu inquired.

"About six hours," Nurisk replied. "Ten minutes fewer than when you last asked."

"I hate waiting." Levu pushed himself up from his captain's chair impatiently and flung his arms as he began walking around the bridge. "I didn't have to wait on my last trip out here."

"You've been to the Cruxfix System before?" Humwe asked. "I didn't think we'd been to the Cruxfix System too many times."

"We haven't, but, yes," Levu said as he sat down in his chair again and opened his eyes wide. "Thirteen years ago. That was the most exciting trip I've ever been on. It challenged my crew, my ship, and most of all, me."

"What happened?" Humwe raised an eyebrow.

Levu looked around his bridge to see everyone except Kolij and Nurisk staring at him with anticipation.

"Very well," he said with a sigh. "I suppose a little story time won't hurt anything. I was on a special exploration mission in the Onuy Nebulae," Levu began, "when I ran into a Sekurai patrol, the kind we'd like to avoid today." He waved his hand dismissively to the side. "There were three explorer class ships. They generally don't venture that far this direction. They just jumped right on top of us and knocked out our communications system immediately. That's possibly the most devastating thing about fighting the Sekurai—other than their smell, of course. I know odor doesn't penetrate the vacuum of space, but once you've battled them hand to hand even just once, you associate that malodorous stench with just seeing one of their ships."

All those aboard who'd faced the Sekurai in battle either laughed because it was true or crinkled their nose for the same reason.

"I swear you can sometimes detect the presence of Sekurai ships because of the stench. Anyway, their targeting systems are very specific and accurate as to what on board systems can be targeted. The fastest help we could find was in the Cruxfix System, so we went there at top speed. I hated to run with my tail between my legs, but I had a ship and crew to be responsible for. We had only been there twice before, and we were hoping they'd remain friendly to us. They had always been very helpful, just as we hope they will be now."

"What happened to the Sekurai ships?" Humwe asked. "Were you able to shake them off? Didn't they pursue you?"

"One of them we destroyed by running him around the dangerous nebulae until the effects of it practically dismantled the ship. We were able to evade that ship's weapons fire and eventually just irritated him enough that he lost his head and ignored that fact that his ship was being torn apart by the nebulae. He just kept chasing us, not caring that we were staying outside the nebulae while he was cutting corners through them to try to outmaneuver us. He kept trying to cut us off by flying through even the deleterious nebulae, and it eventually destroyed his ship."

"Typical Sekurai foolhardiness," Regti observed.

"The other two split up and searched for us inside the other nebula, the one that hinders ships' sensors. Fortunately, sensors were affected enough and we were undetectable until we were on top of one of them and could blast them at point blank range with everything we had. Then we got out of sensor range before they could come about and get a lock on us. We targeted one of the ships repeatedly and were able to use this hit and run tactic until their ship was disabled. Unfortunately, we took a lot of hits and stood no chance against the last ship. So, we decided to stay inside the edge of the nebulae to stay out of sensor range until we could get on the Cruxfix side of the nebulae. If we could do that, we had a chance to get there before the Sekurai. We had to direct all power, including life support, to the engines. They were catching up with us, but we had the distance we needed because they started on the other side of nebula cluster. A Cruxfix ship met us at the edge of their space and escorted us to Crux I. The Sekurai ship went home and we found Nurisk."

"What do you mean, you 'found' Nurisk?" Prak asked. "Did he just turn up?"

"Basically," Levu said with a shrug and a smile. "Nurisk was found by a mining crew in the mountains of one of their rural provinces. No one knew how he got there."

"Or even who I was," Nurisk added. "I don't know why I was there. All I was able to learn was my name, and that was only because it was printed on my jacket. It wasn't long before Levu came along and offered to take me back with him. I had an amnesia of the most serious kind. I couldn't remember anything about my life, and I still can't."

"That's the first time I've ever heard the story," Prak said.

"There's more to it, I'm sure," Nurisk said. "I just don't know it, and I probably never will."

"Those were some interesting tactics," General Regti said. "You actually used a lack of sensor ability as a weapon. We used some similar strategies in the last Sekurai battle."

"I've heard that was a great battle." Prak turned toward Regti in anticipation. "I would've been there, but I was on another mission when the Sekurai attacked. I was actually conducting research on Redron, and by the time we got word, it was all over."

"That was indeed a great battle," Regti said. "We were outnumbered and outgunned, as is usual against them. We needed every man we could get. The Sekurai attacked the Kriline Defense Barrier for only the second time in its history. It had been almost one hundred fifty years since they'd attacked it, and we actually thought we'd quelled their temptation to penetrate the great security guard, but we were wrong."

Kolij and Humwe shook their heads in agreement.

"They came with warships, about six of them; the bulk of their fleet must have been otherwise engaged. They came with dozens of fighters supported by escort ships. Cargo ships were sent in like a flotilla of portable mines. They would be set on autopilot and set on a collision course with our warships. Some we shot down before they met their targets, others we did not," Regti said lowly with a sigh. He drooped his shoulders and closed his eyes for a moment, remembering those who'd fallen. "We lost a lot of good people. The scout ships were just out there to draw our fire. It takes next to nothing to destroy a scout ship, even a Sekurai scout, but they are small, fast, and highly maneuverable; this made them next to impossible to hit. They swarmed us like gnats."

"I remember that," Kolij said, "and immediately when I saw that tactic, I got an idea for a better version of it."

"You mean for their side?" Regti asked.

"Yes, if I had that many scout ships, I would have created a physical wall with them and used that wall as an escort. That way we could only punch holes in the wall and wouldn't be able to target their bigger ships until enough holes of sufficient size were made."

"Good tactic," Regti said, "but why the hell were you formulating tactics for the enemy?"

"It just occurred to me," Kolij said with a shrug and a frown. "I found a better maneuver than they were already using. I thought perhaps we could use that to our advantage. They had imperfect tactics, probably because they were overconfident; if we had perfect tactics, which we did, then we could win."

"Which we did," Regti said with a still mild expression of incredulity on his face. "Anyway," he continued, "unfortunately, we hadn't developed this class of ship, the cruiser. If we'd had some, we would not have suffered so many casualties. The mines that permeated the holes in the Barrier were a great defense; they destroyed many fighters and damaged other ships, but they were no match for their fleet. But, we had our ships there waiting for them when the mines fell.

"First they targeted our fighters. Their fighters were stronger than ours, so we had to gang up on them. This took a lot of time and we were unable to give sufficient cover to our warships from their suicide cargo ships. Eventually, though, we did lessen their fighters enough to have an effect. Some of the fiercest combat was done in the dog fighting. Our boys and girls had to not only coordinate the attacks with their wingmen and work on destroying ships that were more powerful than they were, but they also had to navigate the asteroids in the Barrier. Fortunately, there were only two fighters destroyed by asteroids, but the fighting was vicious. The Sekurai were ruthless and well-trained. They used every maneuver in the book to get away from our gangs of fighters."

Humwe shook his head again and groaned as he remembered what his fighter wing endured that day.

"As I said, because of the time it took to destroy their main fighter line, the enemy cargo ships went unchallenged except for our warships, which already had their hands full with the escort ships. We lost three warships to the cargo ships colliding with them. When our fighters did finally get back, they were able to attack the escorts from the rear and our warships took them on the other side. Every weapon we had was punched into the grouping of escorts. We could see that their line was breaking, and we knew their warships would not hold up to our ensuing assault on them. So, I took another big chance. Our warships were still far enough away from the escort line that I told the gunners to keep firing and the helmsmen to plot an intercept course for the enemy warships. I was ready to send a final message to the Sekurai and tell them to leave us alone. By the time our warships were on top of the escorts, their line was gone and we chased the enemy warships down and our fighters picked off their gun ports. This gave us endless shots and all we did was fire until they were all destroyed.

"Since then, the Sekurai have rebuilt their forces and they are still much larger than ours, but we have the Kriline Defense Barrier mined again. We haven't heard from the Sekurai since."

"They're still out there, but I don't think their thoughts are on us," Levu broke in. "We aren't even their archrival, despite their repeated attacks on our space. They have always been more concerned with the Swisura. There has never been any large open confrontation between those two peoples, but they've had many skirmishes with each other. That particular "war" has never heated up. The only reason the Sekurai have not attacked the Swisura is because they have equal-sized fleets and comparable technologies. A war like that might rip the galaxy in two."

"I remember the order to engage the Sekurai warships," Kolij said. "I was trying to figure out what to engage. Our ship had been boarded by escapees from an escort ship we had just destroyed. Somehow, they got one of their shuttles into our main shuttle bay, and they tried to take over our ship. That's when I was first exposed to the stench; I'll never forget it. That smell was their best weapon, as though they needed another advantage." Everyone chuckled at Kolij's humor. "We had next to nothing as far as power was concerned. Everything had either been damaged during battle with the escort ships or in hand-to-hand combat onboard.

"The fighting was very fierce. There was blood all over the place from the shuttle bay to the bridge. Dead bodies littered corridors and there were scorch marks on the walls and control panels. Some of those who were dead were charred beyond recognition. They ripped their way clear across the ship. It was total warfare in every way, just like it always is with the Sekurai. Our captain and first officer were killed, so I took command of the ship. I wasn't next in line, but I was the highest ranking officer on the bridge. We'd finally been able to drive them out and seal off the bridge while our troops were defending it when the order to engage was given."

Kolij looked around at her captive audience, fully engrossed in her part of the battle.

"We were the closest ship and could at least get the enemy warships' attention while the rest of the fleet moved to intercept, but we had no power with which to operate the engines. In fact, weapons were the only thing we still did have," Kolij continued with a raised brow and higher voice. "So, I gave the order to decompress the shuttle bays and use that for propulsion. The decompression was enough to catch us up to the enemy, but our ship was too damaged to put up a fight. Our fighters were covering us as best as they could, but I knew I would have to set a collision course. Of course, then I wondered how I was going to do that with no power and I wondered how I could disrupt more than one ship. Our only shot at stopping the invaders from getting back to their own space was to break their formation. I ordered a shuttle to be waiting for my remaining skeleton crew, and our tactical officer was coordinating with the me at the helm about which quarters would have to be decompressed to move us into the middle of their fleet. We had to use our own guns on our own ship. We set hand weapons on overload and threw them into the areas in question and raised force fields around the interiors of the rooms. The explosions blew out the windows in the appropriate crew quarters, and this decompression shot us right into their center, disrupted their formation, and allowed the rest of the fleet to catch up and destroy them."

"That tactic is now standard instruction in our military academies," General Regti said. "That saved the battle. One of the most important things about it was that our tactical abilities were good enough to send a message to the enemy. We lost a lot of good people in that battle. I hope we never have to fight a battle like that again, but if we do, Kolij will command our finest warship."

After a long, voluntary silence in remembrance of those days, Humwe, staring off into space, said softly, "I was there too, and I'll never forget what I saw. My fighter squadron was one of the first to respond to the automatic long-range warning system." He recovered himself, looked around the bridge, and took a deep breath through his nose. "We got there just a few minutes before they came into sight. As they got closer, it looked like a line as wide and as deep as the eye could see. There were so many of them, they could have surrounded an entire planet. They may only have sent half a dozen warships, but they sure did send the escort ships and fighters. The very sight of the Sekurai war machine marching toward us was enough to send us home in fear. We knew we didn't stand a chance unless some other help was going to show up soon."

"We got there as quickly as we could," Regti nodded toward Humwe. "You did very well to hold them at bay as long as you did."

"The enemy decided to attack before we could get into position though. Once the minefield was down, they started to come through the hole in the Barrier. When the enemy is bottlenecked like that, they aren't able to put up much of a fight, but once they started trying to send fighters through the asteroids, our forces were spread pretty thin. We could no longer focus all our firepower on one point. We were weaving in and out of the asteroids and trying not to hit each other or run into the enemy fighters.

"We had to make sure none of them got past us in order to avoid having to double back and give up ground. A few of my men tried to ram their challengers. Luckily, they found a way to destroy them in a better way—all of them except one. My number one wingman had to take his target out by ramming his ship into it. Fortunately he was our only casualty. Other squadrons weren't so lucky; some were totally destroyed. The very fact that he was willing and ready to die for his cause made the rest of us feel the same way. We knew we were facing the destruction of our race, and we would have to do whatever we could to survive. Much like—like we are now."

Later, after the mood had been solemn for some time, the *Quia Vita* came to the edge of the Cruxfix System. Nurisk opened a communications channel with Gronil's office and arranged a meeting with one of his officials. The ship was set down on a landing pad just outside the palace.

As the group entered Gronil's palace, they immediately noticed the levels of intricacy and beauty it held. The walls were pure white, and on them hung the weapons of former heads of state. For there was a time when the Cruxfix people were not so focused on knowledge. At the start of the long corridor, for which the palace was known, hung the spear of the first ruler on Crux I, long before there was unification on any of their system's planets, and then a series of swords of various designs. Some swords were broad and thick to show the ruler who wielded it was likely a warrior by trade. Others were more slender and pointed instead of blunt, which would indicate the person was skilled in areas such as leadership, diplomacy, or tactics. There was the occasional bow and arrow that would suggest a more articulate and forward-thinking monarch. The sword, though not used for many years, was still the choice weapon of leaders in deference to days gone by.

In the large rooms were columns about a foot wide at the height of a man. Carvings on the columns depicted previous rulers of the Cruxfix System. An exaggeratedly tall and slender carving of the ruler was on one side, and the other side told of the person's life and major accomplishments.

As the group stood in awe at the sight of all these things, the official to whom they had spoken earlier approached Levu. "We're ready to hold the meeting as soon as you are," he said.

"I think there would be no better time than now," Levu responded. "If Gronil would permit it, we will stay the night and be off tomorrow morning."

"I assumed so," the official said, "and the arrangements to have your ship resupplied and your crew rested are already made. Please follow me to the meeting room."

They ventured across the large square room to an ornate doorway on the opposite side. Beyond the door, which was adorned with a scrolling scrimshaw carving effect of concentric protrusions of rectangles relieved from the body of the door itself, was an office on one end of which was a desk for official business and various computer panels. Behind the desk was an old, large executive chair, and seated in front of the cherry red desk were two smaller matching red leather chairs for guests. The other end held several chairs for meetings with small groups such as Levu and his crew. It was to this end that everyone was directed and told to seat themselves.

"Can I offer you something to drink?" the official asked.

"No," Levu said making eye contact, "but you can introduce yourself."

"Ah, I apologize. I am Klacton, Gronil's chief advisor. He would meet with you now, but he is currently tied up in other affairs with another group. Now, tell me your situation again."

"Nuin, the star opposite our solar system from Redron, has been countering the gravity well from Redron for as long as our civilization has been documenting the movement of the stars," Levu said, "but Nuin is destabilizing, and its gravity is no longer helping our system maintain the delicate balance that allows for our existence."

Klacton nodded, his brow furrowed.

"There was no warning to foretell this natural disaster, and now we don't have enough time or ships to evacuate all our people. We don't know how this happened, but right now we have to worry about the fact that it has happened.

"Your libraries are the largest and most extensive known to exist. We need to know if anything like this has ever happened before and how the problem was solved—or what went wrong in the effort. If it's never happened, we need to come up with a theory as to how to fix the problem. Can you help us?"

"Yes, I can," Klacton said. "I'll go with all of my staff and peruse our library and see what I can find. I'll look into all contingencies. We will meet back here once I've found something."

"One more thing," Levu said. "We've brought a small group of some of our finest minds. They're still aboard our ship. Would it be possible for you to take them in? We hope they can gain access to your database to communicate and coordinate any evacuation possibilities they may come across in their studies."

"Absolutely," Klacton said. "I'll have one of my stewards see to all their needs."

Levu and his company went to their rooms and were brought a meal, as well as made comfortable enough to take a short nap. If it weren't for the severity of their situation, the length of the journey would have made napping much easier, but as it was, that was out of the question.

During the wait, Nurisk searched through the Cruxfix files about his past, trying to fill the void that existed in his mind. He discovered that about a week and a half before he was rescued, a crashed spacecraft had been found on the side of a mountain range just across a large plain from the mountains where he was found. He had no evidence to support any theories, but he thought it was worth investigating—the crashed ship and his being found in the same general area may not have been a coincidence.

After a while, Klacton recalled the group for another meeting. His previously stiff posture was replaced now by one that was slack, his shoulders drooped. He shook his head sadly. "I must confess I have found next to nothing to help you. There have been stars that have gone nova before, of course, but anytime they were connected to inhabited solar systems, the people either moved out long before the star exploded or were destroyed by the event because they hadn't the capability of moving. As for your unique gravitational situation, it's just that—unique. I've found nothing like it in our records."

"You said 'next to nothing'," Kolij said. "That means you have found something that could give us a small chance at least."

"Yes." Klacton paused, then sighed. He slowly raised his eyes to meet those of Kolij. "Have you ever heard of the Orbs of Quality?"

All heads shook.

"The eight Orbs of Quality were constructed here a long time ago. They were built only by craftsmen who were pure of heart and they were blessed by our priests at that time, though they are technological and not mystical in nature. Their intent was to help the development and effectiveness of various sections of our society and stop a terrible war that our people were engaged in at that time. All the goodness, well-meaning, and expertise of those who constructed them was pro-grammed into their neural energy matrices. It was a mastery of neural technology to imbed the best qualities of our best people in the com-puter cores of the Orbs.

"The Orbs brought us out of that war and started us on the path to where we are today as a society. However, the fear that they could be used for ill purposes, though that is not known to have ever happened, caused us to decide most of them should be destroyed and scattered throughout the cosmos. Seven of the eight have been destroyed. Six we destroyed ourselves."

"Then how can any of that help us?" Prak glared at Klacton. "You're talking about gallivanting around the galaxy on some scavenger hunt. I have a wife, a loving, beautiful wife back home. I don't want to spend weeks or months away."

"We had hoped for something more concrete," Levu deferred. "We're used to long shots, but we're also used to solving them by hard work, not a hope and a prayer."

"If any part of a broken Orb touches a whole Orb, the broken Orb will be forged again. We left ourselves a chance to re-forge them by leaving two unbroken. Through the years, however, a seventh was destroyed. You would have to find the Orb that's still intact first. We have their locations and all other information regarding the Orbs on this disc." Klacton handed a small silver data disc to Levu. "There was once, during the process of scattering the Orbs, an attempt to retain them and test their power for evil. An officer on one of the ships charged with distributing the Orbs was found to have been from the most evil faction long leftover from that terrible war. He tried to leave all of the Orbs in one place so he could go back and gather them all later. His attempt was thwarted quickly, but that will explain to you how two of the Orbs, the Red and Black, may be found so near to each other.

"The power of the Orbs is not known, however. We never tested their limits; that was part of what was so scary about them. If you can find them, you may be able to send them into Redron, destabilize the black hole, and cause it to collapse, but, again, I can't be certain of this at all. You may also find that the black hole is too strong. If that happens, your efforts will have been wasted."

"So, we don't know if we can find the Orbs," Regti said pessimistically, "and if we can, we don't know if they can help us."

"What do these Orbs look like?" Nurisk asked.

"They are each a different color, although translucent like amber, and each color designates the specified power of each Orb. As far as general appearance, they are simply each a stone globe."

"That sounds like a good name for our little group," Prak said.

"What do you all think?" Levu asked. "Do we go in search of a fool's hope?"

"What other choice is there?" Kolij answered. "We have no other hope. No one else has even given us a possibility."

"It is a fool's hope," Prak agreed.

"It's also the only hope we have," Levu noted sternly. "I think we have to try to find these Orbs and send them into Redron. They must be powerful indeed if they helped pull the Cruxfix people out of such a nasty and devastating civil war."

"We've already come this far," Nurisk said, "and we came *here* for a reason—because we trust that the Cruxfix people can help us."

"We should just go back home and do what we can to help evacuate our people," Prak said.

"Evacuate to where?" Regti asked, raising his voice and throwing up his hands. "There is nowhere to go! The Cruxfix can't absorb billions of people. Where would we go?"

"We don't even know if the Orbs exist," Prak added. "What if they do exist? What if we do somehow find them in the vastness of the galaxy? Can we do so before it's too late? Are they powerful enough to stop Redron?"

No one had answers to these questions. Prak's misgivings were met only by blank stares and questioning glances. They had no ideas at all.

"I can't answer your questions, Prak," Levu said, "but I don't see any alternative. We can't evacuate; there's nowhere to go, and even if there were, we can't get enough people out in time. If we go back home, we can't make enough of a difference. As long as we have some semblance of a chance, we've got to try."

Everyone nodded, even Prak. Even if they didn't care for the idea, they agreed they should name their group Stone Globe because it fit their new objective perfectly. They decided to leave first thing the next morning and start collecting the Orbs.

Nurisk spent the night continuing to research his past. He had already discovered the account of a crash that took place not far from where he was found. Then Nurisk found something which he had always wondered about. He thought that any survivors would have been taken to some care center as he had been. He went back to the *Quia Vita* to check his personnel record. He compared his blood sample to the Cruxfix System's database and found he was a match with two of the crew members onboard that ship, only one of which survived.

It was always hard for Nurisk, not knowing where he'd come from. In fact, sometimes when he stared up into the dark night sky and wondered which of those many points of light he actually came from, the scar above his right eye still throbbed a little. He was educated in the field of mining and other resources as well as industry and manufacturing, Verdin's planetary strengths. Nurisk had worked his way up through the ranks of professionalism, society, and influence. His place in Stone Globe was well-earned. Though he had fit into Braline society quickly, easily, and quite effectively, he'd never expressed any interest in building a family. This was not out of any obligation, hesitation toward the Braline people, or sense of being unwelcome in any way, but a simple sense of self-isolationism where family was concerned.

The next day Nurisk woke Levu, and this was saying something. Levu was always the first one up and ready to begin the day, especially when he had a mission to complete.

"Levu," Nurisk said as Levu tried to wake up, "I've found something you should know."

"What could you possibly have found out in your sleep," Levu said, still trying to wake up.

"I have a brother," Nurisk said.

Levu was instantly awake. "What? A brother?"

"I compared my blood sample with the records taken from the crew of a ship that crashed near the same time and place I was found thirteen years ago," Nurisk said. "The results show I have a brother. My sample matched two of the crew in the crash. One died, but the other survived."

"Where did the ship come from?" Levu asked as he wiped the sleep from his eyes.

"It came from the other side of known space," Nurisk said, "from a place called the Rongi System."

"We've never been there," Levu said.

"No, we haven't. But, I was also able to find my brother's name."

"Look," Levu said, placing his hand on Nurisk's shoulder. "I know how exciting this must be and how many questions this answers, and how many more it brings up, but we do have a mission to accomplish here. When this is all over and our people aren't in jeopardy anymore, I'll take you to this Rongi System so you can answer all these questions. Okay?"

"Okay, it's a deal!"

"Now," Levu said, "I'm going back to bed. You should get some sleep also. We will not be in so comfortable a place for a while starting tomorrow."

Nurisk began to leave Levu's room when Levu asked him one last question. "What's this brother's name?"

For some reason, Nurisk's scar hurt just a little more than usual as he answered. "Surist."

✗ ✗ ✗

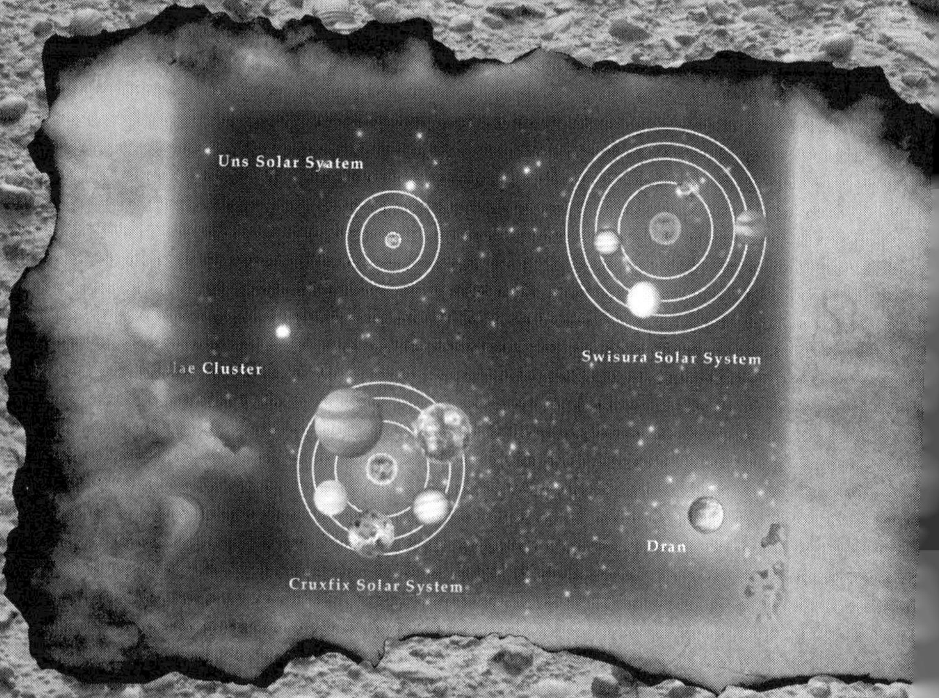

Uns Solar Syatem

Swisura Solar System

llae Cluster

Cruxfix Solar System

Dran

Chapter 9

THE BREWING OF RIVALS

The day after the Orb Seekers and Stone Globe had their separate meetings and decided what they should do, they both prepared to leave the Cruxfix System and set out for the Swisura System. The day was a nice one; it was the kind of day one would set out on an adventure, but the forecast had an ominous and foretelling storm brewing.

The Orb Seekers were gathered and preparing to leave. They were glad they now had some hope, although it wasn't as much as they'd hoped for, and they were ready to get started on their journey, to accomplish their goals, and to return home to their loved ones.

Gronil had come to see them off. "Your ship has been fully repaired and resupplied. I wish I could be of more help," he said with a shrug. "My people aren't militaristic and don't have ships to spare, so I can't dispatch even a few scout ships for your escort. But if there's any way I can help you, just let me know. I'll do what I can. I don't doubt that you'll run into trouble along the way, but I know that your spirits will not be undone."

"You have done much for us," Karak said. "I personally could ask no more of you, but if my people need your help, I will ask. As for now, we must begin our quest."

At that the Orb Seekers made their way across the platform towards the *Malus Tempus* and waved farewell to Gronil. They entered the ship and assumed their posts, from which they had been quite glad to get away for a couple of days, and set the ship on a course out of the atmosphere in the direction of the Swisura System, their first stop.

"That was a welcome visit to Crux I," Hiram said.

"It was more informative than anything," Lithinia said, "but the rest was nice. Now that we know the Orbs exist, we just have to go and find them. All across the galaxy they're scattered, just waiting for us to find them and restore all the glory that has been lost as they have remained dormant for so long."

"This is going to be a great adventure. I look forward to the challenges ahead." Karak sat his flight plan computer down and looked ahead. "Once we've cleared the planet, plot a course for Jisk, the capital planet in the Swisura System. That's where the Green Orb is, the first of eight."

About two hours later, Stone Globe met with Klacton on the same landing platform the Orb Seekers had used. The weather had turned and it wasn't quite as nice as it had been just a few short hours earlier. A storm was moving in, and Stone Globe thought it best to leave now rather than wait until evening in case the storm turned too nasty to take off.

"Everything is as scheduled," Klacton said with a smile. "The *Quia Vita* is ready and so, I hope, are you."

"We're ready to depart," Levu said. "We plan to head for the Swisura System, specifically Jisk, first. That's where the only whole Orb is. Hopefully we can proceed on from there."

"That sounds like the same path I would choose." Klacton looked around at the sky. "You'd better get going, though, before the storm worsens."

"We'll come back to see you once we have accomplished our goal," Levu promised.

"I'll look forward to seeing you again." Klacton smiled back.

Shortly after the crew boarded the *Quia Vita*, the ship's engines were engaged and the course set for the Swisura System.

"We'll have to navigate all this traffic," Levu said as he looked out at the many ships moving about the area. "The Cruxfix System sure is a hotspot."

"There are a few Cruxfix scout ships—and one unknown ship," Nurisk said curiously.

"Open a channel to the unknown ship," Levu said after considering for a moment.

"Channel open." Humwe eagerly operated his console as he was himself curious.

Levu began his message. "This is the *Quia Vita*, a Braline cruiser. We are on a mission of peace and exploration. Your ship is unknown to us. We wish to open dialogue with you and learn more about you, your ship and your people."

"Karak," Lithinia said, "we're getting a message from an unknown ship also in this system. They have identified themselves as Braline."

"One of the peoples mentioned in the records of Station Ynu," Notolla said, reminding Karak of where they'd heard the name before.

"Open a channel," Karak said as he sat up straight in his captain's chair.

"I am Karak Jewill, son of Diwill, leader of the Orb Seekers. Our ship is the *Malus Tempus*, a Rongi cruiser. We are on a mission of urgent mercy with the highest of stakes. Our destination is the Swisura System."

"Interesting," Levu said, having heard Karak identify his group. "What takes you there?"

"An urgent mission to save our people. We find our sun threatened by a deadly galactic phenomenon."

"The Swisura are powerful people, from what I understand," Levu said. "If anyone can help you, it'll be them. We're heading there too. It will be our first time in their space."

"We'll take help from anywhere we can get it," Karak said, "but we're looking for something specific and may not need to involve their people at all."

Levu became suspicious now. "What is it you're looking for in the Swisura System?"

"We are looking for an ancient artifact of great power."

"What sort of artifact? Perhaps we can help."

Karak hesitated. "We are searching for the Green Orb of Quality."

Upon hearing this, Levu's eyes widened as he looked around the ship's bridge at his comrades. Everyone looked back at him with eyes full of surprise, shocked anticipation for the exchange that was about to happen, and total deference to their inspired leader. A long silence ensued before he could overcome his surprise. "Why do you want the Orb?" he asked.

"Our solar system is in great peril," Karak said. "We must use the power of the Orbs if we are to have any hope of saving it. What's your mission?"

Levu rose quickly and approached Nurisk's station. He muted the communications channel. "Nurisk, how far away are they?"

"They're about two hours ahead of us," Nurisk replied. "Almost to the edge of the system."

"I'm open to suggestions," Levu said, looking around his bridge.

"We could join forces," Nurisk suggested. "Perhaps we can help each other."

"Or we could blow them out of the stars." General Regti shrugged. "If they won't cooperate."

"How can you suggest such a thing?" Kolij glared at Regti with a look he would only expect to see from his wife, if he had one. "That's not the kind of people we are. We're a good, honest, decent sort. We've had to defend ourselves many times before, particularly against the Sekurai," she continued as her tone changed from shockingly accusatory to defensive and then to appealing. "We must be true to ourselves and not throw away our honor just because it becomes inconvenient. We're out here to save our people. I couldn't live with myself if we just killed innocent people because they were in the way. If we did that, then we might as well throw away all that would be lost along with our people. We are more than culture, language, literature, art, architecture, and even lives; we're good, honorable, respectable people."

"I agree," Levu said. "It is important that we live honorably. If it were just us, we could decide to let them go and not compete for the Orbs." Levu shifted in his chair and displayed a thoughtfully pained expression. He looked at Kolij and then Regti. "But there's a lot more at stake here than just us. Our entire civilization hangs in the balance, teeters on the brink," he said with a softer voice and held his chin in thought, "hangs by the most tenuous of threads."

This response from Levu was noticeably different than any of the crew thought possible, given Levu's character, though it could hardly be argued with because of the ramifications if they failed to collect the Orbs. It was neither in his nature nor in the example he'd led by for so long to decide so quickly to accept the idea of killing innocent people in cold blood.

"I'm only saying that since they're ahead of us, they will get the Green Orb first," Regti said. "If they won't help, then what choice do we have? It's between us and them. They may not leave us an option."

"Before we do anything we might come to regret, I think we should learn more about them," Humwe said.

"Agreed." Levu pointed a finger straight up. "We will only risk open confrontation if they won't cooperate, but Regti is right—if they won't help or stand down . . . ." Levu could not bring himself to openly agree with Regti's assessment of the situation, but he also could not come up with an alternative. "Reopen the channel."

"Mr. Jewill," Levu said, "I am Levu Earsp and we're on the same mission you are." The Orb Seekers now had their turn to look around their bridge at each other in amazement. "Our people are in danger as well," the message from Levu continued. "Our entire solar system will be sucked into a black hole if we can't gather the Orbs and use them ourselves. It's been brought to my attention that one option is to view you as competition. Another option is to suggest that we assist each other. I would prefer the latter."

"As would I," Karak said. "I find it improbable to believe that two solar systems are on the same quest at the same time for a similar reason. However, stranger things have happened. Our timetable gives us approximately six weeks. If yours is different, then perhaps we can be of service to each other."

"Our timetable is not going to be forgiving, it seems. We have about the same amount of time to save our own solar system, perhaps even a little less."

"I'm not out here to make enemies, but the Orbs are our only chance," Karak said.

Levu had been challenged, though not out of malice or pride, but by the obligation of duty and patriotism of his new counterpart. He looked to his crew for advice and suggestions. He was about to decide which was more important, trying to save his people or attacking in cold blood a ship on an errand of mercy.

"We cannot allow them to obtain an Orb," Regti observed. "We can't risk not being able to acquire all eight."

"Missing even one would derail us," Kolij added. "But I will not condone our instigation of open confrontation. We would be no better than those who've attacked us in the past."

"Their ship is comparable to our own in every way, as far as our sensors show," Nurisk added. "We would do good just to catch up to them, even if we did want to fight."

"I don't want a fight," Levu said without hesitation. "These are not Sekurai. We are not their sworn enemy. If we attack these people— then we don't deserve to live."

"Would your wife and children choose to die along with our entire civilization just because you were more in love with honor than with the lives of all our people?" Regti asked pointedly.

Levu had no immediate answer for this. He knew life wasn't a game of numbers. Numbers were cold, hard, and unsympathetic. A hundred lives were no less important than a thousand. However, the *Malus Tempus* housed half a dozen people while the Braline System was home to tens of billions.

"Reopen the channel," Levu said determinedly.

"Go ahead," Humwe said.

"Neither are we here to make enemies," Levu said, speaking quickly for no other reason than to get the words out before he changed his own benevolent mind. "However, we've decided that, for the preservation of our race, we must have the Orbs. We will do what we can to help you in other ways, but the Orbs will have to be ours. Bear in mind that we will defend our cause and ourselves if necessary. We're not a race of warriors, but if enemies we must become, then so be it."

"Let's not do that," Karak said instantly, hoping against all quickly fading hopes that they could continue to be friendly to one another. "Surely we can help each other."

"Do you have a proposal to make?" Levu asked, eyeing his view screen as he tilted his head toward it.

"I'm afraid I don't," Karak sighed. "Mr. Earsp, we need a solution. We are a peaceful people. We don't war with others out of little reason, but this is hardly little."

"Nor do we."

"What's more, time isn't on either of our sides."

"If we had more time, perhaps we could come up with something."

"You could help us find the Orbs. We would destroy the energy phenomenon that threatens our sun," Karak proposed. "And then you could come and live with us in the Rongi System."

"We can't evacuate our people in so short a time. Besides, I doubt your system can house the tens of billions we would bring even if we could get everyone out."

"It could not," Karak admitted with a sigh, "and the same circumstances are true of our situation as well. But we must find some solution!"

"I'm afraid there's no time," Levu said as he recognized the situation slipping away quickly.

"Surist, what is their tactical analysis?"

"It appears to be comparable to ours," Surist replied.

"I assure you that we can destroy you," Levu said becoming more resolute for no reason other than he was a few minutes further removed from his threat to fight and had become more accepting of it. "You need not consult your officers."

"What was the name of the person you just asked?" Nurisk broke in.

"I asked my science officer about what his sensors read," Karak said as he squinted at such an odd question. "Why do you ask?"

"What was his name?" Nurisk pressed.

"His name is Surist," Karak answered and then became testy. "Why?"

"Nothing at all," Levu said so harshly it came out raspy. "Close the channel!"

"Levu," Nurisk said, "that's my brother!"

"You don't know that!" Levu said.

"That's my brother's name."

"We have a mission to complete!" Levu yelled. "Don't forget what's at stake. Besides, that may be a common name among his people; you have no way of knowing he's your brother."

"Karak," Lithinia reported, "they've directed all power to their engines and plotted an intercept course with us."

"Shit," Karak said under his breath.

Back on Crux I, Klacton and Gronil had gone back to the landing pad to watch the storm and think about the groups they'd helped. "I had an interesting meeting last night," Klacton said.

"So did I," Gronil said. "What was yours about?"

"Some Braline came here with a problem. Their system is being sucked in by Redron because Nuin is destabilizing somehow. The gravitational equilibrium of their system has been destroyed and neither we nor they know why. I sent them on a quest to find the eight Orbs of Quality in the hopes that they could provide the power they need. I told them it may not work, but it was the only shot they had."

Gronil stared at Klacton. "I did the same thing with some Rongi people. Their sun is in the path of a band of very destructive energy. I sent them after the Orbs too."

"Do you mean they are out there under the most severe kind of pressure, fighting not just for themselves, but also for their entire civilizations, and they're after the same thing? They will both be desperate to succeed. Who knows what they'll do! What will happen?" Klacton asked.

"They're both peaceful peoples. Perhaps they will work something out."

"They can't both have the Orbs."

"No, they can't," Gronil said with a look of despair. "They can't *both* have the Orbs."

"What have we done?" Klacton asked in a foreboding voice. "What have we done?"

On the edge of the solar system the two crews were still shocked at what they'd learned and both were full of tension. The *Quia Vita* had increased her speed to catch up to the Orb Seekers.

Karak Jewill was often calm and calculating, and perhaps just a bit cold toward others from time to time. He wasn't short with people because he desired to put them down, but because he was always more interested in getting his job done than he was about protecting people's feelings. This both earned and lost him respect. Now, however, feelings were a moot point.

"This is the *Malus Tempus* to the *Quia Vita*," Karak said. "You have made an aggressive move toward us. It is my belief that you intend to fire on us when you come into range. If you do so, your actions will be interpreted as an act of war and will be dealt with accordingly."

"This Karak Jewill sounds like a man whom I should be sorry to offend," Levu said to his crew.

"In situations such as this," General Regti said, "someone is usually lying because they're out to get something. They usually have some ulterior motive, but here I have strange suspicions of honesty."

"Suspicions of honesty," Prak remarked with a brow raised toward Regti. "Very poetic."

"Yes," Levu said. "If they were just looking for the Orbs as a power source and weren't in actual need of them, they might break off because we wouldn't be worth the fight. Karak seems like an intelligent man; he would not push us too far unless he were also willing to push his own ship and crew that far. It's like making your opponent fight in a corner; it's not the best move. It often galvanizes them and motivates them to fight even harder."

"Never push a desperate foe too hard," Regti said. "If they are telling the truth, we may be in for a long mission."

There was a long pause without reply to Karak's last message when finally Levu said, "Karak, I don't wish to fight you, but it sounds like we may have no choice. There may be larger forces at work causing both our problems. This whole situation seems to be too big of a coincidence. Despite this possibility, we must address the situations in which we find ourselves. I realize you are doing what you know to be right, but I am doing the same. You must understand this. We're both fighting for the continuation of our civilizations, and only one of us can win."

"Is there nothing we can do to help each other or at least to avoid conflict?" Karak begged, now finally realizing that in order for his people to live others may have to die. Though Karak was not at all in favor of the provincial Rongi attitudes that were all too often on display back home, he was much more accustomed to them. The idea of firing on the *Quia Vita* didn't sit well with him at all. He had no desire to attack Levu or his cause, but he had less compunction about doing so in favor of his people's well being, but only a little bit less.

"You're ahead of us," Levu said. "We have to take your advantage away from you."

"It seems that words are of no use here." Karak went steely and cold. He seemed to too easily accept the fact that he might have to kill someone on a quest of equal nobility as his own. "How long until they catch up to us, Surist?"

"Our engines are comparable. It will take them approximately two days to obtain weapons range," Surist said, "and not quite a week for us to reach the Swisura System."

"Two days!" Karak exclaimed.

"Their engines appear to be quite comparable to our own," Surist said. "They won't make ground up quickly, but they will make it up."

"We could do the same thing they're doing," Hiram suggested as he turned to meet Karak's eyes. "I can get the same power out of our engines."

"Yes," Karak said, "but we would still have to deal with them later, and the Swisura could side with them. That would be disastrous. It would be better to quell Levu's threat now than leave it to chance."

"Their ship matches ours in every respect as far as I can tell," Lithinia said.

"Then we will have to use our wits, cunning, and guile," Karak said. "Let them catch up to us, but maintain our current speed. I don't want to arouse suspicion on the part of anyone who may yet be in front of us."

"Don't you think you're a little too eager to kill?" Surist asked.

"I am not eager to kill," Karak said, "but it seems that Levu may not give us any option. We will succeed and protect our people."

In the time it took for the *Quia Vita* to catch up to the *Malus Tempus*, Karak and his crew tried to come up with a way to avoid a battle. They were unsuccessful. It seemed that a skirmish, and perhaps the demise of their cause, was unavoidable.

"Every battle is possible to avoid," Karak said. "Why is there no solution to this problem?"

"The only solution would have been to avoid communicating with Levu," the duke said.

"Well, we can't do that now." Karak continued stirring and stewing, mumbling to himself the whole time.

"We're entering the Uns System," Surist said.

"How long before the *Quia Vita* comes within weapons range?" Karak asked.

"Five minutes. We'll meet near the star in this system."

"They're powering up their weapons," Notolla said. "They're coming to bear."

"Full power to the shields," Karak ordered. "Arm all weapons. Don't fire until I give the word. We won't fire first, but fire we will."

Levu had run his ship hard to reach this point and he was ready for battle himself. "Raise the shields and ready the weapons. Prepare the forward guns for a warning shot; we mean business, but we won't harm them unless they force us. Target twenty-five meters off their ship."

"Warning shot ready," Regti reported.

"Karak is on a channel," Humwe said. "He says if we fire, the blood will be on our hands and he will return fire."

"As long as that blood is his and not ours," Levu said in an uncharacteristically unfeeling way. "General, fire."

The shot fired was a dark blue laser shot that lit up the viewing window on the bridge of the *Malus Tempus*.

"What damage has been done to their ship?" Levu asked.

"None. It was just a warning shot. It appears their ship's shields are comparable to our own," Regti said. "Their weapons are powered as well. They're turning to face us and are returning laser fire."

The *Quia Vita* was jarred momentarily by the blast of the red laser shot.

"Damage report," Levu inquired.

"Minimal," Prak reported. "Our weapons are of nearly equal power to theirs as well as the engines."

"If they won't back down, we'll have to see what that little ship will withstand," Levu said. "Target two torpedoes at their engines."

Regti operated the appropriate controls on his console. "Ready."

"Fire!"

Two torpedoes launched from the *Quia Vita's* forward torpedo bay toward the *Malus Tempus*. They impacted on the enemy's shields with a violent explosion.

"Our shields are down to ninety percent," Notolla reported. "They're firing again. Incoming missiles!"

The ship was again shaken hard by the impact. Sparks flew on the bridge.

"Minimal damage to our ship," Nurisk said. "Shields are at ninety-three percent now."

"What's their situation?" Levu asked.

"They are firing again."

The *Quia Vita* shook from a shot to the engines.

"Engine efficiency down ten percent, Levu," Nurisk said.

"Prepare a spread of torpedoes in conjunction with full power from the forward batteries," Levu said. "Fire!"

Half a dozen torpedoes launched directly at the bridge of the *Malus Tempus* and all forward guns fired sustained blasts amidships and then a few shorter blasts all across the ventral side of the *Malus Tempus* in a strafing maneuver.

"Their ship's shields are down to seventy-five percent; their communications array is damaged, and their life support system is damaged, but functioning," Prak reported. "All their defensive systems are still at full power, though."

The Orb Seekers were in a real firefight now. Some were shaken from their seats, the lights on the bridge went out momentarily, sparks flew from nearly every console, and bits of bulkhead were blown off their placements, but the *Malus Tempus* held together.

"Return Fire!" Karak yelled. "Try to knock out their weapons."

Notolla fired a few more torpedoes. "I am unable to penetrate their shields," she said. "Their shields are down to seventy percent, and they are preparing to fire again."

"This is getting us nowhere," Karak said. "Take us into the star's corona to avoid detection."

Field Marshal Notolla unleashed a blistering laser fire attack. She had preprogrammed a firing plan to target key systems on the enemy ship since they knew the *Quia Vita* was trying to catch up to them. She also fired a few torpedoes directly into their weapons array for good measure. The *Quia Vita's* shields were taken down to fifty-seven percent and their sensors were now operating at reduced efficiency.

"Moving into the star's corona will only keep them from detecting us until they close in on us again," the duke said.

"That's all the time we'll need," Karak said. "Notolla, prepare a remote-controlled explosive and some debris."

"Why the debris?" Notolla asked. "Why not just launch the explosive?"

"So they'll have more than one target to shoot at," the duke suggested. "If they don't knock out the explosive on their first shot, it may damage their ship severely."

"Good idea, but that's not at all what I had in mind," Karak said. "I'm not going to give them that chance. Target the package for the star and fire."

Notolla gave her console undivided attention. "The explosive is away."

"I guess this is our third weapon. Lasers are not effective enough and torpedoes won't punch through their shields," Karak said, really getting his blood up now. "Thrice armed is he who hath his quarrel just! Are they in pursuit?"

"Yes," Notolla said. "They're nearing position."

"Detonate the explosive and put us back on course at maximum speed," Karak ordered.

"They are moving away from us," Kolij said. "They're heading further into the system and closer to the star."

"I'm unable to detect them, Levu," Nurisk said. "Between the radiation given off by the star and our reduced sensor capabilities, I've lost them."

"There has been an explosion on the surface of the star," Prak reported.

"Is there sufficient debris to account for the *Malus Tempus*?" Levu asked.

Nurisk scanned his screen. "I'm not sure. It could be that they went too far into the corona to avoid detection."

"Hold here!" Levu ordered and walked over to Prak's station. "This isn't right. It's the oldest trick in the book. They want us to believe they're dead. Just in case they have something else planned, have all power put to the shields and be ready to leave quickly."

"I'm reading sudden instability on the star's surface," Prak said pointing at his console screen. "It must be the explosion. They must have detonated some special type of device."

"Get us out of here!" Levu yelled.

When the explosive was set off, a great burst of material from the star was expelled from the surface like grapeshot in the direction of the *Quia Vita*. The ship was jostled roughly and thrown far out of position. The crew was thrown out of their seats and across the bridge. Sparks flew and set parts of the bridge alight. Computer panels were blasted completely off the walls. The crew clamored back to their stations.

The *Malus Tempus* was not nearly as close and fared much better, but did not go undamaged.

"What is the damage to their ship?" Karak asked.

"They have lost all weapon control," Notolla reported as readings continued to come in. "Their shields are down and sensors are offline. Our weapons are out, though. We caught just a little of the debris that was blasted off the surface of the star."

"Are there any life signs?"

"Yes, I still read all life signs," Surist said.

"Good," Karak said. "Resume our course to Jisk. We will not bother ourselves with Stone Globe again, I hope, although I fear I'm wrong. Now there's no way they can get to the Swisura System before we can get there, get the Orbs that are there, and be gone."

"Is everyone all right?" Levu asked after the ship stopped shaking.

Kolij and Prak had suffered burns, as the computers at their stations had been overloaded and the panels blasted from the stations. The others seemed a little shaken, but there were no serious injuries.

Levu still wanted to pursue the enemy, and they were definitely enemies now."Status report!"

"Weapons are offline," Regti reported.

"Long- and short-range sensors are down and engines are running on limited power." Nurisk was looking at the readouts at his station through smoke and the occasional blast of sparks from which he protected himself by raising his hand.

"The whole ship is running on limited power now." Prak scowled. "Our shields are down. We have no defenses."

"Are we still able to catch up with them?" Levu asked.

"Are you serious?" Regti asked with one eye closed and the other squinting at Levu. "We can't do battle in this condition."

"We don't even have enough power to push our engines that hard," Nurisk said.

"I recommend that we just sit here and repair our systems," Kolij said. "We have to get the ship back in running order before we can do anything else."

"All right. We've lost this time." Levu squinted at the view screen as the *Malus Tempus* got away. "But we still breathe. We have been outsmarted by Karak for now, but we'll be back. How long until we can be repaired?"

"We can't fully repair this kind of damage on our own." Nurisk shook his head. "We would have to put into space dock for that."

"I think we can get all of our systems back up and running on our own," Prak said, "but we will be at reduced operating capacity from now on. To repair the structural damage, we need help."

"Get on it," Levu said, continuing a change in personality. "I intend to meet Mr. Karak again. I'll track him through the Onuy Nebulae, from one end of Harza's pull through to the other, clear across all of known space, through all its traps and snares ere I let him go. Oh, yes, we will hunt him down, and when we find him, we will take the Orbs from him, no matter the cost."

✡ ✡ ✡

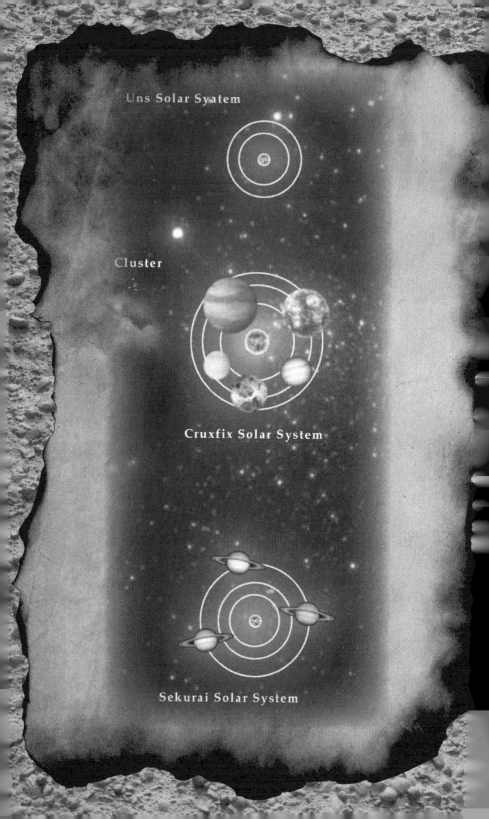

Uns Solar Syatem

Cluster

Cruxfix Solar System

Sekurai Solar System

Chapter 10

THE FORGING OF ALLIES, PART I

As Stone Globe sat stationary in the spot where they'd been bested in battle by Karak Jewill and the *Malus Tempus*, they tried to conjure up a strategy that would allow them to gain the upper hand. Their ship had been badly damaged and could stand no more battle without more extensive repairs. They had been still for nearly a day, repairing the various systems on board the ship.

"I've managed to get the sensors back online." Prak groaned as he reached up from lying underneath his console and raised himself with a grimace. His face was covered with dust, burn marks from failed repair attempts, and various chemical substances. "And the weapons are operational as well, which means we now have some power to redirect to the engines, since they weren't significantly damaged in the battle, although they're operating at slightly reduced efficiency. We can transfer power from one of those systems to the engines if we wish to move, but we can't have all three systems online at the same time yet."

"Moving that kind of raw power from system to system is inadvisable," Nurisk said, narrowing his eyes at Prak. "The transfer systems aren't built for handling that much at once."

"Those systems can operate above the standard capacity by about twenty percent, and we've also hardwired all the systems through a central hub by running a cable from system to system," Prak said.

"Great, something for me to trip over in the corridor," Levu said sarcastically. Without looking at his comrades, he shook his head. "Transfer power from the weapons to the engines, but let's try to get every system running at maximum capacity as soon as we can. I don't want to find ourselves in trouble out here without power. We're already a long way from home, and we're likely to go even farther before this is all over."

"Is there a course I should set?" Kolij asked.

"That's what we have to decide," Levu said slowly. "We don't have many options, and we're going to have to decide quickly if we're to do anything about Karak and his crew. They'll be pretty far ahead of us."

"Whatever we do, it'll have to be powerful enough to counter the Swisura navy." General Regti turned to face his shipmates. "We know the Orb Seekers are heading for the Green Orb in their system."

"We can be almost certain they will be helping the Orb Seekers on their quest," Levu said, "given what we've learned about them from the Cruxfix people."

"We can't counter the Swisura on our own," Nurisk warned. "Our entire navy couldn't take on the Swisura. They're one of the most powerful races out here."

"We'll have to have help." Humwe shook his head. "We can't do this on our own now that we have competition and have taken significant battle damage." He looked at the jagged metal edge of the bulkhead that had fallen just inches from his head.

"All options are open," Levu said, pepping up a little. "Nothing is out of the question. Our navy is otherwise engaged in the evacuation process and not powerful enough to take on the Swisura anyway; that option is out."

"If we could somehow get the Swisura otherwise occupied, it might let us have another crack at Karak and his ship," Kolij suggested. "By that time, they might even have a few Orbs we could take."

"I like that idea." Regti nodded. "We're no longer in position to go scrounging the galaxy for Orbs anyway. The Orb Seekers will collect all the Orbs, or at least several of them, and then we can take them from them."

"We must assume the Swisura will be sympathetic to the Orb Seekers," Levu said. "They would help them, I'm sure. That's their nature, according to what we know about them, and we can't get there first. So who else could we bring into the picture to stop the Swisura?"

"The Cruxfix people also don't have the force necessary," Regti said.

"They also have excellent relations with the Swisura," Levu added, waving his hand dismissively. "We couldn't get them to oppose or even sanction the Swisura."

"The Swisura are sure to help Karak. The Cruxfix people won't step in. Our forces are preoccupied and don't have the strength to counter the Swisura," Humwe thought aloud. "That only leaves one civilization left to consider."

Everyone looked at Humwe with skeptical and treacherous sneers. They knew of whom he spoke—and they didn't like it.

"Surely," Regti said slowly as he eyed Humwe, "you're not serious."

"The Sekurai wouldn't help us if their lives depended on it," Kolij said incredulously and with increasing volume and attitude. "They hate us. I was there in the last battle, and so was General Regti. I saw how much they wanted to destroy us, and we can be sure they don't like us any more now than they did then."

"I am serious," Humwe said quietly. "You forget I was there too. I held my squadron together while their ships were crashing through us like we were nothing. Think about this for a moment, though."

"I have!" Regti dismissed the idea with a perplexed look and a wave of his arm.

"I can't believe you'd even propose such a stupid thing," Kolij said.

Humwe still thought he was onto something. "There's only one thing the Sekurai hate more than us, and that's the Swisura. They've been in more skirmishes with the Swisura than battles with us, and that's saying something. The Swisura are also the only thing standing in the way of the Sekurai obsession with conquering the galaxy."

"The Sekurai might believe we're being short-sighted," Levu said, raising a finger. "Because once they're done warring with the Swisura, there would be nothing to stop them turning their attention to us. I doubt that even the Sekurai would be immediately ready for any offensive after a war so long and hard-fought, but you know they'll be coming."

"It would be a big chance for them to try taking over the galaxy after fighting such a war," Regti said. "The Swisura would see to it that the Sekurai wouldn't be in control of much of anything after such a war. Even if the Sekurai prevailed they'd need years to rebuild."

"Say we do go and—ask them for help." Kolij gagged and covered her mouth. "What's going to stop them from destroying our ship when we first approach them?" She put her hands on her hips and looked at Levu.

"We would have to give them some reason for keeping us alive," Nurisk said with a shrug.

"What if we tell them we would share the power of the Orbs with them?" Prak asked.

"That might dispel any fears they might have about gaining control of the galaxy after the war with the Swisura," Levu said. "The prospect of possessing the Orbs could offset any concern about damage they would take during the war. It would leave them stronger than when they went into the war, and the rebuilding process would likely go more quickly. I think I could get their attention just by telling them they have a chance to destroy the Swisura. I can save bringing the Orbs into the discussion until later, when it becomes necessary to guarantee their cooperation."

"But we don't know if the Orbs will survive the punishment we would put them through in Redron," Nurisk reminded Levu.

"The Sekurai don't know there is a chance they'll be destroyed," Levu said as he turned to face Nurisk with a wry smile. "For all they know, the Orbs are indestructible, leaving them with an endless power source."

"Do they even know the Orbs exist?" Regti asked.

"They've been space-faring for a very long time. I would think they'd be aware of the tales," Levu said, "even if they don't believe them. And we have data on the Orbs that comes from the Cruxfix people. That should be convincing."

"And speaking of the Orbs—" Kolij brought up a star chart on the main screen and plotted the Orbs' positions. "We can't forget that according to the information given to us by Klacton, the fragments from the broken Orange Orb are on Qu'uack, the Sekurai capital planet. This would give us a great chance to go and get it while you're talking with someone about the prospect of war."

"One more thing," Humwe said. "If the Sekurai don't survive the war or if they suffer too many casualties, we would be rid of our only true enemy. We're going to make an enemy of the Rongi, but if we get the Orbs, they'll die off."

"That's just one more incentive for us to do this. Set course for the Sekurai System," Levu said. He took in a deep breath and expelled it slowly. "I never thought I'd be going there for help."

Nearly eight days later, the *Quia Vita*, no longer limping but not at full power, entered the Sekurai System. A Braline ship had never entered Sekurai space. No Braline wanted to go to any planet or station in Sekurai territory because of the smell—and they were likely to die if they did.

"There are six Sekurai scouts on an intercept course," Nurisk reported. "They're not as well armed as escorts, but their weapons systems are hot and they'll be in range in three minutes."

"They're transmitting a message," Humwe said. "It's on audio only."

"Let's hear it." Levu spoke forebodingly from a slouched position and clutching the ends of the arms of his captain's chair.

"Sekurai patrol group to intruding vessel. You have been identified as a Braline ship. Your presence here is unwelcome. You will stand down and be taken prisoner immediately."

"We are prepared to surrender on one condition: we must meet with Empress Mudin at once. We have information she would find very useful," Levu said.

"You have no information the empress would be interested in!" the scout leader yelled.

"I believe she would think differently if she knew what I know," Levu teased with a sly smile. "It concerns the Swisura."

Mumblings and low whispers could be heard in the background of the lead scout ship.

"Silence!" the leader ordered his men.

"Can we at least have your name so I may know to whom I'm speaking?" Levu asked.

"You may not," the leader replied, "but this matter is beyond me. I will direct you to Rorn, our general. We will escort you to Qu'uack, our capital planet."

On the way to Qu'uack, the very center of hatred and malice in the universe, Levu and his crew noticed how enormous the Sekurai navy was. There were thousands and thousands of ships. Some were large warships with escorts and entire flight groups of fighters flying cover missions. It appeared there were constant training missions going on all around the system.

"There must be tens of thousands of people on all of these ships," Prak said, slack-jawed. "Maybe more than that."

"There are all kinds of ships here," Regti added. "This is the largest gathering of forces I've ever seen. I wonder what they're preparing for. I hope they're not getting ready for war with us."

"I would guess they aren't preparing for anything in particular," Levu said. "It wouldn't surprise me if this were normal for them."

Stone Globe felt quite out of place in this part of space. They'd never been this far from home in any direction; they'd never been here, and they certainly never thought they'd be in Sekurai space asking for help. They felt nervous, alone, and vulnerable. As the *Quia Vita* continued on through Sekurai space, Prak's hands shook with every sensor control he touched.

Levu nervously fiddled with his walking stick.

Kolij was strong, resilient, and proud. She stuck her chin out a bit and lifted her nose at the mass of Sekurai warships in view, but then she realized that would offer her nostrils a better angle by which to detect the Sekurai stench. She pulled back.

"We're nearing Qu'uack," Kolij said.

"Once you land, you are to leave your ship and meet with Rorn," the scout leader ordered gruffly. "He will be waiting for you."

"Set us down at the predetermined coordinates," Levu said. "Everyone remain calm."

As the *Quia Vita* was landing on the platform, a large contingent of Sekurai troops flooded the area. Once the ship landed, the troops drew their guns and awaited the order to fire.

Levu and his crew exited the ship as they were instructed. They were met by some very highly decorated individuals, the foremost of which introduced himself as their expected host.

Rorn was a particularly nasty looking man. His skin was a dark reddish color like someone who'd worked outside in the sun all his life. His hair was jet black. The uniform which he wore was heavily laden with medals—some of which, no doubt, had been earned in battle against the Braline. Rorn was of medium build, not stocky and not thin. Neither was he short nor tall, but he made it obvious with his tone and gruff manner that he didn't care for Braline people in Sekurai space, let alone on their capital planet.

"I am General Rorn, in charge of security here," he said combatively. "I hear you have some information that may be useful to us."

"Yes," Levu said, "but what I have to say is for Empress Mudin."

"You will not get near our leader," Rorn said. "If I like what I hear, then I will speak with her. If not, you will die where you stand."

"I'll tell you one thing," Levu teased again. "I can give you a chance to destroy the Swisura once and for all. Now, do you like what you've heard? May I speak with the empress?"

"I will discuss the matter with her," Rorn conceded, gritting his teeth. "You will wait in your ship; we cannot allow you access to our planet beyond this point. If you attempt to take off, your ship will be destroyed before it can leave the ground."

After Rorn left, all of the members of Stone Globe had confidence that they would gain the help of the Sekurai.

"I don't think the empress will be able to pass up this opportunity," Levu said, "and while I'm in conference with her, I want you to go find the Orange Orb. I know it's probably in a million pieces, but you only have to find one. This will put us one Orb closer to victory."

"We won't be able to reassemble it," Kolij reminded him.

"That's okay as long as you can get one piece," Levu responded with a wave of his hand. "All we need is one fragment from it. When we do get a whole Orb, we can just touch the fragment to it and the pieces will all come together from anywhere and that Orb will be re-forged."

"How are we going to be sure that we get one of the pieces of that Orb?" Regti asked, "There may be millions of orange rocks to choose from."

"It's supposed to be a deep but transparent color of orange," Levu said. "It should look like no other orange you've ever seen. I'm betting you'll notice it when you see it, general. Grab up several pieces, if you have to."

"That Rorn guy did say we should stay in our ship," Nurisk said.

"I will take care of that when Mr. Rorn comes back," Levu said.

A few hours later, General Rorn returned after having spoken with the Sekurai empress. He now demanded to speak with Levu and convey news from her.

"Well," Levu said, "are we going to talk with your leader now?"

"You seem very presumptuous that you'll be allowed to see her, let alone live to see the next hour," Rorn said with a sneer.

"I know that none of you, not even the empress, can turn away a chance to destroy your fiercest rival," Levu teased yet again.

"You know us well," Rorn admitted with a squinting scowl. "You, and you alone, are permitted to speak with her. I will take you to her." He turned around to lead Levu to the empress.

"Uh, just one more thing there, uh, Mr. Rorn," Levu said.

Rorn growled under his breath because he wanted to listen to Levu even less than he wanted him in Sekurai territory. "What is it?" he grumbled without even turning around.

"Some of my people would like to do a bit of research on the matter at hand. Can you provide them with someone who can answer a few questions?"

"Your people will stay in your ship," Rorn said.

"It is crucial and pertinent to the same matter I must discuss with Empress Mudin," Levu explained. "We wouldn't want the empress to be hindered by a lack of information."

"Very well," Rorn admitted with an eye roll, still not facing Levu, as he motioned for a guard to escort Regti, Nurisk, and Kolij.

Levu was then escorted inside the palace and proceeded to what he could only assume was the location of the empress. The palace was a circular shape with six rings, each one smaller and enclosed by the one before it. Each ring had only one entrance, and that opening was always halfway around the structure from the previous one. Levu was being taken to the innermost ring where the leader of the Sekurai people was housed. Due to the length of the trip from one ring's entrance to the next, the journey took about an hour.

When they finally arrived at the inner-most level, they came upon a very large and extremely ornate set of doors. The doors were made of well-polished silver and consisted of six panels, three on each door, each of which had carved into it what were deemed the most impressive firsts in Sekurai history. On the top left panel was depicted the forging of the first sword known to exist on Qu'uack. On the other panels were the launching of the first warship onto the sea, the first piece of artillery used in battle, the coronation of the first planetary leader of Qu'uack, including the decapitated head of his rival with his foot perched crushingly upon it, the launching of the first warship into space, and the first conquering of beings from another solar system.

The doors opened to reveal a desk, in front of which was seated a chair. Behind the desk, Empress Mudin's slender frame sat in her own chair.

"Come in, Levu Earsp of the Braline," Mudin said. "Please, make yourself comfortable."

"No offense, empress," Levu said in a skeptical tone, "but let's get on with our business; I have many things to do. I'm here to offer you something you want, and, in return, I am going to ask from you something I want."

"Go on," Mudin said in not so nice a tone as before, realizing her charm would not work.

"As you may or may not be aware," Levu said, "the Braline System's gravitational equilibrium has been compromised. Nuin is dying, and our system will be sucked into Redron."

"I see," Mudin said coldly. "I don't care, and if you think I'm going to help your people, then you're mistaken. There's nothing I'd like more than to see your people crushed into oblivion."

"There is something you would rather see," Levu said as he was coming to enjoy teasing the Sekurai leaders. "The Swisura people crushed into oblivion."

Mudin sat up with an awed expression on her face. "You're right," she said, "but they are very powerful. How could we possibly go into a war with them and expect to come out even a shadow of ourselves as we are now? Even if we were victorious, there would be nothing left of us. Even your puny, backward, little warships could come in and end our civilization."

"Your praise of our military standing in the galaxy is astounding," Levu said in a low sarcastic voice. "But what if I told you that I could save my people, with your help, and that, with my help, you could eliminate the Swisura threat to your expansion?"

"Though I still don't see how, I'm listening," Mudin replied skeptically.

"Have you heard of the seven Orbs of Quality?" Levu asked.

"No."

"I'm surprised. They are stones that are old—very old—and very powerful." Levu leaned in. "They were made in the Cruxfix System over a thousand years ago. It was through their power that they were able to end a devastating civil war that was tearing their people apart."

Mudin stared blankly at Levu as he spoke.

"With their power, we could save our system, but there is one thing in the way. Another group is searching for them too, some people from the Rongi System, and that group has very likely enlisted the help of the Swisura."

Mudin still had not moved in the slightest. She just glared at him through thinly slit eyes and didn't noticeably move even to breathe.

"We need your power to counter the Swisura. If you will help us get all seven of the Orbs, we will share their power with you, and that power will allow you to destroy the Swisura."

"I don't like the idea of helping you," the empress said, coming out of her trance, "and I like the idea of accepting your help even less. However, I do like the prospects and the thought of eliminating the Swisura. You're saying that all we have to do is help you find these seven stones?"

"That's correct."

"It sounds too easy."

"At the outset is does, but these Orbs are broken and scattered throughout the galaxy."

"There's always a catch, isn't there?" Mudin rolled her deep set eyes.

"Yes," Levu said. "What do you think? Will you join our little adventure?"

"I will admit it sounds enticing," Mudin replied, finally shifting in her seat and looking down to her side as she did so. "What exactly will our role be?"

"The Orb Seekers, the other group, will already have two of the Orbs," Levu said. "We will go out and try to find the other Orbs while you keep the Swisura busy. Then, together, we will take those two Orbs from the Orb Seekers and have all of them to ourselves."

"You know we will most likely not gain much ground in a fight with the Swisura, don't you?" Mudin asked as she re-entered her former trance-like state.

"You don't have to," Levu said, raising a hand to dispel Mudin's concerns. "All you have to do is keep them off our backs while we go and look for the other five Orbs."

After a few moment's pause Empress Mudin gave her answer. "Go back to your ship," she said. "I will consider the idea and will let you know within a few hours. I will let you know by either keeping you alive—or by killing you."

Levu began to leave to return to the *Quia Vita*. "One more thing," Mudin said as she rose.

Levu turned to face her.

"I want something from you. Something special."

"What's that?"

"I've been noticing your helmsman since you arrived." The empress exhibited a little twinkle in her eye. "She's awfully pretty."

"Don't you have your own helmsmen?" Levu turned away again, this time with an eye roll.

"Yes, but I want yours."

"What do you mean you 'want' her?" Levu took a bit of an attitude.

"I mean I *want* her." Mudin rose and raised a slender, long-fingered hand to her breast. Levu walked to the doorway, ignoring her. "You will agree to my terms or I will not consider your proposal."

"I can't sell one of my crew for sex!"

"Then your civilization will die." Mudin sat back down in her chair with a wry smile and pressed her fingertips together. She eyed Levu and then asked, "I wonder if I'll hear your people's screams from here."

"Space is a vacuum," Levu said, not having a better retort. "You won't have the pleasure."

"Interesting. Don't you claim to be able to smell us from ship to ship?" Levu had no response. "Give her to me—or you will get no help here." Mudin leaned forward and pointed a finger hard onto her desk to emphasize her resolve. She cocked her head. "It really is interesting, isn't it? We've been trying to kill you for one hundred fifty years and now, all of the sudden, I don't have to do a damn thing for you all to die. I'll just sit here."

Levu hesitated. He had no choice. There was nowhere else to go, and he needed help from the Sekurai. Levu, utterly defeated, just nodded. He then turned and walked out the door.

Levu left to go back to the *Quia Vita*. It felt safe there, even though there were over a dozen plasma cannons directed at it and ready to fire in less than a second's notice. Truly, there was nothing safe about anything Levu and his crew were doing. There was no safe place to go to. They were surrounded by danger, and this was danger of the most dangerous kind. Levu was quiet. He couldn't believe he'd agreed to Mudin's outrageous demand, but he'd had no choice.

While Levu had been meeting with Mudin to discuss plans, Kolij, Regti, and Nurisk were escorted to an area near the coordinates of the Orange Orb as provided by the Cruxfix information. As they closed in on ground zero, Regti gave Kolij a look and they jumped their escort. Beating him over the head several times, they overpowered him quickly and easily, and then drug him into a wet gutter in a nearby alleyway. Nurisk wasn't necessarily a fighter like Kolij and Regti were, but he had grabbed up a stray board and whacked the guard a few times for good measure.

"That was even easier than I thought," Kolij said, wiping her hands together. "He didn't even have time to go for his gun."

"Yeah, but we touched him with our bare hands," Regti complained. "Now I'll smell like Sekurai for a week."

"Awww," Kolij teased him.

"When you two get a minute," Nurisk began, "we need to find the entrance to this subterranean vault. It's got to be where the Orb fragments are; the coordinates lead that way."

A few minutes later, Nurisk's handheld computer had directed them to an old cellar. They busted the lock and went down the damp steps into the dark crypt. As they reached the bottom of the steps, the cellar became more of a cavern. Only the door was manmade; the steps had been carved out of the natural rock face. The cave was not lit at all; the trio had to pull out their light sticks from their pockets to see anything.

"The coordinates are leading me over here in this general area," Nurisk said. "We're looking for a deep translucent orange rock."

Regti walked over to the nearest wall, which was partially caved in by this time. An ancient room beyond the wall could be seen through the gaping hole. "I'm guessing the ceiling in here may not be altogether stable given the condition of this wall. There are bits of it lying everywhere."

Nurisk examined the wall and its remnants closely. "This wall has been here for a very long time, centuries, I'd say."

"I think I've found something," Kolij said as she joined Regti near the wall. "This protruding stone appears to fit the description, but it's stuck in the wall. It's part of the wall. I don't think we could get it out without bringing the whole place down around our heads."

"It's only a piece," Nurisk said. "Surely there are other pieces around here too. Perhaps some of them are loose here on the ground."

They sifted through the various rocks and found several that matched the descriptions of the Orbs. They gathered up several of these and Kolij put them in her pouch.

"What's going to happen to this cave when we finally do re-forge this Orb?" Regti asked.

"What do you mean?" Kolij gave Regti a look that demonstrated she didn't know or care.

"Well, this cave isn't exactly stable," Regti noted. "When we re-forge the Orb, any pieces of it that are part of the wall will be removed from here, and they'll come together at the point of contact between this piece and the whole Orb we use to re-forge it. Some structurally important pieces may be taken out of this wall and this whole cave could collapse."

"Yes, and . . . . ?" Kolij asked.

At this, Regti realized he didn't care either, and they made their way back up the stairs with their collection of rocks and through the darkness toward the landing platform where the *Quia Vita* waited.

When Levu returned to the *Quia Vita* from his meeting, a surprise was in store for him.

"We have something that may interest you, Levu." Kolij handed him an orange rock. "Behold, the Orange Orb—or at least one of its fragments. We'll need a whole Orb to re-forge it."

"It is beautiful," Levu said. "Just as we were told it would be."

The fragment was about one tenth the size of what the Orb would be if it were whole. It was as smooth as silk on the outer edge and jagged and torn on the inside portions. The color was of the deepest orange, pure and bright. The outside was devoid of all blemishes or discolorations. There was no question this was a part of the Orange Orb of Quality.

"The plan worked perfectly then, I assume." Levu looked expectantly at Kolij.

"Indeed, it did," Kolij said. "It wasn't easy, but it worked. We ditched our guard and followed the Cruxfix directions precisely. We brought back several other pieces of rock that are smaller versions of this piece. They are of the same color and may belong to the Orange Orb as well. We wanted to be certain we could re-forge it and not have to come back here."

"My end of the bargain worked as well, I think," Levu said. "She said she would consider the plan and decide in a few hours. I told her there were only seven Orbs. Hopefully, that will leave us with some breathing room if something goes awry. Then even if they do win the war with the Swisura and steal the Orbs from us, they won't have them all. They won't even know of the existence of the eighth Orb, and they'll be so busy warring with the Swisura they won't go to the Cruxfix System to do any research on the Orbs." Levu's attention shifted as he was trying to avoid looking Kolij in the eye. "You said you ditched your guard? How?"

"We jumped him in an alley and left him in the gutter," Regti answered with a shrug and a smile. "We ditched him."

"I see; nice work," Levu said.

"They will be more aggravated at us than Redron is now," Regti said jokingly. "We may have to move to another galaxy."

"We would hole ourselves up inside the Kriline Defense Barrier," Levu said, still distracted. "We'd be okay. Now, tell me how you managed such a feat as to get the Orange Orb fragment."

"The location of the Orb was exact, just like you said it should be," Nurisk said. "Prak and Humwe stayed here and monitored our progress while Kolij, Regti, and I went searching. We found ourselves in a cave underneath the city, and the destination provided by the information was beyond our reach. There was a wall where the Orb should have been, according to the coordinates. The room had been sealed many, many years ago.

"So, we scrounged through the debris lying on the floor and found these pieces of rock. We knew we only needed a part of the Orb, because once we get a whole Orb we can just touch this piece to it and the Orange Orb will be forged again. There were other pieces lying around on the ground; we picked some of those up as well. Others were actually part of the wall."

Later that evening, after supper, Rorn and another Sekurai general came aboard the *Quia Vita*. Rorn spoke with Levu and said he'd come for Kolij. Levu was instantly irritated and on full alert. "You don't come aboard my ship and ask to take a member of my crew. I'm responsible for her and each of the people aboard my ship."

"If the empress is going to enter into an alliance," Rorn said as he coughed harshly at the thought, "she's going to insist on proper planning. General Snar, here, is going to talk to you about getting some upgrades done to this little ship of yours. And you know why I've come for Kolij."

Despite his mistrust and high levels of internal angst, Levu remembered how much he needed the Sekurai, so he agreed to Rorn's request and showed him to Kolij.

Once he was with Kolij, Rorn took an unusually disarming demeanor. "Our empress has a proposal to make."

"Oh?" Kolij asked.

"It's an indecent one."

"Indecent?" Kolij said as she leaned back away from him and raised her hand to just beneath her neck.

"You see," Rorn began with an unassuming tone, "the empress wants you."

Kolij paused with a curious look. "She wants to spend a night with you," Rorn said, not playing games any longer.

Kolij's mouth gaped open and her eyes grew wide. "I'll never," Kolij finally said. "No!"

"She *wants* you. And she will have you, or your crew will get no help here. You came here because you need us, remember that." Rorn gave Kolij an especially serious look. "Your captain has already agreed. He had no more choice than you do."

Kolij was about to protest, having regained her presence of mind, but she remembered losing the first battle with the Orb Seekers. The task before Stone Globe had become too big for them. They desperately needed allies. "What does the empress want?"

"You will come with me. You will actually spend a night with her. It is to be a sexual encounter to her liking. I can't be clearer."

"You can't be serious," Kolij said, feigning a laugh.

"The empress is serious, and therefore so am I. Our agreement is completely dependent on this." Rorn stood up and assumed a strong position to demonstrate that he meant what he said.

Kolij's smile changed to a horrified and oppressed expression.

"There are no questions. There are no warnings. There are no demonstrations of our power or our resolve. This is not a discussion. You will come freely or your cause will die here and now."

"I can't do that," Kolij said, maintaining as much calm as she could muster.

"Then your people will all die," Rorn said uncaringly as he turned to leave.

"Just tell me one thing. Why does she want me?"

"I assume she's interested in a new experience, something different than what she's accustomed to. She's been bored for some time. If you do not agree, I will leave and send you on your way. We will watch as your entire solar system is sucked into Redron. There will be no second chances. You will decide now."

"I wouldn't be of any use to her. I-I...don't know what I'm doing. I haven't—"

"Irrelevant. She orders and I obey. She will tell you what to do." Rorn removed his communicator from his pocket and held it up to his face, ready to report.

Kolij stared at Rorn. She wasn't accustomed to being in such a position. She was out of options. After a moment, but without a word she got up and slowly followed him.

Rorn took Kolij by the arm and walked her away. Kolij was appalled at the thought that a Sekurai was touching her, but she knew she'd better get used to it quickly. The *Quia Vita's* ramp door closed behind them.

Levu locked himself in his quarters the rest of the evening and all night.

Kolij entered the empress's quarters. Mudin, already disrobed of her outer garments, still only displaying the slightest hint of a bosom, walked to the door to escort Kolij in and lock the door behind them. "Welcome, my child," she said.

Kolij, ever strong-willed and stout-hearted, just stood there, frozen and crying.

The next morning Rorn brought Kolij back. None of the other Stone Globe members knew what had happened. They assumed she'd gone to bed early and had been on the ship the whole time. She staggered up the ramp, her clothes fitting somewhat more loosely than normal, and stumbled down the corridor of the *Quia Vita*. She had a deeply unsettled look on her face, and her hair was a disheveled mess. She'd been crying, and in no small amount. She fell into her quarters and lay there on the floor, doing nothing, not even crying. There were no tears left to cry. Her spirit had been crushed; she was defeated. She had a thought or two about taking a shower, but could not bring herself to move for quite some time.

Levu went in to see to her for just a moment. She could not look at him, but spoke to him just long enough to tell him a few sentences about what had happened. A foreboding look came across his face. He patted his friend on the shoulder, left Kolij on the floor, and left her quarters, closing the door behind him.

Levu, thinking about his uneasy alliance with the Sekurai and about what he'd done, perched himself up against the bulkhead of the *Quia Vita* with one foot tucked up under him against the wall and his knee sticking out straight away from him. Hanging his head low, his chin resting so low on his chest that his hat brim was nearly vertical, and with his eyes closed, it was clear that something was troubling him. He was uneasy, to say the least. Ironically, the cause of his lack of ease was the successes they'd just had as a team in forming an alliance to help them save their people, despite a personal defeat that Kolij could never undo.

"Why do you look so down?" Regti asked.

"I just made a deal with the devil," he responded with a sigh realizing the road he and his colleagues were going down. Never would they have even thought to venture to the Sekurai System, let alone enter into an agreement with them. The Sekurai were the greatest threat to the Braline, only to be outdone by Redron's pulling in of their entire system. Nevertheless, here they were making an alliance with the scourge of the galaxy, a race bent on war and conquest.

Levu told his crew what had happened.

"You did *what?*" Regti asked Levu. "You agreed to *what?*

"How could you possibly let that evil woman have Kolij?" Humwe was disappointed in Levu for the first time.

"It was either agree to her terms or we'd have to leave with no alliance, no help, and no chance. I had no choice, and neither did Kolij."

All of Stone Globe knew exactly what Levu meant when he said he'd made a deal with the devil. It was something imponderable to them until just a few days before. They were sacrificing all they were to try to save all that they had. They had to find seven more Orbs, and the mission was already reshaping them—into what, they did not know—nor did they care to know.

"Just one thing before you go, Rorn," Levu said, trying to put the indecency behind him. "Could you provide us with a scout ship? We wish to spy on the Orb Seekers and have advanced information on their plans."

"Yes, I will see to it that you're provided with a stolen Swisura scout ship. That's the smartest thing I've heard anyone say in days." Rorn flashed a quick smile full of yellowed and crooked teeth. Bad breath beyond all proportion expelled from him.

"Well, that was exciting," Prak said sarcastically after Rorn had left.

"I rather like him," Regti said. "I think I've found a new role model."

"I detect sarcasm," Levu said, trying in vain to recover himself after the deal he'd made which might have resulted in the destruction of his best friend.

"No," said Regti in the same tone as before, "surely not."

"Nurisk," Levu said, turning away. "I want you to go on this spy mission. Perhaps you can convince your brother to join us, if he is your brother. Even if you can't, though, you are to bring at least one whole Orb back to us. Your scout ship will be faster than the *Quia Vita*; we'll meet you in sector D:4 just outside the Onuy Nebulae. From there we can be of assistance in the battle or at least stop the Orb Seekers from gaining any ground."

The *Quia Vita* took off from the launch pad and began its route to the furthest shipyard in the Sekurai System, where they were to be re-supplied and upgraded. They were also scheduled to take on board a stolen Swisura scout ship for Nurisk's special mission. Once they reached the shipyard, the upgrades began immediately. The commanding officer of the shipyard had already received his instructions and was very much on top of things. Levu wondered if he got to work so quickly because he wanted to get rid of his Braline guests or if this was just his regular working pace. The tempo must be quick and effortless in order to maintain the massive Sekurai navy.

"I have a Swisura scout ship here," the officer said. "Do you want it in your shuttle bay?"

"Yes, thank you," Levu said in a hollow voice. "That would be great."

The officer had the ship moved into the shuttle bay. The two shuttles already present there had to be rearranged to make room for the scout ship. One was moved against the wall of the bay, and the other was nearly touching the first, and still the new ship was practically on top of them.

The ship was of a very simple design. The white scout ship was shaped somewhat like an egg lying on its side when viewed from above, except it was thinner when viewed from the side. Levu thought this appropriate, since the Swisura were a very peaceful people. He also found it ironic that he was going to engage in a war against a people, though not quite an ally, toward whom he certainly felt no ill will, and do so with a sworn enemy at his side. This made him sick just at the thought. He didn't know how the plan would play out. The price he and his crew would pay was no longer the only thing on his mind. Now the well-being of a great many more people would be placed in jeopardy. A great war between the galaxy's two largest forces was about to begin.

"All right," the officer said as he wiped his hands on a towel and walked over to Levu, "You're all ready to go."

"Is there anything my pilot will need to know about the scout ship?"

"No, it will fly similarly to your own ships, just faster and more powerful. I've uploaded a manual to your computers. You're not just going on a joyride. It wouldn't hurt if the expected pilot learned a little something about the ship's systems and maintenance requirements before he tries to take it into battle."

"Okay. Thank you very much. We will be on our way and out of yours," Levu said. "By the way, what did you upgrade on our ship?"

"Most things," the officer said. "Your weapons are now much more powerful and so are your engines. You'll definitely be superior to the Rongi ship. I would have upgraded the weapons even more, but your ship doesn't generate enough power to support those systems. The sensor range has been increased and the shields should hold their own better, especially against any Rongi ship."

"How do you know we're fighting the Rongi?" Levu asked with a questioning eye.

"They tell me everything I need to know when I get an order," the officer answered with a shrug. "You never know when the next piece of information you didn't get could've come in handy. I was even provided with specifications of the kinds of ship's systems your people use. We've captured and studied Braline ships before. Your ship is of a different design, but it operates on the same kinds of systems. The upgrades were relatively easy."

"I see," Levu said expressionlessly.

"You should have the Rongi ship at your mercy," the officer continued. "You are now vastly superior in every technological way."

"All right," Levu said softly, turning to board the *Quia Vita*. "Thanks for your help."

"Happy hunting," the officer said.

As Levu boarded the *Quia Vita* he began to think about the officer. There was something different about him, and he couldn't quite pinpoint what it was. He entered the bridge and sat down. "Take us out of here," he said, putting the details of the recent events behind him a little too easily. "Set course for the Swisura System. We should be able to destroy the Orb Seekers without much problem now. According to the commanding officer of the shipyard, we're vastly superior to their ship, and all our battle damage has been repaired." He frowned. "There was something different about that officer though."

"What would that be?" Regti asked.

"I don't know. I can't put my finger on it. He actually seemed rather personable—kind of respectable."

"I know they're our allies now," Regti said, looking at Levu as though he was trying to keep his leader's feet on the ground, "but they aren't our friends."

"No, I know." Levu shook his head once to the side as he closed his eyes. "There was just something different, and I'd like to be able to say what that something was."

"I think you're being paranoid," Kolij said emotionlessly as she slowly returned to her post.

"Yes," Prak said. "The next thing we know, you'll be telling us he didn't smell."

"That's it!" Levu bellowed. "That's what it was. That great natural defense and deterrent—it wasn't there. He didn't smell."

"He didn't smell?" Regti said questioningly.

"He didn't smell," Levu said.

ҳ ҳ ҳ

Swisura Solar System

Chapter 11

THE FORGING OF ALLIES, PART II

On the four-day journey the rest of the way to the Swisura System, the Orb Seekers were able to repair what little damage they'd sustained during the battle with the *Quia Vita*. What was foremost on their minds was how they would convince Prelate Luric, the leader of the Swisura, to help them find the two Orbs that were located inside Swisura space.

"I think we should just go in and take the Orbs." Notolla shrugged. "They have no meaning to anyone but us. Surely the Swisura wouldn't mind."

"That's not the spirit in which we do things," Karak replied. "Besides, we may need help from the Swisura later on."

"Why don't we just tell the prelate everything and let him make a decision?" Hiram asked.

"I don't think that would be wise either," Surist said. "I think we should just ask for help. Since we have to go to the Swisura System, I did some research on them while we were still on Crux I. The Braline and Swisura are not likely to have met before, although it's possible. We don't want them to take Stone Globe's side."

Everyone looked at Surist. They thought he was promoting a slight bit of dishonesty in suggesting that they not tell the Swisura the whole story. However, they could not argue with his logical rational thought process.

"I'm not sure I like the idea of hiding something from them," Hiram said. "I do understand where you're coming from though."

"Stone Globe has to try to get help somewhere," Lithinia said, "but where can they?"

"That's just it," Surist replied. "The Swisura are the only option either of us has. According to the Cruxfix library records we downloaded while we were there, the Sekurai are the only people with the power to counter them, and the Sekurai wouldn't help anyone without an ulterior motive. Besides, the Braline and the Sekurai are enemies. The Sekurai have attacked the Braline many times with the goal of taking the Strunk Nebulae, the chief Braline source of indimite, on which their ships operate.

"The Swisura have a history of helping people. Their history also shows that if we can get their commitment first, they'll abide by it and help us. Once they make a statement they stand by it, even if it becomes inconvenient. They are impartial and true to their word."

"Do you mean they would fight the Braline even though they have the same enemy?" Karak's eyes met Surist's.

"Yes." Surist nodded. "Their history shows it. Principles aren't convenient and they know it, but they accept it."

"And you've learned all this by studying the Cruxfix database on the Swisura?" Karak questioned a little incredulously.

"Yes," Surist responded. "Their records are quite thorough. The duke and I both thought it best if we educated ourselves on the next leg of our journey."

"The Swisura are some of the most powerful people in the galaxy," the duke said. "Their help would be invaluable, especially in a war in which we have little or no advantage."

"What war?" Notolla exclaimed. "We're not at war! We've fought one small skirmish."

"I wouldn't count on the idea that Mr. Earsp and his crew are out of the race," Karak cautioned. "We've seen how serious they are about their mission. I would imagine we'll be seeing them again. What's more, the Braline have nowhere else to go. No one else would be willing to help them, and those who would be willing don't have the power. It's decided; we will tell the prelate our situation in its entirety and ask him for his help."

The Orb Seekers entered the Swisura System and headed for Jisk at maximum speed. They didn't want to risk Stone Globe gaining any advantage. "We've received permission from the Office of the Prelate to land on Jisk and speak to Luric about the situation," Lithinia reported.

"Set us down on the landing pad closest to the prelate's office," Karak ordered. "Upon landing, we'll proceed directly to him to plead our case."

The *Malus Tempus* glided through the atmosphere and Hiram operated the controls to gently land the ship. "Considering we took some battle damage, I think that landing went well," Karak said. "Let's go meet this Luric fellow."

Luric was a middle-aged man, tall and lanky, like most Swisura. His thin frame supported a light gray suit worn over a white shirt. He'd been the leader of the Swisura people for less than a decade, but long enough that he was well established. The walls of his office were white, but the furniture and settings were of many different colors and types of materials. His desk was a simple clear acrylic desk and was purely utilitarian, without much frame. His office chair was a different matter entirely, however. It seemed to be of a somewhat opulent level of comfort with cushions everywhere, padded arm rests which could be repositioned at seemingly any angle, and a headrest which telescoped upward and tilted forward or backward.

Upon seeing Luric's desk, Karak wondered if Luric could possibly be busy at all, then after seeing the chair, he assumed Luric never left his desk and must, therefore, be snowed under with all sorts of paperwork. The Orb Seekers stood in front of the desk and spoke with Luric, who had gotten up to place his hand on Karak's shoulder, the traditional greeting of the Swisura.

"Welcome to Jisk." The prelate resumed his seat. "I have read the account of your situation. It seems as though you've had quite an exciting time getting here, and this mention of a Braline ship attacking you on your way is quite a surprise. You are here, I think, to ask for assistance."

"Yes," Karak said. "Our foe is after the Orbs as well, and though we've been able to damage his ship and get away from him for the moment, we believe we have not seen the last of him. He is in the same position we are. We've taken drastic measures to ensure our safety and we are still engulfed in the shadow of this latest obstacle. We don't want to kill anyone. In fact, we're trying to save tens of billions of lives." Karak fixed his eyes upon the floor with a gaze of regret. "However, we're finding that our principles of peace may have to be, uh, *revised* if we are to complete our mission and save our people."

"The end justifies the means?" Luric asked, tilting his head back a bit while maintaining eye contact with Karak.

"That always depends on both the means and the end," Karak responded with a steely look. "There is no greater end for us than the survival of our people."

"I understand your situation," Luric said with a nod, "and I am willing to commit our forces and power to your cause. I cannot simply sit by while a civilization's very existence hangs in the balance by such a fraying thread. I cannot guarantee anything in the way of success, but I will do all I can. I anticipate your stay here lasting about four days. It's late today, and I think one day to find and procure each Orb, perhaps two for the Purple Orb. I know some of the story of the Orbs. For instance, I knew of the two in our system. However, I was not aware there were eight in total."

"We believe the only thing we will require your help with is getting this new enemy out of our way." Surist understandingly leaned in toward Luric and raised his empty hands from his lap, palms facing the prelate. "We don't want them killed. In fact, we would help them if we could, but we obviously have our own problems. If you could just keep them away from us and allow us to find the Orbs, you would have served your part. Surely one ship won't be hard to stop."

"It will be done," Prelate Luric said with an agreeable smile. "We'll see what we can do to help the Braline people evacuate too. I feel for them as much as you."

"We should begin looking for the two Orbs in your space as soon as possible," Karak said.

"I will go with you to help you find the two Orbs in our space." Luric eyed his calendar.

Everyone gathered into the *Malus Tempus* and set course for a small, remote island on Jisk. Upon arriving at the location of the Green Orb, Luric educated the Orb Seekers. "The island is inhabited by a primitive people who have never taken part in the technological advancements of the rest of the solar system. These indigenous people are well aware of the culture that has thrived around them; they simply don't want it for themselves. They prefer a simpler way. The Green Orb is a god to them. They have placed it upon a large mantel in the middle of their village. The mantel is very highly decorated with leaves and feathers; the Orb is obviously very important to them."

"And just how are we supposed to get at it?" Notolla asked halfway irritated. "They have it surrounded by decorations and it's practically framed into the mantel."

"This civilization would be devastated if their god turned up missing tomorrow morning," Karak agreed, looking at his team for ideas.

"Perhaps we could synthesize a replacement," Lithinia said.

"Surely they would know the difference." Surist frowned.

"I'm not so sure they would," Luric said, squinting and pointing at the Orb. "This tribe never does anything but look at and pray to the Orb as a god. It wouldn't be difficult to create a very similar looking replacement; all it would have to do is look the part."

"How soon can it be done?" Karak asked, giving Luric a hopeful look.

"If we go back to the ship we can send a message to one of my aides," Luric responded, "He could probably bring a suitable replacement here in just a couple of hours."

"Very well," Karak said as he nodded his head. "That will give us a few hours to think about what we will do to find the Purple Orb on Isk."

In a matter of just two hours, one of Luric's aides set his small, one-man scout ship down next to the *Malus Tempus*. The aide brought the fake Orb to Luric and reported that it met all of the specifications he'd been given in the message. Then Notolla and Karak went to switch the Orbs as quickly as possible. While they were gone Orb hunting, the rest of the crew stayed behind, and Luric and his aide had a private discussion.

"This shouldn't take too long," Karak said to Notolla. "Just switch the Orbs and get back to the ship. If anything happens, just grab the real Orb and run for the *Malus Tempus*."

Notolla walked past the sleeping guard and sat the fake Orb on the ground so she could take the real one from the mantel. Just as she snatched the real Orb, the fake one began to roll down the hill. Notolla tried to put her foot in front of it to stop it, but it had rolled so far already that she could only put her foot on top of the replica. Notolla looked into the bushes to see Karak covering his mouth to contain his laughter. Notolla sneered at him.

Notolla's foot then slipped off of the fake Orb. As her foot hit the ground she lost her balance and stumbled, all while still holding the real Green Orb. The fabricated Orb then began rolling downhill again. Notolla sat the real Orb down to chase after the fake one.

In her chase, Notolla tweaked her ankle by stepping in a hole. She let out a cry that woke the guard, who began chasing after her while yelling and waving a stick. Karak had begun laughing aloud as this happened. Then the real Orb began rolling down the other side of the hill and Notolla was completely beside herself. She picked up the fake Orb, handed it to the guard, who was just happy not to have been caught by his leaders while he was napping on duty. Notolla then ran for the *Malus Tempus* as Karak went over to the real Orb, picked it up, and also headed for the ship.

"So, anyone could have just walked up and done this?" Notolla said when Karak finally caught up with her.

Karak laughed. "Oh, no. I don't think just anyone could have done *that*."

Notolla leered at Karak's amusement and Karak collected himself. "I think this could have been done anytime, yes."

"Then how do we know this hasn't been done before and that this is the real Orb?"

Karak just looked at Notolla, smiled, and said, "Now, marshal, we can't be thinking pessimistically now, can we?"

"Always," Notolla said under her breath. "One more thing. Won't their crops fail now?"

"They probably won't fail," Karak said in a tone that showed he shared some of Notolla's concern, "but they may not see the same abundance they've become accustomed to. The Orb doesn't grow crops for them; they've still had to develop sound farming practices over the years. They'll be fine."

Karak and Notolla returned to the ship with the Orb shortly after having set out on their task. When they arrived, everyone was taken by the beauty of the thing. It was as perfect as had been described.

"Its color is of the purest hue," Hiram said. "I never would have expected such beauty."

"The description of the Orbs that Gronil gave us didn't prepare us for this." The duke's eyes grew wide. "It really is beyond words. Its surface is completely smooth and perfectly round."

"My friends," Luric interrupted, "I hate to disrupt your viewing of one of the greatest wonders of ancient times, but there are matters I must attend to. I have just been informed of a mass militarization of Sekurai forces in our direction. Something bad is about to happen."

The *Malus Tempus* hurried back to the prelate's office to drop him off before going to search for the Purple Orb on Isk.

The prelate was met on the landing pad by several of his advisors and some security personnel when the ship landed. The *Malus Tempus* crew accompanied him to the exit.

"I'm sorry that I cannot accompany you on the rest of your journey," the prelate told the Orb Seekers, "but it seems that the Sekurai want war all of the sudden. I don't know what this is all about, but I would guess that it's not unrelated to your own cause. You must go on to find the Purple Orb by yourselves."

The Orb Seekers said their expedited thank-yous and the *Malus Tempus* raised itself into the air and shot towards the sky as fast as it could. It raced into the upper atmosphere and headed for Isk. The Orb Seekers wanted to get the Purple Orb and get out of the line of fire before the war started. The *Malus Tempus* was no match for Sekurai or Swisura forces, and they certainly didn't want to get caught in the middle of a fight between them.

The short journey of only an hour or two was uneventful, much to the delight of the Orb Seekers. They decided it would be wise to take a shuttle down to the surface in case the ship was attacked. They could defend themselves in space much more effectively than from an aerial assault. "The ship could at least run if it were attacked in space. It maneuvers better when it doesn't have as much gravity to tend with— as well as enemies firing at it," Notolla said.

"I will volunteer to remain onboard and alert you should something go wrong," Surist said. "The last thing we can afford to have happen is the Sekurai coming into Swisura space from a backdoor and finding an unknown little Rongi ship that will make easy prey."

"The information Gronil gave us says the Orb should be somewhere within about a square half-mile," the duke said.

"That's not too much area," Karak said.

"It's also not a small area," Notolla observed.

"This shouldn't take long with five of us searching," Karak reassured. "We're looking for something purple and, if history proves itself again, it should be the most striking purple we've ever laid eyes on. Also, we won't know that we have part of the Purple Orb until we touch it to the Green one and re-forge the Purple one, and we won't know if the Green Orb is genuine until we re-forge another Orb with it. Let's spread out. Keep in touch."

The group scattered in all directions and traveled the area specified. About half of the area was flat plains with short grass. This would not be hard to navigate through, but the grasses could conceal the Orb pieces. The other half of the terrain was a dark wooded region. This area did not have the brush the plain had, but it was very dark due to an excessive forest canopy of tree branches. Nothing grew on the forest floor for lack of light. The floor was just lined with dead leaves and branches.

Meanwhile, on the *Malus Tempus*, Surist was plotting the group's next course and deciding which Orb would be the best to go after next. He hadn't gotten very far when he received a message from Prelate Luric.

"The Sekurai are heading for sector D:4," Luric said. "They're taking up a position just outside the Onuy Nebulae. This is consistent with Rorn's strategies. Rorn is their main naval general. We are going to defend our borders in sector D:5. So far it seems like they know nothing of your whereabouts or even your mission. I just thought I'd let you know what's going on."

"Thank you, prelate," Surist said, "I will inform Karak at once."

After Karak had been updated he made the situation known to the rest of the crew. They agreed that they had to keep searching for the Orb even if they were in the line of fire.

"We have searched the grassland area and have not found the Orb," Karak reported to Surist. "We are now concentrating our efforts on the wooded area. Karak out."

A few minutes later, the sensors picked up a small scout ship approaching the *Malus Tempus*. It was of nearly the same design as the one Luric's aide had used to bring the synthesized Orb to them on Jisk, except this was a two-man craft instead of a single person shuttle. Surist decided to open a channel to the ship. He wondered if it had been damaged and needed some kind of help, but no damage registered on sensors.

"This is Surist of the *Malus Tempus*," he said. "Please respond."

Then a response came that would shake Surist's soul. "Hello, my brother."

Surist waited for the face to appear on the monitor. "My brother died long ago."

The face then said, "I am Nurisk, son of Hurid."

"I don't believe you," Surist said with calm certainty.

"Is a good thing so difficult to accept?"

"Yes." Surist folded his arms across his chest and raised his chin slightly as he offered a challenge. "If you are my brother, then prove it."

"Our father died on Crux I while on an exploration mission. I was found, but not amongst the wreckage. The crash caused head injuries that resulted in an amnesia that has left me without memory of my life before the crash. But then I found something I never expected. I compared the Cruxfix blood sample database with my own sample and found that I am the son of one of the people killed in the crash and a brother to one who was treated afterward. I was found away from the crash site and was taken to a different medical facility. They had no reason to look for anyone I may have been involved with, and I could tell them nothing. They took me in and cared for me.

"Later, Levu Earsp came and took me to the Braline System, where I was reeducated and have since joined Stone Globe. He and the Braline gave me a home. Levu sent me to spy on you and your fellow Orb Seekers. I finished my studies into my past while I passed through the Cruxfix System recently. It took a long time to put all the pieces together, but I've finally been able to find out who I am. Even Gronil's people hadn't put it all together."

"The story sounds believable enough, despite the fact that it is unbelievable," Surist said, trying to keep Nurisk talking, "but why should I believe it?"

"You should believe it because I can prove it to you," Nurisk said. "Even the Sekurai believe in our cause. They are helping us. We must face the fact that one of the two civilizations at risk will likely die, and we should help the one with the best chance of survival. We also can't allow only one of us to survive; brothers should live. We should be on the same side. If we continue on opposite sides, we will eventually have to battle each other again, and brother should not fight brother." Nurisk shook his head as he spoke. "Neither of us could kill the other, but we would have to do so in order to ensure the survival of the culture we represent. Since one of us could not harm the other, we would be at a deadlock and both civilizations would wind up with only a few Orbs. They would both die; *we* would both die." Nurisk paused. "You lost me once, will you lose me again?"

"Your argument is convincing," Surist said, "but it's flawed. Both of our sides have an equal chance at victory. Why don't you join me and help your ancestral people?"

"I'm helping those who've given back quality to my life," Nurisk said quickly and with much conviction. "Without the Braline, I would not be the person I am today. The Braline have a strong sense of honor and duty. On my way here from the Sekurai System, I sent a message to the Cruxfix libraries asking for some information they were more than happy to provide. The Rongi culture seems a nice one with good-hearted people, but the Braline possess a much stronger cohesion at every level of society. We work together better and help each other more. We still have our own personal goals, but we're not as provincial as you. We are the better culture; we are purer, and we are more how I believe people are supposed to be. Besides, we have the upper hand now. The odds are that our two ships will do battle again, and our ship has been upgraded and now has Sekurai technology. We're stronger than you."

Surist began to bend, but did not break. "Even if I converted to your side," he nodded, "I could not betray my people and give you all of our Orbs. It would be out of the question!"

"Then perhaps you could just give us one whole Orb and leave the rest for your companions," Nurisk suggested, opening his hand to Surist. "As soon as there's a second whole Orb, bring it here. There would be two whole Orbs and each group could have a chance. That way you would not harm your fellow countrymen and we would be together again. Doesn't that sound like a fair compromise?

"Surist," Nurisk continued, pleading with his brother, "we must be together. I can't remember it, but I know from the records that our family always explored together. We belong together. The Rongi people don't have that underlying togetherness for all the people in general, but they do have it for family. Come and be family with me once more. The Braline honor family, but they also respect what must be done for the good of their people as a whole. What greater cause could there be?"

Surist paused for several minutes. Nurisk had struck several chords with him. His argument had been similar to what Surist would have expected in a debate between brothers around the supper table. Also, Nurisk had pointed out that the Rongi were provincial and a bit selfish. This was true and it annoyed Surist, just as it did Karak. Despite this, Nurisk had also played that same small-minded card against Surist. He had asked Surist to be equally provincial in leaving his own people and joining him. If Surist left the Orb Seekers, he would be breaking his oath to Karak, Praetor Jarob, and all the Rongi people. He would be leaving a greater goal in favor of family. This was no different than what a full one-third of the members of Rongi Council had done. Smee Glars, Vladdy, and Craden had chosen to stay behind, not only because they didn't believe in the Orb mission, but also because they wanted to help evacuate those closest to them instead of trying to help all Rongi people.

"It does sound fair until it involves stealing an Orb from them," Surist said finally. "It's true that our family has always been loyal to each other before anything else. Perhaps that's part of the opportunistic

Rongi side of me coming out. That familial loyalty is the one thing I've missed most in the last thirteen years."

After a long pause in the conversation, a lot of hoping on Nurisk's part, and much consternation, Surist finally decided. "No, I can't go. Our people depend on this mission. Family is the most important thing to me, but I—we still have family back home. I can't betray them. It would almost certainly be a death sentence for them if the Orb Seekers lose this race."

"Very well, brother," Nurisk said. "I'm disappointed, but we will meet again. When our ships meet in battle perhaps you'll see what I mean when I say we are the stronger. There will always be an open seat here for you."

About an hour later, Surist was informed that a fragment from the Purple Orb had been found lodged in the crotch of a very old tree, and the rest of the Orb Seekers were coming back to the ship. They had to use their blasters to cut the piece free. As soon as the others arrived back on board the ship with the piece of the Purple Orb, Surist suggested that he would forge the Purple Orb while the rest of the crew decided which way to go next to avoid the battle.

"I got a message from Stone Globe," Surist told Karak when the team was back on board. They said they've enlisted the help of the Sekurai. I don't know how, but they said the Sekurai augmented their ship; apparently it's been upgraded. We may not want to see them in battle."

"Why would they tell us this?" Karak tried to guess his opponent's next move.

"Maybe they're trying to get us guessing wrong, keep us off balance," Surist said. "It could be misinformation."

Karak's eyes met Surist's. "I'd better get up to the bridge. You go re-forge this new Orb."

Once Surist was left alone, he forged the Purple Orb by simply touching the purple fragment to the Green Orb. As the whole Orb and the purple fragment touched, the rest of the Purple Orb appeared around the piece he was holding. The pieces just simply appeared where they belonged in the Orb, and it was forged. This was a spectacular sight. Pieces just appeared from out of nowhere, and they did so in perfect placement. The Purple Orb became complete and solid, as though it had never been broken, and all right in front of Surist's eyes.

Surist did a lot of thinking for a while now, and also some talking to himself aloud. "This situation just cannot be. How am I to choose? Talk about being torn!" He rolled his eyes at the situation. He continued on with his work, distracted by events about which he would tell no one. Nurisk had returned, from the dead, for all Surist knew, and Surist was thinking about his offer.

⅀ ⅀ ⅀

Chapter 12

LET THE BATTLE COMMENCE

Hiram, Notolla, and the duke were in the mess area of the *Malus Tempus* having a snack and considering the Orb Seekers' next move.

"The duke and I believe we should go after the Yellow Orb next," Hiram said.

"The Yellow Orb is the one in Braline space, isn't it?" Hiram looked up at the duke.

"Yes, it is," the duke said.

"Why would we want to venture into enemy territory?" Hiram asked. "I thought we were trying to avoid the battle as much as possible."

"We will avoid the battle by going after the Yellow Orb," the duke responded as he sat down and disapprovingly eyed his food. "The battle isn't in the Braline System. It's in sector D:4, just outside the Swisura System." He clanked his fork down and pushed his plate away with a sigh.

Karak slipped into the room unnoticed. He and the duke had just locked the Green Orb safely in the duke's quarters. The Purple Orb was in Surist's room. Karak thought it best to have their Orbs in different places. If one broke for some reason, the other wouldn't be there to be broken at the same time.

"The Orb is on an asteroid called Enarf, which is now in the Kriline Defense Barrier," Notolla began, holding up a map on her flight plan computer pad. "Enarf is on the outer edge of the Barrier, so there won't be a major concern about being in Braline space. It should only take a few hours to gather the Orb and leave the area. We can avoid detection by drifting up on the asteroid, thus avoiding their sensor arrays and mines, which will read engine output as their main form of detection. By the time any Braline ships were sent to intercept us, we could be long gone."

"How do *you* know how Braline technology works?" Karak asked gruffly.

Everyone stared at Karak.

"I'm sorry," he said softly.

"Field Marshal Notolla and I have been going over the tactical analysis of our encounter with them," the duke answered. "Though their ships have other methods of detection, their course corrections in our brief interaction occurred at almost exactly the same interval of time after our course changes. They monitor movement and react accordingly."

"They're used to fending off Sekurai attacks on their space," Notolla chimed in. "It's a legitimate way of programming one's sensors if you've taken up a defensive posture."

"I think we would be wise to be away from here when the big dogs start growling," Karak said as he got up and headed for the bridge. "Make for the Braline System."

They met on the bridge about an hour later.

"I think going after the Yellow Orb is a good idea. Judging by the size and power of the forces in the battle," the duke said, "it will be a long, hard-fought battle, and we should be well on our way to our next destination by the time it begins."

"It's a good plan," Karak said. "If we can find the Yellow Orb, our task would then take us much closer to home to find the other Orbs. At that point, we would be fighting alongside our own navy, and that could tip the balance of any battle which might take place near home. With any luck, Stone Globe will go after the Yellow Orb and find it missing while we go closer to home. We should also count on Stone Globe having a fragment of the Orange Orb."

"If it did play out like that," Notolla added, holding up her right index finger, "with the enemy clear across the galaxy looking for the Yellow Orb, when they don't know we've already found it, and us near home with the Orbs, we would have almost entirely put ourselves beyond the possibility of defeat."

"We'll still have to battle Stone Globe," Hiram said. "They need the Orbs, just like we do."

"They will be coming." Karak said forebodingly as he moved only his eyes to look up from his computer pad. "With the power of the Swisura navy we could destroy them," Karak said in an uncharacteristically callous and careless way. "The *Quia Vita* is powerful now that they have Sekurai enhancements, but it can be destroyed. We would have to chase after them anyway because they'll have some Orbs we need."

"You would be willing to take the war to our own doorstep?" Lithinia eyed Karak.

Karak tilted his head toward Lithinia. "We're going to have to find all of the Orbs soon. So a battle will come, whether we want it or not. It will not be only the Swisura and Sekurai who fight this war; we will become much more involved than we already are." Karak's eyes widened. "And we're already in over our heads."

"Common sense also dictates that Stone Globe will not expect us to venture so close to their territory, and thus, we should be there," the duke surmised. "We should be where we are not expected. Also, due to the fact that they've not been within communications range of their home since they first met us, the Braline navy won't know to consider us enemies."

"That's true," Notolla concurred. "Stone Globe will not expect us to take a course leading so far from home."

"That's the course we'll take," Karak said. "Hiram, plot a course that will take us to Enarf, but will leave us out of sensor range of any ships taking part in the battle. It will be starting soon."

"I'll get right on it," Hiram responded as he operated the helm controls. "We should be ready to leave shortly. It should take about ten days to get there. It's not a short distance."

After a few days of travel, the Orb Seekers passed by sector D:4. They were just past the staging grounds, but Hiram kept the ship out of sensor range. So far, there had been only minor skirmishes; few of the forces that would fight here were arrayed and deployed for battle. There were no warships detected in the sector, but there were some close, he was sure.

The *Malus Tempus* proceeded on uneventfully for a few days and was coming closer to the edge of the Onuy Nebulae. A ship rocketed into their sensor range at astonishing speed.

"Karak!" Lithinia shouted. "There's a ship coming into range. It's moving at an unbelievable rate of speed."

"What is it?" Karak asked.

The duke looked out the viewing window "It's the *Quia Vita*! She's had her engines enhanced—and I wonder what else."

"They've modified more than the engines," Notolla said. "They're targeting us with all their weapons. They must have upgraded their entire ship like Surist said. It wouldn't surprise me if the effectiveness of their weapons was increased too. Last time they matched us shot for shot."

A grave look came over Karak's face. "Run," he said softly.

"I'm redirecting all power to the engines," Hiram said. "They're being pushed to the limit."

"The *Quia Vita* has opened a communications channel to us," Lithinia said.

"Let's hear it." Karak shifted in his seat.

"This is Levu Earsp commanding the newly renovated *Quia Vita*. You will give us the Green and Purple Orbs or we will take them from you. Give them to us and we won't fire on you."

After a moment, Karak said, "Give us a few minutes to—"

"No!" Levu yelled. "That's the oldest trick there is. I will have the Orbs now, or I will take them from you *now*. We already have Orange Orb fragments. That one is already ours, as all the Orbs soon will be."

Karak whispered into Hiram's ear, "Maximum acceleration, maximum speed, anywhere."

"They're pushing the limit with their engines, Levu," Kolij said.

"Keep pace with them!" Levu howled. "They can't run from us. Fire the forward guns!"

The deep blue laser shot went at the *Malus Tempus*, shaking the ship and jolting the crew.

"There's no way we can counter something like that," Notolla said to Karak. "Our shields are down to seventy-six percent."

"Return fire!" Karak yelled. "Give them everything you have!"

Marshal Notolla operated her console furiously and fired three full spreads of torpedoes and a continuous burst of maximum powered lasers at the *Quia Vita*.

"They suffered direct hits," Notolla said confidently, and then her smile turned into disbelief, "and their shields are down to ninety-seven percent."

"How can everything we have only lower their shields by three percent?" Karak asked.

"They're gaining on us and firing again." The duke braced for another jolt.

The *Malus Tempus* was again battered by only one shot from the *Quia Vita*. Sparks flew everywhere on the bridge. The entire ship shook furiously from the force of the blast. The explosive slicing effect of the forward guns blew out an entire section of the *Malus Tempus's* hull.

"A huge gash was made in the ship's hull. Internal airlock doors between sections have been dropped around the blown out portions in order to prevent the rest of the ship from losing compression," Lithinia reported. This effect could have been passed off as a surgical strike of sorts, except that there was an almost careless kind of vengeance in Levu's voice as he had spoken with Karak over the communications channel, and the *Quia Vita's* movements were unbridled and aggressive, like a man gone wild with rage.

"Our shields are down to fifty-three percent now. We've lost some secondary systems," Lithinia reported. "Dorsal shields are buckling. Sensors are operating at reduced efficiency. Our aft weapons are useless; their control matrix is—non-existent."

"Non-existent?" Karak turned toward Lithinia.

"It was in the section that was blown off the hull."

"We're approaching the Onuy Nebulae," Hiram said. "The radiation is beginning to affect our—"

"Take us in," Karak said. "This is what we need. Even if their range is that far enhanced, which I doubt, they won't be able to see us on sensors without coming inside after us."

"How is radiation going to help us?" Lithinia asked. "I know their ship runs on indimite too, which is neutralized by this kind of radiation, but that doesn't help us."

"Sure it does," Karak said. "You see, they can't come in here without their shields and weapons going down, and we're out of range in here. How long can we hold out in here?"

"We could stay here for about sixteen hours before other ship's systems begin to suffer," the duke said.

"They've halted their pursuit," Lithinia said, monitoring her screen. "They're just sitting there waiting for us now."

"You'd better believe it," Karak said. "They have no choice. Their shields are a projected plasma form of indimite, just like our own, which is, as Lithinia so wonderfully pointed out, neutralized by this kind of radiation. Their shields would be down in seconds and weapons wouldn't function either. Neither of us could attack the other. We have sixteen hours to come up with something."

Surist spoke almost to himself. "So, we're just going to sit here, trapped." He looked around thoughtfully for a moment. "I'm going to go check something." He stood and turned to leave the bridge. He quietly and quickly collected the Purple Orb and made his way down the corridor to the shuttle bay. Surist could not have gotten into the duke's quarters to steal the Green Orb, and he wasn't sure if he wanted to. He never even looked back before he piloted a shuttle toward the *Quia Vita.*

"Surist to Nurisk. Do you read me?"

"Yes, brother. Have you reconsidered my offer?"

"I have. I'm coming over," Surist said without a second thought, "and I'm bringing an Orb."

"What did you say to your comrades?"

"I recorded a video last night. I couldn't sleep."

"At least it's not just the result of this little skirmish that's convinced you," Levu broke in.

"It didn't hurt," Surist said. Surist's sarcasm showed that he was still of sound mind.

"I knew you could not deny your own blood," Nurisk said.

After having docked the shuttle, Surist sat on the bridge of the *Quia Vita* at one of its science stations. A lot was going through his mind. He was ready to fight for the Braline, but participating in the killing of his former friends was hard for him to swallow.

"How do you feel about fighting your old mates?" Nurisk turned, eying his brother.

"It is a hard thing, but my mind is made up. I'm here, aren't I?" He had underestimated how this would tear at his heart and just how hard it would be to destroy his former friends.

Surist would be affected in ways other than those that would affect his comrades. None of them had become a traitor. This, piled on top of him, and then on top of the already dire circumstances, would weigh on him significantly, but he never seriously questioned his decision to betray Karak and join his brother. Being reunited with Nurisk was the most important thing.

"Let's get that Orange Orb re-forged," Levu said and then paused and looked around his bridge. "We've never done this before."

"All we do is touch a fragment to a whole one," Surist said as he raised the Purple Orb.

Nurisk had kept a piece of the Orange Orb in his pocket. He touched it to the Purple Orb. The entire Orange Orb instantly appeared around the fragment. The two Orbs were held next to each other, perfectly the same size, just as if they'd been there the whole time. Pieces did not fly through the air; they simply materialized, seemingly out of nowhere.

In reality, the pieces disappeared from where they'd been. The fragment was touched to a whole Orb and the pieces simply reappeared at the point of contact.

The wall in the underground cave on Qu'uack had several pieces taken out of it as a result of this and it began to deteriorate further. Dust was expelled from the wall a few times. Rocks began to shift under the weight. Cracks formed in the wall itself. Then finally the wall buckled under the pressure, collapsed, and brought the whole ceiling down with it. The building above the cave also fell in and the rubble filled the ancient cavern. No one on Qu'uack knew what had happened or why, only that the building had fallen in and been completely destroyed. Even the rubble became dust.

After about an hour, Levu realized he had to go back to the battle to ensure victory there. "We have good tactical positioning to attack the Swisura flank," he observed. "And I wish to hang some Swisura hides on our bulkheads." The gravity of the situation in which he found himself had driven him to have a thirst for blood, a thirst nearly as great as his desire to save his people. Though he knew the enormity of this task would be beyond anything he'd ever faced, he thought his past had prepared him to do the hard things this mission was likely to require. He was the best person the Braline could have chosen to lead this mission, but that did not make him immune to the effects of the stresses and hard decisions he'd already had to make, let alone those that were still to come.

"Kolij," Levu said, "plot a course back to the battle. Last time we were outsmarted; this time we have the upper hand. We've trapped Karak on this side of the galaxy. He won't stand a chance cutting through either the battle or Sekurai space to get back home. They're stuck here with no way out and no reinforcements. We'll be back for them."

"We're going to have to take their Orbs from them sometime," Regti said. "We could wait here and go back to the battle in a little while. The *Malus Tempus* won't hold out in that radiation for even a day."

"No, in a day, the battle could be over if things go decidedly one way," Levu said, "and it may not go quite the way we want it to."

"The course back to the battle is laid in, Levu," Kolij said.

"Send a message to Rorn," Levu ordered. "Tell him to have a small wing of cruisers and explorer ships with fighter escorts standing by on this side of the battle. We'll take charge of the group and try to turn the Swisura right flank."

"The Sekurai won't take orders from us." Regti turned to face Levu.

Levu turned to look at Regti with a serious expression. "They will if they want to win. Just remember, they hate the Swisura even more than they hate us. Tell Rorn we have a chance to turn the enemy's flank."

"What motivates you to leave here and go to the big battle?" Humwe asked.

"I don't know. Perhaps those Orbs are having an affect already," Levu said, not really even believing it himself.

Surist held out an upturned hand toward Levu. "Well, the Orange Orb is supposed to inspire clearer creative solutions. I wonder if it's made a connection with you."

Levu just sat in his captain's chair and stared thoughtfully at the Orange Orb Nurisk held. "I'm uneasy about those Orbs being in my head." Levu had a wary look on his face, but it was possible that the Orange Orb had just inspired a decision that would wind up saving himself, his crew, and his ship.

"The *Quia Vita* is turning around and heading back for sector D:4," Hiram reported.

"Good. Apparently they don't have the stomach for a fight," Karak said, knowing the opposite was true as he sat in his bent, battle-scarred, and now cockeyed captain's chair. "Go on; run away. We can't miss you if you're not gone." He added a dismissive wave as the *Quia Vita* left from view.

Once the *Quia Vita* was well out of sensor range, Hiram guided the *Malus Tempus* through the back side of the Onuy Nebulae to avoid a last-minute detection by Stone Globe. They proceeded to Enarf to find the Yellow Orb.

"We have a clear shot to the Yellow Orb," Karak said. "Now we have to hope the Swisura can at least open up a hole for us to get past the battle on our way home. We'll either have to pass through the battle or through Sekurai space. I doubt Sekurai space is simply abandoned either. They would leave a defense force to look after the system in case anyone should try to take advantage of their involvement in the war right now."

Lithinia added, "The opening of a hole in the battle is a pretty long shot considering that the battle includes irresistible force meets immovable object."

"I've fought battles like that before," Notolla said. "Something has to give."

"How long till we reach Enarf?" Notolla asked.

"Several days," Hiram said. "The battle will probably last about that long."

"Where's Surist?" Karak turned to look all around the bridge. "He said he was going to check on something. I thought he'd be back by now."

None of the Orb Seekers had an answer. They took time to begin searching the ship.

The two giant forces had finally gathered themselves in sectors D:4 and D:5 and were ready for battle. Each fleet consisted of great warships which contained many small fighters inside. Also gathered by the opposing navies were cruiser class vessels, escort ships, and cargo ships. It had taken a couple of days for all of the ships to gather themselves into position. The thought of a preemptive strike had been prevalent in the minds of Rorn and Narvok, the Swisura general. Nevertheless, both decided that there was no hole left open in the enemy's defenses and such an attempt would be useless.

Now was the silence before the battle. These two battle tested warriors had faced off several times before, albeit in skirmishes, and knew each other well. Neither held an advantage based on their previous encounters, but now they were each fighting for more. The Sekurai were fighting for potentially unlimited power and dominance in the galaxy, and the Swisura were fighting for the survival of the Rongi civilization as well as their own.

The Swisura ships were white in color and simple in design. They were nearly all the same basic shape, just different sizes. Much like the scout ship the Sekurai had captured and given to Levu, the Swisura ships were shaped like an elongated egg. Warships were longest with cargo ships to follow. Escorts and cruisers were of the same basic shape except they were a bit wider and thicker proportionally, and significantly shorter. They seemed to have no discernable parts on the exterior of their hulls. This was intentional in their design so as not to give an enemy any specific targets to pick off of any of their ships. Swisura guns were mounted flush with the ship's hull. The Sekurai ships, on the other hand, featured prominent gun ports, torpedo launchers, communications arrays, and shield generators all on the exterior hull of their ships. Because of this, they seemed less smooth and more rigid and hard looking, an effect that was desired because the very look of a Sekurai warship often conjured stories of other conquests and struck fear in the hearts of their enemies, thus taking away their will to fight even before the battle began. This effect was not, however, in lieu of fighting any battles; the Sekurai were formidable foes and were not to be trifled with. Their forces were indeed strong, and they'd proven it many times against worthy adversaries. Narvok was the first to make a move.

"Well, it wouldn't be a battle if we didn't try to resolve the issue with talk," Narvok said without the slightest hint of sincerity. "Open a channel to Rorn."

"Channel open," Scit, the Swisura communications officer, said.

"Send the following message," Narvok ordered. "'We are protecting the Orb Seekers. They are on a mission to save their civilization, and you are threatening that quest. You have no right to interfere with their task. Stand down now, and we will not have to fight this war.'"

"I don't plan on making a war out of this," Rorn replied with a condescending attitude. "In fact, I'm planning on winning so swiftly and easily that this will be only a scuffle. We're not concerned with these Orb Seekers; we're concerned only with accomplishing our own goals. I don't care if you're protecting them or not. If you stand in our way, this battle will rage. It's not too early in the day for the killing of rivals—or irritants. Be on your guard!"

After having made his intentions clear, Rorn decided to unleash his aggressive side and send in his forces. "Now, we fight!" Rorn yelled. "Send in the first wave of fighters. Have the escort ships fall in behind them and target their warships. We will blow them out of the stars and their skies will rain with blood!"

With the Sekurai fighters and escorts advancing, Narvok initiated his own battle plan. "Stand by to detonate quadrants one and two in minefield four. That should slow their advance."

"Should we begin advancing near minefield one, sir?" Narvok's tactical advisor asked.

"Not yet. We'll use the mines defensively. We should not advance until we see an opportunity. The plan is for the mines to do a lot of the work for us."

"The first wave of Sekurai forces is coming into minefield four," the officer said.

"Open another channel to Rorn."

"It's open," Scit said.

"Rorn," Narvok said with his nose pinched to change his voice, "back your ships off. I can smell you all the way over here."

Rorn just growled.

"Detonate the mines!" Narvok ordered.

On the tactical display screen, Narvok watched as the specified mines attached themselves to enemy ships magnetically and exploded. The result was great carnage as the pieces of several Sekurai fighters floated aimlessly in the blackness of space. Other ships were scarred so badly they were disabled and stationary without power. The escorts continued their push despite having taken some damage and only having a few fighters left to protect them now.

"Damn!" Rorn yelled. "Those Swisura mines are going to have to be dealt with before we can do anything offensively. Send an empty cargo ship into each of the minefields. If Narvok lets them through, we will remotely set a collision course to the nearest warship. If they detonate their mines, then we won't have to worry about them anymore."

"Sir," Tirsch, Rorn's communications officer, reported. "Levu Earsp has sent a message asking for a small wing of fighters, cruisers, and explorers to be waiting off the Swisura right flank. He says he's on his way and hopes to outflank the enemy."

"Do it. Any chance of gaining an advantage should be taken," Rorn ordered. "Knowing Narvok, he'll probably find some way to extend this battle and give his fleet every chance to gain a victory. I hate him, but I respect him."

Narvok noticed the cargo ships proceeding to the middle of each minefield and decided to do neither of the things which he was expected to do. "Send in the fighter wings that are lined along the minefields," he ordered. "Destroy those cargo ships!"

"It will take time to destroy those cargo ships, sir," Major Jehn, his tactical officer, said. "Their shields are strong and Sekurai cargo ships have a large number of effective turrets."

"Yes, but it will take longer for Rorn to send reinforcements," Narvok replied.

The Swisura fighters flew in at maximum speed and fired all weapons at the cargo ships. The unmanned cargo ships were operated remotely by the Sekurai battle cruisers. These freighters were not as well armed as warships because they generally traveled with escorts, but they did manage to destroy a few Swisura fighters. The fighters, though, overwhelmed, outnumbered, and outgunned the slow bulky vessels. The cargo ships exploded one after another, and the fighters returned to their posts after their task was accomplished.

Rorn was once again furious. "I can see that Narvok has not lost his touch in quick strategic thinking or his taste for victory. We will have to stop wasting time and bring out the big guns. Send in the siege ships."

Upon receiving this order, several large ships came from just beyond Swisura sensor range and settled themselves behind the Sekurai lines. These ships had only two discernable parts: a power cell and a turret. Each ship's rear section was an irregular hexagonal cylinder with longer sides on the top and bottom. This back portion was where the power was generated for the gun. The gun was a large conical shaped piece at the front of the ships. They were ships built for the destruction of enemy warships and other large vessels. They fired an enormous, concentrated projectile of energy at a target and utterly destroyed it with only a few shots.

"Order them to target the nearest warships and fire when ready," Rorn said.

"Fleet command to siege craft, identify the closest warship and attack," Tirsch relayed.

The sight of these huge and menacing siege ships brought fear into the hearts of the Swisura fighter pilots. The Swisura did not yet know what these ships were capable of or what their intent was, but they were sure it wasn't going to be good. Because the Sekurai and Swisura had never escalated their distaste for each other into open war, these siege ships were not known to the Swisura. Although Narvok was worried, he was able to control his fear and continued to lead his troops in battle.

"Attention all fighters, be prepared for anything," Narvok alerted. "We don't know anything about these new ships yet."

At that moment the siege ships had charged enough power to fire, and fire they did. The Sekurai ships fired a shot that lit up every window and view screen of the entire Swisura fleet. The bright purple balls of energy were hurled towards a warship near the front of the Swisura line. One blast hit the lead ship and it was racked by the force of the shot. It shook violently, and the crew was thrown to the deck. Power momentarily fluctuated and sparks flew all throughout the ship.

When the blast was over, the captain asked for a damage report.

"Our shields are down to thirty-nine percent," the first officer responded. "We still have weapons, partial power to engines, and sensors, but our shield generator is out. The thirty-nine percent is all we're going to get. We can't take another volley half that size."

"Relay that information to General Narvok. The least we can do is provide information before we die."

"Those ships aren't firing anymore, though," the officer reported. "Perhaps they are a one-time thing."

"I doubt it. We don't get that lucky," the captain said. "Any ship that fires that kind of blast is going to take a few minutes to recharge."

"General Narvok," Scit reported, "that ship can't take another hit."

"Tell them to come around to the back of the line," Narvok ordered. "If Rorn thinks he's the only one with surprises, he's in for a dandy. Send the dreadnoughts in underneath those siege ships. Tell them to destroy every one of them, whatever the cost."

Narvok watched as his dreadnoughts, previously hidden by their stealth shielding, approached the siege ships from below. This stealth shielding was a combination of an energy shield, which redirected sensor beams off into space while sending no signal back to the scanning ship, and the fact that the dreadnoughts had no structural angles facing directly toward the angle from which a sensor beam could approach. All surfaces of the outer hull on a dreadnought were curved; there were no straight lines at all, and at no point along any curve was a sensor echo going to be sent back to the scanning ship. All scanning beams were deflected in some other direction.

The captains and crews of these dreadnoughts knew the gravity of the situation was heavy because the command ships could not counter the kind of firepower the Sekurai siege ships possessed. The dreadnoughts came in firing at full power and setting space ablaze with their bright green laser shots. They targeted the siege ships relentlessly, ignoring any fighters they'd been targeted by. Each siege ship took a lot of hits and boasted strong shields, and despite the assault that had been launched upon them, they continued to fire at Swisura warships. The dreadnoughts had come too close to the siege ships to be fired upon by them. Any destruction of those dreadnoughts by the impressive blasts from the siege ships would result in the destruction of the Sekurai artillery also. The dreadnoughts had settled themselves just below the siege ships.

The siege ships aimed at freshly targeted Swisura warships, since some of the first ones had moved out of range, but eventually many Swisura warships would at least have their shields damaged significantly and would be at a disadvantage for the rest of the fight. The shot from the siege ships was again unbelievably strong and it blasted one new target's shields down to twenty-eight percent.

Narvok knew his dreadnoughts' shields could withstand a lot of fire, but he couldn't fight a battle with only them. He had to preserve some of his warships. "Up to now, only our warships have been targeted," he said. "Move them off of our right flank out of range of those siege ships. Expand our left flank in a telescoping maneuver all the way to the Consraka Nebula Cluster. I don't want the Sekurai trying to slip in and turn our left flank. Now Rorn's secret weapon will be destroyed from behind his own lines, and they won't even have a target with which to get revenge. I just hope those dreadnoughts can hold out a while."

"We have a new problem, sir," Major Jehn reported. "The Sekurai warships have spiked their energy output. It appears they're creating a shield shell around their entire fleet. Our dreadnoughts are now hitting the shell instead of the siege ships, and they are still taking fire from enemy fighters."

"Tell them to concentrate on the fighters then," Narvok said. "At least we can lessen the Sekurai gnats and go after the big dogs later. What kind of condition are the dreadnoughts in? Are they taking as much fire as we projected?"

"The one in the worst condition has had its shields taken down to eighty-nine percent, and they're still too close to the siege ships to be fired on by them."

"Good," Narvok said. "How far does that shield protrude?"

"Its forward extent is just in front of our few remaining mines, not in range of their effect," Major Jehn reported.

"Well," Narvok sighed, "we can't get any other ships within range of the shield without also coming in range of the siege ships. Now we wait for the dreadnoughts to tear down that shell."

"We could move wings of our fleet around the minefield," Jehn suggested with a shrug.

"That would take too long," Narvok replied, shaking his head. "I sent the Dreadnoughts around at the beginning of the battle, and they're only just now getting there. Besides, that would open up a better chance for the Sekurai to attack our homes. There would be significantly less between them and our system."

The battle tore on for some time in this manner. The dreadnoughts impressed Narvok by engaging a large portion of the small, maneuverable Sekurai fighters and slowly tearing down the shield shell whenever time permitted.

Rorn was pleased with the effectiveness of the shield his ships had generated. Both sides were waiting patiently for the next phase of the battle. They were strong, fierce, and intelligent. Both sides had thus far deadlocked one of the biggest battles since the Sekurai/Nilg war.

The Sekurai could not cross the minefield, and the Swisura dared not get in range of the siege ships they still did not fully understand. They were deadlocked.

However, Levu was about to emerge and unveil his plan in the hopes of crushing the Swisura. He hoped his attack on the right flank of the Swisura navy would end the war almost before it started.

"How long till we're in range?" Levu asked impatiently.

"About five minutes," Prak responded.

"We can't wait that long," Levu said. "We've been traveling for a day, and we have no way of knowing how the fight is going."

"I can't push the engines any harder," Kolij warned.

"I don't care! Do it anyway!" Levu yelled in a whine that demonstrated a lack of self control that was unusual for him. "This ship's tough now."

After a few minutes, the *Quia Vita* entered sector D:4 and found the ships Rorn had sent. The small taskforce of Sekurai ships were just out of Swisura sensor range waiting for Stone Globe to arrive.

"Where are the fighters I requested?" Levu asked, annoyed. "All we have are cruisers, explorer ships and escorts. I wanted some fighters too. Ask them where the fighters are!"

"They say the fighters could not be spared," Surist answered. "They lost several at the beginning of the battle."

"Contact the group and tell them we're attacking the Swisura right flank now." Levu pointed sharply at Surist.

"They report ready," Surist said.

The *Quia Vita*, along with two other cruisers, three explorers, and three escort ships advanced on the right flank of the Swisura. Soon, though, they realized they'd made a big mistake. The group smashed into the right side of the Swisura fleet only to find that many of the warships had been diverted to that side.

"How did they know?" Levu yelled with a whine and displaying the same expression a child shows when denied something. "We can't take on every Swisura warship in their navy! How could they have known?"

The *Quia Vita* and the small group of eight ships that accompanied them were in the middle of the Swisura warships before they knew it. They tried fruitlessly for quite some time to gain any advantage and destroy a few warships. They were able to lower the shields a bit more and destroy a few escort ships, but not nearly enough to turn the Swisura flank. Most of the warships had been hit by the Sekurai siege ships, so they had taken significant damage to their shields, but Levu and his escorts were unable to break the enemy's lines with such a small force.

"General Narvok," Major Jehn said, "a few Sekurai ships of various classes and one Braline ship have begun attacking our warships."

"How did they get around there?" Narvok walked over to take a look at Jehn's console.

"They must have taken the long route beyond our sensors, sir," Jehn suggested, "but they are neither powerful nor numerous enough to destroy our warships."

"They didn't expect us to have those ships there, did they?" Narvok wondered aloud. "Why would they? If Rorn's siege ships hadn't forced our warships to that region of the battlefield, those ships could punch a small hole in our defenses, perhaps enough for Rorn to take advantage of. It turns out to be a wonderful stroke of luck for us. We'll eliminate those ships easily. Have the warships form a sphere to surround them and destroy them. This will have been another small defeat for Rorn in this battle."

"This is impossible!" Levu shouted with a grimace as the *Quia Vita* took yet another hit from a Swisura warship. "Humwe, tell the other ships to get back behind the Sekurai lines if they can. We can't do what we wanted to do here, so let's just go ahead and target the White Orb next. Kolij, plot a course out of the battle. Full power to the engines! Divert as much power as possible to the shields, Regti! We're ramming right through their lines."

"Perhaps if we found a moon whose gravitational pole we could hide above and thus deceive the Swisura sensors, we could perform repairs before we proceed," Nurisk suggested.

"Kolij, do it," Levu ordered.

"Course laid in," Kolij reported. "Engines at maximum."

"We were outsmarted by Karak," Levu said. "Then we trapped him half a galaxy from home, and now we've been driven out of the battle. We have to do better. However, we have two Orbs and we're about to take this battle right into the heart of the enemy. Send a message to General Rorn. Inform him of our situation and tell him we're going to make repairs and then move to Rongi space."

After a moment, Humwe said, "Rorn has responded saying he will order the Sekurai navy to Rongi space in order to protect us should we run into their forces."

"Good," Levu said. "I was hoping he would do that. We'll need protection when we land on Vock I and try to take the White Orb."

"We can be sure the Swisura will follow the Sekurai," Regti said. "There will probably be a colossal battle there as well."

"Take the fleet to the Rongi System," Rorn ordered, angry that he was retreating, but pleased the battle was only moving. "We must protect Stone Globe when they get there to search for Orbs."

"Which path into Rongi space should we take?" Tirsch asked.

"Take us through the Strissen Corridor," Rorn answered, his red face squinted at a map at the helm station. "We'll try to keep the Swisura from protecting the Rongi from the *Quia Vita* by drawing them to the side of Rongi space opposite where Levu will be."

"The *Quia Vita* will be no match for the entire Rongi navy," Tirsch observed.

"No," Rorn said, "but the Rongi are concentrating on evacuation right now, and they won't know what the *Quia Vita* will be there for."

The Sekurai fighters were the first to leave. Next the cargo and escort ships moved out. Only when all others had moved out of sensor range did the warships head towards Rongi space.

"Where are they all going?" Narvok asked as he watched the Sekurai fleet disperse. "Neither side has accomplished anything yet. Why would they be leaving the battle?"

"Their course would suggest they're heading for Rongi space via the Strissen Corridor, General," the Swisura tactical officer said. "The *Quia Vita*, that Braline ship, moved off behind our lines. We've lost them now, but their last known course was taking them toward Rongi space."

"They must be going into the Rongi System to get an Orb," Narvok said under his breath. "We'll have to make an attempt to stop the Sekurai navy there. Order the fleet to intercept the them as soon as possible. If we don't, they'll rip the Rongi people to shreds."

"So, who won the battle?" Major Jehn asked.

"Yes," Narvok responded, knowing he wasn't answering the question. "Both sides accomplished tasks. We allowed the Orb Seekers to get away, but couldn't keep the Sekurai navy from assisting Stone Globe. And the Sekurai have occupied us and allowed Stone Globe to continue their mission."

"So the Sekurai accomplished all of their goals and we didn't," the major observed, looking a little defeated.

It was now Narvok's turn to growl as he glared at his officer. "We are conceding this now useless battlefield," he said curtly, "and the Sekurai have gained a useless victory. Who knows how the next battle will go?"

The duke of White came onto the bridge of the *Malus Tempus* with a dejected look on his face. "I've come across a message in the main computer I think you all should see. I haven't watched the whole thing yet."

The duke brought up the message on the screen at his console and everyone gathered around it. It was a video and audio message with Surist speaking. "My comrades and countrymen, in times like these we must often make decisions that don't seem wise at the outset. And we also must step back from the situation and examine it from an objective perspective. I have done this, with the help of another, and I've come to the decision that I must leave you.

"I know you all think I've betrayed you, but in a way we will all betray ourselves and each other on this quest. I don't have all the details on just how Stone Globe managed to convince the Sekurai to help them, but they have. Our little feud has become a much more prominent detail; it has spread into open war between the powers of the galaxy. Every power in known space is now involved in this conflict.

"New information has come to light concerning my brother, whom I believed I had lost. Nurisk was thought to have died in the crash on Crux I thirteen years ago, but I tell you now that I have met my brother. He lost all memory of his life before the crash and has been gathering information to try to piece his life back together. After the crash he was taken in by the Braline people and he now owes his allegiance to them. I've decided that I cannot oppose my brother and that our reunification is more important than anything else. Our two sides were balanced, so I couldn't decide which one of us should alter his allegiance. Then I was informed that the *Quia Vita* has been modified and now has several advantages over the *Malus Tempus*. You know they have Sekurai technology now, so avoid them—avoid *us* at all costs. Due to this, Stone Globe has a better chance of success."

All of the remaining Orb Seekers' eyes were locked on the screen, listening intently to Surist explaining himself.

"I know this sounds like a poor explanation for such a drastic measure, but my family comes first, especially since I have no closer family. Also, the chance of survival must come first. I'm taking the Purple Orb to Stone Globe. You still have the Green Orb, so we each have the ability to re-forge the Orbs we find. I cannot ask you to forgive me, only to understand what I've done. I have deserted you, but I have not destroyed you, and I'll always remember you."

The Orb Seekers stared at each other or at the screen in amazement as the message ended. They were speechless for several moments. None of them knew what to make of this sudden turn of events.

Eventually Karak growled. "Where is that ship?"

"They're a long way from here by now," the duke said. "They've gone in the direction of the battle."

"I would go find him if we had the time," Karak said with a sneer, "We could at least take back the Purple Orb."

"And we could destroy that ship and all those on board," Notolla added through gritted teeth. "They certainly deserve it."

"You would kill Surist?" Lithinia eyed Karak and Notolla, surprised.

"Yes," Karak said instantly, losing his usual understanding attitude. "He's a traitor now and he should be killed. At least the others chose to stay home in the first place, but he has betrayed us. If I get the chance to destroy him in battle, I'll take it."

"He has a point, you know," Hiram said, raising his upturned hand to Karak and looking him in the eye. "Some members of Rongi Council chose not to come on this journey because they wanted to focus all their attention on their families."

"He made a promise to go on this journey and do whatever he could to help the Rongi people," Notolla said, her annoyance only being outdone by Karak. "Those who decided not to accompany us on this mission made that decision first. He has made a decision and not followed through with it. I don't agree with those who refused to come, but I can at least respect them. I can't respect Surist now. At least the others stayed back to help with evacuation efforts. Now he is actively moving against us."

"He's betraying his own people," the duke said. "He's basing his decision on a few technical improvements to a ship."

"Not entirely," Lithinia said. "He's basing this decision more on the family issue. Apparently Nurisk owes everything he now is to the Braline. If we've learned anything about the Braline, it's that they have a stronger duty to king and country. I would venture to guess that no Braline who was asked to go on their mission chose to stay home. Surist could not have separated Nurisk from that, so he had to go to Stone Globe to be with his brother. I don't agree with what Surist has done, and I wish he would have talked it over with us first, but I do understand what he's done. I just hope he knows that he'll die for this decision."

"He's taken an Orb," the duke said. "We have to get it back. That has to be our top priority."

"We will." Karak squinted. "We will. And when we do, I will kill him." Karak had never been so single minded or filled with rage and vengeance. He had greater contempt for Surist than would normally have been expected even in this situation. The stresses, continuing battles between forces too big for the Orb Seekers to even comprehend, and what was at stake for their people had begun to eat away at the Orb Seekers, especially Karak, their leader on whom all the pressure rested. "Principles aren't convenient, and he knows it, and he will accept the consequences—when we shove them down his throat."

"He was a great man until this," Notolla observed aloud. "I'll miss him."

"It seems that nothing is certain now, if it ever was," Lithinia said with a shake of her head.

"One thing is certain," Karak said. "Only one of our two groups can have the Orbs. He and Stone Globe will have to come for the Green one. We will meet again—when we fight to the death for them."

As the *Quia Vita* had effectively hidden from the Swisura to make repairs, Levu took the time to properly welcome Surist aboard and into Stone Globe. Surist had proven his worth to Levu already by bringing the Purple Orb. Then he went to the bridge and left Nurisk and Surist to talk.

"Welcome, my brother," Nurisk said with a wry smile.

Surist just looked around the room for lack of anything to say, and then looked back at Nurisk. He leaped upon him and embraced him, reduced to tears.

They spent the entire evening catching up. Nurisk was told of many things from their childhood and explorations before the crash. Surist's provincial motives for leaving the Orb Seekers and joining Stone Globe were reinforced when Nurisk gave account of the Braline/Sekurai conflicts he'd seen and been a part of. Nurisk told him how the Braline worked together so well. If they didn't move as one, they would've fallen to the Sekurai long ago. Cohesion had become engrained into their cultural DNA.

Their discussions and reminiscing were pleasantly interrupted by members of Stone Globe popping in and introducing themselves. Mostly, however, Nurisk and Surist were left alone to talk.

"How do you feel now that you've left the Rongi?" Nurisk inquired.

"I'm sure I'll settle into a new role just fine. It'll just take some getting used to. I know we don't exactly have a lot of time right now. I'll be fine."

"I think so too. We can always use another science officer—and a long lost brother or two."

"Or two? Are you planning on picking up more hitchhikers?" Surist asked as he facetiously looked around the room, thinking he might find another lost soul ready to join the group.

"No; you're it."

After a pause, Nurisk continued. "How do you feel about meeting the Rongi ship in battle?"

"We are going to have to get their Orbs. They only have one right now, but they'll find others. Karak is resourceful, and he has a good crew and a good ship."

"Not as good a ship as this one."

"No, from what you described, this ship is the most powerful and fastest of any outside the Swisura and Sekurai navies." Surist paused, then considered his brother's question. "I'm uneasy about confronting them, but I know it's got to be done." He rubbed his hands together uneasily. "I had to leave them the Green Orb; I didn't have access to it."

"They can use it to gather more Orbs," Nurisk observed. "And then we will take them from them."

"Yes," Surist said with a level of certainty and confidence equal to that with which he had pledged his life to Karak and the Rongi people. He had just taken the final step in both accepting what he'd done and in embracing his new "family."

"It will not be easy going up against them, I'm sure," Nurisk observed.

"It will be a hard thing to do, attacking them."

"Definitely," Nurisk agreed.

"It's all really irrelevant, though. In any situation you do what needs done. You don't avoid doing something just because it's hard. I'll be on the bridge at my post, and we will attack when the time is right. Nothing will stop us. We will prevail," Surist said as he leered with contempt for his former shipmates.

"Karak will want to kill you."

"I will kill him first."

✗ ✗ ✗

Redron

Onuy Nebulae Cluster

Kriline Defense Barrier

Enarf

Harza

Cruxfix Solar System

Braline Solar System

Nuin

Strunk Nebula

Chapter 13

THE YELLOW ORB

The Orb Seekers had taken the loss of their science officer with courage and logical thinking, along with a great deal of anger, resentment, and bitterness. They knew that an already difficult mission had just become even harder, but its necessity remained at the highest level. With the battle of a lifetime being waged, however, they were left alone for a time. They had to take advantage of this lull in their part of the action to plan as best they could.

"Karak hasn't been himself lately," Lithinia said to Notolla with a worried look as the two of them took an early supper one evening. "He's taken Surist's treachery very hard and personal."

"I know," Notolla said sympathizing with both Lithinia's concerns and Karak's behavior. "He's begun to abandon his usual magnanimous attitude and picked up a careless approach to Surist and Stone Globe."

"He's just not acting normally," Lithinia started again, playing with her food. "He's responsible for our success or failure; he's our leader. The circumstances, pressures, and the impending great catastrophe that will befall our people if he fails have begun to affect him."

"He's changing internally to suit what's necessary to be done," Notolla said.

"Surist is one of the most experienced explorers in Rongi history—or was," Lithinia said as Karak walked in.

Karak, blinded by aimless rage about Surist's defection, muttered something about his former science officer.

"You can't carry Surist around with you like a stone around your neck," Notolla said.

"I'll decide what to do!" Karak yelled at the top of his lungs, losing his composure. He made a ring with his hands and squeezed. "I'll find him and I'll kill him! He won't live to regret his treachery! He's condemned us all to death, all Rongi people!"

Everyone was surprised at Karak's reaction as they just sat and stared at him.

"To hell with him!" Karak yelled, and then paused for a moment to reflect on how quickly and how much things had changed. He then continued in a more normal tone while talking with his hands. "Whether it involved a new species, an uncharted part of space, or a keen observance and a quick solution, Surist was among the top people who could be counted on. Now, however, he's betrayed his people. Blood, for him, means more than the very culture and society from which he's come, and to which he'd pledged his life to try to save. He was so quick to chastise some of his fellow delegates to Rongi Council for their refusal to join us, and he had jumped at the opportunity to pledge his loyalty to me and his life to saving his people, and now he's a traitor. Now he fights against us. They now know of Rongi tactics, ship capabilities, the character of those with whom he's served, mission plans, everything." Karak just shook his head as he played with his glass, rolling it between his hands. "Kin always was important to their family."

"Now it's family that's torn him away," Notolla observed.

"I know why he betrayed us, but that's not at all to say I approve," Lithinia said.

"I do not approve," Karak said calmly. "He's a traitor. No mistake should be made of it; if I get the chance, I will kill him."

"You can't pull that trigger," Notolla said calmly and slowly.

"Watch me."

While the battle began in sector D:4 just outside Swisura space, the Orb Seekers traveled a long journey of another four days to Enarf to find the Yellow Orb and continue their quest. Karak and his crew had no way of knowing which side was winning that battle, or if it had even started yet. They were running on the assumption that it had started, but as far as who had the advantage, they were completely in the dark. The two forces, the Sekurai and the Swisura, were hated rivals and they had massive arsenals at their disposal with which to unleash that hatred upon each other.

"We're trapped on the far side of known space," Notolla pointed out with a foreboding analysis. "Once we obtain the Yellow Orb, we're going to have a very hard time getting back to the other side. If we take the northerly route, we'll risk running into the immense battle that would spread across several sectors of space. If we take the southerly route we would have to pass close to Sekurai space. Either way, it'll be treacherous."

"Not only is our information about the battle and the situation dark, but we're traveling through an unusually dark portion of space. There are very few stars in the area by which to navigate," Hiram reported. The region was almost entirely black. "Fortunately, this region of space is not terribly large, according to the Cruxfix database, so we should be able to pass through reasonably quickly. Due to the star charts from station Ynu and the Cruxfix information, we know that Harza, a black hole, is in the area, but we don't have an exact location."

"If we're to be stuck in this lifeless region of space for very long, we would be sure to experience some significant side effects," Lithinia added. "One expects stars while in space, so the absence of them could drive one mad. 'Where are all the stars?' one might whiningly ask oneself, thus expressing the first stages of some sort of deep space psychosis."

Karak himself was another story entirely. He limped down the corridors, tottered onto the bridge, and stumbled into his captain's chair, which was still bent and tilted almost as much as he was jilted. His chair had been rattled loose and the column on which it was perched had been slightly bent out of shape in the last battle with Stone Globe. Karak's spirits were in a shape similar to his chair after having been beaten in battle by a ship far more powerful than his own. And suffering treachery at the hands of a crew member who surely knew their weak points, with a likelihood they would meet again, not to mention being trapped on the far side of known space, had taken a toll. His appearance, however, was a whole other matter. He was tired, with bags under his eyes, dirty with grease and plasma fluid all over his clothes, face and hands after repairing some of the ship's systems, and exhausted. Everyone was tired and dirty.

After the Orb Seekers' most recent encounter with Stone Globe, who, in their minds, were represented almost exclusively by the traitor, Surist, Karak was almost as much bent on revenge as on saving the Rongi people. Once or twice he even considered turning around and going after Surist, completely denying the fact they would be destroyed if they tried to take on the *Quia Vita*. The matter of Surist had become personal with the Orb Seekers. Their eyes always squinted now, if not from exhaustion, then with rage. It was a deep rage that called for blood, the blood of Surist.

However, still possessing barely enough vision and clear-mindedness, they pressed on. Their hearts were conflicted over feelings toward

Surist while also still focusing on their people. They continued toward Enarf, the asteroid upon which they would find the Yellow Orb, while performing repairs to their ship.

"Have you had any luck locating that black hole, Harza, yet?" Karak asked.

"None," the duke of White responded with an annoyed sigh as he closed his eyes for a moment. "It's possible we won't know where it is until we're affected by it."

"I would prefer to remain unaffected by a black hole," Karak said with much certainty. "How long until we reach Enarf?"

"We should arrive in about eight hours." Hiram effected a course correction at the helm.

"Keep an eye on the engine performance," Karak said. "It'll be the first thing affected by Harza. As soon as we start accelerating beyond our current speed, we'll know it has begun affecting us. It will start to pull us towards it."

After a couple of hours, Harza's affect was noticed. The *Malus Tempus* was beginning to accelerate and was being pulled about twenty-five degrees to the starboard. The pull was especially strong and would have eventually overpowered the engines of the small Rongi ship if not for the keen eyes of Hiram, the helmsman, the duke, and Lithinia, the only science officers on the *Malus Tempus* after the untimely and treacherous departure of Surist. Finally, Hiram was able to compensate and hold the ship at a steady distance from the projected eye of the black hole. They were only able to make an extrapolated projection of where the eye was, but once the black hole had come into view, they could make sure to keep away from the event horizon.

"What's our situation?" Karak asked.

"We're holding steady from the event horizon." Hiram made several more course corrections. "But we're moving at a much slower rate than before. I have to fight the pull from the side as well as maintain forward progress. If we keep moving like this, we won't arrive at Enarf for several days due to our lack of speed and the distortion of time as we pass nearer the center."

"What?" Karak's forehead wrinkled and he closed his eyes.

"You see, the phenomenon's immense gravity well causes a different rate of time flow. The closer we are to the center, the more severe time will be distorted compared to the outside. We may only experience an hour or two within the black hole's area of effect," the duke said, "but, more than a day would pass outside, and the further towards the center we travel, the more severe the distortion will be."

"Well, we can't have that now, can we?" Karak said with as considerable an eye roll as his tired eyes could muster. "We don't have that kind of time. What if we were to backtrack our steps and go back out of the black hole and continue from there?"

"That route would take even longer, because we would be going the exact opposite direction as the pull from Harza," Hiram said. "Its force almost equals our own." Hiram made some calculations on his flight computer. "We'll have to lose some time, but I think I can limit the loss by not venturing too far into Harza and projecting a parabolic course away from it."

"If we can't go through or around, and we can't afford to take a day and a half at present course and speed, what are our other options?" Karak asked as he rubbed his tired eyes, irritated at the situation.

"Can we gather momentum from Harza and slingshot ourselves out of it?" Lithinia asked.

"Theoretically, yes," Hiram said. "I've executed maneuvers like that before, but it doesn't always work. If the slightest thing goes wrong, we'll never reach Enarf, or anywhere else, ever." Hiram turned to face Karak. "We have to remain outside the event horizon."

"What would be involved in such a maneuver?" Karak asked. "And can we please not have any more troubles on this trip? Let's figure this one out and then have no more drama."

Hiram ignored the last bit of Karak's whining. He spoke with his hands, making gestures that matched his words. "We would have to skirt on the edge of Harza's event horizon. It would have to be far enough in to gather the amount of momentum which, when added to our engines, would allow us to break the black hole's grip and escape. Theoretically, we would arrive at Enarf in just about half a day."

"Is this ship built for that kind of punishment?" Karak asked.

"I think she can handle it," Hiram said and then paused to look straight ahead, "unless we collide with something else that's being pulled into the black hole."

Karak smirked."That would be bad."

"We could even set the course so the changes would be easy on the ship," Hiram continued as he punched a few more preprogrammed orders into the computer. "It will still shake us around pretty good, though. The only thing is gathering enough momentum to allow us to escape, but not getting in so far that we can't escape."

"Moderation," Karak said. "Not too much in one direction or the other."

"Yes. I will also build a safety into the plan," Hiram said, thrusting a finger into the air. "I will set the course for a position where our normal engine output will allow us to escape, but I will have power from every other system on the ship ready to be put toward the engines in case we're off by a little."

"So this is like trying to slingshot ourselves around a planet or star?" Karak asked, trying to put the situation into terms he understood.

"Right," Hiram confirmed.

"And you have done this before, I hope?" Lithinia's eyes shifted toward Hiram without her head moving.

There was a long pause. Then Hiram said, "Once or twice."

"All right." Karak sighed. "I was hoping to avoid this altogether. Obviously, that didn't happen. Let's go for it."

It took a few minutes to lay in the exact course through the area of the black hole's gravity well. While this was being done, the duke remembered something about the Braline predicament that had sent them on their mission. "Weren't the Braline dealing with an emergency involving a black hole? Wasn't it something about a black hole that sent them to the Cruxfix System to begin with?"

"It was a different one, not Harza," Hiram said, not taking his eyes off the programming of the flight computer. "If you bring up the Cruxfix database, it'll probably tell you what black hole may be in the area around their system."

"I have it here," Lithinia said, looking at her screen. "It's called Redron. It's a lot larger than Harza, here, that's for sure. It seems Redron's pull on their system is counter balanced perfectly by Nuin, an enormous star that's much closer to Braline space than Redron is."

"But that star is destabilizing, wasn't that right?" the duke asked.

"That's right," Lithinia answered. "They're trying to avoid falling into the black hole. I'm sure their plan was to gather the Orbs and send them hurtling into Redron to stop the gravitational pull on their system."

"How would that work?" Notolla asked.

"It might not." Lithinia tilted her head toward Notolla. "But then we're not sure that sending them into a shockwave of destructive energy will work either."

"What if they can't stop Redron from pulling them in?" Karak wondered aloud.

"They would be pulled into the black hole and unable to escape," the duke answered. "There would come a point where their ships could no longer maneuver out of its gravity well. They would be stuck there forever."

"Till they got sucked into the eye of the black hole, right?" Notolla asked.

"No," the duke continued in a very teacher-like way despite the fact that the ship was shaking and could be dragged into Harza at any moment, "they would never make it to the eye."

"Because the gravity would crush them first?" Notolla asked again.

"No, let me finish. Time moves at a slower pace when affected by greater gravity. With that much pull on them, their time would move significantly slower. Time outside the black hole would progress the same as we're currently experiencing, but time inside would move much, much slower, although those within wouldn't notice because they would be part of the phenomenon."

"Like how you don't notice the rotation of a planet you're standing on," Lithinia added.

"They would never actually reach the eye of the black hole," the duke said forebodingly. "They would continue to move towards it, but the closer they got, the slower time would progress. They would be stuck there forever, never reaching the center, and never being able to get out."

At this realization, the entire crew understood how the Braline people needed saving. They needed the Orbs desperately, just as the Rongi people did. They gained a newfound respect for their adversary—not that they could do anything to help; they were in no less precarious of a situation than the Braline.

While the duke, Hiram, and Lithinia were making sure they had everything prepared and accounted for, Karak and Notolla discussed the plan to get the Yellow Orb. It would have to be a quick job because of the time they would lose in fighting Harza's pull.

"Notolla, I'll want you and Hiram to stay here on the *Malus Tempus* while Lithinia, the duke, and I go onto the asteroid." Karak pointed to each crew member as he said their name. "I hope to have the Yellow Orb before any Braline scouts find us, but that's unlikely."

"We can stay on the side of the asteroid opposite the Braline ships," Notolla suggested.

"That's wise, but it probably won't be very effective," Karak said. "Surely they're monitoring their space extensively. I want you two to stay here so you can engage their forces in battle if necessary and Hiram can provide evasive maneuvers that'll allow you to hold them off while we're searching."

"I don't think it would be wise to engage in a battle so far from our allies," Notolla advised.

"I don't think it's wise either," Karak agreed, "but we won't get another chance at this. Avoid battle until it becomes impossible; stall however is necessary. It shouldn't take too long for us to locate the Orb."

"We're ready to initiate the plan," Hiram said. "We've taken everything into account, and I've made preparations to redirect power from wherever is necessary."

"Well, we have a long journey ahead of us." Karak resumed his seat. "Let's do it."

"I'm changing course to head for Enarf and compensating for the gravity well," Hiram reported as he continued to operate his station. "We already have enough momentum to avoid being sucked in before we've passed the center, which is off to the port side."

"We're gaining speed rapidly, but at the rate expected," the duke said as the ship began to shake harder. "We're approaching the maximum anticipated speed."

The ship shook violently as it approached its apex speed. The vibration was very strong and only got worse as the ship progressed. The crew hung onto their seats to keep from being thrown out of them. Computer pads fell from their perches atop consoles.

"Are you sure the ship can take this vibration?" Karak asked.

"Of course! I know the limits of this ship. We're going to be just fine," Notolla said as she looked around with wide eyes, not believing her own words.

"Structural integrity is holding," the duke said, "but not by much."

"We've passed the projected center," Lithinia reported, not wanting to look away from her console. "We should start to slow down now."

"Go ahead and transfer power to the engines, Lithinia!" Hiram yelled.

"The power has been transferred," Lithinia reported. "You now have the power from the long-range sensors, weapons, shields, and life support."

"We're breaking away from the belly of the beast!" Hiram yelled, getting excited. "This is what a helmsman dreams of! We're slowing fast, but I think we'll make it."

The vibration eased and ship operations returned to normal as they distanced themselves from the black hole.

"I thought I was going to shake right out of existence," Notolla said sarcastically, placing her hands all over her body to make sure everything was where it was supposed to be. "One more vibration and I think I would've shattered into a million pieces and rolled around on the floor. I probably would've gotten stuck between computer banks and circuitry knots—maybe squeezed through the molecules of the deck plate and come out on the level below."

"We're on the bridge in the nose of the ship, deck one," the duke said coldly. "There are no decks beneath us."

"Good thing it stopped when it did, then." Notolla nodded quickly a few times.

"We're in the clear now," Hiram said as he locked in the rest of their course to Enarf. "Our calculations were close, but not perfect. We were aimed a little too far to the starboard. Any further the other way and we would've lost our lives."

"The Green Orb would have been destroyed with us too," Lithinia added.

"Let's forget about what might have happened and go find the Yellow Orb," Karak said, shifting in his seat and looking away from those who were seemingly more concerned about what hadn't happened than about what they were going to have to do now.

"We should arrive at Enarf in about half a day now," Hiram said, leaning back in his chair.

Upon reaching the Kriline Defense Barrier, the Orb Seekers were in awe of such a structure. The sphere of asteroids was thick and dense, but not so dense that a small fighter couldn't get through. The trouble for such a craft would come not in the spacing between the rocks but in the navigation of them. "It would be very easy to crash into an asteroid because they're so dense and compact," Hiram said, pointing to the screen at his console. "Another navigational hazard is how fast the asteroids are all moving. It would be very difficult to program a flight path to get through a hole in the barrier, other than the ones meant to allow the Braline to venture beyond their solar system. Their extremely fast orbit means the barrier only needs one level of thickness and doesn't have to be solid, though it's pretty tight anyway. There can still be small holes in the barrier because there's an impossibly narrow window to get through."

Enarf had been the home of the Yellow Orb ever since the Cruxfix people decided to disband the group of Orbs, break most of them, and scatter them throughout the known parts of space. Enarf, however, had not always been in the Kriline Defense Barrier. It was moved into the structure as part of its construction about one hundred fifty years earlier. Up until that time, Enarf had been a free floating asteroid in space. The Cruxfix people had left the Yellow Orb on this asteroid because they felt that a stray asteroid in the middle of space was more than innocuous enough of a place so as to keep from drawing attention to itself. Thus the Orb could have remained hidden for a very long time. The Cruxfix people had, however, kept up on its location, as they tried to do with all the Orbs. They wanted to make sure the Orbs didn't fall into the wrong hands, as the Orbs had been created to serve the necessary purposes of good. In case they were needed again, they would be able to find the Orbs if they continued to monitor their whereabouts.

The Orb Seekers found Enarf, the asteroid on which the Yellow Orb rested, exactly where the information on the Orbs in the Cruxfix database said it should be, and proceeded to scan for signs of the Orb.

"The sensors' effectiveness is very low," the duke said. "The combination of the metals in the rock must be dampening the signal."

"So how are we going to find the Orb?" Karak asked. "We can't expect the thing to just be sitting down there. Besides, we know it isn't intact."

"If we can't pinpoint the location of the Orb, can we at least narrow down a certain area to search?" Lithinia asked.

"That's what I'm trying to do now," the duke said as he operated a series of controls at his console. "I think I've got the residual power signal from the Orb. It's a good thing Gronil told us these things had a power matrix inside. We know there's something to scan for. We've never seen this type of power. I don't understand it, but then I don't need to either."

"It should be the only power source down there," Notolla said.

"I've got it." The duke clapped his hands together lightly in satisfaction. "It has the same power readings on our sensors as the other Orbs we've encountered. I've narrowed the search grid down to a one hundred square meter area."

"All right," Karak said excitedly. "Let's go."

"I think it would be wise to take the Green Orb with us," Lithinia suggested.

"Why? What would that help?" Karak asked.

"We may not be able to find a piece of the Orb just laying around down there," Lithinia explained as she extended an open hand, "and if we do find one, we could at least touch it to the Green Orb to find out what it is instead of bringing a bunch of rocks up here to test them out."

"Good thinking." Karak turned to leave the ship.

Karak, Lithinia, and the duke of White shuttled down to the surface of the asteroid to search for the Yellow Orb. They wore oxygen atmosphere suits when they exited the shuttle because the large rock had no atmosphere. The suit began at the helmet with a large clear face shield through which one could see. The rest of the topmost portion of the suit was a grayish color. The body of the garment was entirely white and very plain. They were air-tight and loose-fitting. They consisted of only one piece and extended down to the feet with the lower portion of the same hue as the upper parts.

Even the boots were attached to the legs. The way one would enter these suits was through a seal which ran down the front so one could step in. The seal was broken only by a chemical called bicondritium. Bicondritium would be applied to the seal and temporarily neutralize the bonding agent that held the suits together. Once the effect wore off, the edges would regain their adhesive quality and bond instantly, forming a perfect seal when they were touched to one another.

The necessary environment was maintained by a small pack kept inside the suit.

Having precious little gravity forced the group to tether to each other. One would hold on to whatever was available, at first the ship, a rocky crag, a hole in the surface of the asteroid, or whatever was available. The others would then telescope outward, still tethered to the first until they found something to hold on to, then the original anchorman would venture out. They also anchored themselves with grapples in case the anchorman's hold was broken loose.

They began looking for yellow rocks of any size, but had very little luck in finding any. No one found any rocks whose color was as full and bright as the other Orbs they had already seen.

While they were on the asteroid searching, Notolla and Hiram were having troubles of their own. They'd come into sensor range of the Braline patrols sooner than they'd hoped. The patrols just so happened to be scouting that part of the Braline System about an hour and a half after the *Malus Tempus* entered the Kriline Defense Barrier. First, Hiram tried to hide the ship behind a few asteroids to avoid detection, but the Braline ships had already noticed them.

"They're hailing us," Hiram reported.

"I'll handle this," Notolla responded.

"This is a Braline patrol," a voice said over the communications system. "You are intruding on Braline territory. Please state your business."

"We were passing by on a routine exploration mission when our engines experienced a malfunction," Notolla explained. "I can assure you that we will be on our way as soon as possible."

"Our superiors would prefer you not just stay out here unaccompanied," the Braline scout replied. "We must respectfully request that you follow us to one of our shipyards."

"Then why don't you just stay here with us until our engines are repaired?" Notolla asked.

"Our duties are pressing," the scout leader responded. "We have a mission to complete."

"If you can wait about an hour or two, we'll have sufficient engine power to move towards one of your shipyards," Notolla said.

After a moment the scout responded, "That is acceptable. We will wait with you."

"Thank you for your patience," Notolla said understandingly. "I will inform you when we've repaired our engines adequately."

After the conversation was over, Notolla worked out a plan with Hiram to get away from the scouts once the Yellow Orb had been found. "When Karak informs us that the Orb has been found and forged, we'll cut our stabilizing engines and be slowly drawn in by the gravity of the asteroid," Notolla said. "That should draw the scouts' attention and give our crewmates a shorter distance to travel to get back aboard the ship."

"How are we going to get out of here once everyone is onboard?" Hiram inquired. "We aren't as fast as they are. We don't want to destroy them."

"That's Karak's problem."

Meanwhile, Karak and his companions had spent about two hours scouring the asteroid with no success. After that time, Lithinia began simply rolling the Green Orb on the ground, keeping her hands on it the whole time for fear it would drift off the asteroid in zero gravity, hoping it would touch a piece of the Yellow Orb and forge it. She did this for nearly an hour and covered almost all of the hundred square meters the search area had been narrowed down to when she finally accomplished the task. When the piece of the Yellow Orb was struck, the different parts of the demolished Orb simply materialized at the point of contact between the whole Green Orb and the Yellow Orb fragment. The entire Orb was in place, just innocently lying there on the ground as though it had always rested there.

Lithinia picked up both Orbs, and opened her communicator. "Notolla, we have the Yellow Orb and are preparing to shuttle back to the ship now."

"Wait!" Notolla said. "We've been accosted by some Braline scouts. We have a plan and will initiate it now. Wait until we're closer to the asteroid before you come back to the ship."

"Just give us a signal," Karak said. "We'll be ready."

"Hiram," Notolla said as she raised a finger and then dropped it to signal her verbal command, "cut the stabilizing engines—now."

"We are falling towards the asteroid," Hiram said as he monitored their progress.

"The Braline are hailing us," Notolla warned. "They've noticed that our orbit around the rock is deteriorating."

"We're about two hundred fifty meters from the surface," Hiram said.

"Karak," Notolla spoke into the communications microphone, "you may start your approach, but be quick about it."

"We're on the way," Karak responded. "We should be there in less than a minute."

"You'd better say something to these testy Braline." Hiram was getting antsy.

"*Malus Tempus* to Braline scout, this is Field Marshal Notolla. We're having a small problem with our stabilizing engines now, but we seem to be fixing it. We had to take them offline and restart the system to get our main engines back online."

"Perhaps you would like some assistance," the scout offered.

"No," Notolla said quickly, "we have the solution and it is being implemented now."

"The shuttle is back in the docking bay," Hiram reported urgently, but in a low voice. "Karak should be up here shortly."

"Was that a shuttle that just now boarded your ship?" the scout asked skeptically.

"We had to send someone out in a shuttle to do some repair work on our engines," Notolla lied.

"Your story is getting sketchy," the Braline scout leader observed. "Why didn't you mention this before?"

At that moment Karak, Lithinia, and the duke of White reached the bridge.

"Cut that communication line," Karak ordered. "Get us out of here. Set course for the Sekurai System and engage the engines at full power."

"Course plotted and engines engaged," Hiram said.

"We aren't as fast as these scout ships, Karak," the duke informed.

"We won't have to be fast at all once they find out we are going towards the Sekurai System," Karak said as he settled into his familiar command chair. "They will immediately break off their pursuit." Karak shifted over to his right and the cockeyed chair swiveled around toward that side. Karak glared at Notolla. "Next time make the seat pedestal stronger." Notolla just smiled.

"Why are we going to the Sekurai System?" Notolla asked with a worried look.

"We're going there to get these Braline ships off of our backs," Karak responded. "After that, we're heading for Station Ynu."

"It would seem almost like home compared to all the places we've been recently," Lithinia said.

"Don't you think going to the Sekurai System is trading a small problem for a huge problem?" The duke's eyes grew wide.

"Yes," Karak agreed, "but if we don't solve this small problem, we'll never have any problems—ever again—at all. Solve the current problem now, and then tackle the others. Besides, I want to make sure the Orange Orb is not in Sekurai space. I believe Stone Globe probably got it while they were there securing their alliance with the Sekurai, but this is going to be our only chance to find out for sure if the Orb is there or not."

"We're being tailed very closely by those scouts," Notolla said. "Our firepower is superior; we could destroy them and head straight for Station Ynu."

"I would not even consider firing a warning shot," Karak said, showing a vestige of civility despite all that had happened to him and his crew. "They will not fire on us unless we actively harm them, and I have no intention of doing that. All we have to do is run and the situation should solve itself."

"And I think that's happening just now," Hiram reported. "The Braline scouts are breaking off and heading back for their own space."

"Good," Notolla said. "Now we can proceed unhindered for a time."

"Inform me as soon as we're in range of any Sekurai ships or stations," Karak said. "We still have to obtain six Orbs. Our work is less than half done."

✗ ✗ ✗

Sakurai Solar System

Station Ynu

Sniguri Nebulae Cluster

Chapter 14

FLYING INTO THE WEB

The Orb Seekers had traveled for four days after leaving Braline space. They were tired and they were losing track of the insufferably long days. Their road wasn't expected to get any easier though. The closer they got to home and to the deciding point of their mission, the more trying their situation was expected to become.

Hiram turned to report. "We've not yet encountered any Sekurai ships. As soon as the Braline scouts realized we were heading for Sekurai space, they backed off and went home."

"They didn't want to infringe on Sekurai space and risk open war," Notolla accurately suggested. "The Braline have no idea that Levu Earsp negotiated a peace, albeit an uneasy one, I'm sure, with the Sekurai. As far as the Braline scouts knew, they were just pursuing a rogue ship that had done nothing wrong except fly into their space and leave."

"They have no idea that Levu and his crew need our precious cargo," Karak said thoughtfully. "The *Quia Vita* has long been out of communications range with their home. As far as the Braline people and leaders know, they are to continue with evacuation efforts, and Levu and his crew are out here on their own. Neither they nor our people have any idea of all the bustle that's going on in the vast outer regions of space."

"I would imagine that nearly all of the Sekurai navy is currently engaging the Swisura forces in sector D:4," Karak said, peering out of the main window on the bridge. "I thought they would have more defense because of the war, if for nothing else."

"That's the only reasonable explanation for the lack of ships in the area." Notolla raised her hand to her chin.

"We're in sensor range of Station Sek, the main defensive Sekurai post," Hiram reported, pointing to the screen at his console.

"And I'm now picking up a few scouts on sensors," the duke of White said.

"Keep an eye out for any of those ships that may come our way," Karak said warily.

"We're nearing the sensor range of a warship that's in orbit around Qu'uack," Notolla said, "but we're out of the scouts' weapons range for the present."

"Do we know what types of signals obstruct their sensors' effectiveness?" Karak asked, turning to the science stations. "If we're going to fly through Sekurai space, we're going to need some advantage, and I would like to go through unnoticed, if possible."

"All of their systems are very advanced compared to our own." The duke turned toward Karak. "But they would likely be susceptible to a network of jamming rays."

"In that case, prepare a series of probes designed for jamming," Karak ordered, moving toward the front of the bridge. "We will launch them and disrupt their sensors long enough to get into the system, get the Orange Orb, if it's still there, and get out."

"Surely the Sekurai will destroy the probes as soon as they find out what's jamming their sensors," Lithinia suggested with raised eyebrows.

"Yes," Karak responded, raising a tight fist. "That's why we must be quick."

"How much time do you suppose we will have?" Lithinia asked.

"It will take them nearly an hour to determine the problem if their technology is comparable to the Swisura." The duke shrugged. "And then another hour to destroy enough probes to make our jamming net ineffective, but those figures are only estimates."

Notolla turned to face Karak. "The probes are ready for launch."

"Good," Karak said. "Launch them and initiate the web. Let's hope this works."

Out of the *Malus Tempus's* forward torpedo bay were then launched a series of probes, which spread out in every direction. Together these probes would create a network of jamming rays and render the Sekurai sensors ineffective. The main question was whether or not the web would operate long enough to ensure the Orb Seekers safe passage through the system while they attempted to find out if the Orange Orb were still on Qu'uack and, if so, allow them to gather it.

"The probes are launched and the web is operating at full power," Notolla reported, keeping her eyes on the readouts at the tactical station. "It seems to be working. The probes will continue to spread to the furthest extent at which they can still operate at maximum capacity.

They will even follow us and keep us in the middle of the network while we move further into Sekurai space. They're very handy, these probes."

"If they stay with us, won't that clue in the Sekurai as to where we are?" Lithinia asked.

"It would," Notolla answered, extending an upturned hand and then pointing out into space, "but these probes disguise themselves in addition to anything with specified signatures within the network. The Sekurai won't be able to see the probes or us."

"So, they inhibit targets with specified signatures and they can also mask certain signatures?" Karak shrugged. "There's something new every day."

"As long as we have the necessary signatures to input to the probes' computers," Notolla said. "We got that little piece of information from the Nilg database and confirmed it on Crux I. These are generally only meant for use in small groups or even just one. The idea was to attach one to each of our deep space probes. This would keep them from being destroyed by anything hostile that we've encountered before. We've also thought about using them to disguise our ships in the Consraka Nebulae to get by Agri, but we haven't been able to test them yet."

"What do you mean you haven't been able to test them yet?" Hiram gulped.

"Well," Notolla started slowly, her eyes moving from person to person on the bridge, "we haven't been able to test them yet—at all—ever."

"Great," Lithinia said sarcastically with raised brows. "We're guinea pigs."

"Let's hope it holds long enough," Karak said solemnly. "Take us in."

During the better part of the next hour, the *Malus Tempus* traveled behind the shroud which her crew hoped would protect them for enough time to allow them to complete this leg of their mission. They assumed that Stone Globe had already acquired the Orange Orb, but this was going to be their only chance to get it if it was still on Qu'uack. Their journey had taken them to the heart of one of the most powerful empires the galaxy had ever known, and the most evil.

"We're approaching Qu'uack," Hiram reported. "Shall I assume a standard orbit?"

"No," Karak said, turning his head thoughtfully to one side. "Remember, one of their ships is in a standard orbit. Take us into a high orbit. We'll be fine as long as the probes are still operational. We can't take up a lower orbit, or people might actually see us from the planet's surface."

"I'm scanning for the power signatures emitted by the Orbs," the duke said hurriedly. "So far, the sensors aren't picking anything up."

"How are the probes holding up, Notolla?" Karak asked.

"They're all still there and the net is fully operational," the marshal responded.

"It won't be like that for long," Lithinia butted in. "The Sekurai haven't found any of the probes yet, but they have identified their sensor problem. I've been monitoring communications."

"We have to make this quick then," Karak looked at the duke. "How long before you're done scanning?"

"At such a high orbit it may take a few minutes," the duke answered.

"You may not have that long," Karak said.

"I'm detecting a fluctuation in the net," Notolla reported urgently. "One of the probes is under attack."

"Which probe is it?" Lithinia asked, a bit overwhelmed.

"The first one we set," Notolla answered. "It isn't the one nearest us. We'll be undetectable until there are only four of them left, but we have to stay inside the net to remain undetected."

"Why four?" Karak asked, looking questioningly at Notolla.

"We are large enough of a three-dimensional object," Notolla began, talking with her hands, "that if we want to remain hidden, we need to be inside the larger three-dimensional net. Any three points can create a shape on one plane, but it requires at least four points to create a shape in three dimensions."

"My scans are complete and I haven't found any signal of an Orb," the duke reported. "However, I have found another warship. This one is in our orbit and is just now coming into view after being obscured by the planet."

"Increase speed and set course for Station Ynu," Karak said, returning to his chair and bracing himself. "We still have the probes. They should at least get us out of the system."

"Another probe has been destroyed," Notolla said urgently. "The net is weakening. They aren't going to hold much longer."

"Will that warship in our orbit be able to detect us when they get in sight?" Karak asked.

"Not unless the network is gone by then," Hiram said, "or someone looks out a window."

"We're fast approaching the minimum number of probes required to maintain the net," Notolla urged.

"Get us out of here!" Karak yelled.

"I'm reading several Sekurai ships coming into sensor range," the duke reported.

"Two more probes have dropped off my screen," Notolla said quickly.

"This plan is unraveling quickly," Karak said.

"We're only one probe away from losing the network," Notolla observed urgently.

"The network of probes has been disabled," Notolla said after another moment. "We are now open to detection."

"And we are being intercepted by that warship," the duke said. "It's right in front of us."

"Hard to port!" Karak yelled. "Any nebulae in the area? We need a place to hide fast."

"The Sniguri Nebula Cluster is off our port bow," the duke answered. "We've seen this nebula before."

"Set course for the nearest nebula," Karak said. "Perhaps it'll shield us from their sensors. Don't forget, though, that we'll have to put all the power to the shields to survive."

"We won't be able to stay in there for very long either," the duke reminded Karak. "Whatever we're going to do, we have to do it quickly."

The Sekurai warship changed its course and caught up with the *Malus Tempus* just before it could enter the nebula. The ship was shaken by the blast of the large and powerful Sekurai weapons, but it was not soon enough to damage anything except shield strength as the Orb Seekers were already on the edge of the nebula.

"What's the damage report?" Karak asked.

"The warship took our shields down to seventy-two percent, and it's going to get worse all the time we're in here," Notolla reported. "They did no damage to the ship itself, though."

"What's the status of our pursuers?" Karak inquired.

"The nebulae not only inhibit sensors but also communications," Lithinia said. "I can't receive any of their channels, but their last order was to 'destroy the intruders,' and they had sent all of their ships still at home, including the empress's ship."

"They must know who we are," Karak said. "Mr. Earsp must have told them all about us and our ship. That's why they're sending everything they have at us."

"We're going to have to navigate by sight while the sensors aren't working." Hiram pointed to his useless navigational controls.

"If we were to exit the nebula cluster on the opposite side, how long would it take for the nearest Sekurai ship to overtake us?" Karak excitedly wheeled round in his captain's chair.

"We could stay ahead of them for about a day," Hiram answered. "Their scouts and escort ships are faster than us—and they would eventually catch us."

"And how much time would be required to reach the weapons range of Station Ynu?" Karak asked, eyeing Hiram.

"We are approximately three days away," Hiram responded, shaking his head.

"We would be dead by then," Notolla said.

"Not necessarily," Karak said, holding up a finger, "We did send messages back home from Station Ynu. It's possible that our people have a presence there by now. There may be a few ships that can help us."

"If we had those ships just come here and protect us on our way out of the nebula, we would have a chance," Notolla said. "It depends on how many ships we have there. To wage an effective battle with just a few dozen Sekurai ships, it would take our entire fleet though, and we can be sure our entire fleet isn't there. In fact, most of them are surely helping with the evacuation."

"But it would buy us some time," the duke said, his eyes meeting Notolla's. "If we can get to those ships, they can protect us while we make for Station Ynu. They might slowly be thinned out, but they could take some hits for us and allow us to get there with our Orbs."

"I was thinking we would meet any ships halfway," Karak suggested. "We would not survive in this dangerous nebula until they got here, even if we could get a message out. We would also save a day or so by doing it that way."

"How do we know our people sent an expedition?" Lithinia asked. "We're only assuming they've gotten the station up and running at full strength and can offer us some help. Also, how do we know those old weapons will still be effective against the Sekurai ships?"

"Well," Karak said, "surely Praetor Jarob sent an expedition and then started evacuating to the station as many people as it could hold. I would think we have a presence there by now."

"As to whether our ships are numerous and powerful enough or not," Notolla said, "our main goal is simply to use them to provide a distraction. Having a force large enough to wipe out all of the enemy's ships is a bonus."

"I think it's our only option," Karak said, looking around the bridge for a better suggestion. "Set course for Station Ynu and send a message to the station once we've cleared the nebula. Inform them of our situation."

"How close to the edge are we going to have to be before the sensors start working again?" Karak asked cautiously.

"They won't get any readings until we're completely out of the nebula," the duke responded.

"All weapons are ready," Notolla said, "but they will be of no use if there's anything like a warship out there."

"Notolla, you've just given me an idea!" Lithinia's eyes grew wide. "If we fire a torpedo directly forward, we would be able to see any detonation in front of us. The sensors wouldn't be necessary. We would simply be able to see it straight ahead."

"I could set the torpedo to detonate if its sensors detect any enemy craft within a specified range," Notolla suggested.

"If we see a detonation, we could simply find another area from which to exit the nebula and try again," Hiram added.

"It sounds good," Karak said. "Fire a torpedo directly ahead."

"Torpedo away," Notolla said as she hit a few buttons on her console.

"It's approaching the edge of the nebula," the duke reported. "It has exited the nebula, and passed through without detonating."

"All right," Karak said, "take us out of here along that same path at maximum speed."

"Engines engaged," Hiram reported as his hands flew across his console. "We will achieve full acceleration just as we clear the nebula."

"We are now approaching regular space," the duke said. "We will exit the nebula in just a few seconds."

"I have communications channels again," Lithinia said.

"Sensors are working properly now," the duke reported. "We got out of there just in time, too. There are three enemy scouts to the starboard side and a warship to the port side."

"Oh, well," Karak said. "Our destination is in neither of those directions—it's straight forward. Full speed ahead!"

"Those Sekurai ships are pursuing us, and they're gaining on us," the duke said with a sigh.

"I'm transferring power from weapons to the engines," Hiram said. "We're going to have a problem though."

"I don't want problems," Karak said with his adult voice, but in a childish manner.

"We won't make it to the rendezvous point before they catch up with us," Hiram said. "We're going to have to fight them."

"That's not an option." Karak shook his head. "We have to outsmart them or run from them. We can't fight them—they're too powerful. I want ideas."

"I've already sent the message to the station," Lithinia said. "I'll monitor for a response."

All day long, the Orb Seekers fought a losing battle by trying to outrun their Sekurai pursuers. Power from all systems had been diverted to the engines in order to get as much speed as they could, but despite all their efforts the Orb Seekers were unable to attain a speed as great as the enemy ships. The Orb Seekers could not reach Station Ynu before they were overrun.

They also didn't know how many Rongi ships would be coming to their aid, if any. No response to Lithinia's message had been received because the Sekurai had jammed the communications frequencies almost as soon as the *Malus Tempus* left the nebula. It was going to be close as to whether or not they would make the rendezvous point before they were overtaken. Their only hope was that the Rongi leadership had sent a force large enough to hold off the Sekurai, and that they were fast enough to be of help.

"Our pursuers will be in weapons range in two minutes," the duke said forebodingly.

"Transfer power to weapons," Karak ordered, steely-eyed. "We'll make our stand here."

"Our weapons are fully charged," Notolla said.

"The first scout ships are now in range to fire on us." The duke adopted a cringing expression and tightly closed one eye as if expecting a blast.

"We're receiving a message from the warship," Lithinia said.

"Let's hear it," Karak said. "We need to buy time. Let's keep them talking."

"Rongi vessel, you are ordered to stand down," an intent female voice said. "You are in possession of some valuable tools, and you will give them to us or we will take them from you."

"First of all, whom do I have the honor of addressing?" Karak inquired. "I would at least like to know who's threatening me before I give anything away."

"You're speaking to Empress Mudin of the Sekurai Empire," the voice said. "Now, you will hand over the Orbs or be killed."

"You do realize we need these Orbs to save our civilization, don't you?" Karak asked.

"I don't care," the empress said.

"And you also know we've been through a lot to get them," Karak said. "It would be rude to ask us to part with our possessions."

"Again, I don't care," the empress said, "and I'm not *asking* you to do anything. I'm ordering—and I'm threatening."

"We will stop at nothing," Karak said.

All was then quiet for a moment, but only for a short moment. The empress had realized that Karak meant he would fight to the death, because that was what was at stake either way. So Mudin gave them her response.

"Sekurai warship coming to bear, Karak," the duke said worriedly.

"Power up the laser guns and load the torpedoes." Karak gripped the arms of his chair. "Full power to the shields and stand by for evasive maneuvers."

"The fighters are attacking," Notolla said as the first wave of the enemy fired on the *Malus Tempus*.

"Evasive maneuvers now!" Karak yelled.

The shots missed the *Malus Tempus*, and Hiram brought the little ship around to bear.

"Return fire," Karak ordered. "It'll take everything we've got to destroy one fighter."

"Targeting the nearest enemy," Notolla reported. "Firing!"

The closest fighter was hit by the full blast of the *Malus Tempus's* weapons and was damaged enough to break off its pursuit.

"I'm detecting six enemy fighters coming in," the duke said.

"Evasive maneuvers!" Karak yelled.

This time Hiram was too late. The blast hit them straight on and crippled their shields.

"The shields are at thirty-four percent," Notolla reported. "Our shields didn't have time to fully recharge after the damage they took in the nebula, and that blast was from all six of those fighters at once. Our shields won't survive another hit like that."

"The empress's warship is in range and is powering up her weapons," the duke said.

"All power to the engines and aft shields," Karak said urgently. "Get us to Station Ynu!"

"We'll never make it," Hiram warned.

"We have to try," Karak urged.

"The warship is firing," Notolla said.

The weapons from the Sekurai warship were devastating. Blasts from all gun ports, which were too numerous for Notolla to take time to count, emitted purple shots that lit up the blackness of space. Some emissions were of a slicing nature and others were some kind of energy projectile which had a concussive and explosive effect.

Fortunately, the *Malus Tempus* was moving at a speed great enough to force about half of the warship's guns to be inaccurate.

"Our shields are down and our weapons are offline," Notolla reported with a defeated tone.

"The enemy continues to pursue," the duke said.

"We aren't going to win this one, are we?" Karak asked of no one in particular.

"It's looking like our journey is at an end," Hiram said.

"Lithinia," Karak said, "you're good with creative solutions. Got anything for this?"

"Yes," Lithinia said, perking up with an idea, "if we can't destroy them with conventional weapons, we can eliminate the problem by unconventional means."

"I get your meaning," Karak said, "but instead of initiating the self-destruct sequence, we'll take a much more interesting approach."

"What do you have in mind?" Lithinia gave Karak an untrusting look.

"Set course for the empress's ship," Karak said intently. "All power to the engines."

"Course set," Hiram said.

The *Malus Tempus* then turned about and attempted to avoid all the fire coming its way. Hiram was weaving the ship to and fro, trying to dodge the weapons fire coming at them. All of space was alight with the firing of the Sekurai ships. Only the superior navigational abilities of Hiram were capable of avoiding destruction up to now, but they knew at some point even Hiram's skills would not be able to match the Sekurai firepower. This was the point they'd reached, and they reached it sooner than they'd hoped. The Orb Seekers wondered how anyone, even the Swisura, could absorb that kind of firepower. Their entire mission seemed to be crumbling to dust before them now. Just as it seemed that all was lost and the hope of saving their race from extinction was all but gone, Karak looked around at his valiant crew and silently appreciated their sacrifices and efforts. No words of thanks needed to be said. "Ramming speed!" Karak yelled. If they couldn't win, they weren't going to go out without causing some damage.

"The sensors are picking up a fleet of ships heading our way," the duke said quietly.

"Great," Karak said sarcastically. "How many are there now?"

"They're still coming into sensor range," the duke said, his voice shaky. "I can distinguish approximately one hundred fifty different ships and counting."

"Impact with the empress's ship in fifteen seconds," Hiram warned.

"What kind of ships are they?" Karak asked.

"They're still too far away to tell," the duke said.

Karak paused to think. "Evasive maneuvers!"

Then, right in front of their eyes, a Sekurai fighter came to bear at point blank range. It sat there, momentarily hanging in space for a period of time no longer than that of the pilot's ability to react and operate the firing controls on his joystick, but that split second seemed to be frozen in time because not even Hiram could get the *Malus Tempus* out of the way of this enemy's guns, and everyone knew the ship couldn't take another hit.

The small fighter's laser emitters lit up as its powerful weapons were being fired. Just as it did so, a great blackness, which was as black as space itself but somehow different by having a bit of a gray highlight, flew between the two ships. The shot from the Sekurai fighter made an impressive impact of bright colors and devastating effect, but that impact was not rendered upon the *Malus Tempus*. Then three more small black shapes came from behind the enemy ship and shot it to pieces. These black ships had an unbelievable firepower; it was as impressive as that of the Sekurai ships.

"What was that?" Notolla asked.

Karak shook his head. "No idea. But we should take advantage of it while we can. Get us out of here!"

"Karak," the duke of White said slowly, "these ships are Nilg ships. We made it to the rendezvous point at the same time. There aren't any of our own ships here, though. Only Nilg."

"They're engaging the Sekurai forces," Field Marshal Notolla said, "and they're doing so quite effectively."

The Nilg ships cut and thrashed their way through the Sekurai navy like one of the most feared forces in the galaxy was nothing. They attacked in groups and never gave their opponents a chance to fire a shot. The black ships were agile and fast. They were able to avoid laser gun shots at close range and then come about to destroy the ship that had dared fire on them. They were able to match the Sekurai fighters shot for shot, and, in fact, they were better.

However, the largest task was still to come. The empress's ship was the largest and best-armed ship ever built. Every time the Sekurai Empire conquered another world, the empress wanted to be there in person—and these Orbs were like new worlds to her. The empress's ship was the most powerful, effective, and menacing in the entire Sekurai fleet. Her ship would be the biggest test to this point, and Karak was up to the challenge even if his ship wasn't.

"The Sekurai are in shock at the sight they are now being forced to see," Karak said. "The Sekurai thought the Nilg had been destroyed centuries ago. To see a force this large must be scary in itself, but when you see it's from a race that had been destroyed so long ago, it must be completely unnerving."

"The results from the battle would indicate that," Notolla agreed. "The Sekurai are running for their lives. The Nilg ships have inflicted massive damage on them. More than half their ships are annihilated."

"Karak," said the duke, "I've been able to get the weapons back online and give us fifteen percent shields."

"Then let's use them," Karak said lowly and with much attitude. "Despite the fact that they've been surprised, the Sekurai are war veterans and are dangerous to the end. We can't have them getting back into this battle and causing trouble later, so let's see that end a little quicker. Take us into battle! Guns blazing, marshal. Fire at will!"

"It seems that the Nilg ships have not only come in force, but also with some strategy," Notolla said. "They've cut off the Sekurai from getting back home. The Sekurai fighters have all been destroyed. They are now concentrating on the empress's ship, which is trying to get away, but not toward Sekurai space."

"What do you mean, they're not retreating back home?" Karak asked.

"They're moving away, but not toward home. I don't know where they're going." Notolla shook her head with a perplexed look. "They must be moving off toward something."

"It doesn't matter anyway," Karak said. "Marshal, target their weapons and fire at will!"

Notolla was looking at a sensor readout that showed the ship was covered with laser turrets and torpedo launchers. "Which one should I target?"

"Whatever's closest."

"Oh, right."

The *Malus Tempus* rushed into the battle at full speed and with all weapons hot. There were no other Sekurai ships in the area now, and the Nilg ships were attacking the great warship.

Time and time again the ship was charged, and time after time the charges were withstood and repelled. It seemed that nothing could be done to destroy the great beast. But between some of the most desperate minds in the galaxy was concocted a plan that would have to work.

The Orb Seekers had to do something quickly. They had to get this great Nilg fleet to help the Swisura and perhaps to protect the heart of Rongi space. They still had no idea how the battle in sector D:4 had gone. They didn't know if Rongi space was safe or not. They hadn't a clue where the *Quia Vita* was or what Stone Globe was doing.

"One thing I've noticed," Notolla said, "is that each time the ship is attacked from different sides, the firepower is not enough to damage it. However, when the ship is attacked by all of our ships from one side, it diverts all its shield power to that side."

"If we could attack it on a side where an important system is," Lithinia said, "while the Nilg ships attack it from the opposite side, the shield power would all be on the side of the Nilg ships."

"If we were detected in our attack, they'd leave enough shield power on our side to repel our offense," the duke observed with a look of incredulity.

"I can disguise our engines' emissions as normal pockets of gas from a destroyed fighter—perhaps one of theirs, to ensure they don't defend against us," Hiram said. "It'll only work for a short time. We have been damaged badly enough that I can't keep up such a charade for long."

"All right," Karak said. "Now, on which side do we attack?"

"The best target is always the engines," Notolla suggested.

"If we destabilize the engines, we blow them up, and if we do that, we blow up the ship," Karak said. "Let's hope this works."

"I'll link up and coordinate the attack with the Nilg ships," Notolla said. "This should be fun. I've never had a fleet like this at my disposal."

"You know what I find most interesting about this?" Lithinia asked.

"What would that be?" the duke asked dryly.

"The fact that there are only fighters here. There are no warships or escort vessels, no cruisers or scout ships. They're all fighters."

"Interesting," Karak agreed. "We'll have to get some answers when we get back to the station."

"I've sent a message to the Nilg ships," said Notolla. "I've gotten no response, but they are forming to attack the side of the warship opposite the engines."

"Attack," Karak said.

Then the Nilg navy attacked from the side opposite the engines while the *Malus Tempus* waited with armed torpedo launchers. Hiram had been successful in disguising the *Malus Tempus's* engine emissions, but due to the damage the engines had taken in battle, the disguise would only hold for a short time. As soon as the shield energy was transferred, the Orb Seekers went in for the kill.

"I don't want to fire until we're at point blank range," Karak said. "We may not get another chance to do this."

"There are no shields on this side," Notolla said. "None at all."

"The engine camouflage is about to give out," Hiram said.

"We are at two hundred meters," the duke reported.

"Fire," Karak said softly.

A pair of torpedoes were fired.

"Fire," he said softer than before.

Shots were fired again.

"Fire," Karak said even more emotionlessly and expressionless than he had before. "Fire."

A moment of breathless silent suspense gripped the crew.

"The torpedoes were a direct hit," Notolla said.

Another period of suspense took hold of Karak and his people as they waited to see the effects of their torpedoes. Everyone looked on intently.

"The ship's engines have destabilized," the duke reported, monitoring emission readouts. "Their power is fluctuating heavily. I don't think they're going to be able to fix that one." A great smile ran across the duke's face. "She's going to blow, I promise."

"Set course for Station Ynu," Karak said. "Get us there as fast as possible, and have the Nilg ships go after the main Sekurai fleet."

"Engines engaged," Hiram said.

The crew still monitored the empress's ship. A series of small fires burst out from the engine area. Once the engines had been completely destroyed, a cascading system failure spread through the entire ship. Now every system on the ship overloaded and blew out every hatch, access port, window, and shuttle bay on the entire ship. It busted into pieces, and then the weapons on each piece exploded in terrific fashion. The ship was so heavily laden with weapons that each piece of the now dismembered battleship was its own armory. The connected systems of laser turrets and warhead launchers each went off and lit space up like a firework show. A massive explosion was caused when thousands of missiles, torpedoes, and bombs went off at the same time. Every last bit of oxygen on each part and in all the storage tanks of the old war mongering vessel was burned as fuel for the blasts.

"The empress's ship is destroyed," the duke reported with a sigh of relief.

"It's been an interesting day, ladies and gentlemen," Karak said. "It's been a hard fought, deadly, eventful—interesting day." Then he paused and smiled. "We may have to do this again."

The Nilg navy had arrived barely in time to save the Orb Seekers from certain destruction. The Orb Seekers would head to Station Ynu for repairs and to collect the two Orbs that were in the vicinity of the station. Their cause had lived to see another day, but what the days ahead would hold was more unforeseeable now than ever.

☆ ☆ ☆

Chapter 15

AGRI

Despite trapping the *Malus Tempus* on the far side of the galaxy, or so they thought, Stone Globe had been unable to procure the Green Orb. The *Quia Vita* headed straight for Rongi space to find the White Orb. But directly in the path of Stone Globe had been the battle between the Swisura and Sekurai. They had taken up a position of hiding above the electromagnetic pole of a moon in the Swisura System and they made repairs while they were there. They'd stayed there for several days to make repairs after their failed attempt to turn the Swisura flank. Now Stone Globe decided to be where their opponents least expected them.

"We don't have to go completely undetected," Prak said as they watched the remaining Swisura defense forces move about the system. "We only have to get into the Consraka Nebula Cluster before they can catch us. With our newly enhanced engines, that will be easier than ever. And I do believe the Swisura are already rather occupied." Prak nodded angularly toward Levu with a raised brow.

"The Swisura engines are still more powerful than our own," Levu observed, cocking his head. "Are you sure we'll be able to outrun them to the cluster?"

"Yes," Kolij said, "as long as we aren't detected too soon."

"This is going to take work from all of us in our specific areas." Levu shifted in his captain's chair, excited for another challenge. "Prak, you try to mask our signatures so we can go undetected. Kolij, get us to the closest nebula as quickly as possible. Let's all hope we make it. Surist and Nurisk, you two work together to eliminate any extra emissions we're giving off."

"Eliminating extra emissions may be a bit difficult," Surist said to his brother, "if you still like that spicy food you always used to."

Nurisk's amnesia prevented him from remembering, but he did manage a chuckle.

"You know," Surist continued, "I could have fun with this. I could make up a whole bunch of stuff about you, all things you don't remember. You wouldn't know if I was being honest or not."

"You're already having too much fun with this." Nurisk rolled his eyes.

"I remember that one time—" Surist began.

Nurisk shot him a look that could only have been inherited from their mother and Surist turned his attention toward his station.

"So, as long as we cut to a minimum the emissions that allow us to be tracked, we should at least be able to get to the closest nebula before we're even seen," Surist said. "If we're seen, I think we can get into the nearest nebula before we're caught. We will have to battle Agri though."

"What's an Agri?" Humwe asked, not even looking up from his console.

"Not *an* Agri," Surist corrected in an ominous tone as his countenance became foreboding. "Agri is her name."

"Ok, who's Agri?" Humwe asked again, this time looking at Surist.

"That's a very difficult question to answer," Surist said, meeting Humwe's wondering eyes. "Agri is—a great space creature, for lack of a better term. She is of unknown origin and, just like many ships that enter it, seldom leaves the nebula cluster. She is powerful, calculating, cold, and heartless. Put simply, she has the looks of a large bird of prey and she destroys everything she can. We should definitely avoid her."

"Like a spider in a web," Humwe said with uncertainty.

"Exactly," Surist agreed. "She's a leviathan, a behemoth in space. She seems to just sit there and wait to attack anything that enters her lair. We know very little about her, though. Almost every ship or probe that's been sent in has met Agri, and none has come back through the cluster after an encounter with her—except one ship."

"You're trying to scare us," Levu said dismissively. "We don't have time for ghost stories."

"No," said Surist lowly, slowly, and more serious than ever as he swiveled around to face Levu. "I'm not trying to frighten you; Agri will do that all on her own. Only one ship has ever faced Agri and come back in one piece, and then only barely. Hiram, the Orb Seekers helmsman, piloted a ship into battle with Agri once. He managed to make it out alive, but his ship was nearly destroyed. It is possible to get by Agri by not encountering her in the first place, but the odds of that are slim to none. Only a few ships have been through the nebulae without seeing her. She's deadly; we should avoid her."

"I still see no other way, though," Levu said, eyeing the back of Surist's head after he'd turned back around. "We have to get into Rongi space quickly and complete this next phase of our mission. Could we go around the nebula? I know it's large." Levu looked at a stellar chart.

"No," Surist said, "we'd be in sensor range early enough to be met by the Rongi navy on our way to the system. The shortest way into the system without being detected from far away is to go through the Consraka Nebula Cluster. The cluster butts right up against the edge of the solar system. We—sorry—the Rongi have a reasonably extensive network of satellites and probes around the outside of the system that could detect us earlier than we would like."

"Well," Levu said with a sigh, "again we must make a tough decision. Let's do it."

"We need to be ready to take evasive maneuvers if we're detected before our plan allowed for it," Levu said. "We don't want to be taken by surprise. How long until they'll be able to see us?"

"About ten minutes," Nurisk said, "but it'll take them another ten minutes to catch us."

"We'll be inside the nebula before then if I can squeeze just a little more out of these engines," Kolij said. "Can I pull a little bit of power from the life support system?"

Nurisk looked toward Levu and received a nod in reply.

"I'm transferring ten percent of the power from life support to the engines, but be careful about pushing our engines that hard," Nurisk warned. "Our engines can handle it with the Sekurai upgrades, but the structural integrity of the *Quia Vita* wasn't made to handle that much thrust being applied; it was made to a one hundred twenty percent tolerance of our engine output, not Sekurai engine output."

"It won't have to hold up for long," Kolij reassured with a note of confidence, and then very unsurely looked around above her. "I'll dial it back as soon as we're inside the nebula cluster."

"It looks like our plan has succeeded," Levu said. "Continue on this course and speed."

"Our plan has succeeded *thus far*," Surist corrected. "We still have to battle Agri. That will put us to the test, I assure you."

After just a few minutes of travel, the *Quia Vita* was detected by some Swisura scouts, but, just as Stone Globe expected, there were no ships dispatched to intercept them. Such ships would not have been able to catch them. So, the *Quia Vita* was allowed to enter the Consraka Nebula Cluster unhindered, but they would not pass through it unscathed.

"The Consraka Nebula Cluster is the largest cluster of nebulae in this part of the galaxy," Surist began. "It's composed of orange nebulae on the side closest to the Rongi System. These Nebulae dampen all emissions, making all ships undetectable. This has a two-way effect; ships cannot be detected and sensors can't detect any ships outside these orange nebulae. Only by a visual account can a ship be seen by another. In the middle of the cluster are the brown-colored nebulae, which emit intense radiation that tears down shields and destroys ships. The radiation in these nebulae is so strong that it will eat the very hull of a space ship. On the side from where we entered are the pink nebulae, which enhance the shield power and sensors' sensitivity due to the high concentration of indimite. Some nebulae should be avoided while others will help."

"Is there a way through the cluster that would allow us to avoid all unhealthy nebulae?" Levu inquired.

"Yes," Prak responded, "it's a reasonably direct route with only a few detours, but it will still take a couple of days to travel, and that's if we don't run into any surprises. I wouldn't recommend speeding through this thing. The paths between the nebulae are very narrow, and we should take our time in traveling them. We may still scrape the edges of some nebulae on our way. We don't want to find ourselves fighting a radioactive nebula that's tearing down our shields."

"Let's go then," Levu said. "Due to the relocation of the battle, I think we have some time for this little part of our journey."

Stone Globe reached the edge of the first pink nebula and traveled into it with ease. The close proximity of different nebulae made it difficult to maneuver, but it was only a minor challenge for Kolij, who had navigated less impressive ships in and out of wings of Sekurai fighters before, in addition to having flown through the Kriline Defense Barrier many times. When the *Quia Vita* reached a transition area from one type of nebula to another, it was a very rough obstacle course to navigate. There was a different force and pressure on the ship's shields each time it passed from one type of nebula to another. When the ship was in the middle of this kind of crossing, it was jostled significantly.

On each side of the ship, one could view a multicolored array of light, which provided some of the most beautiful sights any of the crew had ever seen. The colors mixed with one another to form previously unseen hues. The nebulae also intersected to develop some interesting shapes. Part of the time, the ship was passing through corridors that seemingly were created with purpose. These hallways allowed for close observations and inspired many exclamations by the crew.

Shortly after entering the first stages of the pink nebula cluster, the ship was suddenly shaken and tossed about violently, but they hadn't crossed from one kind of nebula to another.

"What was that?" Levu asked urgently.

"Shields are down to seventy percent."

"That, my friends," Surist said, "was Agri. She seems to be—aggravated. We've been spotted and attacked."

"Why didn't we pick her up on our sensors?" Prak asked, incredulous of the notion that they'd been attacked. "Something that big should have registered long ago."

"I don't know," Nurisk said, "but I'm tracking her now. She's pretty big and obviously powerful."

"The substance she fired on us seems to have been a type of acid," Prak reported. "It's potency is almost more than our shields can handle. They can only take a few more hits like that, and then we'll be defenseless."

Agri, in her diabolical levels of patience and knowing the effects of the various nebulae and the paths through them, waited to strike again. She moved around in the cluster and waited for the most opportune moment. It was hours later that such an opportunity presented itself.

"I'm detecting our Agri!" Prak alerted.

"She's coming about!" Nurisk said.

"Full power to shields!" Levu yelled. "Arm all weapons."

The beast stopped directly in front of the ship and stared at the *Quia Vita*. It was her intention to stare down the crew and dishearten them. Despite her tactical superiority, however, Stone Globe would not show any signs of fear. They'd been through too much for that.

"Let's put a stop to this now," Levu said. "Fire a laser shot down her throat. Full power from all forward batteries! Let's see how tough she really is."

"Firing," Regti said.

The usual blue laser from the *Quia Vita* fired on Agri, but with no effect. Agri was able to react and maneuver very quickly, and she escaped the shot as soon as it was fired.

In response, she fired more acid to further weaken the ship's shields. Due to the blast resulting in system overloads, sparks flew aimlessly on the ship, but again the crew was undaunted despite the ship's little remaining shields. A small fire started up at the rear of the bridge.

"Our shields can't take much more of this," Regti said. "I don't know what that acid stuff is exactly, but it sure is effective."

"She has also perfected her technique over the years," Surist said, almost admiring their would-be destroyer. "There's only been one ship that's survived battle with her."

"No pessimism allowed," Levu warned Surist. "We'll be the second ship."

"She's heading right for us," Kolij said.

"Back us off," Levu ordered. "Pull back away from her. Give us enough distance that we're out of the range of her acid."

Agri then went away again and left the *Quia Vita* alone until Stone Globe crossed the border from one nebula to another. Each attack had caused the *Quia Vita* to retreat back a little into the nebulae through which they'd already come. This cost them precious time, disheartened them, though not significantly, and it also allowed Agri more area in which to attack again. The next day, she did just that.

"She's coming about again," Prak said.

"Prepare a spread of torpedoes," Levu said calmly and in an uncaring way. "I refuse to be stopped by spit."

"Ready," Regti said.

"Fire!"

Half a dozen torpedoes exited from the ship's torpedo launcher and spread out so as to hit the creature in multiple spots from the tips of her wings to her body to her head. The spread was so wide that Agri wasn't able to move out of the way fast enough, although she did manage to avoid some of the torpedoes with an agility that was exhausting just to watch. Agri was hit by the blasts and was knocked off course. On that pass she was unable to spit her acid on the *Quia Vita*, but she wasn't harmed, just stunned—and angry.

"I'm not reading any change in life signs coming from her," Nurisk said.

"Plot a course for the edge of the nebula," Levu said. "I don't want to be in her way when she's aggravated."

"We'll be there in a few minutes," Kolij said.

"She's pursuing," Prak reported anxiously, "and she's gaining on us. The shields won't hold up to many more attacks."

"She's spitting her acid," Regti said.

"Evasive maneuvers," Levu ordered quickly.

The *Quia Vita* took a glancing blow from the acid, and the ship's shields were down to fifteen percent. Agri had caught up with the little ship and was coming to bear again. Her large, predatory figure was silhouetted against a bright orange nebula as she came upon the *Quia Vita*.

"That sight was beautiful and deadly," Levu said. "Like so many other women I've known."

Kolij turned toward Levu with a wry smile. All of the sudden, the more fearful creature to Levu was inside the ship rather than outside. This interaction with Levu was the first time Kolij felt normal since her forced encounter with Mudin.

Agri then retreated and waited yet again. She had forced them back a little deeper into the nebula. She was playing with them like a cat with a mouse. She'd been toying with them for three days now on what was supposed to be a much shorter journey. Every time the *Quia Vita* would get close to the Rongi edge of the cluster, she attacked. They would fight against her, but their evasive maneuvers sent them back the way they'd come. She came back around later that day.

Agri spat again and took the shields down. With relative ease, a virtually unknown space creature had taken down the shields of the recently refitted *Quia Vita*, the most advanced ship in the known galaxy outside the Sekurai and Swisura navies.

"I've analyzed the acid," Nurisk said. "It naturally eats away at plasma. I don't know exactly how it works, but it does, and very effectively, too. I wouldn't have the technology to get this information if we hadn't upgraded the ship in Sekurai space."

"Well, we don't have to worry about the acid," Kolij said. "We're down to the hull now."

"She's hovering over us now as though she were another ship waiting to dock with us," Prak reported with a perplexed look.

Suddenly, the ship shook wildly and out of control. It began to buckle under the structural stresses. A horrible screeching sounded on the ship's hull. The crew was tossed about on the inside of the ship; everyone landed on the port side of the bridge. No one knew what was going on for a few moments. When they finally looked up to see what had been done to their ship they noticed that equipment, tools, and crewmates had been strewn all about the deck.

"She seems to be cutting into our hull with some—type of—claws or talons," Nurisk stuttered.

"How can a space creature have claws?" Levu asked with a look of skepticism. "It's ridiculous. I can't believe this."

"Nevertheless, it's true." Nurisk's eyes grew large.

"I'm tired of this," Levu sighed uncaringly. "General, fire at will. I want that creature out of my way, now!"

General Regti fired all weapons at point blank range. Two full spreads of half a dozen torpedoes each landed home, and sustained discharges from all ventral guns also hit their marks. This barrage of powerful weapons had a devastating effect on Agri. She was seriously injured and writhed in pain in the middle of the nebula. Her attack was the last thing on her mind, while revenge became the first.

"Get us out of here!" Levu yelled. "I don't want her getting mad and chasing us. Get us to Rongi space. I've seen enough of this Agri creature."

"It's too late for that," Nurisk said. "She's already right behind us. She's coming up for another attack."

"We'll clear the last pink nebula in two minutes," Kolij reported with anticipation. "Do something to buy me just a little time."

"Put the engines to full power," Levu said.

"We still won't be able to outrun her," Kolij warned.

"We don't need to," Levu responded. "I have an idea. Transfer all power to the engines."

"Engines are at maximum power."

"Agri is acting weird all of the sudden," Prak said. "She's unable to maintain a constant speed and she's spinning out of control."

"That's what she deserves for messing with us in the first place," Levu said carelessly. "Take us in close to that last brown nebula and dive away at the last second. The glow and blaze from the overdriven engines is what has blinded and burnt Agri. It's exactly what I planned on."

"We're pulling away from the nebula," Kolij informed.

"Agri isn't changing her course," Prak said. "She's flying into a radioactive nebula."

"She won't last long in there," Nurisk uttered just loud enough for the others to hear, "especially with the injuries we inflicted on her at very short range."

"Her readings are fluctuating," Prak reported. "She seems to be unable to correct her course."

"She's making no attempt to leave the nebula," Nurisk said. "Her corkscrew dive is unchanged."

"She's physically breaking up due to the radiation," Prak updated. "She isn't going to make it. Sensors are no longer registering life signs from her."

"It's unfortunate that such a great mystery of a creature has been killed," Surist said, "but if we don't get back on track there'll be many more deaths before this ordeal is over. That brown nebula will be her burial ground."

"I couldn't care less," Levu said, without the slightest concern. He had just killed the only known member of her species. But he was glad the battle with her was over and was ready to move on. To him, because of the changes that had taken place in him due to the wearing nature of their mission, she was just another obstacle to be hurdled.

"We can be in Rongi space in a matter of minutes now," Kolij said.

"What made you think of using the ship's engines to burn and blind Agri?" Regti turned to Levu with wide eyes.

"Don't know." Levu was watching the various nebulae pass by on the view screen.

"Could it be the Orange Orb again?" Surist speculated.

This got Levu's attention and he turned to face his crew's newest member. "Hmm? Oh, I suppose it could be."

The influence of the Orbs was indeed significant, as they had been told. At this thought, everyone was quiet for a time. They weren't sure what to think about the Orbs swaying them one way or another.

Kolij broke the unnerving silence as everyone was thinking about the power of the Orbs. "We're sitting on the edge of the nebula cluster, and we're getting readings from Rongi space."

"What's the status of their navy?" Levu asked.

"It's deployed and spread out throughout the Rongi System," Nurisk responded. "There are over one hundred ships out there."

"Oh, is that all?" Surist asked.

"How many are there supposed to be?" Levu asked.

"We couldn't take on that many even if we were still at full power," General Regti advised.

"There should be many more," Surist said. "Rongi ships are no more or less powerful than Braline, but the fleet should be much larger than that."

"What are they all doing deployed?" Levu asked Surist.

"I would assume they're evacuating their people," Humwe surmised.

"Some must be gone from the system, evacuating people to somewhere," Surist said, answering his own question.

"Are we in range of their sensors yet?" Levu asked.

"We have been, since we exited the nebula cluster," Surist said, recovering from a bit of absent-mindedness after the killing of Agri. "They must just not want to pay us much attention right now."

"They have no idea who we are or that we're the enemy," Prak said. "We're no more than a blip on their sensors. They don't know they should be watching out for us."

Levu's face now took on an expressionless, heartless, careless countenance. "We'll soon draw enough attention to ourselves," he said menacingly. "Has there been any move to stop or intercept us?"

"None yet," Humwe said. "All their communication lines are preoccupied with the evacuation."

"Good," Levu said in a diabolical tone. "Hold here for a while and make repairs. I don't want to go in there against that many ships without being prepared.

That night, after making a lot of repairs and trying to get the *Quia Vita's* shields back up to an acceptable level of strength, Surist lay on his back in bed in his quarters. First, he had his hands folded behind his head, a posture that might indicate he was relaxing and quite pleased with himself. Then he furrowed his brow and moved his hands so his fingers were interlocked at his waist. He twiddled his thumbs as he thought. He thought about Agri, about how she was the only one of her kind known to exist, and about how she was now gone.

Levu had crafted the plan that destroyed her. He could have just wounded her enough to get her off Stone Globe's backs. Of course, she had chosen to continue to pursue, but he didn't back down either; he persisted until she was dead. Surist knew that wasn't the kind of man Levu was. He'd seen the first signs of change in Karak too, before he left the Orb Seekers. Karak would never have fired on a ship on an errand of mercy, but he did when they first met Stone Globe.

Surist, too, had undergone a transformation. He hadn't entered into his oath with Karak believing events would unfold as they had. He thought his brother was long dead. To find out otherwise shook him in ways he didn't even know were real. He shifted his hands from his waist to upon his chest.

Nurisk knocked on the frame of his brother's open cabin door as Surist continued to fiddle with his hands. "Come on in."

"I just wanted to see how you were doing."

"Doing well. You?"

"Tired, but other than that I'm fine."

"How are the repairs coming on your end?" Surist asked.

"We have shields up to ten percent and the shield generators are charging them. We should be above fifty percent by tomorrow morning."

Surist hadn't moved from his bed or even looked at Nurisk. He continued to wring his hands.

"You're deep in thought," Nurisk said. "I shouldn't have bothered you."

"Perhaps you shouldn't have brothered me."

"What does that mean?"

"I don't know," Surist said as he felt sorry for saying something whose meaning even he wasn't sure. "I shouldn't have said it."

"Are you sorry you left the Orb Seekers?"

"Not at all," Surist said, finally making eye contact with his brother. "Everything is changing so fast, though. This mission has taken me places I didn't even know existed, inspired me to do things I didn't know I was capable of, and taught me more than I thought there was to know. It's overwhelming."

"Yes, it is. We're very close now. We need the White Orb, and then we'll have three."

"And then?"

"And then we go on searching for the others. Karak and his crew undoubtedly have some of them. So, they've done some of our work for us."

"Are we going to kill them too?" Surist asked rather pointedly, but still without attitude.

"I suppose that depends on them."

"How much is it all worth?"

"It's worth thirty-three and a half billion lives. That's how much it's worth."

"I know." Surist sighed, remembering what was at stake.

"If you're not completely on board with everything Levu asks of us—"

"No, it's not that at all. The necessary success of this mission is not in doubt. It just seems to be coming at a very high price."

"Life is expensive, not only to live, but also to keep from dying," Nurisk said.

"I know." Surist sighed again.

"I'm going to bed. If you need to talk, you know where to find me."

Nurisk then left Surist's quarters and went to his own, not to sleep, as the night decided, but to think, as he had found Surist doing.

The next day everyone was as well rested as they were going to get, and they gathered on the bridge to execute their mission to gather the White Orb.

"We'll sit here and continue repairs," Levu said. "Regti, I want you to be ready to encounter resistance. I assume they won't like what we have to say."

"We'll be ready," Regti acknowledged.

"This is not the kind of people we are. We're better than this—or at least we were before we started this little escapade." Levu settled deeply into his captain's chair and brought his hands up to his face and touched all the pads of his fingers together. "We're going to take the White Orb from them, however we have to."

"What're you planning?" Regti asked.

"This is going to be the hardest thing I have ever done," Levu said gravely, almost as an aside. Levu's voice grew still lower and he smiled maliciously as he looked with intensely piercing eyes at the view screen which showed the Rongi capital. "But it will be tougher for them."

☧ ☧ ☧

Dran

Strissen Corridor

Snek Cluster

Strant

Ghor

Station Ynu

Chapter 16

THE BATTLE OF DRAN

Narvok began replaying the audio of his captain's log. "This is a critical and lively time when the fabric of the galaxy hangs in the balance. You might not think the situation could look any more bleak, but I think a great and telling battle might be fought in the least likely of places—the middle of nowhere. In our first battle, the Sekurai accomplished the task of ensuring that Stone Globe got out of the line of fire and on with their mission, but we were somewhat less fortunate. Though we were able to defend our home, the destruction of which was not in the immediate plans of the Sekurai, we have no idea where the Orb Seekers are, or even if they're alive. The battle was more or less a draw, but any victory, no matter how small, could mean the difference between winning and losing the entire war."

Narvok poured himself a drink and sat down in an easy chair in his quarters. He took a sip and then closed his eyes and leaned his head on the back of the chair as the log continued.

"Our two great navies have parted company, but only temporarily. The area of space where we fought before is now strategically useless to our respective clients, Stone Globe and the Orb Seekers, and thus, it's been vacated. All indications are that General Rorn is leading his fleet to the Rongi System in the hopes of eliminating the small and weak Rongi navy so as to make way for Stone Globe to procure the White Orb. I hope that by this time the Orb Seekers should be nearly ready to head for home for the same reason, if they're alright. We head to the Rongi System to escort the *Malus Tempus* home and reinforce the Rongi navy against the Sekurai assault."

Narvok leaned forward in his chair deep in thought, running his finger around the rim of his glass. He looked through his cabin window and stared out at the stars.

Rorn sat in his captain's chair on the bridge of his command ship, his arms folded across his chest. He glared at the view screen. "Prepare to take the fleet into the Strissen Corridor. We must draw the Rongi fleet away from the *Quia Vita*."

One of Rorn's tactical officers turned to face him. "General, why did we not escort Stone Globe all the way to Rongi space?"

"Rongi space could not be accessed easily or quickly from any route starting at the point of battle in sector D:4," Rorn answered without even looking at his officer. "To go straight there would mean navigating our entire fleet through the Consraka Nebula Cluster."

"Surely you're not concerned about the Agri creature," the officer replied.

"Concerned!" Rorn bellowed. "Do you impugn my courage?"

"I'm sure we could easily have destroyed the creature," the officer quickly back-pedaled.

"We don't want to lose any ships to her or to the deleterious effects of the nebulae," Rorn explained. "To go around the Cluster would have meant taking the long way around, and we don't how much time we have because we don't know where our allies are."

I do hope to avoid fighting inside the Strissen Corridor if possible," Flahr Ky Gen, Rorn's chief tactical officer, said, "With stray asteroids floating within the corridor and considering the narrow walls, navigation would be treacherous enough without having to fight enemies at the same time, and the fleets would have to pass through in a line, rather than a large group."

"We will enter the corridor on the end closest to Station Ynu." Rorn turned away from the conversation.

"We should take that station for ourselves one day," Gen remarked.

"Useless," Rorn interjected. "It's in the middle of nowhere. We destroyed the Nilg; that's all that matters. We've left it as a warning to all those that might cross our border there."

"I thought we would have had some message by now," General Narvok said. "Has there been any sign of the Sekurai fleet?"

"None, sir," Major Jehn, his executive officer, replied. "They may have adopted some type of stealth technology."

"We have no way of tracking them; they could be anywhere," Narvok said, running his hand through his hair. "We've always been able to detect them before." He exhausted a heavy breath and looked at Jehn. "I think it's always good to know where the enemy is."

Another officer spoke up, "We're nearing the star, Dran, general. Its radiation emissions are affecting our sensors. We won't know where they are until they are in our weapons range."

"Try to compensate," the general replied. "I don't want to get caught without accurate sensors. That would be embarrassing. Get us to Rongi space as soon as possible."

It was at this time that a voice came over the communications system on the bridge of Narvok's command ship. It said, "I know where you are. Do you know where I am?" It was the voice of Rorn, leader of the Sekurai navy, Narvok's rival general and most lethal adversary.

Narvok gave a prearranged signal to Scit, his communications officer. "Rorn," he said, "I thought you might be heading for the Rongi System. It seems you're just as predictable as I remembered. Where are you?"

"I'm standing right beside you," Rorn said.

At this statement Narvok jumped back and made a quick visual scan of his bridge. After realizing no unauthorized personnel were there, Narvok said, "No one gets on my bridge or on my ship without my knowing."

"The hesitation in your answer suggests, though," Rorn said with a chuckle, "that you at least looked around your bridge." After a pause, Rorn continued, "If I'm so predictable why don't you tell me where I am?"

Narvok gave a look to Scit again and received an affirmative nod.

"Well, I regret that I will only be able to kill you once for your atrocities," Narvok said with a determined look right before he pointed sharply to Major Jehn.

Then, with that signal by Narvok, the entire back quarter of the Swisura fleet shot every weapon in their arsenals at a location that was able to be targeted due to the communications signals coming from that point. They were just on the edge of weapons range. Upon the impact of the weapons, a series of great explosions occurred. Many of the Sekurai ships took damage to their shields. A few smaller escort and cruiser class ships were destroyed by the barrage. The Swisura fleet had fired at every ship that was in range, and had an unobstructed firing angle on the area from which the communications signals had come. They were only able to hit the ships that were on the front lines of the Sekurai deployment, but they did significant damage to them.

"It's not stealth technology at all. They knew our sensors would be affected by the radiation coming from Dran," Narvok said, "so they waited just outside of our limited sensor range. Get our long-range sensors back up. Take power from wherever you have to. I will not be caught in a battle without proper line of sight! I'll be damned if I'm going to have to stand near a window just to see what's going on out there!"

"Fighters coming in," Jehn reported.

"Order our fighters to hold," Narvok said. "We will let the enemy exhaust their emotions before we charge them. Have the cargo ships begin laying a minefield behind our lines, leaving only a small gap between the minefield and the entrance to the Strissen Corridor. Once the mines are laid, we can move behind them and use them as a defense while also protecting the entrance."

Meanwhile, Rorn was having problems on his command ship. People and equipment had been strewn all over his bridge. His ship had been hit hard, but it was structurally unhindered. It was nothing that the experienced and battle-hardened Sekurai crew couldn't handle. "How did they find us?" he asked. "Get our systems running again! Move us to the back of the fleet while we make repairs! Order all ships to attack at once! Send in all fighters!"

With that order, Rorn unleashed a blitzkrieg, the power of which even he was not fully aware. He was usually very deliberate and calculating in his execution of battle. This was typical of the Sekurai—they were never ones to just move their horde in and destroy. They captured ships and took prisoners. They adapted technologically. They weren't just war mongers; they were smart. This was what irritated Sekurai enemies the most—other than the smell, of course.

The Sekurai warships were on their way to line up right alongside with the enemy's equal ships. This was going to be a ship to ship battle. The fighters were engaging each other in dogfights of massive proportions. Hundreds of fighters all in one fireball would maneuver in close quarters and crash into each other just about as often as they would destroy one another with weapons fire. Even the siege ships were getting involved in their usual unthinkably destructive manner. This time they ganged up on Swisura warships. Instead of one siege ship targeting one warship and taking a few volleys to destroy it, a few of them would target the same ship and destroy it with one shot from each, thus not giving them time to move out of the line of fire.

The fighters, however, were the first to clash. They met between the two fleets and attempted to make some sense out of all the fire coming at them. There were hopeless gang attacks on both sides where one wing of fighters would be under attack by numerous wings from the enemy. Some ships never saw their ends coming—they just broke apart and dropped off the map without a word. There were also those who went head on and looked their attacker in the eyes. They would fly right for one another and fire every shot they could. In these battles, if both stayed in the run, it became a question of which pilot was the bravest and would not pull away. Sometimes both were destroyed upon collision.

While the Sekurai won many showdowns with their bravery—or foolhardiness, the Swisura used tactics to win their fights. In several instances, the Swisura fighter would pull away first only to reveal another fighter behind it which would chase the Sekurai fighter to its doom. The Sekurai did, though, have a similar plan. In a seemingly one-on-one face-off, the Sekurai fighter would have a few of his comrades fly in a perfect line right behind him and extend out to his sides when they reached weapons range. These tactics caused many fighter pilots to lose their lives.

The fighters were so engrossed in each other's activities, and in staying alive, that they were unable to pay any attention to the warships that were battling each other directly. The bright green and purple fire lit up all of space to show everyone what war was really like—beauty in color, until the color of blood was all anyone could see. Each side lost many ships and soldiers, but it would be a while before either side secured a benefit.

After a long period of dog fighting, Narvok realized this battle would not be decided without making more drastic moves. His first idea was to fight a purely defensive battle. However, if the Orb Seekers walked into this battle, they would come in behind the Sekurai line. This could spell disaster for the entire operation. Narvok knew he needed to get to Rongi space as quickly as possible. He would have to do something special to remove the Sekurai from this part of space.

"Risks must be taken in life," he said in a motivational tone to prepare his bridge crew for his next orders, "and the more that's at stake, the longer the odds must be."

All of Narvok's bridge crew looked at him with uneasy eyes.

"Order the center of the front line to slowly disintegrate," Narvok spoke again. "Have one in every three ships retreat to the flanks to lengthen our line and hold there as normal. Make the center of our line just a little thin."

The communications officer relayed the orders and the ships began to disperse. After a time of maneuvering around one another, one third of the warships from the center of the line had been moved to the edges of the fleet. The extreme edges of the Swisura fleet were longer and the center was now less densely packed than it had been before.

"What's he doing?" Rorn asked.

"Perhaps the Swisura want us to bust through their center and try to bypass them completely," Flahr Ky Gen, the tactical officer, suggested. "Then, if we survived with enough ships, we would be ahead of them and on our way to the Rongi System. It's a kind of gauntlet system. They would be firing at us from all sides."

"That would indeed be a bold move, even for Narvok," Rorn admitted, squinting suspiciously. "It's a big risk on both our parts. If we made it, we could get to Rongi space quicker, and Levu and his crew could get the White Orb. On the other hand, if enough of our ships did not survive the risk, we would not be able to continue this war."

"I wouldn't recommend taking such risks," Flahr Ky Gen warned.

"I agree entirely," Rorn concurred nonchalantly. "Send the fleet directly into the heart of the Swisura line. We will crush them and leave them in our wake."

Gen gave Rorn a look of utter confusion.

"Order the fleet to move at full speed as though we were going to blast through their front line." Rorn moved to Gen's console and pointed to his map. "Then have them come to a full stop right in their middle. We'll form an impenetrable sphere of warships and destroy them."

"We would be fighting on all fronts, general," Gen warned.

"Do you think we won't be anyway? Our fighters are already going at it, and our siege ships are firing. Narvok is only waiting for the proper time to send in his dreadnoughts again, thus offering them yet another front. If we can maximize our successes before that happens, we will have the upper hand. We will fight on our terms and in our timing. I will always dictate the terms of battle if I can. I will force the issue."

While the Sekurai fleet was preparing for and initiating the sudden move, the siege ships were in rapid fire mode. They were attempting to thin out the Swisura line as much as they could before the close fighting occurred. Their devastating blasts wiped out entire warships that were unable to perform evasive maneuvers once they found they were being targeted. Some Swisura ships escaped the great firepower, others did not. Ships had a few minutes to get out of range once they could tell they were being targeted. These siege ships made a great addition to the enemy fleet and made it very difficult for the Swisura to fight battles against them.

The explosions were vast and breathtaking, and often caused damage to adjacent ships as well. One after another, ships would be warned to move out of the line of fire only to be warned again a short time later once the siege ships had targeted them again. This made it nearly impossible to maintain the line the Swisura had formed, and it was part of the reason Narvok wanted the minefield set up. It was also in his plan to first get out of range of the siege ships and then to suck them into a trap and destroy them along with the rest of the Sekurai.

Meanwhile, the Sekurai fleet advanced on the weakened center of the opposing line. The situation looked a little less sure than it had only a few hours earlier. To the crew on the Swisura ships, the sight of the entire enemy fleet advancing on their position was dreadful. If the sight of the ships themselves was not enough to scare a person, a great mass of them moving toward them struck more fear than was required to take away a well-trained soldier's presence of mind. On top of this, to then have the Sekurai war machine moving slowly but discernibly closer and carving a blazing swath right through their comrades was enough to cause one to take full leave of his or her senses.

"He's doing exactly what he should," Narvok said, smiling. "He's falling into our little trap. Let him come."

"Our center will not hold up to this attack, sir," Major Jehn warned. "There are too many."

"Are the siege ships within range of our flanks?" Narvok asked.

"No," Jehn replied. "They're barely in range of our center, but I think that's the idea, sir. They want to bust our center apart."

"So," Narvok continued, partially extending his hand, "if we were to pull our center back, they would have to move their big guns."

"Yes," Jehn agreed. "They wouldn't have to move them very far before they would be in range of the flanks."

"It will be enough," Narvok said with a gratified look.

"Pull the center, or what's left of it, back in a 'V' formation with the ends of the edges connecting to our flanks," Narvok ordered, talking with his hands as a visual. "The point of the 'V' should point toward the Rongi System and should reach behind the minefield. That'll keep them out of range longer and our weakened center will be reinforced by the mines. Tell our ships to arrange themselves as walls in this 'V' pattern, not just lines. We need to present ourselves in 3-D. That way the Sekurai can't just fly over or under our fleet, and we'll have the option to come at them from above or below as well."

The ships then matched the speed of the oncoming Sekurai warships and escort vessels and retreated into the described formation. They would only be able to go so far, though, or they would separate themselves from the rest of the fleet. This formation was no ordinary battle line.

"General," Rorn's science officer said, "the Swisura center is retreating already."

"I knew the cowards would run," Rorn growled. "They're scared of us! Now, finally, after all these centuries, we can destroy these people. They will never again be in our way. Order the fleet to form a sphere here with the majority of the firepower on their center where they're already weakest."

"Now," Narvok said, "have our flanks curve and form two large arcs and move forward, closing around the Sekurai fleet."

The extreme edges of the Swisura line moved forward, followed by the next furthest ship, then the next, and so on, until two large portions of a circle were formed and met around the backside of the Sekurai fleet. Rorn, his ship, and his entire fleet had been surrounded.

"Now bring our center back into a curve and complete the circle," Narvok ordered with anticipation of the maneuver being completed. "Open a channel to Rorn's ship."

"Channel open," Scit reported.

"Rorn," Narvok began, "I have your fleet surrounded. You have no possible chance to escape with a victory here, if you escape at all. I will give you the option, though, to preserve your lives. If you merely return to your space and stay out of the matter of the Orbs of Quality, you will not be fired upon. I hope you will end this conflict. Do you agree to these terms?"

"Send no reply," Rorn said, rubbing his hands together. "We will have a surprise for them shortly. Is the fleet in position?"

"The last ships were just placed and are ready," Tirsch responded. "Everyone is prepared."

"This is indeed a good stratagem on Narvok's part," Rorn said, "but he's spread his forces too thin. We will first destroy their former center, where the ships were already few and battered. Order all fighters to engage the nearest enemy in that area and all ships to fire at will!"

A great barrage of color and power blasted the Swisura ships. Some support vessels were destroyed. Nearly every ship in that section was damaged.

So, the battle raged yet further. This time, though, it was done in even closer quarters than it had been before. There was little room for maneuvering ability. Only the fighters could make quick adjustments and squirm out of tight situations, and sometimes not even then. The trail of laser shots from one warship to another was practically a continuous beam from several emitters flying at high speed towards the nearest enemy vessel. The siege ships continued to blast away at the Swisura capital ships. Ships were now in such close quarters that they had a hard time moving out of range once they'd been targeted by Rorn's massive artillery ships. If enough of them did move, they would open an expanding hole in the Swisura lines.

Out of the ventral and dorsal sides of the surrounded Sekurai fleet came the fighters. They came in waves—waves of hundreds. They attacked everything they could and destroyed their targets as quickly as possible. The only thing left once a wave of these gnats had gone by was a mass of charred and broken ships. Because they were purely offensive-minded, they took some casualties, but the devastation they left behind had an effect similar to that of a siege ship.

"Sir," Flahr Ky Gen reported with the typical smile of a victorious Sekurai, "our warships have reached the thin part of the enemy's line and are commencing the attack."

"Good," Rorn replied, showing his long, yellow, crooked teeth again. "Once the fleet has busted through the center of the Swisura line, we should be able to get through and reach Rongi space and wreak havoc before this enemy can regroup and come to their aid." He snorted. "Narvok thought we'd just try to ram through. He didn't count on us stopping by to pay him an extended visit. He should have counted on my superior knowledge and experience," he said with a sneer. "Oh, no, my friend, we conquer for a living!"

"Our warships report weak resistance in that area," Gen said, "but the rest of the fleet is experiencing heavy casualties. We must get through now if we are to—"

"I know we have to bust through quickly," Rorn said. "What's the matter?"

"G-general," Gen stuttered as his eyes went wide, "the sensors have detected the Swisura dreadnoughts. They are coming to reinforce their center. Our ships are also reporting that they're encountering a minefield there. It must have been just behind their lines. Once they executed their enveloping maneuver, they enclosed the mines just inside the line. Their center just went from being their weakest point to their strongest. Our forces are shortly going to be greatly overmatched there."

"How long until those ships are in range of our own?" Rorn asked quickly. "Can we train the siege ships on them?"

"It will be approximately one minute until they are in range of our ships," Gen reported, trying to regain his composure, "The siege ships are taking heavy fire where they are right now. They're under attack by the Swisura warships in that area."

"Get those ships out of there!" Rorn yelled. "Order all ships to retreat immediately."

"Retreat to where, general? We're surrounded."

"Back. Retreat back. Ignore the enemy ships. Just get us out of here. Full speed to home."

As soon as Rorn gave the retreat order and the ships moved quickly towards Sekurai space, Narvok knew he'd take a lot of casualties. The Sekurai had been placed in a situation where they had to fight for their lives—one of the most difficult circumstances to offend against. When one sees the end, he fights harder to avoid experiencing it. Narvok knew he could win this battle, but he had to eliminate every Sekurai ship in the fleet because if some did escape, they'd cause trouble later. The Sekurai would just come at Rongi space from another direction. It was the amount of time this would take that scared Narvok. The Sekurai fleet was in disorder and some of it would shortly be destroyed, but Rorn would regroup and pursue. He knew it.

As the fleet was retreating, another surprise came in to alleviate this threat. Rorn had already flown his fleet into one ingenious trap set by Narvok, and he would now send his navy into another trap fortuitously planted by Karak Jewill.

Rorn's ship was at the front of the retreating fleet when the sight made itself clear on his view screen.

"What are those?" a young officer asked. "I've never seen anything like them before. Are they our reinforcements?"

"Not hardly," Rorn said forebodingly as he staggered to his feet. "Those are Nilg ships, the likes of which no one still alive has ever seen."

"I've read about them. I thought we wiped them out centuries ago," the officer said. "I was told they put up one of the greatest struggles of any race we ever encountered."

"They were destroyed," the general responded with a look of unbelief on his face, "or so we thought. It was all our people could do to maintain the fight against them. That war took decades to win. How could a dead race come back to life only to destroy us now?"

"General," Flahr Ky Gen said, trembling. "The two fleets are in weapons range. We have the Swisura fleet at our backs pursuing us, and now the Nilg ships at our front. What do we do? How do we win?"

"We don't win," Rorn said, falling into his chair. "We die. There is no escape from this." Rorn slowly turned his head away from the view screen. His bravery had run out.

The great black ships sliced through space and targeted any Sekurai ship they found. This time it was the Sekurai who were left in a pile of floating debris, not the Nilg, as they had been six hundred years earlier. The Sekurai were surrounded and attacked from every angle. There was nothing they could do. Most of the Sekurai pilots and officers had frozen at the sight of such an old enemy coming from nowhere to destroy them. They knew of the Nilg from their training and history; this was not an unfamiliar sight, but they'd only ever seen accounts and depictions in flight simulators and historical records, never the real thing. The real thing was utterly impossible.

They could only look on as their friends and comrades fell around them, and when their time came, they were simply beaten. Even the best of the warriors managed only a few maneuvers before they were shot down. Their presence of mind had been taken away from them to the point that they were mindless sheep surrounded by two allied packs of wolves. The entire Sekurai fleet was so disheartened and taken aback that they were speechless, motionless, and dead.

Rorn's capital ship was destroyed like any other at some point in the battle. He was not taken out first because he was viewed as a threat to the operation, nor was he killed last so as to antagonize him. His ship was simply destroyed without much of a fight, as though it ever had a chance, and he became just another casualty of war. One of the greatest generals of his race's history and, indeed, in the galaxy's history, he was killed as part of a nearly mechanical process without a second thought. Rorn had no dying words, just death. Some legends, probably started by some Swisura fighter pilots who participated in the battle, told that they actually saw Rorn, or what parts were left of his dead body, floating aimlessly in space shortly after his ship was destroyed. These legends were largely not credible, but similar things had been confirmed in the past.

One by one the Sekurai fleet was destroyed, and totally annihilated they were. Not one survivor was allotted to those evil people. Each one of them died with the sight of a long dead enemy in their eyes. The Nilg fleet just swallowed them up with one swift blanket covering. The entire Nilg part of the battle took only a few minutes. The Sekurai had never been defeated to this extent in any battle, and they'd never lost a war—until now.

Once the last Sekurai ship was eliminated, the Swisura observed the Nilg ships moving off under automation, on their own, and without command. This was puzzling, but the Swisura had to get to the Rongi System quickly, and that's where they headed. Narvok assumed the Orb Seekers would follow shortly, though he still didn't know where they were. In case they needed some assistance, he sent three fighter escort ships in the direction the Nilg fleet had come from, for he thought Karak might've had something to do with this pleasant surprise. It was Narvok's supreme hope that Levu and his crew had not gotten by Agri, but his instinct told him otherwise.

✗ ✗ ✗

Chapter 17

THE BLUE ORB

At precisely the same time the decisive battle in the Swisura/Sekurai War was being fought outside the Strissen Corridor, the Orb Seekers were moving toward Station Ynu. "I sure am looking forward to some rest off of this ship," Lithinia said.

Karak made eye contact with Lithinia. "This ship has done us well."

Notolla nodded in agreement toward Lithinia. "Yes, but I'll welcome a few hours of new scenery on the station and some delicacies from home."

"Station Ynu is a very different place than when we last saw it," Hiram observed as the *Malus Tempus* limped her way toward the Rongi outpost.

"When we left the station last, the entire area was derelict," Karak added. "There was no life; it was an old, derelict space station long abandoned."

"Even the air was stale until the we turned the power back on," Notolla said, her eyes growing wide with the sight now. "The place was unkempt and powerless. Now look at it."

Now, since a Rongi warship and its escorts had arrived a few weeks earlier, the station was alive, bustling and functional. As the *Malus Tempus* made its way closer, they detected not the dead and desolate area they'd left nearly a month before, but a fully manned and stocked outpost awaiting their arrival. It was an oasis in the middle of a desert, and it was no mirage.

After he and his crew got the communications system working again, Karak had sent word to the station about the battle with Empress Mudin and her fleet. "Station Ynu," began Karak, beaten, battered, and filthy, "the Sekurai offense is likely to be headed for our home. The fleet of Nilg ships has gone in that direction as well, with what intent, I don't know."

"Our people have no hopes of defending ourselves against such a powerful enemy with the sole purpose of destruction," Station

Commander Nal said with a worried look. "The Sekurai would leave devastation in their wake. I've studied the records since arriving here."

Karak shifted in his seat at the thought of Sekurai ships in Rongi space. "I sent a message home when we first left the station in hopes that the praetor would send an expedition to investigate the abandoned station. I had no idea the station would play such a vital role."

His hopes had come true, and his carefully thought-out actions had paid off, even though some of the crucial parts, such as the Nilg ships, had not been in his plan at all. The Orb Seekers were greeted with escorts from the station, and they were astonished at what they saw when they docked and went aboard. They greeted Commander Nal upon docking and disembarking.

"I cannot fully express my gratitude for your help, Commander Nal," Karak said.

"I knew you might need it. We had to do a lot of work when we first got here," the commander said with a sigh, "but we got the place up and running. We were amazed to find a few dozen ships here when we came out of the Strissen Corridor; we simply didn't believe the shipyards would have been operational. All the ships in the fleet you've seen are running on automatic. We don't have enough men here to man them all, even if we could control them. They're running themselves, and I would say they're running amok, but they seem only to be targeting our enemies. The ones we've kept here for station defense are manned. They were built after we took control of the shipyards. It was a good thing you set those shipyards in motion before you left—otherwise you'd have been killed by that empress's ship."

"We didn't set the shipyards in motion," Karak said instantly and without thought. At this point in the journey, nothing phased him. "We just left the life support on and docking ports ready to accept your arrival." He frowned. "The ships worry me greatly."

Commander Nal developed a grave look on his face when he realized there was a massive uncontrolled fleet of ancient but powerful ships on the loose destroying entire fleets. The Nilg ships had destroyed the empress's ship, annihilated the Sekurai home navy, and then set course straight for Rongi space—for what purpose, none of them knew.

"How did you get the station in order as quickly as you did?" Hiram asked. "It must have been an interesting mission, considering the evacuation activity that must be going on back home."

"Praetor Jarob decided it best to have a fallback plan in case you failed," Commander Nal answered. "We've been adding to the defenses of this station, exploring the space around it, evacuating as many of our people to this place as we could, building ships for defense—which you've seen on your way in—setting up trade routes from home to here, and scouting for you."

"We read in the logs of this station about the Sekurai and thought you might run into them, if they were still a civilization to be reckoned with, so we prepared to assist you. Based on the information the logs provided, we deduced that the Sekurai Empire might stretch to somewhere near here. The bit about this station being a buffer between the Nilg home world and the Sekurai was quite telling. And those ships that were already built when we got here were an impressive sight. We didn't know what to make of them. The shipyards just kept producing them. They were automatically producing them; they needed no labor whatsoever. Apparently, Nilg technology was much farther advanced six hundred years ago than ours is even now. Those shipyards must have been stocked with all the parts to build an entire fleet of ships, and build they did. Eventually we did gain control of the shipyards too. That took some playing around with the computer, but we got it done and began cranking out a few ships and manning them for station defense."

"We very nearly met our end," Field Marshal Notolla added, pausing to look around like the station was somehow home, but not quite, "several times. It's been tough this last month or so."

"I'm glad to see you here," the commander said. "Your ship is being seen to as we speak. We thought you might be coming home this way, since you had an outpost here to run to. That's why we got the station running quickly—and it was the perfect place to start evacuating to. We knew you would only stop here if you needed to; otherwise you would head for home nonstop."

"Let's just hope Levu hasn't caused any trouble," Lithinia said, almost as an aside. "With that enhanced ship and his strategic brain, he could really wreak some havoc at home."

"Who?" the commander inquired.

"That's a long story," Karak said with a shake of his head. "Perhaps we can discuss it later, over our first good meal in nearly three weeks." A forced smile appeared on Karak's face. "I'm afraid it's been a very long and tiresome journey. We could all do with a bit of a rest."

"In the meantime, Lithinia and I can take care of gathering the Red and Black Orbs," the duke of White said. "The Red Orb is in pieces just outside the defense turrets around this station and the Black Orb is a little further out past the other side of the station, but it's in pieces in space as well."

"Yes, go ahead," Karak said, nodding. "I'd like to have them whole and on hand as quickly as possible. We'll have to head for home first thing tomorrow. We still have a lot to do." He sighed as he looked at the floor, a little distracted. "The deck plates don't vibrate on a station like they do on a ship. That shaking used to bother me. I guess I'd gotten used to it. Everything changes."

"I'd like to see them safely aboard as well," the duke said as he smiled and put his hand on Karak's shoulder to bring him back into focus. "Four Orbs doesn't sound as good as eight, but it sounds a whole lot better than two."

The duke and Lithinia went out in a scout ship while the *Malus Tempus* was under repair to collect a piece from both Orbs whose fragments had been scattered in the space around station Ynu. They took the Green Orb with them so they could forge the Red and Black Orbs. Even from outside the station, they could easily see the great differences their people had made to it.

"There's life there now," Lithinia observed. There were ships coming and going, and these ships were recognizable; not strange Sekurai ships bearing down on them, not Cruxfix patrol vessels accusing them of having entered their space from the wrong direction, and not even the friendly Swisura ships that were of such odd design. No, these were proper Rongi ships. The defensive turret rings had been extended, augmented, and more rings of Rongi turrets were added to the station's repertoire with which it may have to defend itself.

Once Lithinia and the duke compensated for centuries of extremely mild spatial drift, they were able to find the Orbs quite easily. The Red

Orb was between Station Ynu and the Strissen Corridor. The *Malus Tempus* would have passed near the Orb "wreckage" when they ventured to the station the first time. The Black Orb, on the other hand, was on the far side of the station and farther out in an empty region of space.

"The differences in the station are remarkable, don't you think?" Lithinia asked, trying to spark conversation. "It must have taken some doing to get it all up and running so quickly."

"We could never have done such a job if we had a lifetime to stay here," the duke responded as he looked back at the station. "I'm sure it took several teams of engineers, a lot of man hours, and tons of supplies."

"It's unfortunate we can't take time to rest here," Lithinia added. "I'd like to see the station more extensively."

"You're right, it's very unfortunate," the duke said. "But I think we'll be back here, one way or another. I'd like to learn more about what went on here all those centuries ago. Maybe a little visit will be in order if we can get back home, defeat the Braline ship, gather the Orbs, and see if they'll destroy this band of energy that threatens Tris."

There was a bit of a pause in their dialogue when they realized that as far as they'd come, they still had no guarantee of success. They still had a great deal of work to do.

"I hope it's just for a visit," Lithinia finally said, "and not as a last outpost for our people. I'd hate to run into the same fate as the Nilg, especially when we're this close to meeting our goal for this mission. And, honestly, I'm tired of calling it a mission. This hasn't been like any mission I've ever been on. We've been shot at, threatened, betrayed, started a galactic war, been up and down emotionally, and we're not done yet."

"It's been trying, that's for sure, and you're right, it's not over yet. We can still fail."

"We're nearing the position of the Black Orb's pieces. How do you want to go about this? One of us can go out in a suit."

"I have already prepared for these Orbs. I thought they might be a little tricky. The cargo area is ready," the duke said knowingly. "I'll just open the hatch and you bring some pieces into the bay by reversing course."

The small craft then halted with the cargo hatch open. A few pieces were brought inside the ship by default as it reversed and swallowed up space dust and debris along with a few black rocks. The duke went to the cargo hold and gathered up the pieces. He then returned to the fuselage with some pretty black rocks.

"Why didn't you go ahead and re-forge it?" Lithinia asked. "We brought the Green Orb."

"I thought it might be nice to show Commander Nal how these things are reassembled," the duke answered. "You remember how stunned we were when we first saw a broken Orb re-forged."

"All right, that's one. Let's go get the other one. Hopefully, this will go easily also."

As they traveled to the coordinates of the Red Orb fragments, their conversation continued.

"I'm hungry," Lithinia said. "What do you suppose Commander Nal will have for supper?"

"Rongi food. That's all I care about."

They both laughed at this, but not only had it been weeks since they'd had a good meal, it had been even longer since they'd had familiar fruits and vegetables that were agreeable with their digestive systems. They hadn't experienced a home-cooked Rongi meal since they'd left home.

"I miss my kids," they both said together.

"What do you miss most?" Lithinia asked. The duke gave her a blank look, suggesting the answer was fairly obvious.

"No," the duke said. "Honestly, I miss the familiarity of home. I knew where things were, where I was going, what I was going to be doing with my day and my week. I even miss the tension of wanting to be at home with family, but also wanting to get out of the house full of women and spend extra time at the office."

"I can understand that," Lithinia said with a chuckle. "My kids are still little. I wonder if I'll be able to tell how much they've grown. I wonder if they'll recognize me at all."

"Oh, I'm sure they'll be very glad to see you. We're coming up on the coordinates of the Red Orb fragments."

The same process was repeated in gathering the Red Orb. The small mission went easily and the duke and Lithinia returned to the station in time for supper with the commander.

The table had been prepared with foods of such a variety that everyone found numerous things they were thankful for. There was much discussion about the Orb Seekers' mission. The commander reported that the last known course of the Nilg fleet was taking it into the Strissen Corridor.

"They were out of our sensor range some time ago, and they went out of communications a short time before that—not that there's anyone on board to communicate with," the commander said.

"I am pleased to report, however," Commander Nal said, "that the *Malus Tempus* will be fully repaired and ready by morning. My chief engineer gave me the word just before supper."

"That was fast," Notolla said.

"We made it our top priority. We didn't know how long you'd have before you had to get going again. Now, you said you were going to tell me about some character you met out there among the stars."

"Yes," Hiram said. "We first ran into Levu Earsp just beyond the Cruxfix System. There we discovered that he's on the same mission we are. His civilization is in trouble too. Their people face the same fate as ours—not in the same way, but a catastrophe threatens a star that is part of a delicate gravitational balance. Their entire solar system will be sucked into a black hole if they don't get the Orbs."

"We battled just past the Cruxfix System and were victorious through some very unorthodox strategy from Karak," Notolla said.

"Then, after they had allied themselves with the Sekurai, their ship was enhanced, and we were no match for them," Hiram said. "We had to use the retreat strategy effectively."

"Always a very interesting strategy," the commander said. "I have always admired those who can use the retreat effectively. It shows stealth, cunning, guile—"

"It shows we were in over our heads before this mission even started," Karak interrupted, not without attitude.

"Based on how things progressed, the next logical step would be for them to go to our territory, just like we did theirs," Notolla said.

"Commander Nal," Karak said, "tell us, how is the situation back home? How many people have we been able to evacuate?"

Nal's pleasant smile disappeared from his face as though he was hoping to avoid that very question, though he knew it was inevitable. Everyone deduced the answer was not going to be one they wanted to hear.

"Not good," he said simply. "The Band continues on its projected course. Many theories about what to do have been thrown around, but none have proven logical or practical. That's why we're evacuating people to this station as quickly as possible. We're already beyond capacity here, and eventually we'll run out of supplies here anyway. The navy and government are working around the clock trying to come up with some answers, but so far, they have very little to go on."

"But this station can't hold enough people to preserve our culture, let alone the entire population of the system," the duke said. "We would eventually be reduced to a databank."

"It can't hold enough," Nal said grimly. "Not even a drop in the bucket, really. We have resorted to doing 'everything we can' instead of what will work. I don't mean to put the pressure on you, but if you fail, our lives and legacy will end."

"We've been under immense pressure of late," Karak said, "We haven't buckled, and in fact, we've grown from it. We won't back down now. We will succeed. We've met with some success already, but we won't stop now."

"If what you say is true and you have killed the leader of these evil Sekurai, then we have a glimmer of hope," the commander said, "but you still need to obtain the last six Orbs. Some of them you may find, but if this rival of yours already has two of them, you will have to take them from him, and that seems improbable, considering his ship is far more advanced than anything we have."

"Actually," the duke said, "we've been doing some work. We now have four Orbs."

Now Lithinia raised the Green Orb from its resting place at her feet. The duke of White then touched a small Red rock to its surface, and the Red Orb was forged right in front of everyone. The commander was beside himself at the sight. He'd never seen anything like it before. Not only did the entire Red Orb simply forge itself before his very eyes, but the color of the stone was exciting. It was of a deeper red than blood pouring from an open wound. A piece of the Black Orb was touched to the Yellow Orb ever so slightly now and instantly formed a black ball of rock that was glassy and smooth on the outside. Their majesty captivated the station commander to a point of near hypnotism. Once he was retrieved from this state of deep thought and amazement, his attitude had changed a little.

"I still say you'll have a hard time of it," he said, "but if what I've seen here is any indication of the power of these things and your ability to procure them, we may yet have a chance."

"Then you will understand why we need to leave in such a hurry," Karak replied. "The Blue Orb awaits us next. We must leave tomorrow morning."

"Everything will be prepared for your trip," the commander said. "Your ship will be repaired, as I've said, but I'll see to it personally that you're supplied sufficiently."

The next morning, the Orb Seekers gathered in the hangar where the *Malus Tempus* had been docked the day before and repaired. The ship was like new. It was ready to complete its mission, procure the last few Orbs, and carry them to Rongi space.

"I thank you for your assistance, commander," Karak said as he and Nal placed their right hands on each others' right shoulders. "I think we should make it home in short order now, and with a much smoother ride. The ship had taken much damage, and it was quite an interesting ride here from the battlefield just outside the Sniguri Nebulae."

"Hopefully you will find the Blue Orb quickly and get it to our people," Nal said, "I had more information downloaded into the *Malus Tempus's* computer that may not be of help to you, but it should explain some things. I think you'll find it interesting."

"If we're successful, I'm sure we'll return when we can stay and rest longer," Hiram said. "It looks like you've fixed up a very nice place here. I might like to establish a residence here after all this is over."

"Yes, and we didn't get to see the half of it," the duke said.

"Time is of the essence," Nal said.

"Yeah, yeah, yeah," Karak mumbled as he walked away and boarded the *Malus Tempus*. "Time is always of the essence. It's essential to find a time when time is not of the essence."

With that, the Orb Seekers loaded themselves on the ship and set course for Strant, the location of the Blue Orb. The small asteroid was located on the Cruxfix side of the Strissen Corridor on the end closest to Station Ynu. The journey would not take long, but finding the Orb in the middle of the immense radiation could prove difficult.

The *Malus Tempus* flew through the large defenses of Station Ynu and headed for Strant. The crew was on the last stage of their journey, and they knew it. They were all anxiously awaiting the thrill of being back home among their own people, but there was much to be accomplished in the meantime.

"How long until we're in sensor range of Strant?" Karak asked impatiently. "It's about time we got there."

The duke looked at his computer. "If I remember the level of interference last time—"

"Oh, just answer my question," Karak interrupted.

"We're just about there," the duke said dryly.

"We are coming into a large area of wreckage," Hiram reported. "It's difficult to navigate."

"Cut our speed," Karak said, annoyed at slowing down. "We don't want to have a collision. Can you identify the debris?"

"I can't yet identify any markings on the pieces," the duke responded, "because there is so much of it. The mass of the debris field is consistent with that of an entire fleet of battle ships, and a large fleet at that."

"What destroyed them?"

"Now that I can tell you. They were shot down."

"Interesting," Notolla interrupted. "I thought they were shot up."

"I think the appropriate term is 'shot around'," the duke said, "The scattering of the debris indicates the victor surrounded the loser. It must have been an impressive enveloping maneuver."

"Is there any indication as to which way the victor ran?" Karak asked. "That might give us an idea of who won."

"No," the duke said. "That will take some time to figure out. I'll have to recalibrate the sensors to search more specifically through all this radiation interference."

Karak sat motionless for a moment. "I think you'll find the most recent battle between the Sekurai and Swisura was fought here."

"How do you know that?" Notolla asked.

"I'm not sure." Karak's expression showed he was thinking deeply, but was uncertain about his thoughts. "Intuition, perhaps. I think the Nilg were here too, and I think the good guys won."

He wasn't yet aware of it, but the Red Orb had made a subconscious connection with him. It was through that connection and the Red Orb's allowing clearer deduction about the outcome of battle that Karak came to this conclusion. They would have to conduct sensor sweeps to find out more precise details.

"Notolla, you and Hiram stay here and find some answers," Karak said. "Lithinia, Notolla, let's go find an Orb. Hiram, set us down on the rock to drop us off and go explore for information about this battle. I want as much information as you can get. If it was a battle between the Sekurai and Swisura, it's important to know the outcome. I'll signal you once we have the Orb. And if either of you finds a long-lost brother out here, shoot him down—or up, or whatever it takes!"

Karak then took Lithinia and Notolla and the newly forged Red Orb onto Strant in search of the Blue Orb. The asteroid was so small that it was hardly large enough to imagine an Orb being placed on it. Soon, however, Karak and his crew would find that the size of the asteroid did not make finding the Orb any easier. There were other factors of irony working against them.

They exited the *Malus Tempus* in their environmental suits and gravity boots with grapples and tethers, the same as those in which they searched for the Yellow Orb on Enarf, and turned to watch the ship launch itself back into space. The blackness of space was quite extraordinary with the asteroids, ships, and massive debris field set against it. Due to the lack of an atmosphere, the detail of everything was clear and vivid. The *Malus Tempus* could be seen as it circled the wreckage area in pursuit of much-needed answers. They observed three Swisura scouts coming into the area and were glad to have reinforcements.

"All right, let's make this quick," Karak said. "Remember, these suits are made for repairs on the outer hull of the ship, not for asteroid exploration. We need to be careful—we don't want to rip any holes in them by pulling against a jagged rock."

"That'd be our luck," Notolla said.

Karak, Lithinia, and Notolla turned around to face the surface of the giant rock on which they now stood. To their surprise and extreme disappointment the entire face of the asteroid was littered with blue rocks. The surface itself was blue—and no ordinary blue. It was almost the shade and concentration of the color they expected to find in the Blue Orb itself. Even if a fragment of the Orb in question were seen, it would be nearly impossible to discern it from any other ordinary rock on the asteroid. It was as though the Blue Orb had been shattered to dust and covered the entire surface of the asteroid.

"I thought this would be fun," Field Marshal Notolla said. "Now I think it will only be troublesome."

"Considering the size of the asteroid," Karak said, "I thought this would be an interesting but short mission."

"And now it looks to be a challenge and a use of what little time we have left," Lithinia said. "I would suggest bringing in reinforcements."

Karak nodded.

"Karak to *Malus Tempus*," he said, speaking into his suit's communication system.

"We're here," Hiram responded. "Three Swisura fighters have just arrived. Narvok sent them to escort us back home. They're giving us an account of the battle now. Is everything all right down there? Are you all okay?"

"Well, technically yes, but things just got interesting. Have your escorts land their fighters here on the surface. There'll be just enough room for them, but I think we will need a few extra pairs of hands."

"They're on their way," Hiram said.

The fighters landed on the small asteroid a few minutes later, and the pilots exited their craft after grappling the ships to the surface to avoid them drifting off the asteroid. Once they took a look around, they were as surprised at the sight as everyone else. They first remarked at how beautiful the asteroid's surface was. Then they were told exactly what they were looking for and their reactions changed considerably.

"Okay, folks," Karak said with an irritating sigh, "the Red Orb is lying on the ground over there in the center of the area. Just find a blue rock, which shouldn't be hard, and throw it at the Red Orb. If it touches the Orb and forms a Blue one, we can go. If not, try again."

Notolla picked up a blue rock and touched it to the Orb. "Darn," she said with no emotion when it didn't form the Blue Orb.

This was how the afternoon was spent. Instead of taking an hour or so to find the Blue Orb and talking with each other about what all had gone on recently, they were trying to find the right rock. They were having a contest to see who could hit the Red Orb with the next rock they could pick up, but it was rather unexciting. There was some talk about the happenings in the battle, but it wasn't how everyone had imagined it. It was irritating.

"Generally, I wouldn't mind spending an afternoon throwing rocks at things," Notolla said, "but we are sort of in a hurry here."

Almost half a day had gone by with no luck. The group started on one side of the asteroid and tried to work their way to the other end. For a while, some of them had the impression the goal was to get all the way to the other side without finding a piece of the Blue Orb.

"This is intolerable!" Karak exclaimed as his most recently thrown blue rock hadn't forged the Orb. Though the respite had been nice, the entire group was still under a lot of stress, especially Karak. He'd been showing more and more signs of it. He'd been increasingly short with his answers, rather withdrawn, impatient, and, in general, just not his usual self. Having to search all over for this Blue Orb wasn't helping matters.

As they were a little more than halfway through their selection of rocks, one of the escort fighter pilots threw a blue rock and struck the Red Orb with it. Everyone had become so accustomed to disappointment and to seeing their projectile rocks deflected off the target Orb that they didn't notice that this latest shot had forged the Blue Orb. The pilot who threw the rock simply turned around to pick up another stone to hurl in that general vicinity. The rock in Karak's hand actually disappeared. "What just happened?" Karak asked no one in particular. He just looked at his empty hand. "I would've sworn I had a rock in my hand."

"I think I've found it," the pilot said, unsure even of himself.

Everyone looked over at the Red Orb and saw the Blue one sitting there next to it just as though it had been doing so all that time.

"I guess that rock I was holding was part of the Blue Orb too," Karak said.

They all gave each other incredulous looks, picked up the Orbs, and called for the *Malus Tempus* to come and pick them up. The fighters took off from the asteroid and resumed their formation waiting until the Orb Seekers were all aboard and ready to go.

"I would like to meet up with our allies and thank them for their help," Karak said as he returned to the bridge. "Let's head for home."

"Those are welcome words." Hiram had a tear in his eye as he set course for home.

While Stone Globe was still weaving through the Consraka Nebula Cluster and battling Agri, the Orb Seekers were heading for Rongi space. The ship turned and made its way through the Strissen Corridor. It would be another several days home through the Strissen Corridor, just as it had been to Station Ynu when they'd left home. The Orb Seekers were glad to be going home, and they couldn't wait to get there.

Even the short stay on Station Ynu was a bit troubling for the Orb Seekers. They were glad their discovery was working for their people, but the experience helped show some negative things as well. Their mission was not nearly over. More to the point, however, was the fact that they had gained so many new experiences in such a short time that they felt like it was difficult to relate to their own people. The Orb Seekers had been changed by their adventures, for good in some ways and for bad in others. They were worn down, tired, and overwhelmed.

The Rongi they met at Station Ynu were in the military or sciences. They were explorers, and yet they were so small-minded, knowing only of home. Commander Nal and his officers had no real clue what dangers lay out there in the vastness of space. Other than Agri, they hadn't encountered anything "out there" before, and Agri was just something the Rongi people largely avoided. Karak and his crew hadn't had that luxury. They had to face the endless perils of deep space exploration. Their quest to save the Rongi civilization had set them apart from their own people. Karak knew this in his subconscious; he hadn't put it into so many words yet, but he detected that his relations with his own people had changed in an irreversible way.

⅀ ⅀ ⅀

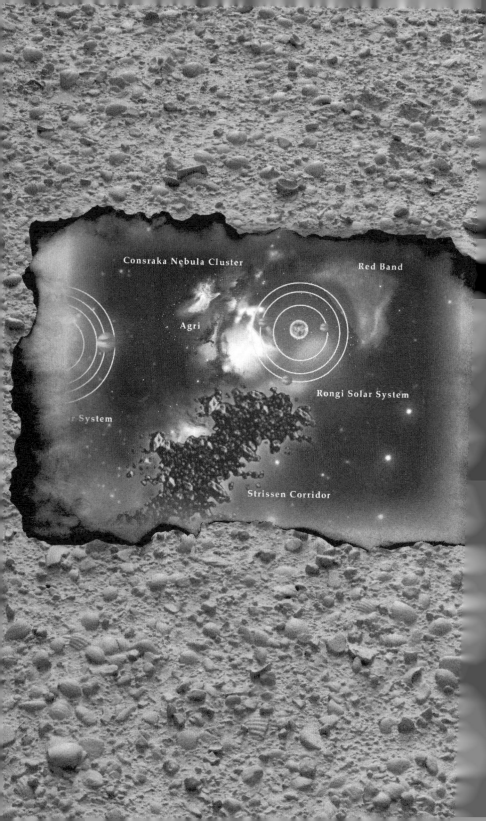

Chapter 18

THE WHITE ORB

After the destruction of the creature Agri, Stone Globe began repairs on the damage to their ship. Agri, the most unexpected of all the challenges that Levu and his crew had faced, other than the Orb Seekers themselves, had done a number to the *Quia Vita*.

"The damages to the *Quia Vita* are extensive, despite her enhancements," Regti reported to Levu on the bridge. "Without the Sekurai upgrades we would have been destroyed. That creature's vicious talons latched onto and ripped out numerous power cables and caused system overloads throughout the ship. We've had to bypass those systems and rig exposed wiring on nearly every deck and in almost every corridor in order to get power to the necessary systems."

Levu finally turned to face Regti blankly. "Agri was a fearsome creature. Now, though, her book is closed. Or, perhaps, her story was only a chapter in the great many volumes which tell a small part of the history of the galaxy. Either way, her story is over, and she's gone, relegated to story, legend, and the mists of time. We have drawn first blood in Rongi space."

Levu rose from his captain's chair, picked up his staff, and thumped it on the floor. "Now we must turn our eyes to another target. The war is not over yet."

Stone Globe knew nothing of what had happened concerning the Nilg and the Sekurai empress or the entire Sekurai fleet. Nor did they know the Swisura were heading for Rongi space at the moment. In addition to this, no one at all knew where the Nilg ships had gone. This was a mystery, but no one had time for it just now.

Stone Globe had to accomplish the task of obtaining the White Orb, which was housed in the capital city on Vock I, the planetary headquarters in the Rongi System. The Rongi hadn't had a clue, until the Orb Seekers were given a copy of all Cruxfix information concerning the Orbs' locations, that they had been sitting on an Orb of Quality for many centuries. Even now, the Rongi government and people were not aware, only Karak and his crew knew. It was a fate of happenstance that the Rongi had gone to Braline space to collect the Yellow Orb and the Braline had come to Rongi space to gather the White Orb.

"Upon entering the Rongi system, we will come to a magnetic minefield," Surist said, "and then the system's automatic defenses."

"I have the minefield on my sensors," Prak said. "We'll have to do something about it. The ship won't survive if we try to go straight through. There are too many mines. If they weren't magnetic, we could navigate through, but they would latch onto our hull and destroy the ship, even if we were running at maximum operating efficiency."

"Just another obstacle," Levu sighed, tired from the journey. "You'd think we've been through four lifetimes of obstacles on this journey, and still have enough impediments left over to stub our toe really good."

"We're nearing the mines now, Levu," Prak said slightly impatiently.

"Yes, yes," Levu responded irritably. "Move us to a safe distance from an explosion that would occur in the middle of their present location. Launch some debris from one of the badly damaged decks, and make sure the metal is magnetic. Those mines can be neutralized easily."

Humwe saw to this personally. He gathered a large piece of the bulkhead and a few other pieces totaling sufficient mass, which, when all was pieced together, was enough to attract all of the mines in the area the *Quia Vita* needed to sneak through, and loaded it—along with some other debris for good measure—into one of the torpedo launchers.

"You can fire from the starboard launcher anytime," he said as he returned to his post.

The metal chunk was then shot toward the minefield just like any other torpedo, except at a greatly reduced velocity. When it got within the mines' magnetic range, they gravitated towards it and eventually clung to it. It was the clinging that activated the detonator within each mine. The time delay was only a few seconds. Not all of the necessary mines had made it to the debris before those that made it first exploded, but more than enough were in range of the initial explosion to cause other mines' detonators to go off as well. Once all the necessary mines had been set off, it was safe to proceed into Rongi space.

"We're approaching Vock I," Kolij said after a few minutes of travel. "We are now being hailed. They're asking us to identify ourselves."

"It's about time someone noticed us," Levu said with a wry smile. "We won't respond just yet. We'll make them think. They have no idea who we are or what we want."

"The automatic defenses have been armed," General Regti reported. "We have incoming."

"They're preset to engage ships that don't identify themselves," Surist informed.

"What does this defense consist of?" Levu leaned toward Surist.

"Five large torpedoes with heavy explosives that will detonate on impact," Surist said.

"Can we shoot them down?"

"Only because of the weapons improvements the Sekurai made to our ship. Without the upgraded sensors, weapons, and targeting systems we would have to run; those torpedoes could destroy us even now."

"I want you to knock them out," Levu said. "Take them offline, but don't destroy them. I want to capture them."

Regti targeted the torpedoes with the forward laser batteries of the *Quia Vita* and fired a wide beam, medium intensity burst, which was of greater power than the typical blast from a Rongi ship, and each projectile was disabled in one group with one shot. They were now dormant, their explosives disarmed, and simply still gliding toward the *Quia Vita*.

"Bring those torpedoes aboard," Levu said. "Make sure they're rearmed and ready to fire as soon as possible."

"Those shots would be of little use to us," Regti said. "There are five of them, and there are hundreds of Rongi ships."

"Proceed, and don't forget to install Sekurai tracking and warhead yield enhancements in them," Levu said emotionlessly. "I have no intention of using them on their warships."

Humwe suddenly turned from his console sharply, "Surely you aren't suggesting—"

"No, I'm not suggesting that we target their sun," Levu said defensively and loudly, showing the stress of his situation. "I'm suggesting that, if we can't solve this situation diplomatically, we clear ourselves a path on the surface to get to the White Orb."

"That would mean killing innocent people," Nurisk said. "We could never do that! Then we'd be no better than the Sekurai."

"No!" Levu rose from his captain's chair and jumped toward Nurisk with clenched fists. "We're already as bad as the Sekurai because we've allied ourselves with them. We will tell the Rongi navy that if they make any move against us, we'll destroy their major cities." Levu then calmed a little. "But I can't see that being forced upon us. After all, they're trying to save their people as well. Then we can have the location of the White Orb cleared of all people who could try to stop us from taking it."

"So, you're bluffing?" Kolij questioned.

"I'm bluffing—unless they call my bluff," Levu answered.

"What if they don't clear out?" Surist asked. "Are you going to kill my family and friends?"

"You're already a traitor!" Levu screamed at Surist as he finally absolutely lost his composure. "What do you care?"

The bridge remained quiet for a time now and Levu regained self control. Kolij, one of his oldest and best friends with whom he'd served many times and under great pressure, had never seen him like this. He was an emotional being, very passionate and dedicated, but he'd never launched at one of his own crew before. And he'd never before hurt her ears just by yelling. But Levu calmed.

"Humwe, send the Rongi government a message," Levu ordered. "Tell them we're coming down to their museum of history and we're going to take an artifact. If they attempt to stop us, we will destroy them with their own torpedoes. Send it now."

"How many people are in that city?" Surist asked.

"Over eighteen million," Nurisk answered.

"I said earlier that what I might have to do would be the hardest thing I've ever done," Levu began. "If the people in that one city try to stop us, then thirty billion will die because of our inaction. I've never killed an entire city of people before, and I'm giving them the chance to avoid it now. Even though one life is priceless, thirty billion sounds a whole hell of a lot worse than eighteen million." Levu calmed again, almost speaking to himself. "'Compromise' can be the dirtiest word with the most devastating consequences; it is simply the nature of sentient beings."

"You sound just like Mudin when she says, 'I don't care,'" Kolij observed without thought.

Everyone knew that, despite Levu's apparent careless disregard for life, he was right. Thirty billion casualties were less acceptable than eighteen million. His comrades, also tired, worn down, beaten up, and still anxious, could not help glancing at each other around the bridge of the *Quia Vita*. They saw a change in Levu they never thought they would. He'd been such a diligent, magnanimous, and heartfelt man for so long. Now, however, he was rationalizing the killing of millions of innocent people who were themselves fighting against time to stay alive.

While Regti was in the torpedo bay, Kolij, Prak, Nurisk, Humwe, and even Surist wondered if any similar change had happened to them in the past few weeks. Being the people of principle they thought and hoped they were, they would have talked some sense into Levu by talking him out of this extortive and murderous plan, but they were no longer the same people they'd been either. They were not the same people who had left the Braline System with nothing more than a hope and a small, weak ship. They were not the same people at all. Their captain was carelessly ready to kill, and they were indifferent in their readiness to let him.

After Regti in the torpedo bay and Nurisk on the bridge had spent time trying to get the torpedoes ready for their mission, Levu wondered why the Rongi weren't moving to at least find out what the unknown and threatening ship was doing in their area. Surely they weren't so wrapped up in their evacuation to not inquire as to the nature of the strange vessel making demands.

"Levu, we've received word from the Rongi government," Humwe reported. "They say they've evacuated the area around the museum and will not attempt to interfere with us."

Levu sighed and briefly closed his eyes. "Regti, target the other four torpedoes for the most heavily populated parts of the planet. I've already set the computer to fire them if we're targeted by any weapons. As long as we aren't interfered with, no one will get hurt. I really don't want to see anybody else get hurt either, but we have to do this."

"The torpedoes are set and ready to launch. They won't be able to shoot them down due to the enhanced target tracking system. The torpedoes will maneuver to avoid being shot down."

"We'll shuttle down to the planet. Kolij, take us right next to the installation where the White Orb is," Levu said. "This shouldn't take too long. Nurisk and Prak, stay here in case anyone gets any ideas."

The Braline shuttles were the exact same shape as the *Quia Vita* herself, but much smaller. The small pyramid shaped craft flew into the atmosphere and glided through the clouds as it continued to descend until it hovered closely over the museum where the Orb's pieces rested. The shuttle took a front row parking space as it landed just outside the front door.

"Regti, scan the area," Levu said once the ship had settled. "Make sure no one is around. I want to know they've kept their word."

"The sensors show the surrounding area is clear. There doesn't appear to be anyone around."

"Okay, let's go get ourselves another Orb. Get the ship ready to take off as soon as we get back. Let's be quick about it, too."

Levu then exited the shuttle with Regti, Humwe, Surist, and Kolij. They entered the museum and found a map of the establishment just inside the entrance. The two halves of the White Orb were displayed in a glass case at the very heart of the building. So, they proceeded through the corridor and took the turns the map indicated.

They passed by several unique artifacts and displays detailing the history of the Rongi people. There were pieces of artwork from every inhabited planet in the system. Levu and his group did not have time to tour the facility, but they did take note of some items as they hurried past. There was the first piece of literature known to exist on each planet. These were collections of stories and epics that exaggerated tales of history that had been passed down through the generations. There were several pieces of armor and weaponry, most of which was worn or wielded by important individuals. Other displays were of scientific firsts such as medical equipment and manufacturing tools. These items spanned through the ages and the many thousands of years from the earliest artifacts to some more recent interstellar accomplishments.

Alongside the two Orb halves, which were until now a mystery even to the Rongi people, were several objects of great historical significance. These were the crests of each planet's leaders when the galactic alliance of the solar system was formed. It was because of these individuals that the Rongi were one people. In the very heart of the case sat the White Orb's sections, there on display because of the striking color of the pieces and for the somehow perfect division of the sphere into two exactly equal halves. Evidently the Orb's greatness had once been known to the people of Vock I, but it would've been stored in safekeeping had its power been truly realized in today's era. This was one object which they managed to keep, despite its having been cloven in two at some point, without being able to preserve the legends and stories behind it or the significance of it. Generally, things worked just the opposite. The legends would remain and, in fact, be spread with exaggeration, embellishment, and self-indulgence on the part of the storyteller, whereas the physical object would be lost.

"All right," Levu said with great anticipation, "let's get this thing into one piece and get out of here. I'll feel much safer once we're on our way home."

Kolij pulled the Purple Orb from the pouch that hung from her belt and prepared to hand it to Levu. He used his walking stick, and in one quick, fluid, experienced motion he smashed the glass case and it shattered all around. This destructive motion was made by Levu without a care in the world for anything that did not suit his purposes. Glass shards were strewn about the case and floor. The museum alarm blared.

Levu picked up the two halves of the White Orb. He set them on a nearby table and held them up to each other as though the Orb were still whole. One could not tell the Orb had ever been broken when it was held like this. The crack which separated the halves was invisible.

Kolij approached with the Purple Orb and set it on the table on the end opposite the broken one. She guided the Orb as it rolled on the table toward the white fragments. Levu continued to hold the pieces together perfectly as the Purple Orb came in contact with the White pieces. As they touched, nothing happened. Levu and his crew members looked at each other as though they'd been tricked, but when Kolij picked up the pieces of the White Orb, they were no longer pieces. The Orb had been forged after all. The usual effect of pieces materializing seemingly out of nowhere didn't happen because all the pieces were already there.

"Okay, people," Levu said hurriedly, "let's get out of here."

Kolij, carrying the White Orb, started to walk away with the others, but then she dropped the Orb. It was shattered this time, however, and the pieces scattered along the floor away from the central spot where the whole Orb hit, like ripples on a pond when a stone is dropped smack in the middle. Some pieces slid under display cases, some lay on the floor, some bounced and disappeared. Now that all of the Orbs were re-forged, they were all more easily broken.

Levu heard the Orb bust on the floor. He knew what had happened even before he turned around. He looked at Kolij such that he had never looked at anyone before, not his kids when they looked him square in the eye and did something he'd told them not to do only three seconds before, not his wife when they had arguments that could curl the carpet, never. It was a look of death.

"How can you be so clumsy?" he bellowed with a growl so deep and so loud it hurt his own throat. "What are we supposed to do now?"

Unable to say anything else, Levu's eyes squinted as he glared at Kolij. He scrambled for his blaster. Kolij recoiled considerably. He jerked his gun from its holster and pointed it at his longtime friend. At the last moment, he stopped himself, just barely regaining control. He put his blaster back on his hip.

The weight of the situation combined with the momentary inconvenience had blinded Levu to such a simple solution of re-forging the Orb again just as they had done a moment ago.

"We can re-forge it!" Regti yelled. "We just have to touch the Purple Orb to it again, and everything will be fine."

Levu loosened up. He sat the Purple Orb down on the sheet of White Orb dust that now blanketed the floor of the museum, and the White Orb was instantly re-forged again. Neither he nor Kolij said anything to each other.

Levu simply turned to leave as he had before, and Kolij followed after a momentary pause as she considered what had just happened.

They hurried down the halls and through the museum. They just wanted to protect their new prize and get to safety aboard their ship.

In a few moments, the shuttle lifted off the ground and flew through the sky of Vock I as it made its way back to the *Quia Vita*.

The whole crew had changed, but not quite to the extent Levu had, for he also had them for whom to be accountable. The weight of several worlds was squarely on his shoulders. It was more than any person could handle, but Levu had done better than anyone else could have. As he was stealing the White Orb from Karak's people, the only person alive who could possibly relate to Levu's situation was Karak himself, and he was the enemy.

"I don't want to be here when Karak arrives," Levu said as they returned to the bridge of the *Quia Vita*. "Kolij, plot the quickest course to the Consraka Nebulae and engage at full speed."

The *Quia Vita* reached a position of sufficient radiation within the Consraka Nebula Cluster so as to hide them from view effectively.

"We're now masked by the radiation coming from the nebulae around us," Kolij said shyly. Now for the second time on their journey she didn't want to look Levu in the eye.

"Hold and wait here," Levu said as he pressed the tips of his fingers together just in front of his face. "This is where we will lead Karak when he arrives.

"But if Karak doesn't know Agri is dead, will he venture out here?" Regti asked.

Levu nodded. "He will come. Trust me; he will come. He has to; he needs our Orbs." He took in a long breath. "It won't be too long before the fate of both our peoples is decided."

☥ ☥ ☥

Chapter 19

THE MEETING OF THE ORBS

In the deep, dark lair of a dead beast, the *Quia Vita*, battered and damaged, settled and waited, assuming the place of the former and longtime occupant of the nebula. Levu felt as though he were the spider in the web, just waiting calmly, patiently for the next meal to come or the next opportunity for him to strike. Now he knew what it felt like to be Agri—he only hoped his fate would be more to his liking than the one he'd rendered upon her. Though she was dead, he and his crew still feared to turn their backs on the nebula cluster; they constantly looked over their shoulders, even on the bridge surrounded by old friends and colleagues. It seemed that something foreboding of a blacker and deadlier nature awaited them. Little had been known about Agri; she'd never been studied. It wasn't even a scientifically proven fact that the creature was female, but it was always referred to as 'she.'

"Karak knows we have to get home with the Orbs, the same as he," Levu said, "and he will be coming. Because we made it into the system through the Consraka Nebula Cluster, it can be reasoned that we killed Agri. Which means this path is now the safest option instead of the deadliest. He will look for us here, and here is where we will fight him."

After a pause, Levu continued with certainty and attitude. "I want a decisive ending to this rivalry. This ship is more powerful, and we shall duel against Karak, to the death if need be, inside the edge of the cluster. The *Malus Tempus* and her crew will be all alone in the cluster against a superior foe, the stakes for each incalculable and all on the line." Levu wanted this to be the final confrontation between himself and his greatest rival. He'd battled twice before with Karak. This would be the third time they'd done battle against each other, and both were determined it would be the last.

The *Malus Tempus* was rocketing back home for various reasons now. The crew, anxious to complete their mission, had endured a long and tiring journey, and it wasn't over just yet. They had made enemies and formed alliances; they had suffered loss and achieved victory, and they'd even started one of the biggest wars the galaxy had ever seen, but they still hadn't accomplished their mission. They also felt an increasing urgency to get the Orbs, all of them, to the Rongi System to save their people if they could. They had pushed their engines to the limit again.

It was likely that Levu would be there waiting for them, having resolved to take the Orbs from them, but they still had a few hours before they arrived home.

"So, what was that information the captain gave us back on the station?" Lithinia asked.

"It was an explanation of me," the duke of White said.

"I didn't think there was such a thing," Notolla joked.

"It's not really relevant to our journey, but it's intriguing," the duke began. "My position on Vock I is the duke of White. I never understood where the 'White' came from, but now I know."

"What's it for, then?" Hiram turned to face the duke with a furrowed brow.

"It actually has to do with the history of the Orbs," the duke continued. "It doesn't detail the story of the Orbs, but it explains why my predecessors and I have been called the dukes of White.

"When the Orbs were scattered throughout the galaxy, some of them were found by the people of the planets on which they were left. The White Orb was the second one the Cruxfix people left intact instead of broken. On Vock I, a horrible and bloody war was raging between the two continents, one in the north and one in the south. A great strike force was sent to obtain the White Orb for the southern continent. Each side thought the Orb was a source of power and would give them an advantage, and, thus, a victory in the war.

"The Orb was deemed so precious that the general of the attacking army, Hrak, saw to the matter personally. And the defending army's general, Timter, who had originally found the Orb, was there to personally defend it. This was the only time the two men ever met. The armies battled for days, weeks, in fact, before they were done. No outcome was reached, and no ground gained.

"On the last day of the battle, the two generals met face to face at the Orb and they both determined that it would belong to him or no one. It was by Kinsel, the sword of Hrak which is now housed in the same museum as the White Orb, that the Orb was struck and split into two perfectly congruent sections. The Orb lay on a bed of primitive explosive powder. When Hrak struck the Orb, a spark ignited the powder. That's how the seventh Orb was destroyed, but not shattered, only split in two.

"There were only ever two pieces of the White Orb. The two halves of the White Orb were taken and put in the museum where they now lie—or, at least, we hope Levu hasn't captured them yet. Through the ages, the legend of the Orb died off. People stopped telling the story, so it was forgotten. Since the Orb was placed there, the keeper of the museum was called the duke of White. It was this keeper's job to make sure nothing happened to the Orb pieces, but that, too, was lost. When people stopped trying to get to the pieces for evil purposes, the position became irrelevant, but it had gained a certain notoriety. So new duties were given to the dukes and they, too, forgot the Orb. The story faded away."

"How do we know all this if it was lost?" Notolla asked.

"The Nilg were consulted by the Cruxfix people about a suitable place for one of the Orbs to rest when they decided to disperse them," the duke answered. "Vock I was where they suggested, and they continued to keep an eye on the Orb fragments for centuries until their own demise. They were among us for some time without our knowing. That's when the Nilg learned our language. When we sent a message to Station Ynu, their communications system recognized our language and responded accordingly. The Nilg presence in our system ended shortly after the Sekurai/Nilg war began. Apparently, what little Orb information we did have came from the Nilg."

It was only a few hours after Levu took up his position in the center of the web that the *Malus Tempus* appeared on sensors. Levu was surprised at what he saw. He expected the *Malus Tempus* to be alone.

"Levu," Prak reported, "the Orb Seekers' ship has arrived on the edge of the system. But they aren't alone; they're being escorted by a group of three Swisura fighters."

"That makes things more interesting," Levu said, stroking his beard. "We need a diversion to break those fighters away from Karak."

"What if we fired one of those torpedoes?" Regti asked.

"No," Levu said. "Then they could pinpoint our location. We will have to wait for an opportunity to present itself. They will have to separate and search if they hope to find us before a very long time—and time is one thing neither of us have."

Meanwhile, on board the *Malus Tempus*, Karak was talking with Praetor Jarob over a communications channel trying to assess the situation.

"At last check, they were heading for the Consraka Nebula Cluster," Jarob said. "I would imagine they are gone with those three Orbs now."

"I don't think so," Karak corrected. "They need the five Orbs we have. They'll be waiting around for an occasion to strike so they can take these Orbs away from us and get them back to Braline space."

"Then perhaps it would be wise to bring your Orbs down here and then go find the others," Jarob suggested.

"I would usually agree," Karak said, "but if we get those Orbs in fragments, which will happen if we have to destroy the *Quia Vita*, or if Earsp is defeated and decides on a scorched earth policy, we'll need at least one whole Orb with which to forge them again. Besides, bringing them down to you would take time, and we can't afford that."

"Whatever action you choose to take, do it soon," the praetor warned, looking away for a moment to check his other computer. "The Band is only a little more than a day away."

"Alright, we'll make it quick," Karak said half serious and half joking. "I'll ask Levu to just be a nice little boy and give up his toys. Hiram, take us to the edge of the cluster."

It wasn't long after the *Malus Tempus* reached the cluster that Karak realized they were going to have to go in after Levu. They didn't have time to wait for Levu to come to them. The Red Band was too close to just sit and do nothing. But this was exactly what Levu wanted, and Karak knew it. While the *Malus Tempus* had her three escorts, the *Quia Vita* would be outmanned, outgunned, and outmaneuvered. However, if Karak and his group could be drawn into the cluster, they would have a hard time communicating and getting sensor readings due to the radiation. With the *Quia Vita's* Sekurai equipment, Stone Globe would be more powerful than each of the ships they would be going up against, but less powerful than the group combined.

"We won't be able to communicate well at all in that mess," one of the escort pilots said. "We'd be best to stay out here."

"We can't just sit here," Karak said. "We have to get those Orbs and be home in less than a day. I'm sure that Levu can hold out just beyond our sensor range for longer than that. I don't know exactly what his timeline is, but I do know what ours is and we don't have time. We have to go in."

"If we do go in, we should be sure to stay within sight of each other," the pilot said. "Make sure you have someone at each window to—"

In mid-sentence the pilot's message ended without warning. His ship, which was clearly visible through one of the *Malus Tempus's* bridge windows, exploded.

"One down." Regti operated his console to try to target another ship. He had to align the shot by eye due to the intense radiation in the nebula. The *Quia Vita* was on the exact edge of a large and particularly dense nebula, where they couldn't quite be detected, but they could still see out of the nebula with the naked eye. Targeting sensors, along with most other sensors, were not functioning well. He warned Levu that he was extremely unlikely to be able to repeat the feat.

The blast was quick, precise, and far too effective for the Orb Seekers comfort level. The Swisura scout ship was shattered, reduced to pieces floating innocently out from the center of the former ship. Parts of the pilot himself were seen silhouetted against the great blackness of space. For that brave soul, that cold, dark abyss and vacuum would be his grave.

Each of the other escort ships immediately broke off from their positions and executed evasive maneuvers. They shot off with great acceleration. One corkscrewed to a point far above the *Malus Tempus*, whereas the other performed an identical exercise in the opposite direction taking up a relative position beneath.

Karak, however, had something much more aggressive in mind. "Charge the nebula!" he yelled, pointing to no specific place on Hiram's stellar map. "Order those fighters to move in above and beneath us. We'll outflank the enemy and surround him. That should end the battle quickly enough."

More shots were fired from inside the nebula, but Hiram was able to maneuver around them once he had the ship moving. Hiram sent the ship hurtling toward the nearest nebula. The crew were pinned to their seats by the force and Hiram's corkscrew maneuver spun them around significantly. The *Malus Tempus* was grazed twice by the powerful laser shots.

Lithinia shook a little as she turned to Karak. "We've just now entered the nebula."

Karak had plans to get the Orbs, though. The *Malus Tempus*, thanks to the wonderfully random and thus unpredictable maneuvers by Hiram, was able to get inside the edge of the nebula rather easily. Once inside, their sensors were cut to a very short range. They could detect very little, certainly nothing specific. They were blind, but the *Quia Vita* wouldn't be any better, for they had gone deeper into the nebula to avoid the Orb Seekers.

At this point, the two Swisura fighters were spotted above and below the *Malus Tempus*. They could all see each other and kept this formation to search for Levu.

"Bring us up a ways behind one of the fighters," Karak ordered. "I know what he will do."

Levu could not yet reveal himself for open combat. He was still outnumbered three to one. Despite the fact that the *Quia Vita* was the most advanced ship in the nebula, she was no match for the combined firepower of two Swisura scouts and the *Malus Tempus*. It was unlikely, too, that he would have the opportunity to strike again as he had before. His enemy was ready for him now, and they were performing a well-planned and well-thought-out search.

"We're in a rather dense portion of the nebula," Kolij said. "Shall I hold us here so as to continue to avoid detection?"

"No," Levu said. "It's a law of physics that objects are more likely to find one another if one of them is stationary. We need to keep on the move for now, looking for any tactical advantage." He turned to Kolij. "It's entirely possible they have maintained a vertical formation identical to that which they took when we destroyed the first fighter."

Kolij just nodded and operated her console. "I'm bringing us to a point consistent with your assumption."

A moment of the thickest, quietest tension began as everyone eyed the view screen. "I've filtered out as much of the interference as I possibly can," Prak reported.

Regti squinted at the screen. "I think there's something right in front of us."

"Hit it with all forward batteries!"

The *Quia Vita* fired its guns with all available power and the explosion was such that it was clear on the screen. They had taken out another Swisura fighter.

Just as Levu and his crew had leaned back in their seats, thoroughly satisfied with themselves, the *Quia Vita* was jarred impressively. The *Malus Tempus* had taken up a position behind the fighter escort, just as Karak had ordered, and blasted away at its enemy with its full arsenal.

"Evasive maneuvers!" Levu yelled, realizing he'd fallen into a trap.

"I knew Levu would assume we hadn't changed our formation. He snuck right up behind that fighter alright, and we did the same to him!" Karak hadn't a thought for the Swisura fighter pilot who'd just given his life for the Rongi people. Again, all would stew in the intense waiting.

An hour passed. No sign was seen of the *Quia Vita*. Kolij had done well in plotting courses that did not allow the *Quia Vita* to be found, but late in the second hour, Notolla waved her arm.

"What is it?" Karak whispered, going to his side.

"Something in the distance there." She pointed at the window.

"What did you see?"

"I don't know, but it doesn't look like something that should be in the nebula."

"We can see the scout from the window," the duke said, "so it isn't her. It could be the *Quia Vita*. It could also be a Swisura ship that's entered the nebula to help."

"Did it look like it could be a Swisura ship, Notolla?" Lithinia asked, with considerable tension in her voice.

"It could be," Notolla said, "but I can't be sure."

"Has the scout seen it?" Karak asked.

"I signaled her to look, and she spotted it as well," Notolla responded, "but she wasn't sure what it was either."

"Motion to her that we will all go and investigate," Karak ordered. "Let's see if we can find out what that is."

So, with the *Malus Tempus* at the head, the two ships moved towards the area of the unidentified craft.

"It's the *Quia Vita!*" Notolla said.

"Have they identified us yet?" Karak asked.

"Their course appears to be unchanged," the duke responded, "but the radiation prevents an accurate reading."

"Can we open a channel to Levu?" Karak asked.

"It would be patchy at best," Lithinia said. "I might be able to clean it up a bit."

"Do what you can."

"Channel open."

"Levu Earsp, this is Karak Jewill. We've been searching for you for a while."

"Prepare two salvos of torpedoes set to high yield," Levu said. "We'll even the field yet."

"Torpedoes ready," General Regti said as he operated the appropriate controls.

"Fire!"

Half a dozen torpedoes per spread, one for each pursuing ship, were fired from the aft launcher of the *Quia Vita* and detonated in the faces of both pursuing ships and their crews. The blasts rocked the ships hard and gave the crews a ferocious jolt. On the *Malus*

Tempus, sparks flew due to overloaded systems. Screens went blank for a moment. Bulkheads were blown off their placements and one hit Hiram squarely on top of his head. He was knocked unconscious. Karak ran up to take the helm. The scout was hit even harder and was jostled violently, spinning out of control and having been blasted in a direction that sent her uncontrollably away from the fight. Lithinia left the bridge.

"What's our damage?" Karak asked, as he initiated evasive maneuvers.

"The scout appears to have been taken out of the battle," said the duke. "The torpedoes fired at us detonated a little farther away than those fired at her. Life support is operating at reduced capacity. Shields are still useless in here." He looked up at Karak. "We'd better inflict some damage on the *Quia Vita* while we can."

"Let's show them we aren't here to play. Give them sustained fire for thirty seconds from every forward battery on this ship."

Karak turned the *Malus Tempus* to aim its forward weapons at their foe and Notolla barraged them with shot after shot for half a minute. At the same time, torpedoes launched at the *Quia Vita* as quickly as the launchers could be reloaded. The emitters on the forward guns were exceeding their heat limits due to the heavy sustained fire at full power. Karak was not playing around. He had to get the Orbs and he didn't care who or what got in his way. There was a complete lack of hesitance from him in issuing the orders that could well lead to the destruction of the *Quia Vita* and the deaths of everyone on board. The entire area was lit up like a pyrotechnic display in the night sky. Little or nothing could be made out during the barrage.

"Weapons are overloading," Notolla urgently reported.

"See if you can target some of those dense gas pockets with your last shot or two!" yelled Karak.

Notolla wasn't able to hit the gas straight on, but she was able to ignite some stray fumes that lead to the pockets. When they exploded around the *Quia Vita* on all sides, the result was the immobilization of the *Quia Vita*.

Lithinia came back to the bridge carrying the Blue Orb. She looked deeply into it as she knelt next to Hiram, whose head lay in a pool of his own blood. Lithinia, with no medical training whatsoever, grabbed a medical kit and began tending to Hiram's injury. The Blue Orb had effected its influence on Lithinia, who had hoped it would do so. Lithinia, in turn, applied the inspirations from the Blue Orb to her treatment of Hiram's wounds. The Orb did not tell Lithinia what to do, but it did offer her clarity for the situation. She knew to raise Hiram's head and bandage his wounds in a particularly effective way to stop the bleeding.

"The *Quia Vita* has sustained damage to her sensors and engines, but I have no way of knowing the extent of the damage. The interference is too much for our sensors," the duke reported.

"That's a tough little ship," Hiram said, picking himself up and assuming his station once more. The crew looked at Hiram and found themselves in grateful disbelief of what had just happened. But there was no time for words; they were deep in battle.

The *Malus Tempus* was rocked again by another discharge of the *Quia Vita's* forward batteries.

"I'm reading a massive power build up. It's so large that its registering on sensors even through the radiation. The *Quia Vita* must be powering up her weapons for a serious attack," Notolla said. "Brace for impact."

"Evasive maneuvers!" Karak yelled. "Fire torpedoes!"

Hiram made a few quick adjustments, creating random movements to avoid the largest part of the firestorm while Notolla fired as much as she could. The *Malus Tempus* only took a few glancing hits. The *Quia Vita's* systems were seriously damaged, but weapons were operating at capacity.

Hiram did well avoiding fire, especially since the *Quia Vita's* engines were down and her targeting systems would be affected to at least some degree by the nebula. Notolla was able to get some shots off every time Hiram's maneuvers had them facing the *Quia Vita*. The *Quia Vita* was slowly taking damage and would soon have to resort to another plan.

At that moment, a great crash sent the *Quia Vita* hurtling. The Orb Seekers had realized the *Quia Vita* wasn't mobile and brought all their weapons to bear again.

"Life support is failing," Prak reported. "Our entire sensor network is fried, structural integrity is compromised, and the engines are out. Weapons are all we do have."

"Open a channel to the *Quia Vita*," Karak said.

"Channel open," Lithinia acknowledged.

"Levu," Karak said, "by the look of your ship from my window, you've been roughed up a bit."

Kolij whispered into Levu's ear that she had maneuvering thrusters back online.

"I still have enough weapons to kill you with," Levu blundered, even though he knew this was no longer a viable option.

"You wouldn't get one shot off before we blasted you out of the stars," Karak said. My people need the Orbs, all of them, and you have three. You will now drop those Orbs into space and leave them behind you. You will then go on your way." Karak moved closer to the microphone. "Or we will destroy you and then take them."

"My people need these Orbs as much as yours," Levu pleaded.

"I don't care," Karak said as emotionlessly as Empress Mudin had said to Levu when they first met. "If my people weren't in dire need, I'd actually help you. But my own people's interests have to come first. Now, the Orbs." Karak held out his upturned hand and poked a finger from his other hand into his palm.

"Levu," Karak continued, "we have you. The only way out is through failure or death. Choose failure, and at least you will live, and you can go help evacuate as many of your people as possible."

"We've already lost too much time!" Levu yelled, unable to hold back tears. There was a pause after this outburst. Everyone on the open channel sympathized with Levu's situation.

"This mission was supposed to save our people, not cost us precious time. We couldn't have evacuated enough anyway." It was at this point that Levu realized the total unrelenting gravity of his situation. A unique quality of hindsight had set in. He couldn't have known things would go this way, but now he couldn't be at all surprised that they had. For the duration of their trek, there had been hope of success. Sometimes it was small and fleeting; other times it seemed as though they couldn't help but accomplish their mission. But there was no way out of this one.

"Failure or death," Levu whispered, echoing Karak's words. Life seeped from his eyes. His tone changed and his expression went blank. Even the White Orb's power to affect his sense of morality couldn't compete with the level to which Levu had descended. His humanity had, completely without influence from the White Orb, taken him farther than that Orb could help him to recover from. "And what if I choose death?" he asked, equaling Karak and Mudin's emotionless quality.

"Then you will die," Karak said instantly and uncharacteristically. "Would you really choose that end for your crew, who have gotten you this far?" Karak asked after a pause.

"Would you leave me nothing to show for my efforts?" Levu asked.

"I would certainly leave you your life."

Wholly unsatisfied with Karak's offering of his life, a thing left meaningless to him because so many of his people would now be let fall to their deaths, Levu then took the controls from General Regti and prepared a preprogrammed automated firing sequence designed to bring down the full onslaught of the *Quia Vita's* enhanced arsenal upon Karak Jewill, now the source of all evil and the target of all hatred. He set the wheels of the *Quia Vita's* massive Sekurai arsenal, including the five augmented Rongi defense warheads, into motion. The Sekurai may have recently been destroyed by the Nilg and Swisura, but their legacy could still be felt if it were delivered by the *Quia Vita.*

Levu had began this journey as a benevolent, kind, loyal good deed-doer of a man. But now had transitioned into a vengeful, hateful, spiteful, repulsive man. The transformation was complete. Levu tilted his head slightly and looked down at the hole in the floor for his staff. A shard protruded from the hole, broken in the melee. The rest lay strewn on the deck. He spoke to himself, still over the open channel. "In the effort to do a good thing, a great man has become the very emblem of horrible, detestable vileness in the galaxy. It was all to save my people, but I failed, and, in so doing, I've destroyed myself." Levu again could not look up to face the opponent that had finally defeated him, let alone to face his valiant crew. He'd moved further and further away from that which he was, and had been taken, by circumstances and decisions, without which the whole endeavor would have failed far short of this decisive moment, to an unrecognizable, loathsome man who was not even deserving of pity for how far he'd fallen.

And at the last, at the very last, the end of desperation, Levu, in his heart, thrust upon his mortal foe the equivalent of a lifetime's buildup of hate, malice, and unwavering and utter contempt, though it had only been built up over a short few weeks' time. "I despise you, Karak, with a blinding fierceness and with an unrelenting and careless wave of all-consuming and unmitigated vengeance." He was consumed not by his desire to accomplish the mission, not by the holiness of his quest, not by the justness of his cause, not even by the necessity of success and the fate which now lay unalterably ahead for his people, but by his inability to accept the unchangeable fact that he'd already been beaten.

He would now unleash a barrage that would otherwise be unmatched in all the conquests, in all the wars, in all the galaxy were it not for the brazen enemy who lay immediately before him, but utterly beyond his reach. Levu's fists tightened. The grudge he clenched onto with his clutches as though existence itself depended upon their holding more tightly than was possible and for the eternity of eternities had become woven into his soul and spirit and it ate away at him in the most thorough of senses. It gnawed on him; it eroded everything intangible that filled the shell of his body until his will, essence, and substance of his personality and character were no more and had all been replaced with unholy emptiness and nothingness, save for levels of hate and hate and hate that were the awestruck envy of the devil himself.

He reopened the channel with Karak. "I take to hell with me enough knowledge and character that relates to your own, as we are linked in likeness and on the understanding that your fate must therefore be inextricably tied to my own, to secure your eternity there alongside my own pitiable soul. We are the same, and thus will our fates be the same. Karak, today completes the establishing of the link between our two tortured and despicable souls, locked in this fray by which ever-fleeting life tenuously hangs in the balance. I will pull you down with me through the depths of the furthest, most fiery, blackest inferno, to the coldest reaches of hell's chasms and there, for all times, we will battle once more and forever until eternity closes in around us and finally snuffs us out."

His crew, unable to bring themselves to stop him due to how he'd led them so far from home and so close to their goal, sat and listened. They could not agree, for they had not fallen so far as their leader, but they also could not challenge his words or actions, for they, too, had changed, and not at all for the better. Their souls had been penetrated, infected, and irreparably altered by this mission and the oppressive weight of it that bore down on them. They knew of this alteration and were not pleased with what they'd become, but they had become it nonetheless. They'd betrayed the very things they sought to protect. They knew what shape their fate would take due to Levu's decision now, and they quietly rejoiced in the fact that they would not have to live with themselves as they had become. They took some small measure of comfort in the fact that their families would remember them for what they had been, and not the monsters they'd devolved into.

Surist sat at his console and stared blankly at its screen. He had begun as a member of the Orb Seekers, but he had betrayed his oath and his own people in favor of joining his long lost brother, Nurisk. The strain of provincial thinking, which he'd sworn off and which had annoyed him at Rongi Council to such an extent, was the very thing that motivated him to betray his people. But he could not have made another choice; his conscience would not have allowed it. If he'd stayed with the Orb Seekers and been on the winning side, he would've fought against his brother and then watched Nurisk die. There were no thoughts of the Rongi people during this short time of reflection for Surist; this was the culmination of his selfish and provincial thinking.

As those last words of Levu's were uttered, Levu reached for the firing controls and conjured up in his mind a picture of his family back home. He saw his wife, the woman he loved more than life itself, as she was today, having gone through life with him. He could not honestly say that she was young and pretty as she had once been, but, to him, she was beautiful. He also saw his children standing with her, though he did not perceive them as the young adults they were now, but as small children who had no question of the love their parents had for them. The entire faded and somewhat blurry picture in Levu's mind lasted for only a fraction of a second. It was distorted by a haze, and he couldn't even be certain he'd seen anything at all. At the same time, he activated the firing sequence at the *Quia Vita's* tactical console.

Just as the unleashing of the ship's weapons was to be brought down on the *Malus Tempus* and the laser emitters flared, the *Malus Tempus* launched every weapon they had at the *Quia Vita*. Having already sustained massive amounts of damage, it never got a shot off before it was totally obliterated and reduced to dust.

Almost before the *Quia Vita* was done exploding, Karak gave an order. "Hiram, take us to the debris field. Prepare to take on wreckage. We need those Orbs." Karak had no thoughts for Levu, but only for the Orbs. He had become a man obsessed with saving his people, a good thing, to be sure, but also a man who'd become numb to the plight of the Braline and to everything and everyone else.

Karak and his crew had undergone a similar change as Levu and the rest of Stone Globe. They'd been to the far side of known space and had seen and done things they never thought they could. They had taken part in a great war that had torn the galaxy in two and seen the destruction of two entire races, the Sekurai and now the Braline. They had been good people who did evil things in order to accomplish a necessary goal.

The *Malus Tempus* moved to the position previously occupied by the *Quia Vita* and took into its launch bay as much of the debris as possible in the hopes that pieces of the White, Orange, and Purple Orbs would be among the remnants. The duke, Notolla, and Lithinia went to the cargo hold and turned off the gravity plating. Dust, which was all that was left of the *Quia Vita* and her crew, floated aimlessly in the room. They had taken the five Orbs they'd collected and flung them across the hold through the weightless dusty debris hoping the whole Orbs would come in contact with at least one particle of each of the Orbs that were destroyed in the explosion of the *Quia Vita*.

One by one, the Orbs were re-forged and made whole. They were re-forged in midair in the cargo bay, and as this happened, they were included in the effort. This was the first time in at least a thousand years that all eight Orbs were intact and in the same place at the same time. Hopefully the reunion would be a happy one. However, there was work to be done. The Orbs would have to be taken to the Band to see if their power matrices could somehow counter its destructive forces. Even though the hardest part of the mission was over, still no one knew if they would ultimately be successful.

No one was happy about the way Stone Globe's mission had ended. Ordinarily, Karak would have done what he could to help Levu and his people, but, as it happened, one side had to win and the other had to lose. They couldn't both have the Orbs. The Rongi still could not be sure if the Orbs were powerful enough to stop the Band as it headed straight for their sun, but they now had their chance to find out. Stone Globe had done the best they could. The Braline people, excepting what few were able to get out of their system before it crossed the event horizon of Redron, would not die, however. For them, in the black hole, time would slow and would keep on slowing forever due the effect that gravity has on time, but it would never stop. They would never be wiped out of existence. In fact, they would continue forever, long past when other races and peoples currently occupying the galaxy had gone by the wayside. But they would never escape the clutches of Redron. The black hole would soon have a permanent grip on them. They would never be able to explore the galaxy because they couldn't escape the gravity well. They would be locked there, doing nothing, slowly, forever.

Karak sat in his captain's chair thinking deeply as he stared out of the main viewing window as the *Malus Tempus* made its way back to the Rongi capital. The look on his face was contorted with concern. He was quiet. He no longer had the clear-mindedness to have occur to him the question of what he would have done had he been in Levu's position at the end. If Karak had been rendered and outgunned, would he have handed over the Orbs and gone to help evacuate more of his people, or would he have fired and gotten his entire crew killed as Levu had done? Karak had emerged victorious for his people, at the price of his self respect and his stable mental condition, and Levu had learned the insufferable nature of defeat. At the end, was there no other difference between them? Were they not really the same, only with one of them being relieved of the burden of having to live with all the things he'd done? Was not the only real difference between them nothing other than that one had won and the other had lost?

𝕏 𝕏 𝕏

Chapter 20

LIFE AND DEATH

After it was all over and the Orbs were in the hands of Karak and his crew, everyone went their separate ways. The *Malus Tempus* was set on the shortest course for Vock I to meet with the praetor and Narvok, who had finally arrived. A plan would be formulated to use the Orbs to stop the Band. It was a destructive phenomenon of compressed energy that propelled itself through space destroying everything in its path. It would otherwise have been an awesome sight to behold. As it had come much closer, uncomfortably closer, in fact, the Rongi had learned more about it and had gotten a better look at it and received more sensor telemetry. They already knew it was primarily yellow and orange in color with some red shades thrown in. A massive quantity of plasmatic tendrils was given off by the front line of the Band, similar to electricity arcing, but without anything to arc toward, just being emitted into empty space in random directions and intervals. A wake of discharge tailed behind the front line, presumably either more discharge because of the excessive energy levels that could not be contained within the main body of the phenomenon or some type of "exhaust" emission left behind in the wake of the Band.

"I'm sorry I was late," Narvok told Karak as soon as the Orbs were reunited. "Going around the Strissen Corridor was best with a whole fleet. My fleet will now head for Braline space to help with their evacuation if we're not too late already. We don't yet know where they may be able to go, so scouts have been sent out to explore options, but for now, the immediate concern is to save as many people as possible. They can live on ships for a time, if necessary."

Both the Rongi and Braline had evacuated as many people as they could to their fleets with enough supplies to sustain them for a short time, but they would need to find a place to settle soon. The Rongi were waiting until they were out of harm's way to unload their ships and send their people back home.

"We've never been sure the Orbs would solve our problem," Karak said. "It was always just a hope and a theory. We should wait to send our people back to their homes until we know the Orbs will dissipate the Band."

"I agree," Jarob said. "We must be sure this will work."

When the Orb Seekers arrived on Vock I to meet with Praetor Jarob, they were given a new name. "You shall now be known as the Orb Finders," Jarob said with open arms and a huge smile.

None of the crew liked the name. Names meant nothing after their long and tiring journey. They all rolled their eyes at the romanticized notion of renaming their group, but they said nothing. There would have been a galactic celebration in honor of their achievement if there had been time, but opening the large main doors of the Memorial Scout for a triumphal entry would have to wait.

"Karak," Praetor Jarob began, "congratulations on defeating the Sekurai and the Braline. It must have been difficult for you, considering the position of the Braline people."

Karak just gave a groan that implied the praetor could not possibly know everything that his crew had dealt with on their mission. "None of us think anyone will ever realize what we've been through. We just killed the only group of people who could relate to our current state of mind. This has been the most trying time in any of our lives. We have explored, done battle, been betrayed, established alliances, thought and talked our way out of death and danger at seemingly every turn. I think I can speak for all of us when I say we feel a little out of place even now, at home, in our greatest moment of triumph. We've been farther and seen more than we thought possible, and it has changed us."

"Well, anyway," Jarob continued, "the work isn't over yet. The Orbs still have to be sent into the Band. We'll send a warship with a well rested crew to drop the Orbs in the path of the Band."

"Absolutely not!" Karak's head jerked toward his praetor. The Black Orb, which enhanced leadership qualities, was possessed by Karak, and therefore, guided his decisions for his crew and his people. Karak's leadership qualities, which were already substantial, were now even greater. "My crew began this mission and we will see it through."

Karak turned to leave and walked toward the *Malus Tempus,* followed by the rest of the Orb Finders.

So, without another word, Karak boarded his ship again and set out for this Band of Death that had been the catalyst for the greatest expedition the Rongi people had ever mounted. It was only proper that they should finish the mission they'd started.

The *Malus Tempus* stood in front of the Band—a spectacular sight, indeed. Though primarily a yellow-orange color, its solid red areas were a rich, deep red that was surpassed in clarity and vividness only by the Red Orb. Plasmatic discharges were seen in great numbers and powerful intensities. The Band was indeed powerful. It was obvious why it was feared so greatly.

"The readouts are off the scale," the duke said with a tone of disbelief. The death and destruction that could be caused by the Band were obvious. "I'm detecting a large fuel source composed of cobalt, manganese, and even some iron."

Hiram's face contorted."How are we supposed to stop something that looks like that?"

Lithinia held up the Orange Orb and looked at it. "What are these shiny rocks supposed to do against that monster?"

"I've never seen anything like it," Notolla said.

"If you're all done gawking in amazement of our enemy," Karak said as he looked at each of his crew, "we can finish what we started." Karak calmly settled back into his captain's chair. "Take us right up in front of it, Hiram, but keep us out of range of those discharges. Then match its speed and turn us back toward home just like you were escorting it. Does anyone remember how we're supposed to use these Orb things?" No one answered.

The *Malus Tempus* was infinitesimally small compared to the Band. Even the Sekurai empress's ship would have been but a speck of dust compared to the thing. It was no wonder the band could destroy an entire sun.

"Are the Orbs in the cargo hold?" Karak asked.

"They're there and ready," Lithinia said.

"Open the doors," Karak said in a low voice.

"The doors are open, and the Orbs have left the ship," the duke said after he operated the appropriate controls on his console. "They're slowing and being overtaken by the Band."

"Get us out of here," Karak said. "Set course for Station Ynu. That's where we'll go in either case. We will either have to go there because this didn't work or to escape the fanfare at home. When we've gotten to a safe distance, turn us around and hold there. I want to watch this."

As the Orbs were engulfed by the Band, they disappeared from sight. The Orbs were shortly consumed by the Band and nothing was seen of them. Karak and the rest of the Orb Finders monitored the situation.

"Is there any change in the Band?" Karak asked hopefully.

"None yet," the duke said.

"How long does it take to have an effect?" Notolla asked.

After a short time of silence, which occurred because no one wanted to believe the Orbs weren't going to work, Notolla had her answer. "I'm detecting power fluctuations in the Band," the duke said. Then his eyes grew wide as he examined the readings at his console. "The Band has begun to expel much larger bolts of discharged energy. These are longer, broader, and thicker."

"This doesn't look good." Field Marshal Notolla couldn't take her eyes off the threat.

The Band put on a fantastic firework show that exemplified great strength and power. Surely now, if not before, anything that got in the way of the output of the Band would be destroyed. The band slowly broadened and lengthened, changed in color to a shade of red that was proud of the Red Orb, for it was richer and deeper. The wake behind it grew as well as the Band exuded greater force.

For a moment, Karak looked around at his crew. "We may have created a force that would rip through the universe with even more destruction than would ever have been done."

"I'm picking up continued fluctuations from the Band." The duke was poring over his console. "Something's changing. The Band is growing erratic. Its outbursts are even more irregular now, and its course seems to be fluctuating."

Lithinia looked back at the main viewing window and pointed; she could not speak. The Band began to form holes in its front. The blackness of space could be seen through the holes. Then everyone noticed the threat they had struggled for so long to destroy was, in fact, dying. The Red Band of Death was breaking apart.

The duke continued to monitor the situation. "Energy output is falling fast. There are no more tendrils of energy emanating from the Band. It's almost completely broken up." The Band had given off one last groan of defiance before its end.

Soon the Band had dissipated to the point where it could hardly be recognized. The threat to the people of the Rongi System had expired. The final stage of the dismantling was rather spectacular. It consisted of a gigantic explosion which expelled all remaining energy in the Band. The blast was bright yellow and red and sent a shockwave a distance that took it near Rongi space, but it didn't reach the area with enough force to damage a ship. The *Malus Tempus*, the nearest ship, was given a moderate jolt, but the crew acted like nothing happened because this blast was not at all like anything they'd felt in the past month.

"It got within half a day from Tris before the beast was killed." Karak leaned back in his seat comfortably. "The Rongi people are now safe to return to their homes and to their lives. The Rongi fleet can be given the order to turn around and take their refugees back home."

Karak quickly lifted himself from his chair in triumph and began to walk around the bridge. "Well, I think we can leave the area."

The duke rose from his console and walked up to Karak from behind, looking at him from behind his shoulder. "There'll be a welcome home party."

Karak's shoulders slumped and his head hung. "I don't want to be the center of any kind of attention, especially some kind of welcome home party." He much preferred to settle down on Station Ynu away from all the attention and in the place his crew had discovered anew and unwittingly somehow set in motion one of the most decisive elements of the last month's expedition.

"We should go in there to see if the Orbs survived the blast," the duke said. "I don't know if anything could have survived that blast, but if they did come out okay, perhaps they could be taken to the Braline System to help those people."

The Orb Finders went into the area of the dissipated Band. They were, once again, trying to find the Orbs. When they arrived, they looked for many long hours, but to no avail. There was nothing to be seen of the Orbs. There would need to be at least one whole Orb in order to re-forge the others, and no intact Orbs were detected. There were no traces of anything. No remnants of the Band were found either. It was as though that area of space had never seen action of any kind. All the material must have been converted to energy and heat and dissipated into space. There was no foreseeable hope for the Braline people now.

Karak could not have been more devastated. He now felt for the Braline people, and for Levu specifically, as much as he would have felt for his own kin had they not survived. He had previously cared very little in a genuine sense for the Braline predicament, though he sympathized with their situation. The successful completion of the mission had instantly triggered the beginnings of the restoration of Karak and his crew, a restoration both crews dearly needed, and the benefit of which Stone Globe would not see. The Orb Finders would never again be the same, but now that the pressure was off they could begin settling back into as much of a normal life as the Orb endeavor would allow. Their transitions into people who were uncaring and loathsome concerning the fate of Levu and his crew would never be completely undone, but they would form some kind of coping mechanism to deal with it all as best they could. The first step was to remove themselves from the situation entirely, and successfully completing their mission was a thing to that end.

"Hiram," Karak said quietly, "get us to Station Ynu."

When Narvok arrived, he saw a series of Braline ships lined up to take on more people and more supplies. Unfortunately, the gravity well was becoming too great for some ships to maneuver inside the solar system. A few of the smaller ships had already been rendered useless by the force. The larger ships were still going, but could only move about sluggishly. The larger, more powerful ships were ferrying people and supplies to the less powerful ships that waited beyond the reach of Redron's gravitational pull.

"What's happening here?" Narvok asked over a communications channel with the lead Braline ship.

"This is Captain Tegrun," a Braline captain said. "This will likely be the last chance to get anyone out of the gravity well's range of extreme effect."

"Very well," Narvok said. "Let's avoid being caught in there. How many runs can we make for people?"

"We've been getting people out and then transferring them to the ships that can't move inside the solar system. Then we go back for more. We were told that each of our ships were only able to safely make one more run by the time we got here," Tegrun said, "but we've made three trips anyway. The last time we barely got out alive, and I'm contemplating another trip. We probably won't be able to get out of the gravitational pull if we go back in. Currently, none of our other ships will be able to make another run for more people after they've completed this one."

Narvok then sent in his entire fleet to secure as many people as possible. His ships had nowhere to drop people off, so Narvok's capital ship was the last ship to carry out any Braline escapees. Every ship available had been dedicated to the procedure, but the Braline still lacked tens of billions. Over thirty billion people were still in the system, and there wasn't a single ship known to exist that could go in and save them, nor was there any process or procedure that could counter such a force. By this time, even the Swisura ships could not have made it through to execute another run.

"How many did we get?" Narvok asked.

"We don't have an exact number yet," one of Narvok's officers said, "but we got everyone we could."

"General!" a Swisura science officer yelled. "There's a ship going back in to make another run."

Narvok started, "Order it to stand down and return—"

"It's not one of ours," the officer said. "It's the *Quia Vita!*" The officer paused. "No, it's another Braline cruiser escort. They must have built a second one while Levu and his crew were on their mission, but this one doesn't have Sekurai upgrades."

"They can't possibly expect to survive."

"It looks like they're going to try."

"Determined to the last," Narvok said under his breath. "Damned fool. Open a channel. We have to stop him."

"Channel open," the communications officer said.

"This is Narvok. What are you doing? You'll get yourself and your crew killed. You know that just as well as I do."

"It's better to go down trying than to watch people die," the captain answered. "Everyone else is making the defeatist assumption that they can't make another run. My crew has made this choice."

That was the last message from the Braline ship. Due to the effects of the massive gravity well from the black hole, years down the road they will probably still be trying to get out of that black hole's gravity, but according to Narvok and his crew's perspective, the *Quia Vita's* sister ship, which was never christened, was lost beyond the event horizon.

The Braline who escaped have said that that ship and its crew aren't dead, but this would be a stretch of an interpretation. The crew of that ship, as well as the crew of the *Quia Vita*, despite their failures, became immortalized, both in the minds of their people and in their own little corner of the universe. "The pure-bred Braline person will become extremely difficult to find in a few generations," Narvok observed. "They will have to intermingle with other races to preserve their families."

More urgent, though, was the restructuring of their government. King Brale LXXII and his family chose to stay and not to try to escape the pull of Redron. He, along with tens of billions of others, did not survive, and he left no heirs. The entire Braline society was shattered. Nothing was left except a couple hundred thousand stragglers. Hope was not a thing for these battered and beaten people, though they would make some small amount of their own hope later.

It wasn't until Jarob actually came to Station Ynu a couple of months later that he again saw Karak. The praetor gave the excuse that he wanted to see the new acquisition to the Rongi domain, but he really wanted to go to see Karak Jewill. Karak hadn't come home and hadn't returned any of Jarob's calls. They walked the corridors of the station, just going for a stroll with all the hustle and bustle of putting the finishing touches on the station.

"You haven't come home yet," Jarob pried passively.

"I don't think I will go home," Karak answered, not looking at his leader.

"Our people are grateful to you and your valiant crew."

"I'm honored, but I only did what anyone would have done. I just so happened to be the one you asked to carry out the mission."

"Except it wasn't anyone else who did it. I chose you because you were the best one for the job. It didn't hurt that all my advisors recommended you. Besides, the people here must be thankful too."

Karak whined just a little. "It's not as bad. It's more relaxed. Fewer people, and everyone is busy setting up their own lives and getting this station fully operational."

"The Braline effort failed. They got so few of their people out." Jarob only looked at the floor.

Karak said nothing.

"We couldn't send ships to aid the Braline because our ships were too slow to arrive there before the gravity well from Redron became too strong, and that we also continued to evacuate our own people in case the Orbs were ineffective against the Band. We have, however, sent supplies of various kinds with the last few Swisura ships to leave Rongi space. Medical equipment, food, some technology, and relevant information are all being sent to try to make the journeys and transitions easier. We're also sending a team of ambassadors to try to open peaceful relations with the Braline."

Karak gave no answer.

"You're thinking about Surist."

"And Nurisk. And Levu," Karak said, his eyes moist.

"He couldn't help what happened."

Karak scowled. "I know that. I'm just glad they got as many people out as they could. It's just the fact that so many people had to die."

"Surist made a choice, and so did Levu."

"What about them?" Karak asked.

"Levu decided that he could never have rescued enough people in an evacuation effort, so he did the only thing he could. He fought for his people."

"That's not what troubles me. He became something different in the end, as did I." Karak looked up and then stopped walking. He looked Jarob in the eye. "He became the sum total of despicable hate in the universe. He hated me for beating him. His last words were—characteristic of a different kind of being, not of himself. I can't help thinking that I may have become something very similar if things had gone, in the end, for us as they did for him. Death was his only option at that point. What he had become shouldn't have been allowed to live, and he would have agreed with that. Perhaps that's another reason why he chose to fight at the very end, when he knew he couldn't win." Karak returned to walking and Jarob followed suit. "I'm glad the Braline were able to get some people out," Karak finished, finding the silver lining.

"You think you became what Levu did."

"I did."

"Then perhaps you think you shouldn't be allowed to live either."

"Perhaps not, but I'm doing ok here. It's just going to take time, and I'll never be the same."

Jarob shrugged. "Yes. They didn't get much of the Braline culture out." He raised his eyes to meet Karak's. "Art, architecture, some literature, relics, and a whole lot of people were lost. They did, however, find a place to go."

Karak perked up. "Where?"

"They went to the Sekurai System. That unmanned Nilg fleet went off in that direction after they destroyed the Sekurai navy near Dran. They went on automatic. We don't know how. It's a mystery, but what we do know is that the Nilg won the war against the Sekurai that started so long ago. The Nilg ships destroyed the Sekurai. They left the solar system intact, but they killed every single Sekurai there, based on the Swisura reports. The Swisura went there to investigate and found what the Nilg fleet had done and they learned all this. There are no more Sekurai in that system, so the Braline went there—they will now inhabit the Sekurai System."

They paused for a few minutes now and just walked in silence. Jarob could tell his visit was helping Karak, but not as much as he'd hoped.

"The last message the Swisura got from the Braline System said King Brale had been thinking about the decisions that had led to that last day, the day his people were lost. He felt all alone among tens of billions of dying people.

"It's a shame we had to fight them. I think they're good people."

"I agree; they are good people. They didn't deserve to die."

They arrived at a small dining establishment, one of few operating on the station. Jarob motioned Karak to enter.

"I may have some new perspectives and additional insight," Karak said with a deep sigh, "but I'll never be the same again. Sometimes we have to do things we would otherwise find unconscionable. No one should have to make those kinds of decisions. Even in this time of accomplishment, ensuring the survival of our race, and even making new friends, I can't help feeling for those who didn't make it, whether they died in the war or—or were traitors, even more so for those Braline who now face a slow torturous un-death in the black hole. One of us survived and the other one died, and we—I—will have to live with that. We both needed the same thing, and only one of us could have it. You know, victory should be the most profound emotion we feel. But sometimes the price of that victory is too damned high. It always provides the utmost feeling of greatness—at first. The rest—I'll leave up to posterity. I guess it's the difference between life and death, the cost of living—the price of survival."

𝕏 𝕏 𝕏

About The Author

Jeremy David Williams is a jack-of-all-trades and a master of none or a Renaissance Man, depending on how the mood strikes him on a given day. Living in the middle of nowhere in central Illinois, he has nature at the ready. Whether it's a hike in the woods, mushroom hunting, geocaching, or staring up at the stars in a clear night's sky, he's always looking, always learning.

He lives alone with his dog, Surrell, a German Shepherd, but the development of this novel has been a long time coming, and the process has seen 3 beagles and a blue heeler come and, unfortunately, go. Jeremy has been an award-winning woodturner, is an aspiring young painter, and now a novelist. He has consumed both fiction and non-fiction. Having read every Sherlock Holmes story and novel written by Sir Arthur Conan Doyle, clues to a few surprises are planted in this work. The calm deliberation with which Edgar Alan Poe wrote some of the world's most suspenseful tales has inspired Jeremy to portray the severity of a situation while not causing the reader to become consumed by the circumstances. Having always tried to do the right thing, and only meeting with partial success, moral dilemmas are at the heart of this work also.

Among other things, Jeremy has enjoyed walking miles and miles early in the morning, shooting pool late at night, and playing chess all hours of the day. Being an excellent judge of character, he has surrounded himself with those who represent the best qualities of humanity and has then included their characteristics in this story.